Praise for SIEG

"This story is a **powerful**
It's the result of the boys' traumatic ~·····
horrific circumstances, and the emotional and psychological
damage they carry into adulthood. It is a story of brotherly
love and personal demons that shape their lives, the choices
they make, and their relationships. Readers will be riveted
by the attention to detail regarding life in Germany during World War II. I highly recommend *Siegfried Follies* to
those who enjoy well-written, compelling, and emotionally
engaging sagas." —*Tracy Roberts, WriteFieldServices*

"Alther has the potential for becoming a highly acclaimed
writer. He writes with realism, and is proficient in articu-
lating intellectual subjects of culture, philosophy, the arts,
music, and education.
"*Siegfried Follies* is a novel which addresses a powerful and
haunting period in world history, a story that will be of special interest to avid readers of World War II and Holocaust
literature. Alther writes with sensitivity on the subjects of
seeking ancestral roots, family, community, and the complex
issue of self-identity. This is memorable writing that will
disturb the reader long after the final chapter."
—*Readerviews.com*

"Little does Franz, a German orphan, know his kind and
perhaps rash and dangerous act of saving a Jewish boy from
certain death will lead to an unlikely thirty-year-long friendship. If you enjoy reading about the Holocaust, survival in
spite of all odds, **and sweeping, epic stories of love, jeal-
ousy, betrayal, and redemption,** you'll definitely want to
add *Siegfried Follies* to your reading list today!"
—*Bestsellersworld.com*

"Two children grow up together, learning the world as it is, and we watch them mature as they make their way from home to home, country to country, until separating and finding one another again in America. They discuss their lives and all its meanings, done in such a way that feels spiritual but doesn't beat you over the head with the author's message. The drama between Franz and J is real and unforced. As children they are unable to understand the chasm that divides them as a Nazi and a Jew, but as they grow up after the war, their differences manifest themselves. They move apart physically as well as emotionally, each responsible for his own inner journey.

"*Siegfried Follies* is laden with the symbols of this journey. The soldier dolls that J makes to sell for food feels eerily reflective of how Nazi Germany made dolls of its people. Labeling them, setting them to work, and trashing them at their whim. Similarly, towards the end, Franz will identify himself also as Jewish, having grown up under J's influence, and realizing they are one and the same. The depth of research and attention to detail give Alther's epic journey of time and family a relevance and ultimate triumph.

"*Siegfried Follies* is a gripping and memorable read **on the perseverance of the human spirit even through the most scorching prejudice.**" —*BookReview.com*

"For Franz and J, the two exactingly drawn men at the center of Richard Alther's **heartbreaking saga of Nazi brutality and the weight of the past,** nothing is ever lost except innocence and — almost but not quite — hope. What a pleasure to read an ambitious novel that resonates so powerfully with historical truths and with the struggles of people for whom history is the central fact of their broken lives."
—*Richard Stevenson, author of the Don Strachey detective series*

Siegfried Follies

ALSO BY THE AUTHOR

The Decade of Blind Dates

For Ray Repp

Siegfried Follies

A Novel

by

Richard Alther

REGENT PRESS
Berkeley, California

ISBN-13: 978-1-58790-204-8
ISBN-10: 1-58790-204-4
Library of Congress Control Number: 2010927586

First Edition

0 1 2 3 4 5 6 7 8 9 10

Manufactured in the U.S.A.
REGENT PRESS
www.regentpress.net
regentpress@mindspring.com

When the self weeps because it has lost,
the essence laughs because it has found.

— ABU SULAIMAN

Part One

*Sons of the great
or sons unknown,
all were children
like your own.*

— JACQUES BREL

1945

Chapter 1

Franz was riveted by the head nurse barking orders in the children's ward. "We need one of the older boys to empty chamber pots." And before she could finish surveying the room, he shot up his hand. *I can do it, I can do it.*

"Franz? Very good."

He followed Nurse Zerbst to the utility room. How grand the size of the hall! How huge the closets where the mops and buckets were stored. Franz was thrilled to step outside the wing restricted to children in the birthing hospital, and with *Head* Nurse Zerbst. Nurse Zerbst instructed him in operating the gleaming, silvery pull-cart, then reviewed procedures for emptying, rinsing, returning the equipment. His heart raced, memorizing her every move.

"And now, Franz, the lavatory."

The plumbing, the sinks—everything was so much more complicated where the mothers were stationed. The halls and rooms, he noticed, continuing the tour with Nurse Zerbst, were not as dazzling white as when he first arrived. The women from the work camp used to scrub the floors and woodwork. Once one had collapsed, and he finished a section around the fireplace for her, although he was scolded—not for his work but helping her to her feet. This confused him.

Franz accelerated his step to keep pace with Nurse Zerbst.

He was pleased to have such errands. He knew they were good training, although he missed the marching practice and class work at school living two years with foster-parents. He was too old now for the Lebensborn, the wards of wailing children. But his school was destroyed, his foster-father killed, and he had to remain a while longer. Probably until the war was over. *Then what?*

"God help me! Ahhhh. Ahh."

The screams of the women in birth pains echoed wildly through the building. Franz flinched every time, despite the nurses saying the yelling was normal.

The children gazed up at Franz as he returned to the large ward steering the shiny steel trolley, straining a bit at the awkward motion but soon mastering it. A work camp woman had managed with arms no thicker than a broomstick. Many of the children here were ill, but Nurse Zerbst said that was expected, with their not eating the vegetables and crusts of whole meal bread. The pots were mostly full of thrown-up food, after the cod liver oil. He liked cod liver oil. In fact he savored it; he knew it went right to his muscles.

"Nurse Zerbst," said Franz. "I am finished. Shall I return to cleaning trays?"

"Ah, yes. Yes," she repeated, focused on stashing things in the linen cupboard.

Franz returned to the tray cleaning station. He was helping to fight the war, this he knew. He could not fire a gun but he was one of the few males in this great building of women and children. The women with big bellies were so helpless, sadly crying all night. *Perhaps I am older than eight.* He liked his new assigned name: Hartmann. Hard man, or tough one!

Franz noticed a curvy "K" embroidered on the rag he was using to dry the trays. It was a "K" on a little scroll, and matched the same letter carved on the ward fireplace. The mantel "K" was painted over with white many times, and was difficult to notice unless you were staring at the other decorations: the wild boar hunt and the wine goblets and the bearded old man praying and reading thick books and the seven-handed candlestick. What a grand home this must have been, he mused.

"Franz! There is a mess in Ward Four. Follow me with the trolley."

Franz charged into the utility room and rolled the polished contraption in pursuit of Nurse Zerbst. Never before, in all of two years, had he been to this section of the building! Young women brushing each other's hair, slumped against stacks of pillows, smiled at him. "Pretty blond one," one teased. Embarrassed, he pushed the trolley faster.

"There!" the nurse pointed and scurried off to more shrieks.

Franz entered a small room with a hideous smell. Someone was buried under sheets, groaning, kicking the end of the metal bed. It was green like pea soup all over the floor. He took a deep breath and attacked the slimy liquid, flecked with bright red. Sick to their stomachs: this, too, they said was ordinary. *No, I mustn't gag.*

He ran out of unsoiled cloths and rinsing water. Franz took a bucket in search of a utility lavatory. His heart pounded, warning him not to venture farther than the end of the corridor. Dare he speak to an inmate? A girl smiled at him and directed him deeper into foreign territory. He heard men's voices, even spotting the uniform of an SS officer carefully folded over a chair in a room with the door partially open. He saw some other children hanging on to women with swollen bellies, whining "Mommy, Mommy." Carrying his bucket, he proceeded to look for a door labeled washroom. He hated to bother anyone else for fear of losing his excellent new job. He slipped into a lav much larger than most. It was lined with uniforms and dressing gowns on pegs and coat-racks. He was about to leave when he heard giggles and running water in another room, just off this one. He peered around the edge of the large door, and stopped abruptly.

"Nurse, you're tickling!" cried the naked man as she bathed his schwanz in the sink with hot sudsy water.

Franz's nose filled with the same disinfectant that was for use on his clean-up trolley. *This* is what it would look like? Amazed, he continued staring: curly brown hair on the officer's head but a snow-white bush crowning his privates. Franz backed out, clanging the bucket against the door, rushing back to the children's ward utility room.

"Not since man first mounted steed, not since rivers of blood first flowed from heroic battles, had the world known such evil as resided in this Hagen," sung the woman's voice over the loud-speaker.

He finished the cleaning, the polishing and replacing of the trolley, just in time for today's story hour. Franz had heard versions of the Nibelungenleid since he was a small child at the Lebensborn. The twisting plot, the horror of Hagen's deed, the eventual revenge: he could never hear enough. How wonderfully valiant was Siegfried, thought Franz, swooning with pride. Here he proved himself to be the most courageous warrior known to mankind, slaying the dragon and winning the treasure of gold. But did he choose to build castles and lie around like a lazy sloth? No! He tossed the gold into the Rhine. He chose, instead, a life of service and protection to the humble. Franz wrung out the slop-cloth once more, his ears fixed on the overhead verse.

"And so Siegfried went forth that fine day in his otter-skin hunting suit, his hat of rare sable, his quiver covered with the finest panther skin for fragrance … "

Not even a sniffle was to be heard at this juncture of the story. Franz's eyes followed the sculpted mantel stories, the loud-speaker bringing them to life once again. He was stooping, the divine hero, to drink from the clear stream to refresh himself, when Hagen stepped forward to take deadly aim.

" … the royal blood of the mightiest warrior-saint spurted so high, it turned the Rhine itself into a horrid, boiling, scarlet flood for fifty days and nights!"

Franz's knuckles turned white, twisting the slop-cloth in frustration. How can I wait for three days, through three installments, for Siegfried's magnificent widow-Queen to plunge the dagger, at last, into the *Devil himself?*

A newcomer arrived at the home; he'd been delivered by his foster-parents, who were very angry. Franz and the boy played together some, although the newcomer would often get hit with the ball because he couldn't hear very well. Soon he was taken to a special place for "non-valuable" children, but Franz overheard a nurse say that he'd been "fixed" in the disinfecting room. At first Franz panicked: *How can I be valuable without foster-parents? But if I'm needed for work …*

Weeks went by. Franz was issued a white smock. He walked more slowly now through the halls. Nurse Zerbst addressed him as orderly. He was given permission to finish the left-over roast beef and sauerkraut on trays of pregnant women who had become sick to their stomachs.

"You'll get the Bronze Medal!" shrieked Gretchen, flopped on her friend Trude's bed, re-braiding her hair. "Your fourth." Franz sat quietly in the corner, waiting to take her tray and finish her mashed rutabagas.

"Nurse!" shouted Trude. "Take this coffee back. I ordered it black."

"Tch. You should have it with cream and sugar, Trude," said Gretchen. "Do you want your hips to go slim?"

In the maternity wing, they had heavier knives and forks crowned with the letter "K." Franz finished the rutabagas in the corner, staring at the wall poster: "Give the Fuehrer a Child for the Fatherland!"

He felt more helpful every day. There were so many messes: the vomiting, the children being less with their mothers and misbehaving, the after-births. He knew they were everyday events, but still he clenched his teeth at the blood.

"You're nothing but a chambermaid! Get your hands off me!" the women screamed at an unpopular nurse. They would throw things and rip their own hair. He knew to clean the windowsills, the bedposts, far under the beds now, without being asked.

One of the wet nurses, Mathilde, called him by his Christian name. "You're one of the lucky ones, little Franz," she once said. "My husband has *seen* with his own eyes the babies put into water tanks and then tossed into bins. Right in front of the mothers! Just because the mother is a criminal, or the child is dark. But the war … there's no room … thank God for your golden hair."

Franz began sleeping on a shelf in the large linen closet. The children's ward was becoming crowded. When one died, they put it in a brown bag and brought it to the refuse collection center, just outside his tiny window. He strained to think of it as mere shriveled flesh. On warmer evenings it stunk, but this no longer made him nauseous. When it was clear at night, like this one, he could watch fire and smoke from the direction of Munich. The whole sky would turn yellow-orange followed by a big rumbling noise, and then it would go pitch black. He'd hold his breath waiting for the next. Of course they would never destroy *Munich,* the very heart of the Reich he knew from his Youth Map. He slept in little bits because Nurse Zerbst wanted the messes cleaned up immediately. "Herr Hartmann," as the wet-nurse Mathilde sometimes addressed him, believed he was growing tougher and stronger every day. He knew the bombs were falling closer, but he also felt safe. The pregnant women said there was more meat and milk and fresh fruit, bread and coffee, here at the Lebensborn than anywhere else for miles. Twice he had sounded the alarm, seeing village prowlers by the refuse heaps. That's why he was rewarded with his special new bed. Mathilde said it was all right, that no one would report him for letting the priest in through his window the other night. The woman with the new baby in Room 106 said she would die if the child wasn't christened. He knew priests had to hide, because they were usually shipped away with the non-valuable children. But he didn't understand why Jesus was so important; women in labor usually cursed him. The last broadcast before story hour was discontinued told about why a Jew was condemned by God to wander forever homeless. It was because he refused to give comfort to Jesus, bleeding and all full of thorns, on the way to the cross. It was wrong, very wrong, to refuse aid to your fellow man. He was baffled why the Jews were so horrible, even to each other like that. Surely Hagen was a Jew, killing Siegfried with his back turned. Franz grew sleepy, in a temporary lull. No sirens, no screams, no rumble from Munich. Even the enemy had to sleep. It was like Barbarossa, the greatest Frederick, still slumbering in Thuringia with his six loyal knights, the line of German protectors stretching through the centuries, one inspiring the next. Now me, Franz, chosen to be a *sentinel* at age eight! He pulled the towels and mattress pads closer, secure in the winning of yet another great war ... the mightiest nation on earth ...

"Orderly!" yelled Nurse Zerbst. "Quickly!"

There was a thin stream of pus flowing from the screaming girl's ear. Groggy, he rolled the trolley after the doctor and nurse, from the ward to the disinfecting room. He knew to fetch a brown bag without their asking; the small bodies he could cart to the refuse center by himself. But this girl: her eyes were open! *And she's as tall as me!* He froze.

"Orderly! The bag!"

Most of the children left in Franz's two wards were very sick. He knew they'd soon die when the darks of their eyes turned gray. The cots were pushed next to one another. The healthy were dispatched to village homes. Some snuck back, because they were beaten or not fed, they said. Franz shared his leftovers. He slept mostly during the mornings when there were more nurses to help. It was getting louder all the time, at night. Droves of local women tried to get jobs in the Lebensborn because there was food. Before, they used to tease the pregnant girls, Trude said, on exercise walks and call them lazy sluts.

Trude was very near to having her baby. It was hard for her to sleep, as it was for her roommate Gretchen. Gretchen claimed to be a prostitute before the war. Now it was against the laws of the Reich to have the baby removed before it was born, or to give it away to just anybody. It had to have a proper home. Without her husband, Franz's foster-mother, once widowed, was immediately disqualified. He no longer could picture her face, although he tried with all this might.

"You idiot, Trude," Gretchen said while Franz was scrubbing their wash-basin. It always clogged with their hair. "Albrecht will never marry you! The regiment needs him to fight. This is what they told Max. 'Wife, children—don't burden yourself with their welfare, that moral responsibility. That is what the Reich is for.'"

"Albrecht is a good Catholic—"

"Don't you read the pamphlets, Trude?" Gretchen mocked. "*We do not want* the Church's influence anymore. How can a man be with just one woman for life, war or no war? I should know."

"Stop!" shouted Trude, her blonde hair falling even more in her face.

"The Catholics force the man to be faithful, and this leads to tension and fewer pregnancies for the Reich. It's unnatural, don't you see?"

Franz stood at the sparkling basin, staring at the drain.

"Well, what does the *poster* say, Gretchen? I've been here three years. I believe it." And Trude recited the Goebbels quote: "'A female bird makes itself beautiful for its mate and hatches her eggs for him. The removal of women from public life—is only to restore their female dignity.' And what if Bach's mother gave up after her twelfth? You see, you are wrong. We are swan maidens," she sang, re-brushing her fair hair.

"You cow!" Gretchen laughed. "You think this is better than what I did on the street?"

"*My* children have Greek noses—the preferred shape. You are jealous."

"There are *no men* to marry, you nitwit. It is five to one in my town of Reinsburg. And that one is usually a deaf-mute, or legless, or … " And both women giggled.

Franz suddenly felt silly in the women's quarters, and started to leave.

Trude stopped laughing. "You, perhaps, have fouled yourself, Gretchen. I believe even filthy thoughts can contaminate your fetus. Perhaps even one of your scum from the street was a Jew! Have you thought of that? You cannot, ever, give birth to a pure Nordic. Do the authorities have *that* on your record?"

Gretchen got up from her friend's bed, startled.

"*Take* your waiting lines of women, with their ugly shapes," Trude announced. "Or the already pregnant and pleading to get in here, and *rejected* with no proof of stock." Now Trude paced the room. "And your wet nurse sows ... and that demented Nurse Zerbst jabbing needles." She touched her fair cheek, flushed now with bright color. *"I have pure blood."*

"What is this racket?" shouted Nurse Zerbst. "Frau Schoner, I heard you curse me."

Trude looked up, her face as drained of color as the porcelain sink to which Franz clung. Several other women collected in the hall.

"I was addressing *Frau* Brunner, *Schwester* Zerbst."

Nurse Zerbst grabbed the handle of the door. Franz thought her clamped jaw would snap her teeth apart. She dashed off.

Franz continued to collect the dirty towels, disinfect the toilet bowls, flush the chamberpots, but the entire ward four stayed on edge. Even the birth-pains subsided.

He was standing at the door to his linen closet as the guards dragged Trude down the corridor. The whites of her eyes had turned pink. "Eight months! I am *eight months* with child. No! *No*," she was screaming, as Gretchen and the other women stood motionless at their doors, as the birth-pains returned but as whimpers.

I must always speak softly, and with as few words as I can.

Franz consumed Gretchen's untouched steamed cabbage and her glass of milk that evening. He could not erase from his mind Trude's look of pure terror as she was hurled into the street. Trembling, he went to Gretchen's side. He stroked her hair and touched her face. She held up a tea cup. "Your eyes, Franzele, are this sky-blue." And she tugged him into her bed and pressed him close to her skin and silky gown. Never, ever, had he felt such warmth and smoothness. He fell asleep but slipped out before dawn, his little prong as hard as a nail.

He watched the work team well past sundown one night, the striped uniforms bending, shuffling, and catching, periodically, the dull glow from atop the tall lamp-posts. They were building a higher wall around the home. They wore rags, he could see, and were taller than he, but much thinner. It took three of them to carry a stone. *These workers are so sick. I could carry it myself.* They must be running out of men.

Franz was promoted, emptying chamber pots now in the central ward. He cleaned the steel table and sinks after every disinfecting. He hoped ending these lives brought relief. No more coughing, shaking, crying in pain. There were two babies just this morning that actually turned blue in the face, eyes rolling upward. "The poor mothers," he wailed to Gretchen. She shrugged and explained the procedure, the injection with the clear liquid so they wouldn't wake up. She said they were "fixed"—the boy whose mouth twitched and the girl who had ears that stuck out like an elephant's. So *that's* why some mothers crept into the children's ward at night, tightly wrapping old napkins around their infant's head and ears.

Franz knew there was a certificate on him in the office files. He had been praised so many times for the color of his eyes and his skin, the shape of his teeth and forehead, the long length of his legs in proportion to his body. "This one— he'll never look like a little ape!" an officer once boasted. Apparently this is why I was chosen for special service, thought Franz as he lay on the linen closet shelf. Maybe I will be a doctor ... so easy to give a shot ... place a hand on a forehead ... He was lulled to sleep by the rhythm of the groans along the corridor, as usual, but also by the ones from the stone-carriers in the courtyard tonight, outside his window. *I wish I could help them, but I'm so tired ...* The grunts of the men became a gentle chorus in a lullaby like one they used to sing in the nursery here, a chorus that repeats, and repeats, and repeats, until all of the children's lids are sealed.

The next day there were bombs in broad daylight. A new nurse came to fetch trays of leftover food when no one was looking, leaving him with just the washing up.

Franz was mopping urine. "Orderly!" He knew to reach Nurse Zerbst before she could locate him. She grabbed him by the collar of his frayed smock and hauled him to the nearest utility room. "You must carry this package immediately outside the LB compound, to 79 Hertzlstrasse, eleven blocks away. Here, study this map. You are to speak to no one. This is a very important job, from the Chief Doctor. You are to leave the package inside the back door entrance, which is open, then report right back to the LB. Here is your permission slip. Now, quickly!" And she left.

Franz was breathless. He knew it would come to this—added responsibility. He studied the map. He had no questions whatsoever. Within minutes he was walking through the gates, holding up his pass. The sky was sickly gray. The Lebensborn driveway was flanked by large square concrete pillars. He could see where flowers formerly had grown around their bases. A name was engraved on one of the pillars: Kramer, with a curvy "K."

A few blocks later, Franz had to avoid dirt and piles of trash. It was so neat around the Lebensborn. Soldiers and housewives studied him, but no one asked to see his paper; he almost wished they would. Most of the buildings and shops and offices on this broad avenue were boarded up. The familiar letters on one building caught his attention: Kramerbank, without the curves this time.

There was a piercing siren. Down the long straight boulevard, Franz could see great masses of dust stirred up from the gutter. There must have been at least two vehicles abreast to make such commotion, speeding towards him now but still several blocks away. He was alarmed, seeing adults stopping up ahead. Should he take cover? He crouched along the cold stone wall flanking the sidewalk as people scattered. The motorcade of rushing loud machines came barreling on, but his gaze was fixed on a small boy in a yellow shirt, maybe half his age, who came leaping out a half-block in front of him. The laughing child appeared in slow motion, as if chasing a tumbling leaf, or a butterfly, as he skipped along the side-walk, then out onto the avenue. Either the dust had settled or the huge trucks were so much nearer now that Franz could read their numbers, see the driver, almost tell his rank. The little boy tossed his pudgy arm in the air, as if to wave, or give the salute. *"Never cross the streets ... "* he replayed his foster-mother's warning. The trucks, the two of them, looked to Franz, huddling on the ground, as if they were gigantic buildings on wheels with tiny slit-like windows at the very top. He could see the driver's face: yes, the clean-shaven face, and the teeth, too, the perfect teeth. Franz dropped the pack-age, stood, and screamed. The little boy was smiling; yes, he turned in the middle of the road and smiled at Franz, waving all the while, and returned a lollipop to his mouth. And then there was dust, and the trucks were past, and it was over. He was glad it was over. And Franz could see, standing on the curb, that whatever blood was quickly sucked up by the dust. There was nothing; just a yellow rag, flapping slightly. They wouldn't need a bag. Anything. It was too late to help. Numb for many minutes, he finally grabbed the package and ran the remainder of his errand.

He was shivering on the shelf that night. *I should have run to the child. There was time!* Eventually his thoughts shifted. He knew there were bananas in the package; they had them for breakfast that morning. He learned, too, on the next trip, that it was her home. There was a "Z," a plain "Z" in a circle, on the faded but tidy doormat.

He decided to take short-cuts, to avoid that spot. He took longer journeys, and discovered more of the surround-ing city each time. Nurse Zerbst seemed not to care as long as the package arrived safely. The guards did not check his pass. He was known to haul the smelliest parcels to the trash area from the disinfecting room; he was acknowledged as a stout worker for his age.

Instead of taking his own naps, he asked to bottle-feed some of the infants who were without mothers. There was only one night nurse for all four wards. The beds and every inch of the rooms were now needed for "the good young blood, the hope of the Master Race!" as one of the posters proclaimed.

If he let the infants nuzzle against him, and actually feel his beating heart, they would eat and fall to sleep more agreeably. He missed Mathilde, the wet nurse. She had been dismissed for eating too many leftovers. Nurse Zerbst had always accused her of stealing soap. Franz knew the pockets of Nurse Zerbst's smock were filled each evening with bars of soap, matchboxes, candle stubs, apple cores, all sorts of things. She would hide them all day under the mattress pads in his closet when she didn't have time to wrap a package for him to deliver.

And in the very darkest hour of night, he often slipped into bed with Gretchen. She held him and stroked him all over, rocking him and making his entire body tingle with warmth and wonderful sensations.

The teeth! He woke up on his shelf and pictured the teeth of the driver, as if he were perched high up in a tower, grinning and looking down on all the litter as he sped onto and over the child. In his fright, he shook an infant by mistake and set it to screaming.

Sometimes the screams were just those of the women in labor on the mattresses lined up along the hall. He had pressed gauze bandages against one woman who was torn and bleeding badly. He could apply fresh ones faster than she could soak them up. Once, between cursing God Almighty as well as the Fuehrer, she smiled at him. "Please," Franz pleaded. "Just curse God, not the Fuehrer, or they might withhold your painkiller."

"This is very urgent!" hissed Nurse Zerbst after she rushed the largest package ever into his lap as he was folding linen. He was tempted to open it, mid-way in his hike to 79 Hertzlstrasse. He was starving. It took him an hour between finding stale crusts, even when he snuck out to the refuse area. But he couldn't, just couldn't, take the chance.

To compensate, on his return from this "urgent" errand, he allowed himself the luxury of resting for a few minutes by the railroad bank. He'd count the cars today. Once he got near one hundred before he saw soldiers on the large platform opposite, and he fled. But now, he felt quite safe, wedged between the broken rocks and piles of powdery brick, because he hadn't been asked for his pass in weeks. *Twenty-seven.* The soldiers were clowning around, punching each other. *Thirty-three.* A smell rose from the hurtling train, almost as foul as his refuse center. *Forty-six.* The windows were boarded up tight, although every now and then there were open slats, perhaps to let the cattle breathe. *Fifty-eight.* Franz kept counting, counting idly away, when suddenly a board was shoved open and two packages heaved out. Arms, there were *arms* in the black hole, flashing by. *Sixty-five.* Food! he thought. Something *valuable.* I must get those bundles without the soldiers seeing, before the train speeds completely by. *Seventy*—and his eyes became glued to one of the bundles that was *moving.* It did have arms! He lost count, hesitated, his mind racing but somehow gone blank. His head was filled with the screech of the train as he stared at a child, its open, wailing mouth oddly silent beside the clanking iron wheels on gritty tracks. The eyes were big and dark as lumps of coal. Franz bolted up. And he scooted as fast as he could down the embankment, the black dust spraying up well over his head, stinging his face. He jerked the child to its feet with one hand and grabbed the black case in his other. He could see the last of the cars approaching. I must hurry! Oh the stench! He lifted the child, as tall as himself but no heavier than a suckling infant. The case had a handle, so that was easy. *Hurry.* He struggled up the steep bank, using all his strength. The train disappeared, as did Franz with his cargo, stumbling into the soot-filled shadows of early evening. A child for the Fuehrer! Give a child to the Fuehrer! he rejoiced to himself, as he groped his way towards the Lebensborn gate.

Chapter 2

Franz paused to rest in a vacant alley two blocks from the Lebensborn, enchanted with his new-found treasure. The boy slumped over the cold ground and curled up to sleep. Franz set down the dusty black case.

The children's ward was so crowded perhaps they would not want another. His elation slipped. And food was now in such short supply. *No reasons a child of the Reich should not have a proper home.* The boy was very dark, even more so in the grime of the city. Franz began shaking with fear as if having done something wrong. *Perhaps he is a non-valuable child. Perhaps he was on a train to a special school. This is not right. I should take him to an officer.* The poor boy had *soiled* himself.

Franz propped the skeleton of the boy against the brick wall, nudging him gently. "Are you a non-valuable child? Please answer me correctly."

The boy opened his enormous dark eyes, but made no further expression. His cheeks were sunk into the bones of his face. And his mouth was drawn so tightly over his teeth that Franz wondered if he could even move his lips.

"What's your name?"

The eyes stayed fixed on Franz.

"Of course, you can't speak German," said Franz, thinking

of the many pregnant women arriving at the Lebensborn every day from all corners of the Reich. They were being sent to headquarters, the heartland, with the war so bad on all sides.

He heard a whistle. Nurse Zerbst would be looking for him as it was nearly evening. The child closed his eyes and pitched forward into Franz's lap. He could feel the beating heart.

"No," said Franz, settling the boy and the funny-shaped valise against the wall. "I should leave you for the authorities to find." He ran back to the gate. There was a new guard, and he had to show his paper. Franz busied himself with chamber pots and dirty linen but remained spellbound by his startling experience.

It wasn't just the sick children crying. The women, also, were yelling for help and begging for pain-killer. His frantic work helped, somewhat, to cloud the image of the blackened boy from the train.

"No, no, now," Nurse Zerbst smiled, rushing by a wailing woman. "It's better naturally!" He couldn't figure out why all this fuss over having a baby. Perhaps the villagers were right: Trude and Gretchen and their friends were pampered no end. *But their pain was real …*

Franz was moving faster than the nurses. He cleaned a dozen trays, flushed four or five pots, lanced several boils in the time it took the older orderly to do just a few. Although he was almost nine, he was getting tall. The muscles of his legs and arms did not yet bulge, but he could see they were about to. Each night he was now feeding and putting to sleep twice as many babies since discovering a way of placing one between his knees and one on his lap. The Reich needed more children! They had just disinfected a boy called Hans, with an earache. Once Hans gave him half a plum—a good ripe plum without discoloration. Franz was running out of energy at the time and had been so grateful. Poor Hans. How lucky I am to be healthy and useful!

Franz was scrubbing a toilet seat caked with the liquid shit of the sick. Suddenly he thought of the little boy with the yellow shirt in the road, the boy he couldn't save and saw crushed by the roaring truck. *So much sadness and sickness and death!* He shuddered and paused, returning to his work with less vigor.

An hour later, Franz found himself sneaking back to the alley with a brown bag from the disinfecting room, plus several concealed handfuls of bread crusts, apple peelings, and chunks of meat gristle. It was quite dark now. The damp spring air was heavy from dust, or ashes, or whatever the bombs stirred up. The boy's eyes were wide open; he was still slumped against the wall. Franz lifted him into the bag and included his strange, oval black case. "You must eat now because it is after supper in the ward." Franz pinched the boy's nose as he had seen nurses do, causing the tight little mouth to open and gasp for air. In went the brown apple skins and seeds, the gristle and the crusts. "There, now." Franz tied the bag loosely and supported it on his back. He could hear and feel the boy retching continuously. I must clean him! But he proceeded, and by the time they reached the gate, the stench was enough for the guards to turn their backs.

Franz made his way to the refuse area and, under cover of shadows, stripped and hosed the child down before shoving his odd bundles through the small window of the linen closet.

He waited until well after midnight, when the few night nurses were busy with deliveries, to prepare a bed in the corner of the children's ward. He found an old infant's mattress smelling of pee, and wrapped it in several layers of plastic. He hid the black case in his closet. The boy was sound asleep by the time Franz arranged him in his new quarters. Back on his shelf, silence at last, Franz decided to drink the little tin of milk himself that he had stolen. *To celebrate! Yes, to celebrate.*

Franz got up extra early the next morning to tell that the boy's heart was still beating and to clean the first breakfast trays for some pear peelings.

"This is not my baby!" a woman was shrieking. "She had beautiful brown hair, and her *ears* ... "

A nurse went to her with pills.

He was the only one emptying pots now. There was mechanical failure with the plumbing, bomb damage he had heard, several blocks away. Large holding tanks were set up in the courtyard, so he had to travel twice as many steps, lengthening his time between checking on his boy.

"Orderly!" demanded Nurse Zerbst. "There is missing linen. Who's been in the supply?"

She watched his activities more closely. He feared losing his job if the child was discovered. All that day, and the following, Franz scoured the hospital for the rare untouched piece of fruit, a perfect pear, hair pins forgotten by the sink, a tortoise shell comb, stick matches of the sturdiest kind. He presented them to Nurse Zerbst, suggesting that she might want to include them in her special package, that it would be shameful to waste them. And she nodded gruffly and stashed them under the mattress pads until his next errand to 79 Hertzlstrasse.

Franz studied the boy carefully one night after the others were asleep, wrapping the napkins tightly in place. He's getting stronger, thought Franz, and swallowing more easily. The chocolate milk was his greatest accomplishment yet—pilfered from the doctor's lunch pail! If only the ears didn't stick out so. The nighttime napkin wasn't working fast enough. "This one looks jaundiced," a nurse had said, pointing to his boy. Franz had panicked, noticing for the first time that the skin was not nearly so pinkish-white, like his own. His nose looked like it had been broken. And his hair, like his eyes, was very dark. The disinfectant! Franz grabbed the boy, still a bag of skin and bones, and rushed him to the lavatory. No one was around, with just occasional flashes lighting up the courtyard and half the sky.

Carefully he placed the boy's head in the sink, and began dabbing the strong-smelling liquid over the hair with a small cloth, the way he had seen the nurses cleaning men's schlongs. He could see the tears, and knew it must be hurting. "I'm sorry, but you will have very good, light-colored hair.

Like corn tassels!" He wished they could speak the same language. Hopefully, in time. He didn't dare turn on the light, but could see enough—see that the hairs were white as snow. If the hair grew longer, then the ears would be covered, and not look so big. The boy was still whimpering when Franz returned him to the ward. "I hope you won't itch so much. That takes care of the lice, too." Franz whispered: "One of the babies died, and I saved you the formula. Please drink quickly." And he unscrewed the lid for the boy. Much of the liquid dribbled down his chin and neck, but Franz settled onto his linen closet shelf that night thoroughly pleased.

The next day the boy smiled slightly at Franz. His eyes were blinking more rapidly. Franz had cleaned all of the lingering patches of filth on the frail limbs.

Franz didn't have to do much bottle-feeding anymore because they were running out of supplies. The women had to nurse with their breasts. This was a shame, said Nurse Zerbst, missing all the important nutrients from the bottles.

Gretchen was still there, but she had three roommates now. Two shared one bed. He missed her teasing him; he missed her hands and silky warmth and, especially, her stroking his stalk. That too was getting stronger. It was wrong of the Catholics, she said, to teach boys it was just for peeing. All of the pregnant women not in labor had to help now with cooking and cleaning. "Himmler's mother was Hungarian!" Gretchen had laughed out loud when Nurse Zerbst wasn't near, after one of his recordings. "She's part *Mongolian*, for God's sake, and he was a *chicken breeder*. Well, here we are girls—cluck, cluck, cluck."

Franz knew she wouldn't be punished. No one even noticed that his boy's hair was as spotty as a leopard's—he had missed more than half of it with the disinfectant. "My little wild cat," Franz called him. But never did the boy utter a word. His large eyes seemed not to miss a thing, though.

Other people were smuggled in, Franz knew. Women had their husbands or boyfriends sneak in after midnight. Franz would often hear them, very late, when he was giving the boy some extra sugar water. He would try to get comfortable on his shelf, the moans of the labor pains mixed with the shouts and moans of the women with men in their beds.

One evening, Franz was startled to see the uniform of an Obengruppenfuehrer in Gretchen's room, one door away! She had moved next to Franz so they could be close. The man had a bottle of schnapps in one hand. He was smiling! Franz retired to his shelf, content that the Lebensborn was so important to the Reich that its very highest officers would chose to stay *here*, to make their babies at the LB Der Eulenspiegel. He dozed off. He bolted upright, recognizing Gretchen's screams. But she was not yet ready for the birth pains. "Stop!" she was pleading. "God in heaven!" He ran to her door watching the soldier, still with his uniform mostly on, slap her in the face, again and again, her sheets on the floor and her legs wide apart and pressed against him. Franz stood there, shaking violently, as other women gathered in their doorways, the women on mattresses lining the hall covering their heads with pillows. He watched the huge form thump up and down as Gretchen whimpered and choked for air, Franz wondering whether to run to the disinfecting room and get a needle of the blue liquid they put into the ones they couldn't control by force, when they wanted someone to be still. He was used to the groans of the women and men, too, when they did their business. "Please God. Please," she was now slurring as other men in the corridor hustled to put on clothes, one dashing into Franz's linen closet and squeezing out through the courtyard window. Gretchen's moaning ceased, he figured it was over, but he slept that night on the urine-soaked pad with his boy in the ward, rising well before dawn to begin his rounds. Three women from the corridor had taken Gretchen's tiny room. The door to his linen closet was open. There she was splayed on the floor, her crotch drenched with blood.

Oh please be alive, he thought, her blank eyes fixed on the ceiling but wide open. "Gretchen. Gretchen!" he cried, to no avail. And then he recoiled. He knew. He had to be strong; he knew what he had to do, above all not cry. He fetched the largest brown bag. It was a mighty struggle— his first adult, tugging her corpse into the coarse canvas. He dragged her to the refuse area without help. He clenched his jaw, bursting with strength through his tears.

Again that night he slept with his boy, Franz's warm arms easily wrapped around the paltry limbs, which were somewhat less cold by morning.

But next night he could not sleep, frightened and shivering on his linen closet shelf. *Gretchen.*

The authorities paid no attention, Franz noticed, to the women's complaints over the theft of their clothing, their missing jewels, money, towels, and soap. Nurse Zerbst no longer asked him to run the errands. She carried home a heavy shopping bag of supplies herself each evening. Out the window he saw the new, younger guards scratching through the refuse area, looking for and finding cigarette stubs, then lighting them with great delight. Franz thought to collect them himself, which he soon was able to trade with some of the women for portions of their wholegrain cereal. The boy was eating more, and joined Franz every now and then on nightly searches for scraps of bread. Once they had their fill of potato skins and canned nursing formula, they would sometimes have a game of tic-tac-toe with cigarette ends from Franz's ample collection on the floor of the closet. The boy's eyes were too slit-like, Franz decided, and so he combed his hair down well over his forehead. But the day nurse had simply treated him as one of the very ill. Franz actually needed the boy's help; there was so much work with the new arrivals. He fretted about older children earning his place. The boy now also slept on the linen closet shelf. He came in after Nurse Zerbst left for the night, and they were up well before her arrival next morning. The ward had become too crowded, and smelly.

There were no more brown bags, and it was days, often,

before the littlest bodies were removed, pressed together and left in a heap. Franz was extremely frustrated that he could not tackle this project on his own; he did, however, take satisfaction from the boy's sturdier gait and growing appetite.

The courtyard refuse area was increasingly dangerous because of the rats. Franz and the boy lived entirely off Nurse Zerbst's daily hoarded goods before she could wrap them for herself. And she had so much, she lost track.

One morning, three truckloads of big-bellied women and small children arrived at the gates. They looked so wild, and lost. In they streamed, through the halls and wards, speaking all manner of languages, snatching blankets off nursing mothers and grabbing pillows. A woman Franz recognized from Room 124 had been shoved from her bed. She was hysterical and bleeding. Her water had burst. The halls were so packed that people were walking all over the women and mattresses and infants. Franz grabbed the displaced woman, her hair sopping wet, and rushed her to his linen closet. He piled the soiled laundry and old mattress pads onto the floor and made her lie down. He raced through the crowd of screaming children, the over-flowing chamber pots, to the disinfecting room. Which liquid was it? Not the blue—yes—the pale yellow! He seized several syringes, small vials and wads of gauze, and made his way back to his closet through the crush of bodies. He recognized several villagers, people now prowling through the rubbish. They were dragging away mattresses, chairs, anything that could be moved. His boy was sitting on the shelf, shivering, staring in a crazed, frightened way, his first real expression Franz had ever seen. The bleeding woman was howling and covered in sweat. Quickly, Franz bolted the door. Then, his materials assembled, he slowly filled the syringes, grabbed and pinched the shouting woman's buttocks, and gave the injection of painkiller. She responded at once, relaxed, and returned to the rhythm of deep breathing.

"We are a product of natural selection ... " came blaring over the loud-speaker, repeating the message he knew by heart.

Franz applied the motions with his small hands against her big thighs, her belly, her sides, that he had seen the midwives do.

"*—the progeny of a race that is thousands of years—*"

"*Orderly! Orderly Franz!*" screamed Nurse Zerbst, pounding on the door. "Let me in for God's sake. I must get my supplies!"

He made the boy hold a wet towel to her forehead as he continued the massage. She was opening now, rather quickly.

"*Alien peoples,*" thundered Herr Himmler's recording, "*have insinuated themselves into our midst and left us their heritage but—*"

"You *must* let me in! I *order* you!"

"The baby has light hair, my frau, so it is of the preferred type!" And Franz wiped the fluids with the gauze as the hole got larger and rounder, as her screams rose ever higher and echoed with those in the hall, the banging on the door, one crashing, head-splitting roar.

"*—because of our blood, one people will triumph, for it is united by the sacred ties of Nordic blood. On the day we forget—*"

He slipped out the purplish-slimy head, gently twisting the shoulders, and then, in a great gush of water, came the infant all flailing and covered with a gluish substance. His boy's eyes nearly popped from their still-sunken sockets.

"*—the foundations of our race—*"

The woman held the child, tears flooding her eyes, while Franz mopped up her legs and waited for the after-birth.

"*—on the day we forget—*"

He reached under the shelf for the boy's hidden black case and, opening it for the first time, quickly stuffed the handful of vials plus Nurse Zerbst's current supply of soap, matches, and potatoes in and around the instrument, a gracefully shaped violin.

"*—the sacred principles of selection and toughness, the germ of death will enter into us.*"

Into the hollow portion, his fingers still flying, he poured his collection of cigarette stubs, for he knew them to be the most valuable of all. She was finished now. He decided to leave her with the problem of the cord—that was the easy part.

"We must always remember our doctrine—"

"Come!" he ordered the boy, seizing the case and opening the small window.

"—blood, selection, rigor, superiority!"

He could still hear the loud-speaker, out in the courtyard.

"Always remember!" the Reichsfuehrer repeated, really shouting at this point, as Franz and the boy and the case slipped through the gate.

"Always remember—always remember—always remember!"

Many of the streets beyond the Lebensborn were impassable. Franz kept his sense of direction, but had to skirt around several fallen buildings and large pits filled with burning embers and thick smoke.

People in a daze were streaming from the center of the city as the boys made their way ever closer to the source of fire and devastation. It seemed to make more sense to go where Franz knew there to be more activity, even though so many were heading the opposite way. He had to slow down for the boy, who ran out of breath. "Hurry!" he urged. "We must find a spot before night."

The boy with the large, dark eyes did not complain. He moistened his lips, his flared nostrils seeming to take in more air than his slightly parted lips, and walked steadily on. As tall as Franz, he reminded Franz of a newborn calf with long spindly legs not yet working.

Time and again that afternoon Franz sent his skinny companion into heaps of stone, between timbers so crushed together that barely a lizard could slide through. They found a potato sack to carry their increasing loot. A few eggs, some small tins of fish, knives and utensils—soon Franz realized it was all too heavy. A campsite was more important.

A tank roared by. Why am I not afraid? Franz thought. He glanced at this poor waif. *I'm responsible for him, for us both. There's no time to be scared.*

White flags fluttered from windows and doors. Bed sheets were fastened at rooftops in some sort of signal to the enemy. The people looked stunned, wandering first in one direction in the street, then another. The boys pressed on in their search. Franz hoped for a large building fallen into a vast wreck, which he thought would make the very best sort of cave. His mind was filled with the illustrations of his storybooks, the brave soldiers taking cover in the thick forest. Again and again, they ducked into cellars through small windows for the perfect hiding place. Franz handed the boy a lit candle so he could thrust his thin arm through a crack to illuminate another possibility.

They paused inside a building that Franz took to be a beer hall. They crouched under the counter, picking up hundreds of cigarette ends—several practically whole! The boy started lowering the lids of his great eyes, slumping against Franz who had to shake him now and then. *Surely I'm safer with him,* Franz thought, *than if I were all alone …*

By the time they continued on their journey through the smoldering ashes of Munich, night was well under way. They collapsed, both exhausted now, in the back of a blackened, wheel-less vehicle until daybreak.

They found a very suitable place in two days. Under great boulders Franz had discovered a narrow staircase, a whole subterranean room well protected by large beams and lined with books and boxes of all sorts. A bit beyond, and lower, there was an opening into a well, or sewer, with an awful smell, so it was perfect as a toilet.

Franz found a supply of water on the next block. He suggested with the sign language he'd devised that they should bathe, having acquired so much soap. Franz removed the pit cover and straddled the opening. He splashed himself from the bucket of chilly water, and lathered himself all over, his teeth chattering.

"Pour it over me," he said, his eyes stinging from the

suds, motioning with a pour gesture.

The boy wrestled with the great weight. Then they switched places. Franz was struck by how bruised the boy still was.

"What happened to your schlong?" he asked. "Why is it all smooth like that at the end? It looks like a little ice-cream cone! Here, you missed this spot on your arm." And Franz scrubbed it, the boy shivering from the icy water, the rough touch, shaking uncontrollably now as Franz exclaimed "Why it's a letter 'J'. You must be special. 'J'. Shall I call you J?"

The boy replied with yet another blank stare.

The people on the street were not afraid of the enemy or the tanks and trucks with their red-white-and-blue marks. Some even grabbed hold of the soldiers, begging for something to eat. Franz and the boy continued to loot houses, root cellars, old shops buried under tons of rubble.

"Here, madam," Franz said, displaying canned beans, clean cloth, and matches to the disheveled woman, her eyes glazed. "For just eight cigarettes." These, in turn, he brought to Herr Schieffer, always on the corner at half-past four in the morning, in exchange for luxuries like tinned meat or cooking fat or, most recently, a pair of woolen socks. And this way, too, his sickly boy slept until sunrise, when dusty yellow light streamed down through crevices into their quarters like broken daggers, when Franz had a slice of smoked meat and brewed medicinal tea for J.

J began itching again, itching until red blisters formed and bled. None of the salves worked, and so Franz held his charge on their mattress of rags until both of them fell asleep. Things were so much better at the Lebensborn, fretted Franz, waking up from a horrible dream. *What's going to happen to us?*

The lines of people up on the street were getting longer every day. They were mostly women dressed in black, but there were others without arms, or limping, or blind—all of them lurching around and clasping each other. Some people stood in line all day for just a slice of canned bread. They would shuffle off, heads down, when the ration headquarters was boarded up for the day. Often on his early morning

errands Franz saw the dead bodies dumped in a doorway before the soldiers could collect them. *Gretchen.* The thought
of her crushed his spirits in a flash. *Gretchen's battered body
… No, I mustn't be sad. I must keep on working if we are to
survive.*

"We should plant these, J," Franz said one early summer
night, fingering their week's collection of potatoes. "No one
has a garden this year. How will we eat this winter?" He
felt the stubby eyes, some sprouting into little white legs. "I
know! There's a good spot under fallen windows—near the
Kramerbank. My foster-mother called it a cold-frame, for
seedlings." He scooted up and out into the twilight, returning an hour later, filthy and well-satisfied.

The enemy, the Americans as Franz now knew them,
had put up posters everywhere. "Turn in all weapons and
hand guns! Penalty!" He tried to translate for J with sign
language, but this was too complicated a message. "I doubt
our people are obeying this," said Franz with pride, anyway,
to J. "I've seen Herr Schieffer accept them in payment for
bread and canned goods. Oh that Herr Schieffer," Franz continued, never taking his eyes off the piles of junk they were
passing. "Giving only two tins of beans for that Luger."

That evening, while Franz and J dined on foul, oily
canned salmon, J suddenly stood, and smiled. Franz stopped
eating, bewildered. J went over to some boxes and produced
a bright brassy trombone in one hand, and a violin, a much
newer one than his own, in the other. Franz reached for the
trombone, with ever more wonder in his eyes, as J quietly
fingered the stringed instrument. Franz had once seen something like this brass in the Youth Camp Marching Band.
Later, perhaps during an air raid siren, he could try to blow
in it and not give away their secret retreat. J plucked softly
on the slack strings.

J's body felt much warmer, Franz noticed, as they settled
under their covers a bit later. Even though J didn't speak
Franz realized J understood all he, Franz, was saying. *I sup-*

pose it's obvious ... all very simple ... food, warmth, sleep ...

One night, Franz followed the path of the candle smoke to the ceiling's largest hole. "Aha!" he cried. He found some sections of sewer pipe which he stacked up and supported with the wires from a broken piano, crushed in an adjacent room. Next, remembering a hideaway scene from one of his storybooks, he stacked several piles of rocks over the ceiling hole so as to distribute the smoke into four thin, unnoticeable streams.

The following morning, while J browsed through more of the books and boxes, Franz followed his way over Nurse Zerbst's map, still perfectly clear in his head, to the place on the tracks where he used to sit and watch coal being unloaded. The station, the tracks, even most of the streets, were a jungle of trash. He found a bucket's worth of lumps in less than an hour. That suppertime they boiled their first water and heated their first tin of pickled cod. J vomited some of it up, but Franz was used to that. The boy's itching was no better: *I must find medication.*

J uttered a cry, a real sound, in the middle of the night. Franz leaped up, lit a candle to discover the rats—seven, eight or more of them, fighting to lick the little tin. "Police dogs will find us!" he announced in alarm, taking great care to wash then discard their tins thereafter, blocks away.

One wall of the room was soon lined with supplies of every description. They had retrieved many tubs of coal. People stood in line for just a handful all day, now that autumn was drawing near. Perhaps it is wrong, Franz thought: J and I are so well off while most suffer. *We should share with a new friend who is also lost ...*

Franz stopped trading in cigarette butts. He now earned them whole, two complete ones, for shining a G. I.'s shoes on the street. There were lots of other boys doing the same, usually older, and men, too, but Franz was faster and more thorough. His business was best between eight and nine at night, just before the soldiers had to return from the bars to their barracks. He knew just where to stand, near the tavern with the largest steins. Some soldiers got very drunk, and gave him the whole pack which they thought was mostly empty but was quite often full! And on several occasions, Franz became bold enough to start the evening trade with those soldiers who couldn't even move, collapsed in an alley. From these he rewarded himself with a brand new pack. After all, he had to remove the shoes to shine them, and then go to the extra bother of putting them back on the feet. J came along as guard, but all too often J panicked at a passing Jeep or a group of singing Amis. Sometimes Franz earned cigarettes from a street woman if he found her a partner.

"Come," he said abruptly in his broken English, tugging on the smiling G.I.'s sleeve. "Red hair, yes, tonight?" His buddy would laugh and shove him along with Franz.

Often he polished the shoes of a soldier who wasn't quite ready to return to the barracks but couldn't find one of the girls waiting in the shadows. Franz knew just where they were lurking. This occasion was good for at least a half-dozen cigarettes, which he triggered by holding up outstretched fingers. Franz hoarded the cigarettes, and carefully stuffed them into the better-preserved cellophane packages of Lucky Strikes which he had taught J to collect in the mornings near the beer-halls. Lucky Strikes brought the best price.

"I think we will be all right for this winter," Franz said one night, munching a Hershey bar from the soldier who said he did the best spit polish in Munich. "Remember the first week when we ate dandelion greens and you threw up?"

J nodded, gobbling his half of the chocolate. "Yes."

Franz stopped chewing. His eyes locked onto J's deep umber ones. He hadn't been using his sign language!

"You understand? What I just said? *You speak German?*"

"Yes."

"Are you a German?"

"I guess. But I can read, from these books, some." Books, in perfect condition, were crammed on shelves lining all four walls.

"Excellent! Could you now, please, J?"

J nodded as Franz lit another candle and set it close to their laps, both squatting on the floor.

"Das Parsivallibretto," J recited, very slowly. "An opera in three acts, by Richard Wagner."

"Oh, Parsifal and the Holy Grail. I've heard that story. This is wonderful!"

And J began reading the first act, about the wounded King Amfortas, Chief Guardian of the Castle of the Holy Grail, who had *sinned*, who had allowed himself to be *seduced* by one of the women in evil Klingsor's garden, and lost the very spear that punctured the Lord Jesus.

"'There is only one knight in the whole world,' cried Amfortas, 'pure enough to withstand the temptations of Klingsor's beguiling paradise of beautiful women.'"

They lit more candles. They split another Hershey bar. The saga of the Grail unraveled, the dangers to its current keepers, and, finally, the innocent wandering boy from the woods, raised in secret. *"Parsifal, the pure fool!* The boy's father was long since slain in battle. How could his mother protect him from a similar death?'"

J gripped the book tightly in his thin hands and continued.

"'Herzeleide, the boy's mother, grieves no more,' reported Kundry the forest sprite. 'As I flew through the woods, I witnessed her miserable death as well, of a broken heart, misplacing her only child.'

"'So he does not know who his father is','" J uttered, choking now on every word. "'Nor can he tell them his own name'."

The blood in Franz's chest and head pounded as never before in his life. Was this his mission, the young Uebermensch, as they had called him for years at the Lebensborn? Was this why, with his parents unknown to him as it was for Parsifal, he had been *selected*, to survive the bombs, to be well-fed, to lead his people beyond all their accidental wrongs, to another day of glory, a second chance? The *next* in the long line of German heroes?

"'Wait for him, whom I have chosen'," J read.

And J. Perhaps he's a Jew, an Untermensch, with his piti-ful ears, and his arm stamped like the courtyard work team with their numbers, only a letter in his case, with his poor skinny arm. *J needs me, and so do the others, for their second chance. Is this what it means? For me with the tall build and desirable hair?*

The words were trembling from J's mouth as he recited this boy's history, Parsifal's innocence, his aversion to weap-ons, reared to manhood in isolation from his parents, wan-dering in hopes of finding his people, and restoring the em-battled spear to its rightful place in the castle of the Grail. Franz was stirred to his very depths as J rushed on with the words, the possibilities. "'Into the brotherhood, only the pure can be admitted!'" Blood … selection, Franz remembered.

"'Mercy, teaches the Grail … He triumphs who meets evil with good,'" J recited more haltingly; he, too, Franz thought, must be shaken by this powerful story.

Blood, selection, vigor, superiority—always remember! Always remember! The words in Franz's head rang like never before.

"'Then blessed by the Grail's power, the knighthood works for *all* mankind.'"

Helping, healing, cleaning, my very training at the Leb-ensborn!

"'Endless, aimless wandering, hacked about by robbers and giants ten times his strength.'" J's dark eyes were water-ing over.

It would be so easy, Franz thought, near tears himself, to set the women free, not bang their bodies. Yes. He himself, like Christ and Parsifal, was chosen because he could with-stand these temptations, and carry the Spear instead …

"'There is only *one* weapon'," said J shaking. "'The Holy Spear, which Parsifal, only Parsifal, reclaims.'"

I want to be a *leader*, Franz thought, and do everything *right*.

"'It is Parsifal, the innocent one, who returns Grace, at

long last, to the sanctuary of the Golden Grail, the cup of *Sang Real*, the collector of the purest blood ever to nurture the earth!'"

J closed the book. He started coughing, his mouth apparently dry from this sudden outburst. He coughed again and again, until his spit showed flecks of bright red, and the Franz brought him a cup of cool water.

"What," J said, sounding more frightened than ever, "is *your* name?"

"*My* name? Why, it's Franz."

They looked at each other a good long while. Franz neatly crumpled the candy wrappers and placed them on the glowing coals. J stared at Franz, still gripping the libretto.

"Shall we smoke a cigarette?" Franz said. "We have so many extra."

"All right," J answered, coughing slightly and nodding approval.

Chapter 3

J was so absorbed in his book that the fire had almost flickered out. The chair legs were all splinters, and they quickly took up in flames. He wrapped the heavy velvet material around himself more tightly. Franz said it was part of the curtain, but he thought it to be the robe of a king because of the ermine collar. They only wore the costumes inside. Upon discovering the closet, Franz wore the court jester outfit to bed, and J often chose the felt-lined wolf skin, but most everything itched. His eyes ached from straining to read in the dim light. Franz had hung some of the larger pieces of curtain up with rope to make the living area, surrounding the stove, smaller and warmer. Their room was no longer a secret, so they could keep the trap doors in the ceiling up on the stage floor open during the day. The Amis didn't mind people squatting in bomb ruins because it made the refugee center less crowded.

J was rapt by the beautiful, painted forest on the floor, the great canvas they had unrolled as a carpet only to find a bubbling brook, lovely plumed birds, trees and lush flowers of all kinds. Their shelves along one whole wall were neatly lined with tins of meat and fruit, soaps and matches, the scissors, candles, knives and bottles, all the treasure from their months of exploration. Cod Liver Oil—Medicines—Kidney Beans—Herring—Sour Onions—Pickled Beets and so on.

Franz had labeled the shelves so as not to misplace a single tin
or tool. Clean blankets, underwear, socks, caps, nightgowns
were folded and stacked on a shelf nearer to the stove, to stay
good and warm. He set their wet laundry to dry on slender
music stands. Presently Franz was doing their bed linen, having learned about scabies from a Red Cross poster.

Franz had fashioned a sink from a kettle drum near the
latrine pit, but J saved smaller percussion instruments for
their musicales. He let his gaze follow the shelves of books
and librettos and scores which he himself had organized over
the months. Nine whole symphonies just by Beethoven. He
fingered the charred pages in his hands. How could anyone
be as pure as Beowulf, as hideous as Grendel? He couldn't
understand—everybody was mostly nice, mean sometimes.
Imagine *one* person, one monster like Grendel, at first a man
and now with fangs …

He got up, shedding the velvet robe, suddenly warmer
with the freshly-glowing coals. He slid the case from under a
stack of silk costumes, and squatted on the floor. He ran his
bony fingers slowly around the case's gracefully curving edges. He traced the frayed black ribbon binding, and he bent
over to smell the leather, the sour fragrance of white skin,
envisioning a forehead that glistened with effort. He pictured
the sawing, hacking, swaying—sometimes gentle but mostly
fierce. The sounds came pouring out, and so did droplets on
stretched skin, causing the bobbing, jerking forehead to flash
like a lantern on a stormy ship. His finger reached the two
ice-cold metal clasps, and he recoiled, trembling uncontrollably. *Am I making this up? Just another tale?* Because every
time he stretched his heart and mind to this source of pleasure, a place of beauty he could almost but not quite capture,
like trying to remember a wonderful dream once awake, it all
blacked out, and his whole body shook. Calm again, he slid
the case back into its special resting place.

"J!" shouted Franz an hour later, bounding down the
narrow stairs. "I found a whole roll of Reichmarks!"

"Very good. Oh, fresh bread!"

"You should keep the money," Franz said, bustling with pots, checking the coals. "The Jews were gifted with money, running our banks, our shops, my foster-mother said."

"We can save it," J said. "What do we need?"

"Take it to a soldier," suggested Franz, his hands flying around the shelves. "See what he offers from the PX."

"Me? Probably hand-cuffs for the little thief."

Franz brought a potato to the fire for cooking. "Next time I'll look for a shorter bread line," he said. "The air was so freezing, every breath was a great white puff."

There was a pause. Then J said: "It's not fair, your working the streets with me here reading."

"I wish I understood English. There was a bright new poster which pictured a winking Fraulein with huge letters "V D." Something about Veronika Dankeschoen. Probably an announcement of a G.I. dance."

J drew closer to the fire, which Franz had adjusted to burn with less intensity. He moistened his parched upper lip, amazed at Franz's dexterous fingers with the paring knife. "Franz. The Romans could never really conquer Germany. The Germans were too—tough. We had invaders from all sides, so that made us—"

"J, please try not to scratch. So," he continued, "don't we already know the Germans were the greatest warriors?"

"The Romans said we were not wandering tribes—that whoever could defend and call home such a bleak and awful place must truly have sprung from it." J twisted his slim hands nearer the stove. He blinked rapidly. "And I also read—"

"Oh! The rubber pistol!" interrupted Franz. "Look, J." And he brandished the sinister wooden contraption with taut rubber straps.

"It looks like a little catapult. The Romans—"

"You probably don't know about weapons."

"Don't point that at me!" J jumped up.

"I'm sorry," said Franz laughing. "You're right to be frightened. Watch." He released the stretched, inch-wide band, which crashed against the floor with a shrill snap. J jumped again. "I saw some older boys fighting with them, and I made one myself."

"I thought toy guns are outlawed by the Amis." J was still shaken.

"What a clever idea, J." Franz's pale complexion colored to rose. "We'll make and sell them to the street children in place of their sticks!"

"I read that *Ulysses* landed in Germany."

"Where could we get more rubber?"

"And the Germans protected the *Pope,* for centuries."

"Oh, J, you are so *brilliant,* with your books and your schemes," said Franz, re-stretching the band.

"Franz! Listen to me. Do you know why we are called Teutons? Well, the descendants from Troy, you know, the Greeks, married a race of giant women here called the Theotonica. We are their off-spring!" J was fingering brass buttons on his sleeves, staring wide-eyed at the fire.

"Thanks to you," exclaimed Franz, re-aiming the pistol, "we'll make a fortune, selling toy guns. Here, have a delicious crust while I fix the stew. Since they are outlawed, the children will want them all the more. Now why didn't I think of that?"

J eagerly sampled the bread, coughing in his excitement. "Franz," he said choking. "The Romans called us *Germani.* Do you know what that means?" J began laughing, although that tickled his chest and made his rumbling worse.

"I made you fennel tea for your cough," Franz said rising.

"It means *brothers,* Franz!" J cried, wheezing, whistling through his dry, stretched lips. "Germani is Latin for brothers."

"It's cold but please drink some."

J took the cup of yellow-green water and sipped it to ease the flaming linings of his chest and throat. "I'll read us some more stories later Franz, all right?"

"Stories," Franz said, twisting the key on a can of blood sausage. "Yes, of course."

Still hunkered by the fire, J flipped a page printed in another language, the Hebrew or Yiddish of the shopkeepers, Franz recognized. J was teaching himself a little more each day. It was vaguely familiar.

Franz licked the lid and polished his prize tomato. "J, with your dark brown eyes you remind me of the man who taught in the boy's academy—chemistry, mathematics, magic. Hopefully we also need warrior types. Strong and brave like the men who pass SS training by tearing out the eyes of a live cat with their bare hands." Franz cringed, and so did J. "I'd *never* do that! But if the Americans started an army for the new Germany, maybe they'd select boys like me, especially ones with straight noses and light hair. Didn't that old hag ask me why I was on line ... didn't I belong to the Amis?"

"I feel much better with this tea. Thank you, Franz."

"The stew will take an hour. Get on the floor, close to the stove. I traded a satin elf outfit for some new itch lotion."

He helped J remove the robe, the sweater and shirts. J knew the circles of red bumps and blisters had spread from the last time. Franz poured a few drops of the strong-smelling fluid onto a scrap of clean cloth and carefully dotted the raised, scarlet flesh. Franz blew and blew, like Neptune of the Sea, and madly fanned with both hands. J uttered not a sound but felt tears spilling over his eyelids. Franz tried to pat more tenderly.

"Our own people can be so mean, J. How the women screamed when Nurse Zerbst poured cold things right from bottles onto their skin! Maybe that's why we lost the war."

The soft touches had pushed J to a glowing place, a warm pool where he could just lie still. He felt only pressure, the weight of a hand. His skin was floating, completely unfolded without a ripple or a crease of any kind.

J was naked, still on his belly, having wiggled out of his lower garments. Franz squatted alongside, continuing the treatment. Gently Franz pressed the now-soaked cloth into the lower back, buttocks and upper legs, intent on avoiding the scabs and largest blisters.

Franz re-heated some stew for him, in the morning.

They had sold seven sling-shot pistols by the end of the first week. J said he would locate and cut up inner-tube tires for the slings, that he may be a banker or professor but he could do that much. Franz collected the best pieces of wood; he whittled and hammered them into several different styles. Some children bought more than one, trading pots of home-made soup or fresh vegetables swiped from their mothers' kitchens.

"The G.I. laughed at me with our growing roll of Reichs-marks," Franz reported, glum. "'Worthless. Zero. Forget it, kid.'"

"We should ask for things useful, even valuables that aren't right now," J suggested. Soon they had several sterling silver sugar bowls, leather belts, even a gold brooch, storing them in the various black leather instrument cases.

One snowy evening, as J was reading aloud from the li-bretto of *Das Rheingold*, Franz picked up a thick stick of charcoal and began absent-mindedly drawing faces on the canvas trees.

J stopped reading. "Let me see."

"No, keep going," Franz pleaded.

"Franz! We're in the enchanted forest!"

"What?"

"Is that Wotan? That you drew on the linden tree?"

"No. These are the soldiers, the sentinels, the tall, straight guards. Aren't they wonderful?"

J continued with the story, the scheming of the evil dwarf Alberich to wrest the gold from the Rhine Maidens. Franz picked up the handle for a slingshot pistol and sketched onto it a helmet and pair of fierce eyes. He wrapped the little key of a herring tin around the waist, a Luger at the ready. J glanced again at the handiwork.

"Franz, you know toy soldiers are verboten. Why don't you make and sell some of them in the streets when the Amis aren't looking? Much nicer than guns."

Franz looked up, his grin widening slowly. "J. We must

save, for you to have a shop when we are older. Your ideas are so good!"

"I think I'd like a whole factory, Franz. Why just a shop?" He pointed his narrow nose in the air.

"No, now you must be serious. To get truly smart you will have to go to school, and I will work in a shop and you will give me the good ideas, and take care of the money."

Franz continued sketching the buttons of the uniform, the boots and then the tinted moustache. J crept into the costume closet with a candle, pulling apart bits of fabric with silver threads and brightly-colored designs.

"Oh, J, this is so exciting," Franz said, his steely blue eyes ablaze. "When I was a little boy, I made a puppet theater just to do my favorite, Hansel and Gretel. That cloth reminds me of the bits of heavy furniture covering my foster-mother had left over. Deep ridges, like on a knight's robe, for my curtain. When you looked from an angle, it was all shiny. I had three different backgrounds—the pretty spot in the woods where they fall asleep, the deep frightening woods where they get lost, and inside the wicked woman's cottage. I'd painted them on cut-up potato sacks with jars of poster color thrown out in my youth group. By adding a little water, they were good as new!" His eyes drifted to the shadows of the ceiling. "Oh, I remember the oven big enough to cook the children ... the magnificent gingerbread and candy-stick cottage, from the *outside*, all sweet and inviting and delicious. This I made from stale gumdrops saved up from my allotment."

J nodded, gathering more material, and collapsed in a heap. He loved it when Franz got carried away. The patter, as now, mushroomed into warm, enveloping swirls that seeped inside his scrawny frame, like lava filling every crack, burning but bright.

"I collected crooked twigs by the hazelnut for mean-looking arms on the trees in the frightening forest. And, oh yes, the stubby knots on the trunk, they were evil eyes! The witch's hair was a clump of dried prickly grass, and her *teeth* ... " Franz smiled through his clenched jaw, obviously delighted by these memories. "The corn my foster-father planted was wrinkled in jagged little pieces. I figured as teeth they could chew the life out of anything. J, that witch just *had* to be the most hideous, cruelest hag ever!"

Suddenly the point of his charcoal drawing stick snapped in half from the pressure of his grip. "Did you ever make puppets, J? Oh right, you can't remember before the Lebensborn, can you?"

By way of response, J fought off a thick, smoldering sadness, but even that did not materialize into something concrete. Finally, he shook his head at Franz and even smiled, as if Franz, his energy and enthusiasm, flooded the tiniest cracks in some bottomless void.

The first week, the soldier dolls were just made of wood. Then J discovered straw could be shoved into dried sausage casings, so the torsos sprouted flexible arms and legs. J's delicate fingers manipulated the needles and threads from their hoard of household goods to include sequin eyes, button noses, feathered helmets and real leather shoes. Girls as well as boys from the street paid with the customary valuables like loaves of bread, but also with thimbles and colored pencils and twine.

Christmas was one month away. Mothers, aunts, and grandparents eventually lined up at the trap door, and bought out their stock of foot-long drummers, infantry soldiers, and Obengruppenfuehrers trimmed in brass.

Once J started to cut up the costumes, the supply of fascinating material pressed their imaginations beyond the armed forces. Sequins were perfect fish scales for the Mermaids of the Rhine. Fasolt and Fafner hissed felt spears of fire from their lumpy bodies of stuffed socks. Noble Siegfried came attired in a patch of the red velvet curtain. The gods Wotan and Freia and Fricka were given wooden heads and moveable jaws, in keeping with the stern commandments they had to utter. J suggested they offer a complete set of the nine Valkyries, with Brunnhilde, the eldest, in a gleaming suit of armor made of two herring tins.

They ran out of storage space for the stream of cigarettes, money, and hardware that were taken in trade. Finally, several children complained they could no longer afford their creations. The spangled uniforms were too fine, and the flaxen shredded ribbon hair on Gertrune made her far too costly.

Franz and J locked their trap doors and, by candlelight within a few weeks, completed all the characters of the four operas of *Der Ring*.

"Show me, king of the gods, your 'power,' you miserable evil dwarf!" J would roar and hold up the Wotan doll, waving his knitting needle spear.

"I'll don my magic helmet, you old goat, and transform myself into a frog, and then try to capture the Ring!" screeched Franz, squeezing the Alberich doll into a soft bundle on the canvas forest floor.

Night after night, when J set aside his books and Franz had completed the cleaning of utensils and bowls, they would begin the next act. They allowed some of the best of their old customers to watch, children who often brought their own dolls and soldiers to join in the chorus. The adults collecting the littlest ones would often linger at the trap doors, staring at the pulsing, bronze-gilt sanctuary under the stage.

Franz wrote the times of their performances on the Veronika Dankeschoen VD posters. "Admission: Six cigarettes." By mid-winter, they took down the curtains and cleared trash for more room.

"There are seats, hundreds of them, upstairs," Franz said one day.

"I know," J said. "But they are covered with broken rocks and—"

"So?" Franz's face lit up.

The rashes and itches were getting better. J was much stronger, although a twig next to Franz. He just wanted to read. He knew the Hebrew alphabet now, and had begun the Torah, the first five books of the Old Testament. It made him feel like a small child with such sounds on his tongue—

Chanukah, Purim, Pesach. Instead of shuddering, the strands of such thoughts were a source of solace.

"Hurry, J!" Franz barked cheerily, hoisting his shovel. "How can we expect people to *pay*, to sit in this *filth?*"

"Haven't we enough cigarettes? This is boring, Franz."

"But you must go to one of the better schools. Have you forgotten, J? You know as a Jew it will take us more money."

J lowered his head. He didn't want to be Jewish, and special. "I will go to the same school as you."

"I'm not going to school. One of us will have to work, to keep a proper home," he said.

J began coughing, stirring up torrents of dust as he swept. Next, he was gagging.

Franz rushed over to J, thumping his back, forgetting the blisters. "Sorry," he said, as J collapsed into one of the ash-covered seats, but Franz soon carried J down their narrow steps for a nap.

The rear half of the huge hall was without a ceiling, under masses of stone. The front half was returning to life, seat by seat, row by row, day by day. J would sweep the debris into piles. Franz would do the heavier work, the shoveling into a borrowed cart and the hauling. The puppet shows of *Der Ring* were cancelled indefinitely as the massive stage above the boys' home was gradually reclaimed.

"I am writing a play," said J one night, sewing vast sections of the velvet curtain back together. "I think we should put on something new."

"But the scenery," Franz moaned. "I want to hang up the stormy underwater Rhine canvas." He was making tickets on the floor to coincide with the usable seats, printing the numbers in his square-like, steady penmanship.

"I'm tired of Wagner. What about something—happier? One of the Italian operas?"

Franz turned red in his peach-colored cheeks. "But isn't it our responsibility to restore the honor of the fatherland?"

"Franz. We lost the war. Our German plays make people

sad."

"Perhaps we will win next time."

J continued sewing the curtain. Franz continued printing the tickets.

"All right," Franz said. "You write the play, and I'll build the scenery."

"We'll both make the puppets," J added.

"And we'll *both* play instruments. I'll play the trombone and drums during the battles, and you play chimes and violin during the love and death scenes. That's another thing, J. You've got to take violin lessons with your family's violin, after the war. And that, too, will cost money."

"School, violin, managing our money … I'll be busy. Maybe I could get appointed Minister of Culture? That is, if my blisters ever heal." Franz wasn't smiling. He just kept printing. He just kept bringing up the violin, *my family's violin*. J looked down at his hands. He had stopped sewing. They were shaking, and frozen. He wanted to shout *no*. He wanted to take the needle and push it through Franz's tongue. He wanted to bend back his brother's fingers, gripping that pen and printing the numbers. He put one hand to his open mouth, gasping for breath, terrified by his rush of thoughts. "I'll—I'll start working more on the play—tomorrow."

"Wonderful!" Franz exclaimed, clasping J's ever-chilly hands, his habit to warm them.

The candle was madly flickering, wax gushing down in great streams.

"Joy!" Franz sung out. "Joy! C'mon, J, sing it with me."

J recognized the familiar Schiller poem he'd taught them, the final anthem of Beethoven's Ninth.

"Joy! Joy!" warbled Franz. "We're a choir of supermen!"

"Joy whose magic reuniteth, all that custom sternly parts," they sang in unison now, J slowly filling his compromised lungs. *"Brothers all whom joy delighteth, reconciler sweet of hearts!"*

Franz wiped his wet lips. "So!" he cried. "We are partners. Isn't that what you said—of the Roman word for Germans?"

"Brothers."

"*Blood* brothers. Let's drink and swear to that! I'll get a cup of water." Franz did so, and returned to the sooty, coppery candlelight, grabbing J's needle. "Give me your hand. C'mon. I'm just going to prick your finger, and mine. A few drops of each into this water."

J felt his eyes pop. *Why? What is this for?* Franz held J's quaking finger over the glass, stabbing his middle finger once, and then milking out a drop.

"Hold still." He stabbed again. "Not yet enough."

J's mouth locked open watching his brother point the needle; he pictured the needle, the silent people holding stiff arms, only his arm was too small for the series. He stared at Franz who was frowning in concentration and jabbing the needle, as he did with the pregnant woman on the hospital floor. J was on the verge of screaming, fainting, fighting, but he couldn't move or utter a sound.

"There. You must have tap water in your veins. See how quickly mine runs?" Franz swished his bloody finger in the glass, turning it a cloudy, fleshy pink. "We each have to drink this."

"Wait," said J, scampering for his moldy violin case. Carefully, he yanked off the two halves of the yellow brass clasp, pressing one into Franz's hand. "You keep one, and I'll keep the other. Always."

Thick dust from their upstairs restoration hung mid-air. In the dull, orangey candlelight, the place looked more all the time to J like his image of a smoke-filled cabaret.

"To us and all our ventures," Franz cried, raising the cup of bloody liquid. "I swear to protect and stand by you, J, for ever and ever!" And he drank half the goblet, proclaiming: "Now, at last, I'm a true German knight!"

J could feel the nausea rising. And the warmth, as always from Franz, which allowed him to hold his gaze and stomach, long enough to repeat the oath and swallow his portion.

1949

Chapter 4

J was glad their room was four flights up because he could watch the children playing tag on the sidewalk and stare at the spires of the Frauenkirche for amusement while reciting his Latin drills. He paused, studying the soft, rounded ruins of the Konigsplatz gateway. Mustn't Herr Helmholtz suspect that Franz and he were just twelve or thirteen, as far as they knew? Yet he did not report Franz to the authorities. *Puriores, puriores, purioribus.* Even if Franz could have qualified for the Gymnasium, it didn't seem right, Franz having to get up at 3:30 AM to turn the dough and fire the ovens, while he, J, could sleep until six. But Franz insisted on being the breadwinner, literally. *Puriorem, puriore.* J watched his slender hand carefully record the tenses now in his notebook. Franz *was* much larger. Perhaps they thought he already completed school. Stop day dreaming! J chided himself, using Franz's voice, and he finished his Latin, then his Greek, next the mathematics and the history. There was still an hour before Franz would charge in with meat and cabbage, bread and fruit, prepare supper and review J's drill books, and then, perhaps, while the stew was simmering, suggest a race to the Englischer Garten.

The amber light of late afternoon poured in, the sun inching closer to the icy mountain ridge directly opposite their one attic window. He waited until the last strands of brilliant gold at the horizon were swallowed by the blue-black sky, the light show over, and then reached for the case under their bed. He assembled the stand, the score, adjusted the strings and lifted the bow into place. His arms wouldn't move, so the notes began in his mind. If he made a mistake, he stopped and started over, even flipping the sheets of the score while his arms, neck and head were locked in place. He could hear Herr Koster yell at him. The jaw of the white-haired old man would twitch in all directions while he pretended to be patient, listening to the barely-missed notes, the incorrect rhythm, pressing his lips tighter and tighter until he would snap "No! No!" And J would try again, and think of Franz scouring caked pans an extra five hours just so he could have this one.

Franz sliced the roll of surplus dough into half-inch thick discs. It looked like he could make at least two dozen. Herr Helmholtz will be so pleased, he mused, which was even more satisfying than the cash. He pressed and rolled each into a rope, then twisted the loops around as he had seen Herr Helmholtz do it. He could even bring a few home fresh from the oven. He wrapped them, hot, in his *Time* magazine and dashed off.

"Work Hard Like Americans! Live Better than Anyone on Earth!" said a new poster. "Discipline Pays Dividends!" Another was handwritten over a faded, scratched one at which he'd repeatedly cringed: "The Jews are the bedbugs of the body politic."

The shops were closed. A cluster of women had collected in front of Herr Grassekemp's butchery eyeing a fresh hanging hog. Why wasn't it open for them? Why would Herr Helmholtz likely get angry if he opened the bakery just for ten minutes while the pretzels were warm? He thought of racing back, grabbing two dozen and selling them on the Marienplatz. "Vote Schumacher, SPD" … "No More Controlled Economy! Adenauer, CSU!" The posters shouted at the early evening pedestrians who would glance up, perhaps, when the smoked pickerel was fifteen cents.

There was a rumble at the end of the block. He noticed an American officer, smiling, shaking his head. Franz looked at his own people, hollering at the tops of their lungs. Several men burst out of the beer hall, steins in hand, and joined in an argument. They all had big bellies and needed a shave. He bolted down the street, moments later scaling his four stories two steps at a time.

"J! See what I got today from—"

"Good evening, Franz."

"Sorry I'm late. I did something extra for Herr Helmholtz." He held up one of his prized baked goods. "Here. It's still warm."

"Thank you."

"You're welcome. And see what else—from Lieutenant Davis, you know, the officer who paid me a mark to scrub his white-walled tires—well, look, J."

J nibbled the fat pretzel and nodded. "Yes. I see, Franz. It's *Time* magazine."

"You know this American magazine?"

"It's in the school library."

"Well, this one we can keep. It should be much better for my English practice than *McCall's* and *Mademoiselle* that the officers' wives leave in the shop, don't you think?"

"I should think."

"Let's eat quickly so I can study the ads."

"The what?"

"The 'ad-ver-tise-ments.' The lovely cars and foods and refrigerators—well here, see for yourself while I fix the cauliflower. Shall I do a quick cheese sauce?"

"That would be nice, Franz." J opened the magazine and read aloud: "You're a going business when you go Pullman. Did you know, Franz, that Germany was once called 'The Holy Roman Empire'?"

"That sounds like puppets of the Pope."

"No, no, we were the great warriors, defenders of the Empire." J gobbled the pretzel. "Franz, we lost this war, but we have mostly won them. You must not worry so, living in defeat. And the Americans … "

"Yes?"

"—will be gone soon, except for some soldiers as police."

"Two slices of Weisswurst, or three?"

"We're to have free elections this summer," said J, "our own government again. Isn't that exciting? Like creating a whole new country!"

Franz served the hot platters, buttered slices of the deep umber pumpernickel, fresh from the bakery and fragrant with molasses. "Herr Helmholtz said he could not get a reliable *man* to tend the ovens and shop in early morning any better than me." He smiled broadly, his pink tongue prodding his upper teeth and gums, fishing for the last morsel of spicy sausage.

"Franz, we have to chew with our mouths closed, or else we are slapped."

"Thank you. And you should eat—you should be building yourself up."

Franz did the dishes and laundered some socks while J sprawled on the floor with the new magazine.

"What scores did you get on your quizzes today?"

"I got very good scores."

"Many mistakes?"

"No mistakes."

"Good! What did you think of the cauliflower? A little tough?" Franz joined him on the floor. "Will you help me, J, with the meanings?"

"If I can." And he recited: "More-for-your-money-buy Mun-Munsing-wear! Munsingwear?" J was embarrassed by the people, a whole *family* in their underwear!

"I get it!" Franz exclaimed. "If you buy underwear, it's a good value. Well, that makes sense. Better than money spent on cigarettes, yes?"

"There's a cigarette advert. Can you read that?" J asked.

"A-B-C-Al-ways-Buy-Chest-er-fields."

"Isn't that clever. You see, Franz?" Always begins with an

'A', Buy, with a 'B'."

"So?"

"Look. In the International News. There's Munich! It says: Streams of ref-u-gees flood into West Germany from the So-viet sector every day. Tem-por-ary quarters have been arranged at nearby Dachau and other con-cen-tra-tion camps because of the severe housing short-age."

Franz, meanwhile, was glued to the page opposite. He read aloud: "Take - one - look - at - that - bull - et - nose - that - air - split - ting - sweep - of - tire —"

"—un-employ-ment at forty per-cent—night-clubs and bro-thels more profitable than fac-tories—"

"—trunk-room and so-fa-deep-seats-so-wide-they-can-be-come-twin-beds-at-night—"

"The al-lies have no right to con-demn the entire German people—"

"— no won-der— Nash — has — rock-et-ed — to — the — top —"

"They act as if we had each eat-en three Jews for break-fast," J read, and paused. Germany was not to blame?

"Oh J, isn't this wonderful? I've never been able to under-stand so much English at once, even talking to Lieutenant Davis."

"Here, Franz, you take the magazine, and I'll work in my drill book."

"Listen to this, J. Fal - sies - to - give - bos - oms - need - ed - build - up. Take a look."

J gasped. "Oh, I have something to read to you, from my social history reader. Franz, it explains—the Jews!"

Franz looked up. "They are teaching this in the Goethe Gymansium? What if you have to grow those curls down your ears? You mustn't be heckled or harmed."

"Please listen. This is *Herder*, a very important German thinker."

Franz rolled onto his back, cushioning his head with one hand and reaching for the last pretzel with the other.

"'We should rejoice—that there are such varied flowers

and peoples on the gay meadow of this earth,'" J began.

"Excuse me for interrupting," Franz said. "But why would women want plastic breasts? All the women at the Lebensborn had more than they could handle. These fantastic Americans—they can sell anything."

"'The Hebrew people were considered from their beginnings as a genetic individual, as One People ... hence the high and resounding tone of patriotism in the Hebrew psalms and prophets.'"

J raced on, reading the last lines, which said that although the Hebrews were considered a nation apart in their dispersion, and not full citizens—he frowned, but continued— despite their parasitic economic condition, they should be allowed to return to Palestine—he stopped reading. He was confused. He was sure it said ... "Oh yes, Franz. Here's the good part. They're a fine and intelligent people, a miracle of the times!'"

Franz rolled himself up, and started to brush his teeth at the basin. "Now if I am to get up at three-thirty in the morning. I wish my teeth were as white as those of the people in the magazine photos," he slurred, his mouth full. "I'll get more copies tomorrow. Perhaps Herr Helmholtz would pay me extra if I could speak better English, tell the officers' wives about the special cakes they can order for the holidays: Pfeffernusse, Stollen, almond butter crescents. Good night," he said, and buried under his half of the eiderdown, but muttered to J that all he could picture were the airplanes, the full-color photos of smiling people on white sand beaches, the wide and low-slung automobiles owned by young men like you'd expect a *general* would drive. "Pan-A-meri-can," he whispered, over and over, in his best English. "Nor-el-co re-frig-er-a-tor. Rayve-Home-Per-ma-nent ... "

J re-read the Herder passage, becoming more and more troubled. As he'd often heard in derision, what *was* so special about the Jews? Maybe it wasn't important. Was Franz a German because he only spoke Deutsch? Would Franz, too, be a Jew if he spoke more tongues, certainly Hebrew? Later,

under the covers, J felt even worse: Jews called *"parasites."*
Franz had said it was a blood-sucking worm. J thought it was
just street talk Franz often picked up, but there it was, in the
Goethe Social History Reader! Suddenly, he was afraid. He
wanted to turn on the lights. The moon was making great
stabbing shadows across the floor.

"You can put your feet on my side, J, and warm them.
I'm awake."

"Thanks." J let his feet slide to meet Franz's burning calves.

"I keep thinking: we have no soldiers anymore, J. No
real men. Look at Herr Helmholtz with his soft meaty neck
and arms, hunched over his swollen gut, complaining all the
time."

"You better be kindly to him, letting us have this flat as
part of your pay. Most people are crammed ten into a room
this size."

"We don't need his pay. You just wait till I learn my
English."

Then what, J shuddered, as he often did when Franz got
aroused by new words and plans. What would be his next
job? Would he move on by himself? J wished the warmth
would travel faster from his feet; up to the knees would be
nice. I should be more athletic, he lectured himself. I should
eat extra helpings of wurst, for sure. These people, the Jews,
they were punished in the war. The war was *because* of them.
The dark-haired, he suspected, like himself, had done something very terrible to the blonds.

"Does yours ever get hard?"

"What?" whimpered J.

"You know."

J froze, and curled his feet back to his side.

"Here, touch it. It feels much better if somebody else does."

J's cheeks filled with flames.

"C'mon. It's not going to bite. It's fun. I used to see some
of the women rub the men like this when they were too near
birth pains to take it inside. It looked so laughable, but, oh,
it's wonderful. Otto, Herr Helmholtz's nephew, showed me

how the other day. When I'm finished, I'll do you. J, please give me your hand."

J trembled, his back still to Franz as he huddled closer to the edge of the bed. Franz took his chilly hand and guided it in place, clamping his own, much larger hand onto J's to instruct him.

It was hotter than Franz's calves. Sticky as well. "This must be like milking a cow," J ventured.

Franz was sighing.

J's arm was beginning to ache, but he was helping Franz. Yes, Franz was enjoying it, immensely.

Franz doubled over, groaning out loud.

"What's the matter? Franz. Did you vomit? What is this? What did I do *wrong?*"

Franz leapt out of bed to the basin. "I must keep a towel by the bed." The water splashed about the basin as Franz rubbed himself vigorously. "That wasn't bad, J. I'll do it for you, sometime, if you want."

"Franz. Wait. You are round at the end, like me. Remember you said about 'my little skull cap'? You have one too!"

Franz had burrowed under the eiderdown, soon asleep. J's batting eyes were wild in the partial moonlight. With the slightest breeze, their small attic sanctuary ominously erupted in creaks like a shrill, angry crow. He shivered, more than before. He wished they were still little boys so they could press together, not just touch feet. J gazed hypnotically out the small window. It was early May, but he knew the Alpine snows would cling to those silver ridges for a good many weeks, maybe not even melting by the first of July. He tried to slow and lengthen his breaths, to be in sync with Franz as Franz shifted deeper into slumber. Instead, J's pulse quickened to the pace of the oscillating, menacing shadows. He could not shut his eyes; could not help but stare pointlessly at the now black and moonless ceiling, miles removed from Franz.

The wheels were revolving in slow motion, at first. Big balloon tires, spanking white walls, rolling gradually faster and faster. My God, it was *he*, Franz, at the steering wheel, so high up in the cabin of the huge transport truck, laughing and shaking his head at the sight of the child. Of course he could see the lollipop, the waving pudgy hand, the little yellow shirt, but did he think these things were for going *slow* when there was a war to be won? Roar on! "Stop!" Franz wanted to cry, his heart thumping until he remembered where he was and who he was, reaching the alarm clock just before it rang, like every day, exactly at 3:29 AM. He slipped into his things, pulled the comforter neatly over J, and undid the door latch without making a sound.

"J!" Franz shouted that evening, bursting through the door with an armload of magazines. "Frau Davis, I mean *Mrs.* Davis, brought me these *McCall's* and *Mademoiselle* when I praised them for English instruction. Look at this one: How-to-get-fine-beef-every-time. Just-look-for-the-Swift-brand! So *that's* what those names mean."

J looked up, but kept his finger on the drill book to mark his place.

"Like Mun-sing-wear. It's a *kind* of underwear. To make it different from others."

Franz craned over some paper with a pencil, scribbling away. J returned to his Latin. Moments later, Franz paused with satisfaction.

"How's that? 'Ask for Grassekemp Blood Sausage, with very special spices. None other like it in Munich!'"

"What's that, there?" said J pointing.

"That's to be a photo of Herr Grassekemp, smiling."

"Smiling? The butcher?"

J continued with his studies while Franz pored over the sparkling pages of color and promises. "Ronson makes light of your gift prob-lem. Jane Russell star-ring in Mon-tan-a Belle. Wow. I think those are real. J, what is this word, please? Mo-dess."

J shrugged.

"This must be important, J. There's a notice in every issue.

But I don't understand. Look at this photograph, these beautiful women."

J looked. They read in unison: "Wrapped, it looks like a box of notepaper, or bath salts, or candy, or facial tissue." J shrugged again. Franz continued: "Act-u-ally, it's Mo-dess in the won-der-ful new shape box. So dis-creet helps keep your se-cret so nice-ly. Now what does that mean? And here, in the March issue, all it says is: Mo-dess Be-cause."

"Maybe it's a mistake."

"A *mistake*? In an *American* magazine?"

"Why don't you ask Mrs. Davis the next time she shops?"

"Good idea, J. Thanks."

"I'd like to try," said J softly, later in bed.

"Eh?" muttered Franz.

"You know." He reached for Franz's hand.

"Ach," Franz laughed. "You feel like a wilted sausage."

"Well, I was ready. Before."

"Wish me luck tomorrow. I'm going to show Herr Grassekemp my advert idea."

"Good luck."

The butcher laughed at Franz. Mrs. Davis laughed at him, too. He stayed up later than J for days on end, reading, drawing, and trying again.

"You again!" exclaimed the butcher, his puffy face turning dark pink. Franz noticed bits of white feathers and fresh yellow gristle clinging to his fingernails as he wiped them on his bloody apron.

"This will cost no money at all, Herr Grassekemp. You could sell twice as much sausage. Please allow me five minutes."

He shrugged, nodding gruffly, and folded his arms. Franz showed him the new drawing, with the heavy dotted lines around the box in the newspaper ad with a big "Five Cents" lettered in the center. He explained that when it appeared in the paper, people would clip it out, bring it to the store, and buy a pound of blood sausage deducting five cents, one to a customer. He just as quickly went over the arithmetic, but didn't say as how J had helped on that. So many more pounds of sausage could be sold, as well as the other non-sale items, plus making new customers, that the cost of the customer savings would easily pay for itself.

Herr Grassekemp said he'd think it over.

Otto Helmholtz, the baker's nephew, had a friend with a camera who developed pictures. Franz took several snapshots of the butcher holding sausage, smelling it, eating it, slicing it, and once, even smiling, all in clean aprons. At least, so far, he hadn't said no. J borrowed a proper tie and a gentleman's vest from a boy at the Gymnasium. They dressed Franz as best they could for his appointment with the advertising manager at the *Muenchen Zeitung,* the morning paper.

"We cannot pay in marks for the space, Herr Director," said Franz, standing on tiptoe to appear older, leaning against the manager's desk.

The man didn't laugh or shoo him away. He studied the ad, the proposition, the wording and the photos.

"But for each coupon clipped and brought to the store in trade, we will give you five cents' worth of the meat of your choice. More people will buy your paper, just to get the coupons."

"Heinrich, set this in type. Very good, son. We'll try it, once."

Mrs. Davis was right about the magazine coupons, bless her heart.

The next day, Herr Grassekemp's Spiced Blood Sausage was sold out by ten in the morning. The director came and, forgetting to count how many coupons were redeemed, collected a fresh goose. Heinrich, his assistant, arrived in late afternoon for two pounds of pork liver. Franz, J, Herr Helmholtz, Otto Helmholtz and his friend with the cam-era, Willy, helped Herr and Frau Grassekemp grind and stuff sausage until midnight.

Franz was bent over much larger papers on the floor. He had a set of red and black grease pencils from the butcher's.

"J, which has greater 'impact'?"

"Impact?"

"Oh, J. Which one *appeals* ... which makes you want to rush to Herr Grassekemp's: 'Save Your Seven Cents Coupon in the Paper' or 'Try New Grassekemp *Smoked* Blood Sausage.'"

"The seven cents one."

"Thank you. I expected that."

Wednesdays became Coupon Days in the *Muenchen Zeitung*. The paper charged a higher rate for regular advertisers because their circulation increased over fifty percent. Franz was hired as Heinrich's assistant.

"Remember in the cellar, when that housewife asked for *our* recipe for bean soup?" said J one night, softly stroking Franz's erection.

"Faster," said Franz. "Harder, please."

"Sorry. This just reminds me—stir for three hours after adding each bean, I told her."

"Like this. Up to the tip." One hand fumbling another, Franz croaked: "Thanks anyway," wrapped himself in a towel, and rushed down to the third floor water closet.

J curled up on his side of the bed, sinking in shame.

J was called Jan Hartmann in school. Hartmann was the name Franz had been assigned in the Lebensborn. Franz and he ate so much better than most families that J had put on weight. He polished his teeth with Ipana brand that Franz went to great lengths to secure from the American PX. He held his own now on the playing fields. Despite his glossy dark hair and piercing eyes, the cut of his chin and the angle of his nose, according to Franz, J was taken for just another bright young German, perhaps a bit more bookish.

His literature class studied *Die Nibelungenleid*. "Herr Professor," said Anders Meineke, "was not Hagen Jewish? Who else but a Jew would lust after the gold sunken that way in the Rhine?" The class snickered while J dismissed a stab of panic with a cold query: how *could* there be two such people, conniving Hagen and valiant Siegfried, in the same royal court? *Am I a German Jew, or a Jewish German? Are not Franz and I blood brothers?* He immersed himself in schoolwork. There was no rush to sort out such a question, so *philosophical* at that.

Franz these days worried he was not paid enough at *Der Zeitung*. It was *his* idea. He should be doing more than oiling machines and writing headlines. It should not matter: people were begging for jobs, for homes, many still starving for decent food. But I was given special training as a child, he reminded himself. It's my *job* to improve things, to make money, to help build a strong economy. I don't need the difficult schooling J and others require. I was called upon ages ago for this opportunity. *And I'd better get busy.*

He remembered J reciting from *Time* that the most successful businesses were nightclubs, pool halls, and whorehouses. He borrowed the camera from Otto's friend Willy. That night, he found his old partner, Marte, the prostitute in the shadows for whom he got G.I. customers as a boy. Now she worked on the Burgholtzstrasse in a green silk dress. She drove a car! By herself! She had a room in one of the fanciest new buildings in Munich. Franz checked the camera then knocked.

The woman adjusted her wig, smiled and looked over Franz's shoulder. She started to shut the door.

"No. Please, I am a friend of Marte's. I *must* see her."

"Sorry, no kids here."

Franz looked her in the eye. He held up the camera. "This is for her. In payment. But I have been instructed to tell her some other, private things from one of your most important customers."

He was ushered down a beautifully carpeted hallway. He couldn't believe Marte had become so rich. The G.I.s could never afford her now.

"Franzele," she giggled, tossling his thick bangs. "Ooo, my, you've grown!"

"I—I wondered if you'd be interested in making some *very* good money—but I see … "

"Oh, you adorable thing. For *you*, I wouldn't charge." She cupped his chin into the mirror and crooned. "It's for you, golden angel with the pretty blue eyes, that they would pay."

"Marte. I would like to take some pictures, you know, without your dress."

She turned down the lights, slipping out of her green silk chemise. "What a treat. Here, lamb. Let's loosen your collar." And she pulled him onto the bed as he straddled her and stared at her firm, beautifully rounded breasts, as perfect as the plastic globes in the *Time* fashion report. She undid his belt buckle and slid off his pants, nuzzling him with her nose, her polished burgundy fingertips, and, soon after, without his protesting, her mouth, her painted lips, and her slippery tongue.

"I—I'd like to get a picture, actually."

"Sweetheart, go right ahead." And she posed, spreading herself one way, then another, giggling in the pillows, gently stretching up and grazing her glittery nails against his stiffness.

Franz could barely hold the camera steady, aiming ever closer at her breasts, her belly, her lovely, moist center which she kept testing with his hard part. He decided the roll of film must be finished. She arched herself up to meet him, guiding him in, directing the pressure, the thrusts, while he managed to lock the shutter and drop the camera onto the bed. Franz was sinking further into the fluids, her throbbing hot chambers. I see, he sighed to himself. It's so much easier, and nicer, this way …

She washed him just the way he'd remembered the nurses had done afterwards with the SS officers.

"Thank you for the pictures."

"Anytime, Franzele," she pouted.

They were developed at five o'clock the next morning by his friend Oskar in the paper's darkroom. Keeping them in a plain envelope, Franz had them sold by lunchtime on Wittelstrasse off the Marienplatz. He took J to a fine fish house for dinner and gave Oskar his twenty percent commission the following day.

J read all the newsmagazines with lovely, difficult words that Franz brought home. And he sped through the free copies of the *Muenchen Zeitung,* always commenting upon Franz's handiwork but devouring the headlines and features and editorials.

One morning, scanning Letters to the Editor, he caught the following: "To the 4,000 Jews in Munich: Go ahead and go to America, even though the people there have no use for you, either. They've had enough of you *bloodsuckers.*" J lowered his lids. He pictured Franz punching someone in the face, calling his brother a bloodsucker. He read on. "Several of the Amis already told me they forgive us for everything except one thing: that we did not gas *all* the Jews, for many are now enjoying life in America. Signed, *Adolf Bleibtreu*— Stay True To Adolf."

J froze. Where is my family? *I thought they were killed in the war. What if…* He slumped. He never had a family. Franz said they were both orphans. *But the violin…*

Next day, J did less well on the soccer field. He walked home from school that afternoon with odd, measured steps. His insides felt twisted, as if he'd eaten something spoiled. He recalled the components of his lunch …

Piercing sirens assaulted him. They were followed by shrill whistles. At first he thought it was an air raid. No, a parade, with shouting. There was fighting, he could see, several blocks ahead. People were racing in front of him. He huddled next to a wall to stop the panic rising in his heart. He didn't feel personally threatened, nevertheless he knew: *they were rounding them up!* Suddenly, he had no strength, to run, to resist. He could hear that word—*Jud!*—being screamed. They were screaming at *him* as he hobbled with head bowed through the mob, the German police, the American Army officers, the Jews yelling and throwing sticks, the drunkards overturning vehicles. It was understandable, what with the hook of his nose, but it was the others they wanted, not him. *He* was Franz's brother, it was all a mistake! He tried to shuffle faster, stopping, breathless, every time he heard a loud crack. He was shoved. He was sure they would at least let him telephone Franz, for verification … someone grabbed the sleeve of his jacket … He yanked himself free and sped away, his pace finally slowing, but not the banging of his heart.

He reached his house and sat quietly in the attic room all the next day as well, telling Franz he was ill. The morning paper reported, on page nineteen, how the Jewish community protest march over the Bleibtreu letter didn't have a permit. The police tried to intervene. The Jews became violent, and began fighting. The paper apologized in its editorial for printing the letter. The Amis military decided not to use force, thinking the German police should settle a domestic squabble. Franz was always glum when his adverts were "buried" as far back in the paper as page nineteen. The article was only four column inches, at that. J felt a little better, and next day walked briskly to school.

By mid-summer, Franz was doing campaigns for every shopkeeper on Gisellestrasse. Franz and even J would get free treats wherever they visited. One early evening, they strolled along the bustling block, their very own block jammed with shoppers, closed now to all vehicles since Franz had appealed to their representative on City Council to declare Gisellestrasse a pedestrian market. Herr Helmholtz the baker was hopping mad at first, but Franz convinced him to try it, to see if uncluttered with trolley cars more shoppers might linger.

"A beer house is opening in August," said Franz as they admired the groups of jolly wurst snackers. "There'll be proper tables over there, with striped umbrellas, and pretty girls with flouncy aprons and a *live band* on Thursday nights. Marvelous, isn't it?"

J was near drunk with happiness. He started to do a little jig.

"Look at that Jewboy," laughed Herr Perldt, the iron-monger.

Franz strode to the man, and glared at him. Perldt quickly stepped aside.

So, yes, I'm a Jew, J thought. And a German, too. We all belong! And he finished doing his little dance.

J caught his breath. "Franz, my new shoes pinch. I hate to complain."

"I should have put those marks in your savings account."

"*Savings* account?"

"You know the Mozart Institute, in Salzburg. I inquired about the fees, and it is very expensive. It will be even more so by the time you are ready. J, you have so much talent. Your people would have been so proud of you," Franz continued, striding on. "I will take their place."

J looked off into the crowd, abuzz with the munching, burping, familiar sounds of his neighborhood. There was numbness in his feet, and it worked its way up. "And will you—join me? Franz? Franz!" J spun around, slightly dizzy.

Franz was several paces behind, tucked into the recess of a still-vacant shop, handing some man a plain Manila envelope, and receiving several crisp Deutschmarks in return.

1953

Chapter 5

J bought a dozen crystallized flower petals and the words Happy Easter in candied lime green. He picked up the meat, the fresh broccoli and the other groceries. He dashed to Frau Baumann's to collect Franz's freshly laundered shirts. He stood on line to deposit Franz's paycheck. He paused to watch the sunset, a somber charcoal sky interrupted by an evanescent plume of icy blue. The sweepers were busy on the sidewalks, their last assignment of the day. By five-thirty in the morning there would be trucks dumping loads of sand and steel. By six, when he was slicing Franz's Spanish melon, the cranes would be in full gear. He tried to guess the workers' accents. Ukranian? Lithuanian Jews? This far south? He bustled along, mentally checking the ingredients: cup and a half of rum, cup and a half of butter, fifteen eggs, toasted almonds, lemon peel, strong coffee for mocha flavor. He wanted it to be perfect. Franz really loved his Bavarian Creme.

The elevator in their sparkling new building delivered him to floor number eight. He put the meat and potatoes in to roast, whipped up the stupendous pudding, and then settled down with his school work. He was about to graduate from Oberschule, the preparation for university. Other boys would have their beaming parents in the audience. For him, there'd be Franz, dressed to kill, with his latest girl.

Absently, J twisted the tip of the textbook page into a little triangle as he glanced out the glossy picture window. *What would Franz say if I received the Albertus Magnus Prize in German Literature studies …*

"J! You will never believe this."

"Hello, Franz. I hope you're hungry."

"I'm going to meet Virginia Mayo!"

"Isn't that an American square dance?"

Franz flung off his leather overcoat and peeked in the oven. "Don't we go to the cinema and read all the magazines?"

"It was the best cut of meat they had left."

"Looks great. J. Virginia Mayo is a *movie queen.*" He kicked off his cordovans, joining J on the sofa with a bottle of beer. "I've got the popcorn concession—I'm executive assistant to the producer—"

"What's this got to do with Grunwald Fabrics?"

Franz laughed. "With this deal I can buy us an automobile—not a VW, but a Chevrolet!"

J smiled. When Franz was in overdrive, J too floated, if briefly, on the cloud.

"One of the biggest American movie companies is making a film here in Munich. They need throngs of people." Franz swung his arm in a great arc. "Parades, riots, factory workers. Grunwald is doing the costumes free, because they're getting a huge curtain contract for a chain of American theaters." He guzzled the beer. "Mr. Grunwald himself loaned me to help the producer, but they're *paying* me, J. Two hundred marks a week! They're giving the extras free popcorn and beer and wurst."

"Did you see in the paper—there were over seven thousand Jewish refugees from the Soviet sector this week. I bet they'd do it for a cup of soup."

"I'm afraid … " Franz hesitated. "The crowds and faces—they've got to look, you know, American."

"Of course," said J, and he got up to check the oven. Franz followed into the kitchenette, sampled the dessert, eyes alight.

After they ate Franz did the cleaning up, whistling along with Eddie Fisher belting out "Oh My Papa" and Teresa Brewer blasting "Ricochet Romance" on the radio. "These Americans," Franz quipped. "They've really got balls."

J dug into translating Schiller's poetry into English, content that dinner was a success.

Later, Franz emerged freshly showered and groomed. "You should come dancing with me and Loralei some night. Stretch those legs instead of that gray matter for a change."

"You should substitute for me in tomorrow's literature exam. Have fun."

J put down his schoolbooks, swallowed by the silence. *How can I live without Franz, yet this is what I crave: being absolutely alone.* He strained to reason why. With Franz, he knew, was a solid identity for them both. *I'm what Franz is not,* he continued, *so together we make sense.* The book of Schiller poems settled like lead in his lap, pushing him further along. *But by myself, though appealing, my mind goes entirely blank. So much waiting to fill it, or is simply nothing there?*

J was determined to get good grades, to succeed at what they agreed was his, J's, job. He pictured himself in class all day, barely finding the strength to overcome his terror of his professors and classmates, even though the answers were right on the edge of his tongue. More often than not, Herr Haas, rigid at his lectern, melded into a man shouting orders, paralyzing him with fear. It was impossible to utter a sound let alone speak up; home with Franz was such a relief ...

Back to the books, thank God.

There was an emergency blood calling near Altmann-strasse, their original neighborhood.

"Name."

"Jan Hartmann."

The nurse carefully printed this on the card, and then recorded his address, age, medical history.

"Blood type?"

"I don't know."

"We'll have to test that first."

He unbuttoned his sleeve as the nurse adjusted the syringe for the sample. He looked down, coolly, at the spot where there used to be a small blue letter. Only a few strange wrinkles of skin remained. He missed the letter "J," but Franz felt J might suffer abuse in gym at school, and engaged a plastic surgeon to remove it. J let his arm lie there, to defy the nurse, to test her power of observation, if this was to be a proper screening. He watched the needle sinking in, never feeling a thing.

"I have type O-positive," said J that night, grinning through a mouthful of potato pancake.

"Very good," said Franz, spearing a hunk of mint-stuffed lamb. "If I recall from the Lebensborn delivery room, that means you're a universal donor." His azure eyes squinted in bald approval.

Franz organized the German and American film crew members into a bowling league. It was a great success, and expanded to Monday, Wednesday and Friday nights. Thursdays were for drinking with his motorcycle club friends at the beer hall, Tuesday and Saturday nights for dancing and movies with Loralei. Sunday nights were devoted exclusively to body-building, to balance, according to Franz, the week's lesser efforts.

J switched to nibbling cold cuts for supper. He was usually alone. Final grades were critical for university placement, and competition at school picked up considerably.

One evening, rummaging through the mess in his bedroom, J spotted the old violin case. It gave him a jolt, a panicky feeling, but basically he was pleased. He perched with it on his bed, recalling his total failure at violin lessons. He wasn't coordinated enough. Or the music—it was exhilarating, but too jarring and frenetic. Especially Bach. J opened the case. He was startled by the curly, glassy finish. How could it stay so polished? It looked like an antique from the Headmaster's library. What was it doing here in all this clutter? He ran his slender fingers over the worn letters on the violin's waist. R, A, D, space, A, R, and I. He'd forgotten those. Maybe he came from a family of rich Italian Jews— traders in silk brocade and patrons of the arts. Chamber soloists. The Radaris. He was enlivened. Gently, he lifted the instrument, uncovering a small black book. *Aleph* was on the first page, *beth* on the second. He thought of the puppet shows, the librettos, Franz's warm hands healing his ravaged skin. But he could never push the memories farther back. *Can't I at least picture her face?* He ran his finger down the delicate curve of the violin. His finger was trembling as he felt it connect to the hundreds of hands that had polished this wood with their playing. He fingered his neck chain with its little brass clasp, his half of the violin case fastener that he had shared with Franz. He knew, in his way, he was as strong as Franz. He was as German as Kant. *Bestimme dich aus dir selbst!* Determine yourself by yourself! *This, too, is buried alive in my being. I can be both—a German and a Jew, if I want.* He seized the little book of Hebrew symbols, shutting the violin case, perspiring now with excitement. He knew his German literature and history backwards and forwards. But he hadn't studied this little black book in years.

He knew Robert Heinrich, another silent one in his school, was a Jew. He had seen the initials "RHM" inscribed on the inside of his silver belt buckle, hanging in the locker room, the "M" apparently dropped.

"Does your family celebrate Passover?" J asked quietly, before morning vespers.

Robert turned scarlet.

"I'm studying Hebrew," J said eagerly, "and would like to hear some."

"Of course, Jan. Come for Shabbat dinner this Friday."

Two days later, Franz was unsettled about something. "I—I might be out rather late tonight, with Loralei. I might—stay at her place."

"That's fine. I—I'm going out myself."

"Good!" cried Franz with a wink.

The Heinrichs' home was in a tree-lined, tidy suburb. Robert took pleasure in pointing out the various heirlooms, hidden for years in secret storage.

"That looks like a Chinese backscratcher," said J, delighted with it all.

"No, Jan. That's a Torah Pointer. The handle's made of olivewood from the Holy Land, and the hand with its pointing finger is pure silver from Yemen. The elders, you see, used it to read word for word. The human hand must not touch the sacred parchment."

"I see." J's eyes were straining to catch every detail. "Do you speak Hebrew?"

"Not really. Just the Sh'ma Yisrael and a few prayers."

J was near intoxicated with Robert's accent, the mysterious sound of just one flipped tongue's worth of the ancient language of the holy brotherhood. *This is my Bar Mitzvah!*

Frau Heinrich, lean, elegant, dark, lit two candles as she rendered a blessing in Hebrew. "You see, Jan," Herr Heinrich said calmly. "The mother has the privilege to light the candles, because Eve, the first mother, extinguished the light of eternal life by disobeying God's word not to eat from the tree of knowledge of good and evil."

J nodded. And he watched her move about gracefully with the food. And he listened to the bespectacled father chanting the Kiddush, the various blessings, the story of deliverance from bondage in Egypt. Robert's sister Leila sat there, smiling sweetly. The words were soothing. *Why, then, am I missing Franz? Why am I hearing rasping, grating chords of a violin? And seeing the moist forehead of a woman?* Soon, he was lost in the Hebrew lullabies.

Later, when it was time to leave, Robert, his sister and parents assembled by the door; they were poised, olive-skinned, subdued.

"Did you lose," J faltered, trying to find the right words, "any family in the war?"

"Oh, yes," said Herr Heinrich. "Uncle Herschel … "

"I meant—daughters—or sons?"

The father smiled painfully, and shook his head no.

"I'm taking Loralei to a party at Mr. Hershenson's. He's the producer." Franz was preening in his new tweed jacket. "I wish you could go, too."

"Maybe they need an urchin for one of the street scenes," J blurted.

"Then we're coming back here. To my room. So if you hear, you know, some noise … " Franz flew out the door.

"Have fun." J let out a deep sigh, and shut the little black book in his lap. He would never become a Just Man, a Righteous One, for his generation of Jews. He'd just as soon polka at the beer hall and have blond hair like Franz. *That's no joke*, he said to himself. *Franz is much more a part of me than anyone or anything else.*

"J!" hollered Franz the next evening from the hallway.

J was sitting in the lotus position, surrounded by books. Solomon, son of David, or was it David, son of Solomon? 4,000 BCE, or 1400 BCE, that Abraham got the message and gathered his family?

"J. Guess what?"

"They want you to star in the sequel."

"Yes, J, I'm in the film!" erupted Franz, fortunately missing the jab. "I've got a part!"

They slumped on the sofa, Franz staring ahead in wonderment. "Well, aren't you excited?"

"Of course," J managed.

Franz grabbed J's shoulder. "It's not fair. I'm having all the fun." He frowned then slapped his hands. "So obvious. J, it's time you had a woman. It's very easy, and feels *incredible.*" He went to fetch a beer. "I will get you a lusty girl, no, two—one for me, also. Enough Hebrew history."

J arched his neck up along with his classmates at the gilded ceiling, the floating rococo cherubs, ribbons, and puffy clouds gracing the grand vestibule of the Nymphenberg Palace.

"It was here," intoned their history professor, "where Ludwig I waltzed with his mistress, Lola Montez, through the 1840s with a splendor, if there ever was one, that could rival Versailles. He was surely the most lavish of the Wittelsbachs, who ruled Bavaria for 738 years."

"Did you know the Hofbrauhaus," whispered Rudi to Heinz, "is 365 years old, the oldest in all of Germany!"

586 BCE, J prodded himself to recall—Nebuchadnezzar leveled the First Temple in Jerusalem.

The boys trotted from the palace upon completion of the tour to catch buses back to the city. J found himself on the platform stepping onto a bus headed in the opposite direction. He watched the bleak gray landscape float by. The road was lined with shuffling refugees, vacant faces returning from center city, another day in hopes of finding a job. The rusted Quonset huts were surrounded by acres of softening spring mud. The sign to Dachau was printed with such diminutive lettering. He found himself on the road, a mile away.

The acrid smell of the people annoyed him, as of course it would Franz. Surely the public baths were in operation. He recalled this lot from the other week at the government office, shoving towards the window, waving angry fists, demanding service and not even citizens yet. He was simply renewing Franz's motorcycle license, waiting in line like most of the rest. Eastern Jews. Horsetraders, peddlers, Slavs; Rumanians, Hungarians, Czech. Flooding the streets, disrupting the peace. At the very least, until they learned the language, couldn't they put them in … he marched on.

"*Arbeit Macht Frei!*" greeted the scrollwork over the gate. The lumbering peasants, parents, professors for all he knew, made way for him as he strolled through the grounds in his crisp blue school uniform. He gazed at the shacks, row upon row, swarming with this new crop of wretched souls. They didn't seem to have the strength to complain, at this end of town.

He meandered on. The barbed wire was all in place, eight years later. The empty guard towers stood sentinel like gaping scarecrows.

He walked. He walked the whole length, and then the circumference, past hundreds of shacks, until he lost count.

Forty years they wandered in the wilderness.

He found Barache X slightly off the main campus. For this there was no sign at all. "Krematorium," he thought it might say. Then at least it could serve as a grave marker of sorts.

It was late afternoon, and ebony shadows swallowed most of the site. The building was locked. The windows were covered with pitch on the inside. Did his family make it this far, or were they shot in their home? How silly of me to hope there would be a list of names. Whatever good would that do? I can't even remember *my mother's face.*

He picked up some pebbles and tossed them singly into the vast ditch, in fact a concrete moat, in case they slithered like bony lizards through electrified fences.

He clenched his hands trying with all his might to make fists, and then let them go limp. *It will never work: my making a home with Franz. I have to find my real family, in spirit if not in fact. I have a responsibility not to fight, not to whine, but to continue!*

He emptied his pockets of coins. He took out the few bills from his wallet, and tossed them on the ground as well so he couldn't change his mind. And then he started walking. He walked for four hours, over hard gravel to the center of Munich, until the blisters broke and soaked his blue silk socks. *Die Juden Sint Unser Ungluch*, read the banner at the famous rally in the newsreel. The Jews Are Our Misfortune. *Stiefkinder mussen doppelt-artig sein!* Yes, that was another, but from his *memory*. Step-children must be doubly good! J kept on walking, walking, past the push-button elevator, up the eight flights of stairs on his bloody feet; he was ready to walk back down if he had to. And one from his people, yes, he was sure. *Vergiss Nicht! Vergiss Nicht!* Do Not Forget! Do Not Forget! Or what if—*what if they're alive?*

"J! Where have you been? It's *Fasching*, didn't you remember our Bavarian Mardi-Gras? The film company's throwing the biggest, splashiest fest this city has ever seen—the entire Munich Stadium rented for three fucking days. Here's Grete! Here's Louise! They'll love your circumcised schlong. I bought our *Chevrolet* today! Hallelujah, comin' to ya. *We're gonna dance all night.*" Franz's golden hair was tumbling like uncorked champagne in time to the blaring radio.

"Dance the Ho-ra!" J started singing. "Light the Menorah! Now's the time for joy-a!" Then he pranced on tiptoe and threw up his arms, doing a jig on his screaming feet.

Chapter 6

Franz was ahead of schedule, so he slipped into the sweet shop to check the day's offerings ... apple, almond, fig. A fruit tart would be his ordinary treat: not too rich and with some nutritional value. Perhaps if he did an extra ten laps in the pool, he could choose the raspberry creme in puff pastry. Hadn't he, after all, skipped toast and jam at breakfast? He dashed back onto the street, briskly walking towards the natatorium.

Franz held his trousers upside-down, found the creases of each leg, and folded them neatly together. He hung his shirt and suit jacket on the hangers provided. He glanced at the sign demanding showering before entering the pool. He had worked intently but quietly at his desk all day ... he could smell no perspiration ... most people ignored ... Inhaling deeply, he plunged into the icy shower jets.

The first laps required an excess of energy. He pictured the burning of waste materials, the ejection of toxins. Somersaulting at the end of the pool and kicking off under water, he opened his eyes and enjoyed his extra surge over the others. He imagined an Olympic coach spotting him, astounded at his age, his speed, his physique, his questionable career in business instead of sports as he, Franz, would smile brightly and zip off in his '53 Chevrolet Suburbanite. He counted to ten ten times for his hundred laps, just over a mile, rarely losing track. His head was crystal clear. His lungs were stretched and deflated like a vigorous bellows, applauding him rhythmically for this opportunity to come alive.

Afterwards, he darted along the pavement, weaving around the slow pedestrians. February, March, April— enough, plough, cough; Franz practiced his English at every chance.

He chose a toffee buttercream éclair and a brandied pear custard for J, and a plain gingerbread cake for himself. He felt terrific. He had a playful girlfriend, his job had all kinds of potential, and his home life with J ran so smoothly. He ducked to his customary shops, feeling the celery, smelling the fish. J was far too busy with tests at school to add meat to those fragile bones. He should fly like this up the stairs for extra exercise; not give in to the elevator, the easy way, thought Franz as he high-jumped the final landing whistling "Man from Mandalay."

Franz scrubbed the rabbit and sauteed the liver. He stirred the onions and minced a caraway seed as a possible accompaniment. Someday he really should make Edda a meal. But she cooked for him, he cooked for J, J earned good grades, balanced their bank accounts, would become a professor— Franz rapidly fixed the salad and then perched on the sofa with his latest *Life*.

"Ballantine Beer watches your belt-line," he repeated slowly to himself. "Brewed to the American taste *and* the American figure." He lingered over the pine-paneled walls, the slim, openly smiling hostess in a cinch belt serving tapered glasses of bubbling, pale golden beer, the men in brightly checkered sport coats and polished loafers, heads back and gently laughing at the joke, the easy friendship between the sexes. Tonight was his night with the boys at the beer house. It was fun but it was so loud, so sloppy. "The '54 Ford takes the drive out of driving." He thought of the squat little cars most people had. Beetles, *bugs*, the Americans had nicknamed them. He read on, wondering if his '53 Suburbanite had ball-joint front suspension …

"Caught you. Drooling over *Life* ads again," said J trooping in. "I thought we were supposed to think German-made."

"I'm practicing my English. I know it's not school-grade, but … "

J smiled and tossed down his books and slumped in a chair opposite, sighing and pushing back wild strands of black hair from his forehead.

Franz pointed to an advertisement. "Look at these spiffy new hairstyles."

"I remember you telling about trying to cover up my big ears with long hair to look less Jewish."

Franz rose and went to the kitchen, wiping the carved oak salad bowl and matching tongs. He folded the linen napkins and set the table with the pewter plates, his favorite for rabbit and game birds.

J hiked his shoes onto the walnut coffee table, reaching for the magazine. "Here's an ad for a flea-killing dog collar. That's an idea for you, Franz."

"What?" He sampled the sauces.

"You know how fussy we are about dogs messing up cars? Why don't you get someone at Grunwald to make a dog-proof backseat cover?"

Franz looked at J, unsure as usual whether or not he was joking. Whichever, if it was J's idea it was worth filing away. "Come sit."

"Very nice stew, Franz."

"We had a buyer from Paris today. Impossible to please. 'Of course, with patterns this plain,' she said, 'we can only look at upholstery possibilities, not fashion.'"

"Great dressing on the celery salad."

"Mr. Farnsworth from London was here, too. Now the plainer the better for the Brits. He'd only nod and smile and ask to see the next sample. Had no idea what the guy was thinking. He was from some underwear company. Imagine the English discussing underpants. Now the *Italians*—"

J wiped his mouth on the linen and replaced it, still folded.

"I heard today from—"

"Eat more stuffing, for God's sake. Of course with the Amis—everything is 'swell' and 'really neat'. There was this fellow from Dallas, and he talked like in Gene Autry movies. He took *our* salesman out for lunch and even came to the Grunwald bowling night!"

"Franz. I got accepted! It's the finest, oldest and most celebrated of all German universities. I've been awarded a full scholarship—to Heidelberg."

Franz stopped chewing for a moment, dumbstruck. He leapt up and shook J's shoulder. "Wonderful!" he mumbled . "Tonight you must celebrate with us at the Hofbrauhaus!"

"I'd just as soon—"

"No, no, a real beer party for J, at last."

"Franz. This means I'll be leaving. Our home."

Franz arched his back, exhaled, and said: "I'll get you a car, another Chevy. You can stay here on weekends. You can study—and I will cook to make up for all the meals you'll forget to eat. Come now, let's celebrate!"

The beer hall was bellowing. Thick smoke made of the wall lamps a bloody smear. The accordion player was pumping away as Franz and J wound around tightly nestled tables, glistening from the freely splashed steins.

"Hey Georg! Hey Herm! Hey Rudi!" called Franz as they reached his regular spot.

"Hey Franz!" they answered in chorus.

"You remember Jan." He rearranged nearby chairs as J nodded to the boys. Georg quickly swiveled his head to the stage, and tapped his free hand on the table as the tuba blasted a solo. Franz ordered two half liters of Maerzenbier, Munich's dark amber, winter-brewed special, and loosely rested his arm around the back of J's chair. The boys were wolfing down the cheese and thin-sliced, salted radish as fast as the clarinet player slid up and down the scales.

"Georg!" Franz shouted over the thumping beat, squeezing J's slight shoulders. "Jan here is going to university."

Georg had straight dark bangs covering his forehead, so it was difficult to read his expression. His eyes were very intense. "Georg, you go to classes at night and weekends, don't you?" Georg stared over at Franz and J. "Perhaps," said Franz, "Jan could find out about your school here in Munich."

J lurched forward, out of Franz's embrace.

"Your friend," snapped Georg, "doesn't look like he'd much enjoy the dueling fraternities." He turned again to the music.

Their beers arrived, Franz wishing he'd thought to order an import, a *Ballantine.*

"Heidelberg is a walled town," J said to Franz. "You can't get more German than a walled city." He took a good swallow from his tankard.

"But I can't picture you in a fraternity, J." Franz sipped the flat, heavy liquid and leaned full back into his seat. He tapped his feet to the polka and watched J enjoy the beer. His friends, too, seemed at ease, the same table every Thursday night.

The evening skipped along. The patrons got louder, the music livelier.

"What are you going to study at university?" asked Herm.

"Literature, I guess," J said.

"I should think philosophy or religion," said Georg. "You seem like the pious type, eh Rudi?"

"I am very pious," J said. "And I am very serious, right now, about swallowing this half-liter whole." And he did.

The boys cheered. Franz felt a wave of relief, J joining in.

"Hog sausage and a *liter,* please," announced J, giggling to the barmaid.

"Who's paying for this round?"

"I will!" J shouted, generously sampling the wurst.

Georg laughed. "Always one hand on the till."

Franz laughed. J laughed. They all laughed.

"Naturally," J said. "Who else was *filthy* enough to handle it? Your Pope," and here J dropped his chin and made the sign of the cross, "wouldn't let *you* folks stoop so low! Gold, coins, jewels—lock them up in the Vatican vault!"

Georg chuckled, then Franz, tentatively, followed suit.

J tossed down the rest of his beer and craned his neck low over the table, cupping his hand in a mock whisper: "Psst. Anyone interested in two percent interest for fifty years? C'mon, guys. I'll make it one-and-three quarters, for friends. Georg, wanna hire me to take your exams? Go to the head of the class for a flat thou. A bargain!" He sat up, near shouting now. "How else can I stick my crooked nose through those carved arches?"

The boys continued to snicker.

Franz, alarmed, stopped tapping his foot. He had to get them singing.

More beers arrived, liters this time, the boys except Franz laughing loudly and acting like storm troopers, tossing up Heil Hitlers to the scowling waitress.

"Did you know," slurred J, "there are e-lev-en million Jews in the world?"

"That's eleven million too many."

"No, but *listen,*" hissed J as if in confidence. "We did away with *half* that many. That's not bad."

"Well, men, we have our work cut out for us," roared one of the others, as J stood and held his stein towards the martial music, lifting his legs, one after the other, in sharp cadence.

The blood in Franz's neck was thundering. He was bewildered, then frightened by the flow of words, the jests, his brother's wild conduct.

"Let us march them to the death camps!" J sung. "The death camps, the death camps … " He stood on his chair as the boys roared approval, pouring the liters down their gullets then stomping along in the mock parade. The nearby tables joined in the singing, the lilting polka, not hearing their words but banging the floor and reinforcing the rhythm. Franz watched in horror as J shoved in a mouthful of soggy pretzels, boiled pork, more gulps of beer. Why didn't he eat this enthusiastically at home, with superior food? His crazy hair was matted down with sweat, and the tails of his shirt hung out in disarray. "It's true!" J screamed. "We have *worms* in our mouth and spit blood. We poison little children and have arms of different lengths." Franz gasped as J hunched one shoulder high above the other. "We are *sorry*, truly sorry, that we started the war. We'll lend you money without interest ... "

Georg, Herm, and Rudi were near hysterical with excitement, beer and tears and saliva running down their beefy red faces. J was wrestling with Herm's shoes. Herm could not stop choking on his own laughs. "C'mon," said J sounding very sober. "I want to kiss them. Let me have them, to spit polish. I'll *lick* them, like new. C'mon, Herm. *Now*, I said! *Hand them over.*"

Franz could only hear the unison of boots and shoes hammering the old floorboards in all four corners of the beer hall. Why didn't J ever share in good times at home? What was so great about celebrating his leaving Munich for better places? Why was he standing *on top of the table now*, rejoicing this way in front of hundreds of strangers ... so happy to be leaving this boisterous, beer-guzzling, nit-witted city but still, his *home* ...

"Stop it!" Franz shouted at J, although his words were drowned out by the throng. He reached up for a shirttail but by then J was doubled over, the spray of vomit more than covering the circumference of the table. The stench traveled well beyond their section of the tavern. The band stopped, and the nearby drinkers and singers hollered abusive words, as Franz carried J out onto the street. He hauled him the several blocks to their apartment building, taking the elevator, this time, to floor number eight.

"I'm so sorry," said J the next day when they were face to face.

Franz shifted on the sofa, his vision gone dull and cast to the floor.

"I know you want me to be happy and singing and straighten my room and help peel potatoes and remember to take out the garbage when it's my turn."

Franz rose and brought J a bowl of carrot soup. "It's very bland. Maybe you'll find it soothing."

"The soup is very nice."

Franz smiled faintly then stood again. "I'll get you some bread." There was color again in J's high cheeks. The soup *was* very good. *Perhaps there's an intercity delivery service … Heidelberg isn't so far away …*

Franz strode through the aisles of the Grunwald Fabric Factory. He was wearing his dark blue serge suit. Edda said it made him look especially blond. He adjusted the silver, initialed cufflinks, a Christmas present from J, and tugged on his shirt sleeves to expose the appropriate half-inch. Blue was not a good color on days he had to change the bulletin boards in the loom shop because of the filaments flying about, but he never knew when one of his superiors would have a new instruction or urgent message for him to post. Franz glided on to the packaging division bulletin board. Mr. Grunwald had personally thanked him for single-handedly organizing the employee bowling and soccer leagues. Three vice-presidents, perhaps as many as twelve of the assistant division managers, called him "Franz" or at least smiled when they passed him in the hall.

"Once a week isn't enough," whimpered Edda as they began their Tuesday night visit. Edda was sixteen, and working full-time as a mother's helper for a visiting American businessman. She tossed her curly brown hair onto his chest, trying to tickle him.

"That feels good."

"You've such lovely smelling skin. It's nicer than mine." She kissed the back of his hand and then with it stroked her belly, squatting at his side on the bed. "See. I'm rougher."

"What does this man do?"

"Who?" She moved his hand closer to her center.

"The American."

"Herr Robinson? Some kind of soap business."

"Maybe it's Rinso White-Rinso Blue. I always thought you smelled so fresh and clean. Hey, where are you putting my fingers?" he mock-protested.

He looked at the nipples on her small breasts stiffening. "Does this Mr. Robinson ever try to have sex with you when you're alone, or when the children are around, for that matter?"

"Huh? Sex around children?"

He withdrew his hand. "Let me hold you. C'mon. Lie down."

"In a minute. Just keep doing that, Franz. Please." She replaced his hand. "Franz, oh Franz." She was sigher louder.

"Oh Edda," he answered, massaging rapidly but gently, teasingly. She wouldn't let him enter her, but this wasn't so bad. She crumpled against him, sighing for several moments. He thought about the end of his penis as she played with it, waving it like a banner at a parade. He liked when it came out of hiding, like now, all strong and spectacular. He liked when it was soft and safely protected by layers of smooth skin. It was odd the way J's was. Wasn't it unmanly to have that skin cut away? A sign of his covenant with God, J had said. Well, it was important to J, and that's what counted.

J was in a quandary about university. Studying was the only thing he was good at, but he was losing interest. Franz had always wanted him to become a professor. He hated the thought of leaving home, yet Franz was so rarely around.

"I went to *church* tonight, with Edda and her parents," reported Franz that evening. "The preacher said we don't need to blame ourselves so much for murdering the Jews."

J looked without blinking at his lifetime mate.

"I mean, it was only a few hundred Jewish people, right? There were gypsies and Slavs and Drekpolacks. Didn't you say about Dachau, those ovens were built and never used?"

J continued looking. He did not feel hurt. Franz was his

brother, his whole family. He could say what he pleased; underneath, nothing would change.

"It's funny, Franz, but before this century we Jews were actually welcomed more in Germany than anywhere else. I guess that's why so many of us made this our home."

Franz squirmed in his seat. "Why must you be special? Why can't everyone *just fit in?*"

"I'm *trying*, Franz. I do at school." He dropped his head. "The beer hall was certainly a flop."

"You know I'm up for a promotion at Grunwald. What should I say if they ask me about my family?"

"Say whatever you want. Haven't we always made up who we were?" J said, feeling uncharacteristically blunt, returning to his bedroom and his books. He was peeved at Franz; more so, angry at himself. *Doing all I can to get into Heidelberg: to please Franz, to please whoever they are looking down on me.*

For several seconds Franz stared at J's door, a sour taste rising from his gut. He went to his own room, and bolted the door. He yanked off his clothes and struck a match, holding it to a candle for soft light, to make it nice and calm. *J thinks too much. He twists things around. He can make me feel so inferior!* Franz was determined to keep things simple, like sex. He lowered himself to the cold floor. Slowly, he began rubbing his cock and balls, growing heavy, getting engorged. He enjoyed Edda's praise, but he didn't need it. These, though, he did. He stroked his neck and cheeks with the silky things he'd swiped from her, similar to a few of the finer fabrics at the factory, but not this smooth. He wanted to drink in the pleasure forever. Could he wait? *He had to wait,* until he could slip them on, until he could feel his crotch caressed by silk, at least for a second or two before exploding ...

Writhing, he knocked over the candle, extinguishing it. He groped in the darkness for the towel and found it, well before the wetness had a chance to crust and stain the beautiful fabric.

He fell asleep, breathing deeply despite the flares and occasional bombs. He could see the night sky turn pale red then pink through his resting eyelids as Gretchen held him close to her belly and lower, before separating her legs. On nights when the linen closet was locked up, he really didn't mind, her body being so smooth and warm, the fresh sheets and satiny gown gently encasing him, sealing out the sirens and the thunder with just a single diaphanous layer ...

The earth rumbled underfoot. He noticed that much even before looking up. The enormous, corrugated tires pounded the pavement: loose cobblestones or flying gravel, debris of bombs, broken crates, these made no difference to the rushing truck. All the might of a convoy in a single, steaming van on its mission. There were people scurrying from the road in all directions, dropping parcels, looking away in horror. Why was he the only witness? Clutching his own parcel, clutching the wall, opening his jaw then locking it speechless. Head on, he saw the driver's grinning teeth, the olive uniform, the tip of the steering wheel, the child's yellow shirt, the waving arm, the boy's pudgy arm waving at him, Franz, in a slow-motion salute ...

"Stop!" he screamed, and sprang up. "Halt!" he kept on screaming.

"Franz," he heard, a distant, hollow voice plus a banging on a door. Insistent, shrieking Nurse Zerbst. "Franz. Open up! Are you all right?"

"Please stop," he shuddered into his hands, soaking them with sweat.

"Franz, I'm coming," he heard from miles away, wondering how he got on the cold linen closet floor, littered with garbage and filth, probably tossed in by scavengers from the courtyard through the tiny window, mingled now with damp discarded linens strewn about in the middle of the night. Rattling, fumbling at the door, waking him up. Labor pains, air raids, shouts and demands forever bombarding him ... He managed to reach and unlock his door. A switch was flicked; a dazzling light blinded him.

"Franz! Holy Jehovah, what a mess. Why are you sprawled there in *women's underwear?*"

Franz worried that his bosses weren't exercising his leadership potential, those qualities he felt in his bones and that J reaffirmed. He was checking the fire extinguishers on his rounds, another of his supposedly important duties. That he was a founder as opposed to a bearer or destroyer of culture was as hammered into him as the air he breathed. If this crop of Germans lost the war, then it was his job to start again, to join with fresher, sturdier stock. Selbstandig! To stand on one's own two feet. This is my heritage.

He wrote a letter to the friendly fabric buyer from Dallas, Texas. He proposed a sales campaign for "Pooch Pad," a dog-proof back car seat cover. He never received a reply.

He asked for extra assignments at work. He decided he was not pushing himself hard enough. One lousy idea, now a laughingstock in America's largest state! He began swimming fifty percent more laps at a stretch, and skipping pastries altogether. He was going flabby. He fucked Edda, and Clarissa, and Ingelene, with equal fervor, for as long as they wanted, caressing, pummeling, licking, lavishing them with as much pleasure as they could withstand. So *self-centered* I've become. He made a gefilte fish dinner for J. He looked up the high holidays in J's vast library and found the recipes. He set up seven individual candles, the holders raised on various ashtrays, to resemble a menorah.

"Good grief, Franz. What have you done?"

"It's a surprise. For Rosh Hashanah. Happy New Year."

"Let's sit down, Franz. I don't know what to say, I haven't seen you in weeks, it seems. We've both been so busy." J leaned forward on the sofa, wringing his hands.

"You haven't been—reading," said Franz. "You've been running around. A *girl,* yes?"

"Well, sort of. I've been to several meetings of Habonim."

"That sounds Hebrew, yes?"

"It's a Jewish youth group. Aimed at populating the—

the Kibbutzim."

"Populating? Good. I'll get us some beer. Is that okay for—Rosh Hashanah?"

"Sure."

"Listen, J," said Franz returning. "I've been thinking hard. You know I'm always the one who says you think too blasted much." He poured the Ballantines into his new tall tapered glasses. "Anyway. I've checked at Grunwald personnel division, and they have a branch office in Heidelberg. It's not a big one, but they're willing—"

"Franz, I'm not going to Heidelberg. I turned down the scholarship."

Franz rested his sparkling glass on the walnut coffee table. "You're not accepting the scholarship? But—you deserve it so much. After all your work, these hard years … " Franz felt dryness shrink his throat, but didn't lift his glass. "Then perhaps you'll study here, at the university. Of course you'd be accepted!" He managed a large swallow. "Maybe not by the dueling fraternities," he laughed, glancing sideways at J.

J smiled wanly. He clasped his slender, pale hands together, the bubbles rising with less speed inside his untouched glass. His lips were working, but no words emerged. He heaved a large sigh. "I've decided to leave Munich, Franz. I'm not going to a university." He looked up, slowly, causing them both to tremble. "I'm going to live and work with my people, in Israel!"

Franz felt his face drain of blood. "But—I thought you were—German, too."

"What do we know? How do we know your parents weren't Poles? They're blonder than we. You know how they took the children to raise here that looked … "

Franz stood, strode to the table and blew out the candles. "After all we've done together … "

"We rescued each other," J managed. "You were like a mother."

"It was my job. It was my responsibility."

J slumped completely into the sofa.

"How will you make a home for yourself?" pleaded Franz.

"I'm sorry. But, Franz. Maybe your parents are alive. Maybe you too have *a real family.* In Scandinavia, or Austria. They found people here from all over the Reich. Oh, Franz." J rose and stood next to Franz, both of them rigid. Facing each other, they embraced and could not let go.

Over J's shoulder, Franz watched the Kugel growing cold, congealing in the red Bavarian crystal dish etched with reindeer and dirndls, wood nymphs and edelweiss.

J stepped apart, squeezing Franz's broad shoulders. "Just think. You could have a mother and father somewhere. Look, we're only sixteen, seventeen, as far as we know. Life is just beginning!"

Franz walked into his bedroom, and quietly closed the door.

J stood outside. "We can write, you know. You'll be making more and more money at the factory. You can fly and visit me on the kibbutz! Think of all the money you've saved for my university expenses, Franz. It's yours. That's how I want you to spend it. I'm sure they allow non-Jewish guests … "

Franz collapsed onto his bed and shut his eyes. He was devoid of thought, yet something steely was stirring in his gut that bore no resemblance to grief.

J opened the door and perched on the edge of the bed. "Look, Franz."

Franz did so.

J pulled out his neck chain, under cover but always there, his half of the brass violin clasp.

J departed a few weeks later, and Franz received his promotion. The promotion meant nothing to him. He was simply going through the motions. Perhaps his supervisors liked it better that way: Franz's quiet demeanor for a change, his blank stares; his punctuality, his lack of eye contact and incessant suggestions.

He was losing weight; this he didn't mind. What reason

to fuss over food without J? He took the elevator instead of hiking the stairs, entering the flat one evening after work. All was in order, how he thought he liked it. No crazy mess of books and soiled clothes in J's room, eerily empty, as if he, Franz, had always lived alone.

Maybe I have lived alone, it hit him as he crashed into the sofa. He took a few swigs of his beer and set it aside— sour and flat. *Maybe J and I always did live in totally separate worlds.* How vain of me to think J has or ever would embrace our German community. In fact, it's not truly right for me, either! He sat up straight. He fondled his half of the brass violin clap, tucked into his wallet. Well, he's sure taught me a thing or two about pursuing your dreams. *Yes. J has his, and I have mine.*

Two months to the day after J boarded the plane for Tel Aviv, Israel, Franz returned to the airport with his own ream of official documents for his flight to America.

Stadtemann, Strässemann, Stendemann … he had fiddled with the papers for days, filling out everything except his name. He was vaguely aware of an earlier one, before he was given Hartmann at the Lebensborn, something starting with an "S." J left for Israel as Jan Hartmann, but Franz knew there was some woman, perhaps his foster-mother or someone before that, in his own, very early years …

He bustled about the apartment, tying up boxes of household items to be given to refugees. He held the red Bavarian crystal serving dish. Did he have room for this memento? He let it slip between his fingers onto the floor. Didn't J recite something about breaking glass at a Jewish wedding bringing good luck? He dropped the new set of pilsner glasses as well, and then carefully swept them up. The valises were strapped. He stared once again at the blank name space, seized with tension and wonderment, then finally printed, in his steadiest penmanship, the words *Frank Mann.*

He had accepted a job set up by Mr. Howard "Howie" Robinson, Edda's boss, who said he'd have no trouble starting in the mailroom with his excellent command of English. Mr. Robinson was Central European Sales Representative for one of the world's largest soapsuds factories, with headquarters and "loads of cheap room and board" located "smack in the guts of America," in Cayahooga County, Buena Vista, Indiana.

Franz had written on a slip the name and address of this company, which J crumpled and shoved into his bursting knapsack. "Now, don't you lose it, so you can write to me and I know where you are. If you waste away in that desert, you may need some 'Hoosier' hamburgers and milkshakes." J simply grinned in reply, his likely riot of thoughts at that moment completely cancelling each other. Franz himself was brimming with conviction.

Franz pushed the down elevator button on floor number eight for the final time. After this, he said to himself, recalling another of Mr. Robinson's nifty phrases, in reference to the mailroom job, "there was no place to go but up!"

1958

Chapter 7

Ĵ sunk one hand into the soft loam to support himself. He grasped the cultivator in his other hand and broke up patches of crust which had baked around the tomato plant. The sun boiled happily in the mid-summer sky, the ninth of Av: specifically, *Tisha be'Av.* J sprang like a jack rabbit down one long row and back another. He could picture the Gush Emunim, the strictly pious ones, in their dumpy, dimly-lit synagogues of Mea Shearim, nodding, fasting, mourning the destruction of the temple about this time of year. He took the end of his cultivating tool and banged straight a tilting tomato stake. Let them worship in the shadows. He looked up, sweat stinging his eyes, to catch his breath. The hazy violet hills ringing Mount Herman, the shimmering flat fields surrounding the simple buildings of Kibbutz Ben-Yaakov, here too was the House of God. Shuli and his other companions bent over in the garden looked like dollops of melting butter under the blazing sun.

J was soaking wet. He squatted and uprooted weeds in his short-sleeved khaki shirt, his short khaki pants, and the heavy work boots which anchored him. He felt like a coiled spring, ready to leap to the next plant when he was absolutely sure the one at hand was sucker-free and securely tied. As it would often occur to him, it was Franz's boundless vigor, now his own. J stood and surveyed his handiwork, four rows down and forty-six to go. It was a vegetable garden for two hundred souls.

"Shuli!" he shouted. "Take a break now."

She slowly hoisted her stooped frame, scowled at him, pawed the air, and returned to her plants.

Suddenly there were twice as many suckers to pinch. The greenery was jungle-thick. He checked his wooden notation stick. Aha, he recalled. The stem-transplanted rows. Stalks twice as meaty, whole clusters of blossoms and developing fruit a good two weeks ahead of schedule. He couldn't wait to report this news to Dov, chairman of the Agricultural Council. Meanwhile, he stretched, twisted, toiled to work the earth, all for the good of his new community, for eight, ten hours of total concentration; he would simply, happily, lose track of time.

"Yod!" Shuli shouted to him, Hebrew for "i" and "z," the closest transliteration of "j." She hobbled along the broad aisles between the peppers and sprawling melon vines, and he followed her for their mid-morning break.

They sipped warm tomato juice in the shade of a dusty olive tree.

"Some heat," said J, not complaining, feeling so mellow in fact to be at her side.

"Be glad we don't have mosquitoes," said Shuli softly.

J smiled and studied her in the flickering shadows. Her face was deeply carved with crow's feet at the eyes plus a zigzag of lines across the brow. She was one of the yushuv, a pioneer, a Huleh Valley original who helped drain the great swamp.

"I shouldn't take this rest," she said, peering out onto the vast potato patch. "They told me, stop at two. What does that give me—six hours all told? How, I ask, can you pinch the beetles and hill the beans in six hours?" She sipped her juice.

"Don't worry," said J. "I'll be done with the tomatoes."

"I worry," said Shuli. She rubbed her hands. "Listen. I used to pick the entire olive crop! *They* say, some big-shot committee, us old ladies should take it easy. Sixty I'm only."

She looked seventy-five to J who was twenty-one or thereabouts, as far as he could ever know. He was in awe of her dedication, her pride in her children, her quiet strength. "It's wonderful, Shuli." He sighed. "I saw all of Israel in the Army. From here to Eilat. I'm so happy to call this home. I could do without the rolls of barbed wire at the edge of the fields."

Home. Five years since Munich, and almost as many since they'd corresponded. J made a fist of dry dirt, for reassurance, he realized. The ball fell to powder at its release. It was he who tossed Franz's latest address. *There's no going back. We are worlds apart, and all for the good.* So why then, he continued, did I cancel the opportunity of simply staying in touch with Franz? He'd be a threat to maintaining my grip on this soil?

"Listen, Yod." Shuli broke the silence, running fingers over her wrinkles. "Hurry you better and speak up for Rivka."

"What's the rush? I've only been here a few months."

"You should have made a shiduch in the Army. We don't have *that* many girls on the kibbutz."

J sketched circle patterns in the parched earth with a finger.

She continued. "Besides. We need the babies."

He stood abruptly, extending his hand to her. Up she rose, groaning slightly. "I'll help with the beans when I'm finished the tomatoes," he said.

"You're a nice boy." She patted his hand. "Soon you'll be working the fields. My oldest Edel will teach you how to operate the ... " Her voice trailed off as she lumbered away.

He stepped into the glare of onion-colored sky. The steady drone of tractors and humming insects pelted him with their rhythm as he returned to work. From a lifetime within dark walls, he was suddenly spilled onto this ocean of blistering acres. He found a slug in a damp haven of foliage and pruned back branches. He supposed Franz was a wealthy American by now from some outlandish, brilliant scheme. J spun a thread of guilt into one of bloated pride, picturing Franz's look of disbelief as he beheld J's strapping body, bronzed by the sun, hardened by the soil. And wouldn't Franz be amazed, intelligent people perfectly at ease *without money*, without their own apartments or bathrooms, with rooms for sleeping and for nothing else? How grand to be working for a common cause. He held up a wriggling earthworm, coiling then springing full length in protest. Just like the floppy side-locks dancing from the near-shaven heads of young orthodox boys as they scooted about the sidewalks. You see. We *are* all the same, he proclaimed to himself, replacing the worm. The Holy Land is *alive*.

J sat next to Allon at lunch in the huge community dining hall. Allon had befriended J at the very start: J was a willing listener.

"Shalom Yod. How goes it?" Allon rolled his sleeves ever higher onto his brown biceps, then planted his elbows firmly on the table.

"Did you know today is Tisha be'Av?" asked J. "One of the holiest fast days of the Jewish calendar?"

Allon exploded his mouthful of soup back into the bowl. "Who gives a rat's ass!" J loved his outbursts, provoked them in fact. Allon would actually listen to him, as well. Allon, the third generation sabra, smeared his bread with margarine. "Religion is a holding pattern for you minority Jews. You had to make your family weaving tallith tassels."

"But I had a mystical experience this morning," said J. "Right in the mud."

"Me too," mumbled Allon, slurping his barley soup. "Up to my waist in the carp pond. 'This is a miracle' I thought. Throw in two fish and zam—no St. Peter or nothing—we get two hundred!"

"I know. You think we Jews are just a cult."

"No! *You* Jews. *We* Hebrews."

J chewed his tomato salad with particular devotion. He wondered if his opinions would grow sharp and strong like Allon's, here in the full blast of Israeli sun. "Is it all right if I keep reading the *Bal-Shem-Tov* at the Children's House?"

"Talking dogs, dancing rabbis—that's okay for kids."

"Hey, Israel's just had its tenth birthday party. We're growing up." J elbowed Allon, who didn't smile.

"This T'Hina is mushy," said a rosy-faced woman near-by. "Don't you boys think this T'Hina's too mushy? Now if I had my own kitchen … "

"Tell the kitchen committee," snapped Allon as J shrugged to the nice lady.

Food, at the heart of his boyhood home, J mused; Franz forever fussing. Here it was simply nutrition. And look at me: sympathizing with these women, *mothers*, over this paste unfit for a hog!

"Now Yod," said Allon, crossing his legs. "Zionism's fine. Personally, I don't need it. I was *born* here. So were my parents. This *is* my country. I am not 'returning.' This is simply my job. I'm a builder and farmer."

"Thanks for sharing your home with strangers."

"Are you being smart with me?" He pointed with his bread. "Now don't get me wrong. I have great sympathy, horror, at what happened to these pitiful people in Europe. I welcome their help. Just don't act like you're doing me a favor picking up the threadbare homestead. *My* family was here in the 1890s."

J forced a smile and a nod. He imagined his own grand-father, settling disputes as the town rebbe, or clearing land in the Ukraine.

"You Jews," Allon continued, "insist on going back, back, back in time! Forget archeology. Let's talk about de-fense … let's talk about how tough we are in spite of your tender-hearted god. This suffering, this obsession with sin … it's ancient history."

J was elated over Allon's involvement.

"Yod, my haver, I want you to march back to that to-mato field and *pray* we find a more successful kibbutz in-dustry than making matchsticks. And stop drooling about that hamburger and Coke on a fast day. I know you religious zealots! Shalom! Happy Tisha be'Av!"

"Wait a second," said J standing, following his friend outdoors. "Do the fish really multiply that fast?"

Allon raised his black eyebrows and shrugged his broad shoulders. "Just making a point. Listen, stud, talking of reproducing. I have decided to marry Devi. She is to have our child next month. We think we would make a good family."

"That's wonderful!" exclaimed J.

"And you? You seem to spend a lot of time with Rivka. When are you moving to her room?"

"We're just friends."

Allon grinned, waved, and joined his tractor crew.

The khamsin, the stinging east wind, blew steadily at J's matted hair, his skin stretched and dried from the brief lunchtime retreat. Ear-splitting gunfire shattered his reverie as he whiplashed and dove into the dirt before he could check himself. *Crack-crack*, it came again, as J rose, wiping particles of sour soil from his lips, recognizing it as rifle practice but still quaking. Staccato shots were ingrained in his eardrums, along with a straining violin. He returned to his knees in the garden, his fingers stained green from pinching tomato suckers. Allon is right. I must address the business end of life. He was sure Franz would have an idea to make the kibbutz money. What to do with these tomatoes, for example, all ripe at once? Hamburgers … *ketchup*, J thought. It took a bushel to boil down into a gallon of sauce. Cider vinegar from their orchard, plus their own orange blossom honey and spices. Ketchup! He'd recommend it to the Agricultural Council. He predicted there'd be almost double the yield because of transplanting horizontally the entire stem for triple the foundation.

He began nodding to the beat of the insect drum, the more intense, mid-afternoon tambourines. The branches of plants just ten feet away appeared to do a belly dance, undulating in the oven-dry heat. He thought of Allon's putting him down along with Judaism. He was pleased Allon took it so seriously. Now Franz, it was the last thing he liked to do: talk about J's ancestral faith. Whenever the topic of Jews did come up with Franz, he would counter with Mercedes-Benz or *discipline*. Such a lunkhead—caring, passionate, but he'll always be a boy. Rather, a man with a simplistic vision, German black-and-white, good-and-bad ... Enough of that! I'm here, and however opinions vary, I'm surrounded by, immersed in, the next best thing to *an actual family*. Bickering, compromising, breaking bread. There. He ended the last row. He could help Shuli with the beans.

Twice a week J read tales at the Children's House.

"Shuli!" her grandson Yuda addressed her as she approached the children's area with J. "Tell my father I did a very good drawing of a molecule in science."

"Hey, Mister Yod!" yelled Arieh, the first one to sit down for stories.

Shuli smiled stiffly, watching her grandchildren squabble and start to jump rope and generally perform. Fathers took their sons for piggy-back rides. It was adults' visiting hour. Shuli sat on a low concrete wall adjacent to the grassy area and held her hands in her lap. J joined her.

"Someday, soon I hope, you'll have your own kiddies," she said. "My Saul he spoils them rotten. Candy he sneaks them from the city."

"I feel like they're my kids, Shuli. We share the same grounds, food, latrine. I feel they're my responsibility, too."

She squinted at him, the sun, even filtered through eucalyptus trees, narrowed her eyes to slits. "You'll make a good husband, a good father, Yod. It's wonderful how you read to the children. You could be napping right now. But you know how people talk. The only man, they say, in the vegetable garden. It's always been women's work. You men aren't good with the children. We women aren't built for constructing the roads and the barns. We tried that, years ago, and what's the point? Now for me, believe me, stooping in the garden all day is hard work ... "

"Shuli!" screamed one of her granddaughters. "Watch!"

"Yes, yes," she nodded, continuing with J. "I'm not about

to fold laundry. Yet. But you, a wiry young man."

"Shuli, I'm going to tell Dov on the Agricultural Council about my expanded tomato harvest, my idea for trench-transplanting a month ahead since the larger root system can reach heat and moisture—"

"You never knew your parents, Yod? They were killed, may their memory be blessed?"

His gaze met hers, and then he lowered his lids.

"A big rosy clan here it's not," she said. "You're in for a disappointment. How do you look on us? Partners yes. Parents no. It's a working collective. You're wasting your time in the garden. I'm surprised Rivka hasn't—"

"Shuli. I'll see you later. I'd better get inside." He dashed off, tired of her same old rant. Scruffy loud kids flocked to his shins before he could reach the bookshelf.

"There's one other little story," J said at the end of the hour. "About why the Jews call today the Ninth of Av, a day of mourning. Does anybody know about this?"

They all swayed their heads from side to side, even little Arieh, J's best customer, whose mother was the Ben-Yaakov librarian.

A bit later, J found Dov outside the tool shed. Huge sweat stains marked his khaki shirt on both sides. He was surrounded by grousing field workers.

"We need a new bucket loader," said one.

"I'd settle for a powered post-hole auger."

J spoke up. "Dov, I've got a proposal for additional income," and he began to elaborate on his tomato plant discovery.

"Save it, Yod, for the town meeting tonight," Dov said and walked away.

In the showers, J stared at his tawny legs, amazed, once again, they belonged to him. But even above the line where his shorts ended there was a distinctly Mediterranean cast to his skin. His hair was coarse and dark, another satisfying identification badge of the brotherhood, whatever he or

Allon wanted to call it.

The young woman dashed up to J in the lounge. She was wearing the standard short-sleeved white blouse, open at the neck, and blue work-shorts. Her thick dark brown hair was parted in the middle, and held back with barrettes.

"Hi, Rivka."

"Hi, Yod!" She caught her breath. "How was your day?"

"Let's sit outside. Supper's not for a few minutes."

They strolled past Shuli, past Allon and his crew, past dozens of their haverim. They found a shady spot near a pomegranate.

"How exciting. Imagine a way to double the yield of to-matoes, the main crop of the garden. I'm proud of you!"

"Is it strange," asked J, eyes cast down, "that I work in the vegetable garden?"

"Silly," she said, tossing a pebble at his chest. "What's more important than vegetables?"

They laughed.

J told her about his plan for a ketchup factory.

Rivka smiled broadly. "What a clever devil. These brain-storms. I suppose your head just swells up out there in the hot sun, blooming with ideas."

He blushed but loved hearing her talk this way. He scanned the flat valley turning deep umber in the setting sun. He could just distinguish the ridges at intervals, the tips of huge ditches both for irrigation and for trapping tanks.

Rivka addressed J's averted eyes. "What's on your mind, friend?"

"I had a good discussion with God today"

"Oh, no," she cried. "Let's eat. I'll race you!"

He sat next to her an hour later as well in the make-shift assembly hall, the dirt floor of their largest barn. " … the amendment to Histradut, the labor federation by-laws, will mean … " He observed the few hundred people, sun-burnt and sweltering even at this hour of early evening. Dark-skinned Sephardic Jews from Barcelona. Chubby, light Ashkenazim from the Ukraine demanding borscht at least once a month. He recalled the kumsitz lamb barbecue and barrels of syrupy homemade wine the women thought was fruit juice, at first. Damned if it *wasn't* a miracle: two hundred seamstresses and civil engineers, probably twenty different tongues, in no-nonsense khaki, holding hearts if not hands under the vast, star-struck summer sky. For the first time in his life, he felt happy, truly happy, even though he didn't have blond hair.

"I am sick and tired," shouted Esther Cohen, "of these black, these dreadful, these colorless shoelaces. Isn't there *anybody* who agrees?" The Polish matrons applauded wildly, setting a school of pigeons streaming from the rafters.

"Do you have any inkling, you nudnik, what washing machines cost? Now, parts for the Caterpillar diesel ... "

"You can't eat underwear, Herzl. Do we want to irrigate the lime trees, or don't we want to irrigate the lime trees?"

J tried to summon Franz's dash, his indifference to ridicule, to speak up if he had reason. He'd been stealing glances at Rivka. Just to look at her filled him with glowing warmth, the inspiration to build the kibbutz into a thriving fortress, the showplace of the reclaimed upper Jordan. She was wholesome, she was kind, she was everything he could ever hope for in a—partner. She looked up at him, smiling modestly. He felt her pride in him, a relative newcomer who was earning respect for his good work. He stood and was recognized, the first time ever at a Ben-Yaakov town meeting, the youngest participant this evening, for sure.

"I'd like to announce," J said clearly, blood surging to his cheeks, "the setting of double the tomato blossoms on the new test tomato crop, through my technique of transplanting the seedling on its side." There was silence. He swallowed. "And I would like to propose to the Agricultural Council—"

"Tell this to the ladies in the kitchen!"

Snickering broke out, and quickly spread from one side of the hall to the other.

"But there is the possibility of marketing the surplus harvest—"

"Fine for Children's House fruit stand—"

"—as ketchup—"

"—we've got fourteen hundred acres to manage!"

J slumped to his seat. Rivka composed her sweet face into a look of utter compassion. "But I never had a chance to explain," and he heaved a sigh, "about the cider vinegar." They slipped out, unnoticed.

He escorted her to the women's dormitory. "Is there such a thing as tomato wine? I bet that would get their attention."

"Would you like to come in, Yodke, and talk some more?"

He froze. She, like he, had a single room, a single bed, and that was it. Kibbutz rooms were for sleeping. The rest of your life was to be shared. In here, there would be no secrets; the walls were paper-thin. Everyone would know if he entered. Everyone would know if he didn't. "Sure," he said haltingly, and followed her.

They sat on the narrow bed. Rivka crossed her feet and folded her hands. J adopted the same posture, but sporadically pushed frizzy hair back from his forehead which didn't require it, and sniffed up his nostrils although his nose wasn't running.

She put her hand on his. "Did you ever try to trace your family, Yod? Through the offices in Tel Aviv?"

"I went in once in the Army. I said there isn't much point. I can't remember my name. They said, tell us what you know, and I said one of them possibly played a violin, in Munich." He let out a short laugh. "Does the kibbutz have a string quartet, Rivka? Maybe my talents—"

"Yodke," she said, squeezing his hand. "I'm sure you'll be voted into Ben Yaakov when your first year is complete. Few young haverim have accomplished so much."

"You think so?"

"They're good people. Lela, you know, would have been

considered a whore on the outside for leaving her miserable husband. Even with her broken wrist. Here, well, as you know, rabbinical jurisdiction doesn't much count."

"I've noticed."

"We are free to be ourselves," she said, leaning closer. "You know my betrothal backfired before I came here." She reached over and rested her other hand on his bare knee. "It's a new kind of life, a fresh start!"

"Rivka," he said trembling. "You make my heart burst with joy." He was drawn to her deep chocolate eyes burning through him, evaporating his fear. She touched his cheek with her soft, cool palm, his face on fire. He placed his sweating hands at the sides of her slim hips.

"Rivka—I love you."

"You are the sweetest man in Ben-Yaakov. Don't listen to them."

He stroked her spotless face and upper neck with his rough fingers. He embraced her, tenderly. He kissed the tears meandering down her cheek. The lids of her eyes lifted gradually, uncovering again the dark, mellow irises which drew him in, smoothly at first then picking up speed as the two of them stood, ripping off their short, simple garments. They joined hands and stepped back, drinking in the wonder of it all. He felt himself swooning at the perfection of her form, this welcome that could match no other on earth. She lay down, and he slowly lowered himself onto her mouth, her nipples, her navel and parted legs. She received him, fully. She was a flood, and he was a desert. They were simply two souls, opposites, locked and floating on the violent sea. He was not alone. On and on, they clung to each other, pinching, gasping, pleading. No, he wouldn't lose her. Never had he felt such joy; he and she, they were almost there. He could hear the breathing through the walls. He could feel the hopes of thousands perch on his shoulders, he could see the wringing hands. No, he mustn't lose it; he could hold it; no, it wasn't leaving him, the lifeline; he could squeeze her tighter and tighter, plunge deeper. He wanted to see Rivka as she was now, but she was playing a violin, she was his classmate Robert Heinrich's graceful mother lighting Seder candles, she was Robert's sister, ruefully smiling at him, she was this woman, some woman he'd always imagined, gripping him, choking him, sobbing, seizing and screaming. They heaved together on the pounding, salty, exuberant sea, and finally flopped back on the bed with a thud.

"You know what I want more than anything, Rivka," he whispered, "on this holy fast day?" She slid her tongue into his ear. "Felafel," he said. "Chickpeas fried in deep fat dripping with grease and crunchy, factory-line lettuce in a white flour pita shell like in the filthiest, most rotten junk-food shack in all of Jerusalem."

For weeks J was giddy, undeterred by all the smirks. I have to tell Franz, it struck him: finally, something to say of myself. He struggled to recall the name, the idiotic American soapworks, someplace in the Midwest. Shameful it's been this long, and it's all my fault. He was encrusted with guilt like crud in an untended oven. His next day off, he caught the bus to Haifa, and spent precious hours in its library, searching for soap makers in the U.S., to no avail.

J spilled a package of green bean seeds by mistake in the garden, and then it flashed. Why *couldn't* things grow in clusters, in big wide rows, instead of standing, skinny as rails, single file? Things don't grow like that in nature. They grow in bunches, dotted here and there, more often in masses. Why am I cultivating all this space within rows, *wasted as aisles?* He examined groupings of radishes creating their own colony, keeping the soil moist, choking out weeds, waving their umbrella greens and shading the broiling sun from the tender fleshy parts. The bulbs are tastier. It's a living mulch. These vegetables, spreading leaf to leaf, are doing a little hora dance! He couldn't wait to hold and kiss Rivka. Just the thought of her inspired him to such heights.

J worked extra hours. This time he kept his discovery a

secret. Over the months, the produce from the garden multiplied. Three times the yield in the very same space with
cabbages, ten times the onions. The Kitchen Committee
proposed that the surplus be sold. The kibbutz garden by
mid-autumn looked like a rain forest. One-third less water
from irrigation and spraying was required. Dov, the agricultural chairman, invited J to draw up plans for successive
plantings of peppers, tomatoes and fava beans for sale to the
National Kibbutzim Cooperative. He was elected to perma-
nent membership in Ben-Yaakov and, a week later, to the
vice-chairmanship of the Agricultural Council.

The kibbutz voted to charter buses for a visit to Jerusalem.
The chatter, the bustle, dribbled away as they wound up and
down the twisting hills ringing the holy city. Rivka and he
stopped their conversation as well with the first glimpse of
the gleaming crown on the Dome of the Rock. All else was a
monochrome dusty yellow, the recycled building blocks for
everything from the Mary Magdelene Church to the Hilton-
King David Hotel. He always expected to see the rocks
bloodstained, at closer range. The bullet-holes were everywhere, but as soft sienna shadows, mere recessed thimbles in
the four-foot-thick walls.

They broke up into small groups. "I'll meet you later, at
eleven," he said to Rivka, suggesting a convenient block on
Jaffa Road. He took a taxi to save time, to allow for a stroll
over the narrow, cobblestone streets. He stared at the old
men with flowing white beards. The boys, with their dangling curls like cocker spaniels, were every bit as full of life,
despite their strange garb. How clearly they were vessels for
the holy word. How tenacious had been their faith in the
face of untold persecution. Banners and posters were strung
up everywhere in Mea Shearim, the largest concentration
of Adukim—the Orthodox—in the world. Discreet dress
on women, the banners urged. No radios on the Sabbath.
Beware the curse of inter-marriage. Admonitions to Ben-
Gurion. He felt the pulse, the arrogance, the passion. He felt
ashamed and selfish, by comparison, to join The Return be-

fore the Messiah. He ducked into the synagogue he remembered from several years ago on Army leave. He took a seat in the shadows. He shut his eyes. He strained to connect, to follow the Hebrew. He didn't have much time. It was Isaiah warning the Jews. *Your iniquities have separated ... you and your God, and your sins have hid his face from you.* They chanted. They slid their individual voices into any silent spaces. *Look unto Abraham, your father, and unto Sarah that bore you ... awake, awake!* He felt on the verge of tears. *Cry out and shout, thou inhabitant of Zion: for great is the Holy One of Israel in the midst of thee ...* He rocked to and fro in his seat, to the rhythm of the men in their wide-brimmed, fur-trimmed hats. It was blinding light outdoors; he had to squint before taking a step.

Yad Vashem had been consecrated five years prior as the Hill of Remembrance. J and Rivka strolled up the fresh gravel path through the Garden of Righteous Gentiles, a tree planted for each of the non-Jewish heroes who risked their lives to save Jews in the Holocaust. *Does Franz count? Was the life he saved worth it? Was Franz at one time noble, or just in need of brotherly love?*

Before J even entered the museum, his mind filled with the stock photography, the parchment skin stretched over clavicles in heaps.

"I'd rather visit the children's art collection," he said to Rivka.

"I'll take the tour. See you later," she replied to his back.

He circled a room for an hour filled with drawings done by children in the camps. There were smiling faces, on stick figures. There were ladders, leaning against nothing, pointing proudly to the sky. There were houses without windows. There were people, holding hands. He strained to see the pain, but the sketches were drenched with hope. He lingered at one, mostly in writing, called "The Butterfly," reading the words over and over and over again. *Such, such a yellow—is carried lightly way up high. It went away, I'm sure, because it wished to—kiss the world goodbye.* He thought of the child's yellow shirt waving in the road of Franz's nightmare. He remembered their vows of faith and drops of mixed blood and exchange of the brass violin clasp as boys. He thought, here in the monument to martyred Jews, of his leaving Franz for the holy land. He wandered back to the bus in a haze of ochre dust.

"I am ready to make a baby with you, Yod," said Rivka one evening after supper. "Shuli told me of a method for increasing the likelihood of a boy."

"Can't we just—"

"But it doesn't matter. I'm sure we'll have several in time. How was your meeting with Dov and the Council?"

"The what? The meeting. Oh, it was fine."

J had been thinning carrots for three and a half hours. Maybe Allon was right. Maybe the idea of being chosen was just in reference to the politics of the day, the limited history of the monarchies, with no reason necessarily to perpetuate it like an albatross through the ages. But what if Allon was wrong? Fourteen centuries of Diaspora rabbis could have their points, too, whether or not the Polish mink hats had turned their minds to mush this close to the Equator, as Allon would jeer. Maybe this Return, the sheevat Tziyon, *was* premature. But what was the point of a secular state? He thought of his sweet Rivka, but instead of swooning, as usual, he found himself wishing she wasn't so insistent on their lovemaking during mid-morning break as well as at bedtime. He chomped a carrot, dirt and all. His jaws worked to the beat of the music in his mind. It wasn't Rachel of Kinneret, it was Bach! The Brandenburg Concertos, the violin … wasn't all this, and Franz, whose last letter years ago he never answered, his flesh and blood too?

"Rivka, I'd like to wait before we have children."

She yanked the barrettes from her hair. "Why on earth not? It's no trouble. The nursery at Children's House—"

"I know. That's what I mean." He choked on these words. "I'm not so sure this is the way that makes sense." He poked at the hard clay packed under his fingernails. "And I'm not sure I'm ready to be a father—the idea of children … "

"There are hundreds to share in the responsibility. How *selfish*—"

"—when there's still fighting … "

They lay together, silent. She fondled him without response.

J got permission to do research in agronomy on occasional weekends in Haifa. For the most part, he would slip into the shul, bathed in lush purple shadows, rocking quietly to the chants.

"Yodke," greeted Rivka one time upon his return. "You remember Mezem?"

"Who?"

"The man I was engaged to. He's coming to visit. I just wanted to tell you. I'll be busy next weekend."

J sat alone on the low wall near Children's House before his next scheduled story hour. Shuli joined him.

"Look. I understand, Yod, really I do. There's no way to trace your relatives. Take the restitution money, the Deutschmarks, for yourself. You've earned them. You don't need to give it to us. Yodke, are you listening?"

He met her eyes.

"You *bring* a family here. Or you *make* a family here. You can't find one in us ready-made. And Rivka she's not going to—"

"Shuli, what are you saying?"

"This is a kibbutz, no less no more. Have you thought of the university? Have you thought of yeshiva, rabbinical school?"

He let her words waft to the ground like feathers: gentle possibilities to consider.

Allon collared him after supper next day in the lounge. He tried to listen.

"We're talking political man here," said Allon, slashing his hand through the air. "Not religious man. There's a reason the tribal Jews became so well-rooted in your homeland on the Rhine."

J nodded, idly shelling sunflower seeds and spitting out the rinds.

"For both Germans and Jews, survival—basic defense—is the common denominator. Let's face it: we're all a bunch of paranoid people in love with ourselves. So Fascism backfired, there. So we're giving Zionism a chance, here."

"I'll second that motion," said Zev, another kibbutz raconteur. "Israel can be the role model for a nationalistic superiority-complex."

J stopped shelling seeds, transfixed by the blank window, his mind in flux. "You know I was raised in a German family," he said idly. "My brother was in a Hitler youth camp." Allon's jaw dropped. "He's been the most important, loving person in my life. He *saved* my life," J continued, as his friends stopped chewing, silenced. "Zev is absolutely right. You're a racist, Allon. Just as much a victim of authoritarianism as the typical Deutschman during the insanity." His voice was picking up. "Look at you, all of us: follow the leader." J shifted his torso to face Allon. "There are two sides to the coin, always. We rabid Israelites stereotype and dehumanize our adversaries to identify and aggrandize ourselves!"

Allon exploded into a spiel. J slouched his shoulders, not believing a word he himself had just uttered. So much verbiage, piled on thick. Maybe Shuli is right, he pondered. I should join the Hasidim in Mea Shearim and finally learn to be devout.

"It's funny," said Robbie Blustein, also listening in. "I can't escape being a Jew in America, or being an American here. I'm glad you guys are trying to figure it out."

A Jew in America, thought J, shuffling alone to his room.

A telegram from Frank Mann dated a year prior and via

the U.S. Embassy in Tel Aviv arrived at Ben Yaakov for "J. Hartmann." But a month earlier, J had departed, leaving no forwarding address. He had cashed in his Deutschmarks held in escrow for Jan Hartmann/Yod Hertzl by the kibbutz treasury, more than enough to purchase his airfare to New York City, as well as several months' of suppers at the Horn and Hardart cafeteria on Forty-Second Street. Still, he had plenty to live on. He was so well off, that two years before, upon discovering his ancient violin was in fact an original Stradivarius, he donated the entire million Deutschmarks from its sale at Sotheby's to the International Dachau Committee. His gift commissioned, among other things he was told, a massive sculpture in twisted steel with a phrase in a dozen languages: *Den Toten, ein Andenken. Den Lebenden, eine Warnung. Lametim, Hazkara. Lachayim, Azhara. To the dead, a memorial. To the living, a warning.* He kept something from his family heirloom besides the clasp still on its chain: a few of the six remaining, non-faded letters on the violin shell. When he filled out the immigration papers this time, he selected the name of Jay Radius; nationality: Unknown.

Chapter 8

Franz opened the imitation wormwood cabinet above his kitchenette counter, scanning the rows of canned goods. He twisted a chicken noodle in the Campbell soup section not facing forward that he might mistake for plain broth. He recalled J messing up their carefully-arranged shelves in the cellar bomb ruins. *Guess I am compulsive about order.* He flipped the pork chops under the broiler, and re-set the timer for four minutes. He replaced the potholders on their hooks, visualizing the selection of vegetables stored in his freezer before opening the door and lingering unnecessarily, wasting electricity. He opened a package of Birdseye lima beans and slipped the block into a pan of boiling water. One minute left on the timer for the chops. He picked up the sponge and collected the shards of ice on the Formica counter-top, the residue from the bean package. He wrung out the sponge, resting it next to the soap dish just as the bell chimed.

The chops were tender. Franz decided to stick with Safeway. Besides, they had the largest rack of Holsum Home Products of any local supermarket. Of course if he was really going to help Holsum Home, he'd buy his groceries at Riteway, study the competition, and figure a way for Holsum to get the upper hand. Such a dumb name for their toilet bowl cleaner: Plumb Pretty. Well, no complaints. *How lucky*

I am. Mailroom boy to traffic man to market analyst in five years—the world's leading producer of household detergents. He admired the yellow, orange, and red bands circling his glass of milk. The colors were so vivid and cheery. Everything in America, even after five years, loomed daisy-fresh. His memories of Germany had dulled to an ashen gray, the mud and dust of defeat. Sure, his last apartment there had been pretty swanky, but all around, for years, was the rubble of destruction, then the grime of concrete mixers and building sites. And there was J, who had shifted in hindsight over these lengthening years from brother to comrade to sometimes-companion. Franz had discarded long ago his wounded pride over J's ditching their correspondence. He truly hoped J had found his family. Franz delighted over discovering one final, succulent morsel that slid cleanly away from the bone.

He did the dishes and wiped the table. He stole a quick glance in the Spanish modern wall mirror, redistributing the wax holding up the stubborn left side of his crew-cut.

"Eye Contact" was this week's lesson for his Dale Carnegie Refresher Course. He sat and opened the book: "Studying the irises will distract and calm you." He was leery, but his boss had suggested it. He sighed, and forged ahead.

Looking up from the lesson he saw that the elephant ear philodendron was doing nicely on the TV console. The phonograph, however, looked spindly on the trio of oak nested tables. He wanted to get one of the new high fidelity systems with matching speakers. He wanted to invite that new girl to his place before she was taken.

He switched on the ten-inch Magnavox centered in a cabinet of cherry veneer. His English was close to perfect, with no accent, thanks to years of repeating radio commercials verbatim and pronouncing the newspaper funnies. Dagwood Bumstead, he suddenly thought. Dick Tracy, Olive Oyl, Mandrake the Magician, it was on the tip of his tongue … Brenda Starr, shining bright, *Sparkle Plenty.* Edward R. Murrow flashed bushy black eyebrows while Franz searched for scrap paper. "Sparkle Plenty," he repeated to himself.

"Much better name for the toilet bowl cleaner."

He was late. He unbuttoned his pink polyester shirt. The Holsum Home bowling league shirt was aqua with black letters. His team, the MA's of Market Analysis, was playing the OF's of Order Fulfillment. The new girl, Dawn, would be there. She was a regular now on the SP's of the Steno Pool. He undid a center button, and rubbed a little more Right-Guard under his arms. He re-checked his crew-cut. He at least had to look the part before he would be considered for a junior management assignment.

He paused at a stop light and fished out the collars of his bowling shirt, adding a little lift to the section at the back of his neck. Not straight up, like a hood. Just a bit of dash.

Franz loved to hear the smashing sound of pins flying against the hardwood lane, especially the ring of them crashing all at once. He stepped up to his lane, toting his monogrammed ball.

"Hiya, Frank!" waved Jim Armstrong.

"Hi, Frank," said Peg Seybolt. "How's the blond bomber?"

"Hi, guys. Great to be seen with you."

He rolled a 202 on his first game. As Franz was waiting his turn, he rolled up the short sleeves of the aqua shirt in a tight, three-quarters-of-an-inch band for a sportier look. He checked his hair in the polished metal part of the clipboard. He knew that Dawn and the Steno girls were sneaking looks, three lanes away. He chugged away on his beer. He couldn't believe the finks that didn't join them bowling. It was almost the best part of working at Holsum Home—the elbows to the ribs, the jibes in good jest, winners buying the losers a final round. He had two strikes in a row. He was determined to slam them home. His pulse was throbbing in time to a mental polka.

"Okay, Frankie, you're up. C'mon boy. We're countin' on ya."

He rested his Miller High Life. He checked to see that Dawn was watching; she was. He wanted a bullet, a cannon ball, right between the nine and ten pins. He felt a surge of strength. The ball, a sixteen-pounder, the maximum weight for a male player, was light as a feather. He realized it was all wrong the split second he took the first step in his delivery. His ball plopped on the alley with that awful, dull thud, curving immediately into the gutter.

Instead of facing the gang Franz shuffled backwards directly into the scoreboard, snapping the one-legged stand in half. Everyone in Order Fulfillment and Market Analysis, as well as Personnel and Inventory in the adjoining lanes, looked on before the games resumed. Franz grimaced with a facial apology as best he could. He found the manager who said not to worry, these things happen, that they'd send him the repair bill. He received some slaps on the back. "Better luck the time ahead, huh guys?" he offered, but found himself slipping to his car after the third game without finishing his beer, without looking up Dawn.

One day Franz climbed to the top floor to the Marketing division. *Marketing.* The very word for him was magic. The shoes were more casual, the secretaries prettier. The men had better postures, leaner builds. He wasn't bored, he reassured himself, posting numbers all day, the network gross rating points, the case sales by Standard Metropolitan Statistical Areas. He actually liked filling a slot in the complex machinery of international merchandising. He loved the smoothly operating blend of people moving up and product moving out. His turn at the helm would come, the most prestigious link in the chain, *Product Manager.*

He'd often ridicule himself at watching his every move in relation to the brass, like his saluting Ami soldiers after they took over Munich: he'd studied their clothes, gestures, trying to learn how they landed on top. He was trying so hard to fit in at Holsum Home. *But isn't it risk-takers, folks with often unpopular but bright ideas, who get ahead?* Franz unbuttoned the jacket of his Dacron checkered suit so as to appear more relaxed. He waited in line for the sixth floor receptionist. She had dark, flashing eyes. He saw Stephen Hockney glide by. *President Hockney's son.* Tall, lithe, in a muted gray, Harris tweed suit, he was here, in PM, Product Management, just because he went to Yale, some famous college. His coat was buttoned. Franz quickly re-buttoned his own, and began to address the receptionist.

"May I help you?" she said by rote, shuffling papers.

"Yes. I have a suggestion."

"For whom? Which division are you? Did your supervisor have a particular brand in mind?" She didn't look up.

"My name is Frank Mann."

"I'm Vicki Fillmore. Nice to meet you. Frank, I recommend the suggestion box on floor—what division did you say you were in?"

She had straight dark hair. Her uncurled bangs looked defiant. The girls on his floor took so much more trouble. The hair that didn't flop in her face was held back by a sexy, thin band of black velvet.

"Did you used to work in the Steno Pool, Vicki?"

She swiveled from her paperwork. "I got this job right from college." Then she smiled as if she didn't mean it.

He noticed the men wore silk ties with tiny stitched patterns—crossed tennis rackets like the skull and crossbones poison warning on labels of Holsum's Drillo Liquid Drain Opener. "Now. What was it you wanted?"

"Ah, I just need the name of the Plumb Pretty Product Manager."

"Dave Hurlihy."

"Thanks. Vicki." He returned to his audit sheets, four floors below.

"Hi, Dawn," he said to the pretty blond at the Coke machine during lunch hour. "I'm Frank. Want to share a Coke?"

"Thanks. But why don't we each get one of our own?"

"That's what I meant!"

"How'd you know my name?" She fingered the pearly buttons of her lemon angora sweater.

He smiled without answering. "Dawn, I need your help. Could you get a Plumb Pretty inter-office memo? Or any one written by Dave Hurlihy, the PM. It's real important."

An hour later, Franz was poring over a fistful of strange documents. He had to hurry, she said, because she "borrowed" them. He labored over his proposal, working in "the label impacts the shopper" and "positioning the parameters of the toilet bowl cleaner franchise." He couldn't find "prioritized" in his English-German dictionary, but was still pleased to have used it.

"Gosh, Dawn, it would be swell if you could type it."

"No problem, Frank." She wet her lips.

He was back at his desk in the bullpen, the vast arena of file clerks and typists and sales auditors and analysts like himself. He checked his watch. He twisted the ends of his pink and ebony chainmail tie. He clipped and unclipped his gold-plated tie clasp featuring the initials FM in Gothic Bold until he realized the men floating around Product Management hadn't worn such trinkets. He tossed it in the men's room trash when he next inspected his nose for blackheads.

Dave Hurlihy called Franz the following day to thank him for the memo; that he would be in touch. That *he would be in touch,* Franz repeated to himself, cruising to all the big discount furniture outlets open that very evening until nine; the US of A was so driven to sell! He decided it was too much of a distance from his flimsy, cardboard-backed couch in the living room to the bedroom. It always backfired when he'd be petting heavily, and the girl would sit bolt-upright. Surely he'd get a raise real soon, now *that he would be in touch.* He bought the biggest Castro Convertible in the showroom. He read reviews of LPs by Ahmad Jamal, Julie London, Stan Kenton: smooth, sweet and sour jazz. *Klutz.* Me and my Pat Boone, Flatt and Scruggs. *No wonder I can't get laid.*

Despite his addiction to "Gunsmoke" and the endless stream of dopey sit-coms, Franz was challenged at being home and alone. His prickly mind would wander. At work he was a whirlwind. He saw himself there on automatic pilot, as if the faster he tread, the sooner the years would fly by, and honest responsibility and creativity would come to rest squarely on his broad shoulders. Yes, so much of America was vapid as cotton candy. Yet his homeland was disgraced. It had taken all his might to erase his accent. Perhaps, he went on, as J had suggested, I'm not even German … a hybrid from the Lebensborn, on fringes of the Reich … It makes sense I've adopted this interracial circus of a country. I can't peg myself as Deutsch. *Nor should have J.*

He flipped the channel in search of distraction.

He sent Dawn up to the sixth floor to report on the shoe styles of Product Managers in detail. They had become pals. Franz had taken her to the Buena Vista Drive-In where they saw Kirk Douglas in "The Vikings." During the rape scene, as she uttered a faint cry, he slid his hand from her shoulder to a breast, and she seemed agreeable. One step at a time, with women, with corporate ladder-climbing.

One afternoon the telephone rang on Franz's desk.

"Frank. Dave Hurlihy here."

Franz tried to swallow, unsuccessfully.

"Frank Mann? Hello?"

He fought to sound at ease. "Oh, hi Dave."

"Could I see you for a sec?"

"Sure thing, Dave. Be right there."

Franz slipped into the men's room to plaster down his bangs which insisted on saluting up in the stiff regimen of the past five years. He loosened the knot of his silk repp tie, patterned with little crossed golf clubs.

"Frank. C'mon in. Have a seat. Like to update you—"

"I'll just—stand, thank you."

Dave Hurlihy smiled, looked again, and seated himself. "You must get a little bug-eyed down there," he chortled, "buried in those books."

"Yes, sir."

"Say, buddy, you seem pretty swift, re: the competitive scene. Perhaps you'd consider tackling a TBC field spot survey for the PP account group … "

Franz gazed at Dave Hurlihy's irises—olive green with nut-brown edges. "Sure, Dave. Sounds like a swell idea."

They chatted amiably for ten minutes. Dave made a phone call to Franz's supervisor, thrusting a tasseled loafer onto his desk.

"Product management," said Franz before exiting. "That's my goal, David. Every department here is important, but secondary ... supportive of PM."

"You're on the ball, kiddo. Just don't get sidetracked into Merchandising," he snorted, "or you'll wind up reporting to that yid, Sy Silverman."

Franz paused, frowning. "You said a Mr. Silverman? There are Jewish people in Holsum Home?"

Dave Hurlihy went blank.

"I, ah, I have very close ties to ... the Jewish community. I'm not comfortable with how you referred to Mr. Silverman." The guy sat stupefied, finally offering Franz the slightest of nods, whether chastised, acknowledging his bigotry, or sizing up Franz as a total dipshit. Franz bolted from the office before he could garble an apology or muted clarification.

I fucked up. How could I break my own rules? How could I say what I really thought? Even a young jerk like me understands *it's just a game.* Play it. Relax. It's America, not the Austrian Empire.

A good month went by. The Castro Convertible had arrived, but Franz had been too busy to entertain Dawn. Dave Hurlihy did not get Franz fired. In fact, Franz received a sixteen-percent raise, and had a windowless but separate cubicle on the fourth floor, two below Product Management, in Market Research. He had less time for sit-ups in the morning, gobbling up bestsellers like "Buying Habits for the American Bathroom."

Franz was incredibly horny; it was time to score with Dawn.

"I didn't know you could cook," she replied to his dinner invitation. "And you're so handsome. I can't believe you don't have fifty girlfriends!"

Franz shifted his new Herman Miller recliner and matching black leather ottoman off to the side, opposite the imitation rawhide Castro Convertible. There wouldn't be any question as to who was to sit where. He made up the hide-a-bed with his new satin sheets and pillow cases sporting the repeated Devil's tail pattern, another *Playboy* mail order special. He cooked a veal and artichoke *ragout* in white wine which could be reheated at a moment's notice. He twisted open all the name-brand liquor bottles so they wouldn't require struggle with the seals. He stacked several of his new, sexy-voiced LP's on the hi-fi turn-style so he wouldn't have to fumble with those, either. And then he slipped a few foils of Lion's Head Lubricated Lambskin Condoms—"the soft touch for a beast of a man" and a dollar each—under the most recent copy of *Playboy* on his new chrome-legged coffee table.

Saturday night arrived. Franz looked into the bathroom mirror and mussed up his new and longer hairstyle into one-inch bangs. He shifted the philodendron in its ceramic cocker spaniel planter a few inches to the left, off center to better feature the stack of LPs, hesitated, returned the plant to its former spot, but twisted so the healthier leaves faced front. He admired the placement of multiple utensils in proper sequence on his table as J had learned at school: hopefully she'll see I'm not a flake. He was still smarting from his disaster at the bowling night, even more so at his too-frequent mangling of American idioms, knowing all too well he likely caught himself just half the time. Back at the bathroom mirror, he dangled his toothbrush from his lips, partially shutting his piercing blue eyes, and swore if he dyed his hair dark, he just might pass for Robert Mitchum. The door bell rang, and he sprang into the hall.

"Hiya, Frank."

"Hi, Dawn! Oh. Just brushing my teeth."

Her smile turned crooked. She was wearing a near-transparent blouse revealing the scalloped ridges of her bra.

"Have a seat. Oh, sit there," he quipped, guiding her by the elbow away from the Herman Miller. "I'll get you a drink."

She sat on the new sofa, and reached for the magazine hiding the condoms.

"Here. Pick out records while I fix the snacks."

"Looks like you've already got records on."

"Those I've heard forever." He grabbed the electric cocktail shaker. "I have some Stingers already made."

"Ooo," crooned Dawn, adjusting the ruffled neckline of her see-through blouse before sipping. "Strong, but nice and sweet."

Franz tasted his drink but still stood. "I hope you like to eat, Dawn. I've been fussing all day." Back in the kitchenette, he arranged hors d'oeuvres on his hot tray with imitation stag horn handles. He set it on the cocktail table, plugging it into the nearby extension cord which he'd arranged for this purpose. Finally he joined her on the sofa, and clicked his glass with hers.

"Here's to the fastest rising star at Holsum!" she tittered.

"Well, if that's to happen, here's to twice the TBC sales with Sparkle Plenty! They're test-marketing my title."

They sipped and nibbled warm snacks as he studied her shapely legs and watched her eyes glaze over. He poured her another tumbler-full and listened to her patter. He grazed her shoulder, felt the silkiness of her blouse, and got aroused.

She leafed through the girlie magazine. "What's Champale?"

"It's ale that tastes like champagne. Want some?"

He went to fetch it as she fiddled with a condom foil, ripping it open. "Oh dear," she giggled. "I thought these were towelettes, you know, like in a Chinese restaurant." He returned to find Dawn near hysterical, watching the lubricated prophylactic sizzle on the hot tray, blowing up to marshmallow size.

"Dandy is candy but quicker is liquor." He laughed, and rubbed her thigh.

She shook a finger at him like a steno pen. "I know you men."

"I'd better get the veal rag-out," he slurred. "No, wait.

That bra is too—boring. You need something more cheerful." And he groped under the bed and produced a silky red lace peek-a-boo bra with large holes for the nipples. "And there's a matching bikini."

"Frank!" she screamed. "That's so naughty. What would Reverend Stout say?" She emptied her glass, and filled both of theirs to the brim. "God, it's even better than Stingers."

He struggled out of his shirt and helped her remove her blouse. Next he flung his arms around her naked waist, nibbling her lower neck, nuzzling his nose into her cleavage. She attempted to stand, for elbow room, to accommodate things and take off her bra. He was wildly aroused at her playfulness, and stood to find the mail order underwear in the growing heap of clothes. He stepped sideways, both feet tangled in the hot tray extension cord, and pitched forward, crashing into an arm of the Castro Convertible. He heard a metallic snap, but paid it no attention.

"You devil, Frank," she drawled, draping herself over the sofa back as he yanked again and again on the handle, to no avail.

"Wait'll ya see the satin sheets. Why won't this open? Damn it."

"Oh, Frankie, I'm so sleepy. Let's just forget dinner and—do it."

"Wait," he pleaded, kicking the hide-a-bed handle and then, on his knees, begging it to open. He reached through sharp metal springs to yank out a sheet, shredding it, cursing, sputtering to himself. His lower arm wedged deep within the bedsprings and wouldn't budge. He closed his eyes, to better concentrate. Meanwhile, Dawn dragged herself to the kitchenette and made instant coffee. A half-hour later, she searched for her clothes amid the clutter. She called to him from the door that she was leaving, but still he didn't wake up.

Franz stepped up his pace at work. His hair was now parted and stayed in place. But another trainee, Walt

Ledbetter with a shit-eating grin, was in and out of Dave Hurlihy's office. Franz saw himself drowning in a sea of market research.

"So, tell me, Frank—it is Frank, isn't it?" said Walt Ledbetter in the cafeteria one day. His hair was much longer than Franz's, with bangs flopping diagonally across his forehead. "Where'd you go to school?"

"School," said Franz, "Well, Ben Franklin Elementary ... "

Walt Ledbetter grinned. "Hamilton College, for me."

"Oh, Alexander Ham—"

"*Hamilton* College. A really fine, small men's school, back east. *Really* strong on liberal arts."

"I like abstract painting, modern sculpture myself."

"Hi, Frank" was addressed to his back in the hall.

"Dawn!" His cheeks went ablaze.

"Listen, don't worry about the other week. It was no big deal. For me. We all drink too much now and then." She was flipping nervously through the pages of her steno pad.

"Hey, you've given me an idea."

Franz rushed to his little office. He was determined to excel at his job, to forget the disaster he had made of his social life. He knew there was a position for an assistant TBC product manager, and he had tons more field know-how than Walt Ledbetter, green out of college. He sketched quickly on a spiral, steno-type pad. He found some Magic Markers, a pair of scissors. He knew the wholesale and grocery chain buyers, too, were bored to death with these statistics. He knew his years of studying slang phrases would pay off. Here, by God, is a way to light a fire under TBC sales ...

"Let's see what you've got there, Frank," said Dave Hurlihy. Franz stood the small flip chart on Dave's desk. It was one ivory, oval-shaped panel resting on a larger one, and, as Franz lifted "page one," it was obviously the mocked-up lid and seat of a toilet bowl. An imbecilic gag, but this was the game, and damned if he couldn't outwit them.

"The Great American Toilet Bowl Clean-Up Campaign," he read eagerly, flipping one compelling sheet of Holsum price deals after another.

"Wow," uttered Dave Hurlihy.

Each flipped "lid" standing upright in fact assumed the shape of a naked lady's rump poised prettily on the "seat," with an extra "PS" statistic to Holsum's advantage, one on each cheek.

"Far out," said Dave.

"Flush away that sluggish bowl cleaner inventory," read Franz off the final lid. "BOTTOMS UP TO TBC SALES!"

Dave withdrew his tasseled loafer from his desk, smiling, nodding.

"Listen, this is great for a start."

"Who could resist lifting that lid … "

"Frank. I'll be in touch."

Weeks went by. Every time Franz saw Walt Ledbetter, he thought of J going to school all those years while he, Franz, pieced together their living. Even back then, J knew that to study, to get smart that way, was the right thing to do. These buggers here just go to college, then directly to the sixth floor. *I've been here five bloody years.*

He cornered Vicki Fillmore, the sixth-floor receptionist, at the water fountain. "Hi, Vicki."

"Hi, Blondie."

"It's Frank. Frank Mann."

"Just teasing. You're so cute when you're serious." She pressed her shoulder-length straight hair to the side of her head as she leaned over to drink. She snapped back up, all pert and pretty. Her ass wasn't half bad. "Did you go to college?" he asked.

"Mount Holyoke."

"Is that a fancy school?"

"Yes."

"I bet you didn't study typing."

"I was an English major."

"English? Hell, I've studied English all my life."

She pressed her carefully painted lips together in a smirk,

and started to march away in her deep burgundy, patent leather low heels. She had skinny legs, no tits, but still he persisted.

"Hey listen, Victoria."

She turned around.

"Could you, er, get me the minutes of a divisional meeting. I'm working on a special TBC report, and I don't want to bother—"

It occurred to Franz one evening, buried in a men's magazine: I can try to screw a secretary on any of the six floors; it's Vicki Fillmore I must master. Been wasting my time, Franz continued. A woman wants a man. So does a corporation, forever in danger of becoming a nursing home of paper shufflers. He flung aside the magazine instructing him on "the fine arts of discovering her hot spot."

He arranged a date with Vicki-Victoria. He replaced the Par-tee-boy Icebreaker glasses with a leather-covered flask, filling it with 100-proof Kentucky bourbon. He got a six-pack of plain rubber Trojans. He piled pillows on the Castro Convertible, and readied his real bed by rumpling the sheets. He yanked open the closet doors to get dressed. He found a crewneck sweater with some yarn ripped loose on one elbow, an Oxford button-down with a frayed collar. He hesitated, naked, his costume assembled, and decided she would never see it in the dark, that it would give him a semi hard-on all night, a big, beautiful, lingering build-up ... the hell with his boxer shorts. He was swollen by the time he even found the red silk lace bikini.

He decided they should start off drinking beer and dancing at Rosie's Roadside, with a neon sign blaring "Live Entertainment." The place was packed with truck driver types. The women sitting on barstools had mountainous hairdos that glowed dull pink from cigarette smoke and low, red ceiling lights.

"It's so wicked! Frank, I love it."

They bopped and shook to "Blue Suede Shoes." They jumped and gyrated to "You Aint Nothin but a Hound Dog."

They stole slugs from the flask. Finally, they were twisting and jerking to the Watusi when Vicki snapped her strand of pearls and Franz crashed to the floor in agony.

"*Good God.* I've done something to my kneecap. Christ. Vicki, don't laugh. My knee. It's in the wrong place!" The pain was excruciating.

"Get up, you old drunk!" Vicki giggled.

"Please," he pleaded. "I can't move."

Burly men began glaring at this pest who couldn't hold his liquor. There were some shouts and shoves.

One of the dames broke into the melee. "Okay, guys. I'm not just your local VD clinic, I'm an RN. What's up with this idiot?"

"Somebody else sprained an ankle to that record. Wasn't that the Chicken Scratch?"

"He was dancing like a loony bird for sure."

They dragged him off to the side.

"It's—back in place," Franz managed between gritted teeth. "I'm okay. Forget it."

"Let her look," said Vicki. "Your knee's the size of a basketball."

"Say, honey, run and get scissors at the bar, or a knife. These pants will never come off."

"Must be a broken blood vessel. Jesus, all that swelling."

"No!" screeched Franz, wild-eyed, at Vicki, the nurse, the barflies and truck drivers, all of them forming a sympathetic, eager ring of spectators.

"Shut up, Frank," Vicki snapped. "You think we've never seen a pair of Jockey shorts?"

"*Please don't.*"

"Relax, Frankie. Here, have another swig. We'll have those pants off in just a sec. Oh, you poor thing."

Franz was clobbered with shame the next week, his knee in a plaster cast. *Asshole.* The humiliation—unthinkable! Screw Vicki. She was just an act. Wanting to be impressed, forcing me to stunts. *What am I but a stuntman, even earning my living this way ...* I had more savvy selling cigarettes and whores as a teen ...

There was a knock on the door to his cubicle. Vicki poked her head in. "Can I sign your cast?"

Franz flushed scarlet.

"Listen. I haven't mentioned it to a soul."

He clenched his fist around a pencil.

"Believe me, I don't give a shit about your sexual fantasies. Hey, I tried falsies, but they kept falling out. Frankie, I think you're terrific. I can't stand all these phonies. C'mon. I'll take you out for a pizza tonight."

Gradually, his pressed lips relaxed into a half-smile. He agreed to the date, she picked him up, she bantered in great high spirits, and a month later she was dating one of the preppies in PM.

Walt Ledbetter became the TBC Assistant Product Manager. The brand name was not changed from Plumb Pretty to Sparkle Plenty, but the toilet bowl flip chart was printed and used by the national rack-job distribution force. Abe Merman, chief buyer of the Howdy Doody Shop-aramas headquartered in Paramus, New Jersey, was first to acclaim the flipping lid. Abe staged an in-store display, a six-foot wide Styrofoam toilet bowl bin, and moved eighty cases week number one. Franz was flown to Paramus for the Grand Opening, staying at a German hotel on East 86th Street in New York City, eating wurst and downing dunkel bier until two AM. "New York's a fun visiting place," he said to the bartender, "but it's not fitting to live here." Chatting with some chaps in his native tongue, he began terribly to miss J. *Damn you, you were the brains of the family ... how will I ever make it on my own?* The Israeli consulate assured him they'd found the kibbutz address for his telegram, and yet—not a word in return. *I can hate his guts. So fucking above-it-all.* Well, Franz burped, I'm the one with money, resources, feet on the ground while J's probably a rabbi by now, studying thousand-year-old Schmaltz. *I should just fly there. Show up, make sure he's alive.* He finished the flat brew, just not the same punch as back home. Franz actually was relieved J was in a kibbutz, helping to build a new land, not lurking in a grimy hell-hole of a city like this. Get me back to the fresh air of Indiana, he sighed to himself, slipping off the barstool. Taking out his billfold, settling his tab, there it was—dull, dented, forever in place: his half of that blasted brass clasp.

Plumb Pretty moved from fifth to fourth in the TBC sweepstakes for the fiscal six months ending March 1959, and Franz was elevated to Assistant Product Sales Promoter for National Chain Accounts. As for his sex life, he knew there was a straight-talking broad out there, full of smarts but no show-off. *I have so much to learn about this crazy country.*

Occasionally, thoroughly down in the dumps, he flirted with the notion of returning to Germany, well, not Bavaria, perhaps Berlin.

Meanwhile, Franz went from fifteen to fifteen-and-a-half in his bowling shirt neck size. He traded in his squat Chevy for a T-bird, and moved to a hillier section of greater Buena Vista, a new apartment complex called Treetops in the quiet suburb of Evergreen Ridge, Indiana.

1961

Chapter 9

J accepted the offer of a spare bedroom for the summer in the Westchester County suburb of Maryville. He didn't know Seth other than as a fellow junior at Yeshiva University. J figured he could read, mostly escape the sweltering city heat. There was a younger sister. The mother worked full-time; she ran a store in their village. This was all J knew, but they sounded like a nice family.

"Such an honor!" exclaimed Lucille Ward, Seth's mother. "From the Holy Land no less." She had orange-red hair, the shade J associated with a Raggedy-Ann doll. She clasped his hand, beaming. "Mo. Hey Mo! Seth's friend Jay is here. Come already and help with these suitcases." She turned again to J, frowning indignantly. "You should have called. You schlepped these all the way from the station?"

"Mrs. Ward—"

"It's Lucille, you college boys are so polite."

"Thank you so much for the room. I hope—"

"Hiya, Jay," said Morris, Seth's father, biting the cigar between his teeth and extending his hand. "Here, I'll get those."

J was embarrassed by the attention, but favored being overwhelmed by extroverted personalities. He could stay safely under wraps.

"So where is that farshtinkener son of ours?" said Lucille,

spinning around in a daze on the plush carpet. "His friend is here, hauled luggage six blocks. Listen, cheese blintzes in the kitchen. You can unpack later. Come, now, while they're warm, Jay. It *is* Jay? Yankel, I want to call you—like Seth's uncle."

J was softening from her chubby energy.

"Oh," cried Lucille. "Here's Holly."

"Hannah." The tall, slender girl held out her hand.

"Excuse me, your highness," said Lucille, shuffling plates. "Mother."

"Are you in college, too, Hannah?" J sat on a stool opposite her.

"I begin this fall, at Connecticut College for Women."

"Too far away! Who finished the sour cream?" Lucille bustled about an enormous refrigerator.

Franz would love this kitchen, reacted J. He probably has one just like it.

The daughter had straight brown hair pulled back and tied with a rubber band, but at the nape of her smooth neck as opposed to a ponytail. Her hands, peeling an apple, were a study in grace. "Do you play the piano?" said J.

"The violin." She blushed.

"There," said Lucille, shaking with satisfaction, serving him a heaped plate. "Coffee?"

"Hi, Jay," said Seth, grabbing his hand and nearly crushing it. He was a large guy, both strong and soft: hefty, Americans called it.

"So where were you, nudnik?" said his mother. "The whole day he walked."

"Hi, Holly. Hi, Mom. The traffic was fierce. Any more blintzes?"

Lucille smiled, wiping hands on her apron.

It was Saturday, J realized. Cooking, smoking, driving. A relief, he supposed, they weren't Orthodox.

"Synagogue?" said Seth later at dinner, slicing sirloin.

"Just wondering," said J. "I thought I'd join you."

There was a pause.

"Jay, don't be shy with the creamed onions," said Lucille. "Mo, pass Jay the creamed onions. I'm with the Haddasah Sisterhood at Yahudeh Eamanu-El. Bridge every other Thursday. Holly, you're not touching your plate."

"I didn't want seconds."

Seth was shoveling in thirds. "Great meal, Mom. Jay, we used to go to shul, three years before my Bar Mitzvah."

"Morris. We bought some Israeli war bonds, didn't we, just last month?"

"Two years ago."

"How much did you give?" said Seth.

"A few thousand," said Mo.

"Is that all?" said Hannah.

"Look," said Mo shrugging. "It's more than most. Besides, we're on the giver list. If anything happens, they'll take us in."

J had no idea if he was joking. Could something "happen" in *America?*

"Jay," said Hannah, her hands folded neatly in her lap. "I hope you'll tell us all about Israel."

"Lots of glazed carrots, folks," said Lucille.

"Mom runs the Hallmark Gift and Card Shop," said Seth.

"Very nice," said J, sipping wine. It was going straight to his head. He was so relaxed, welcomed immediately into the heart of this honest-to-God family. Although, he had to admit: his ongoing ache for Shuli, Allon, for his skin to be caked with dirt, for Rivka's touch …

"We got the nicest line of Rosh Hashanah and Sukkoth greeting cards this week with the Halloween and Thanksgiving shipments," said Lucille. "I swear it's about time the High Holidays had a rack of their own."

"I've got a movie date with Barbara tomorrow night," announced Seth. "Jay, you're welcome to join us. But you don't have to."

"Ooo," said Lucille. "Why not fix him up with that nice Klepperman girl."

"Linda," said Hannah.

J was swooning from the wine, from just knowing he'd be meeting his Jewish-American sweetheart this summer if ever. He couldn't believe his good fortune. Such a reprieve from chemistry, from weeding the kibbutz garden when it was 105 in the shade.

"She's a bit on the tall side," said Mo, using his tongue as a toothpick, contorting the slack skin of his face, his bulbous nose.

"So what," said Lucille. "They'll be sitting down."

Yes, she was tall, and plain, but friendly. J was glad Linda had plenty to say. They sat in the back of Seth's Pontiac Bonneville.

"Have you ever seen a Hitchcock?" asked Linda.

"Pardon?"

"This one's supposed to be his scariest ever—'Psycho.' Glad I'm sitting next to an Israeli soldier! You actually fired rifles and saw somebody shot and all that?"

"Yes."

"Gosh. I may have to close my eyes or squeeze you during the shower scene." She locked onto his face. "You know, Jay, you don't look Jewish."

"Oh, but I am!" She looked confused, and then he added: "You don't either, Linda."

She touched her curly brown hair, relaxed into a shy smile.

The movie theater was packed. The audience responded in unison to the scratches and quirks of the violin soundtrack. The movements of the pretty woman in the motel room couldn't quite hold his attention. He pictured Seth and himself weeks before, slaving in one of their pre-med labs. Now she was in the bathroom and looking in a mirror. Strange it wasn't erotic. She stepped into the shower. It was a black and white film and at first he didn't understand. He expected rape, not a knife. He started to taste cream cheese and toasted onions from their bagels just prior. Comparative anatomy had only used dogs and cats up to this point for dissection. "Oh, my God!" groaned Linda. There were thudding sounds. He clenched shut his eyes, but couldn't dilute the thwacks. Was it a kosher killing, swift and clean? He glanced at the screen, a massive close-up of the shower drain, swirling with black fluid. "No," he uttered hoarsely. He stood, partially yanking Linda from her seat, but she released him. The others remained motionless. The hacking sounds reverberated off the walls, out of the speakers, echoed by the gasping audience. He shoved necks and shoulders; he crushed a woman's foot causing her to shriek in pain. He didn't vomit until the lobby. The car was locked, and so he walked around the block, over and over and over, allowing his mind to slip, impervious, into a tiny black hole all its own.

J browsed among the cards, waiting for Seth who was unloading boxes in back for his mother. He perused the Jewish holiday display. Like all the cards, they were pastel watercolor washes, with a smooth, dreamy quality to the scenes. One featured a boy and girl frolicking in the sukkah, decorating the little harvest festival hut with the etrog and palm fronds and willow branches. They looked like cherubs with their pudgy fingers. A Star of David, on another card, was composed of walnuts, chrysanthemums, and fruits of the season. Yes, he thought, yes! Jewish life can flourish without the diatribes, the barbed wire. Lucille bounced over and caressed him with cheery banter.

It was a drizzly, hot summer evening. Seth had taken some girl to the drive-in. Hannah swam laps in the pool. J sat with Mo and Lucille under a purple and white striped canopy by the gas-fired barbecue.

"Holly, if you catch a cold I'll kill you," said Lucille.

"How 'bout another gin and tonic?" said Mo. He had large lips and wavy black hair combed straight back.

"No, thanks," said J. "This one's plenty." J thought how much Franz would enjoy this gemuetlichkeit, in fact must be thriving on it somewhere in the heartland. The few times he tried to phone information since arriving in New York, he got nowhere, so many Manns but no Franz in the various cities. And there was no way he could recall the name of his company. J pictured knocking on Franz's office door wearing false earlocks and rabbinical garb: *Hi, I'm Franz's brother.*

Lucille leaned forward. "You think Seth'll make medical school? Be honest, now. You. He says you have the most seychl in the class. That's an awful tough school you guys picked."

Hannah climbed out of the pool, and sipped her mother's drink.

"Get a towel! You'll freeze."

Hannah flopped into one of the turquoise padded, white metal patio chairs looking like a drowned rat. She was thin, lanky, no padding, haunting eyes. J liked that. *Maybe I should jump in the pool. It might be worth it just to have Lucille fuss over me, the way Franz used to …*

Hannah and Lucille argued. Then Mo and Hannah checked the pool apparatus. The taste of lime carried J back to Ben-Yaakov. He thought of Rivka, her body, her kind words, her insistence on making babies. Was he ready yet? *Be fruitful, you lucky ones who got away.*

"You have a family?" said Lucille, sucking on her slice of lime. "In Israel?"

"Not really," said J.

Lucille clutched her throat. "You mean you *lost* them?"

J shook his head in the affirmative.

Lucille bit her lower lip, and then placed a hand on his forearm. "Poor bubeleh." Her eyes were blinking, glazing.

"In the war," he said, watching Mo and Hannah uncoiling the pool vacuum cleaner from a small tool shed.

She increased the pressure on his arm. "I try, you know. I try to imagine losing Seth in a war. I panic for a second, then I catch myself. It all seems so far away, Jay. You know what I mean? Am I heartless?"

He squeezed her hand. "No, Lucille."

She smiled broadly, shoving the massive cluster of gold bracelets back up her arm. "I've got the most enormous hunk of lamb. I hope you like it rare. Hey, Mo! Stop schlepping that pool junk and get the meat going."

Lucille and Hannah ducked into the house. Mo pulled up his chair. "You guys, you make it through med school, in a few years you'll each have two places like this."

"It's beautiful," said J.

"Radiology. A hundred grand. Good hours."

"Radiology? I was thinking more of … "

Mo shook his head, then flipped his hand. "Listen. You can never have enough. Just stick with it."

"It seems Lucille has lots of jewels and furs and—"

"We gotta keep some liquid assets." He winked.

"Liquid?"

"You never know," said Mo, rising, shrugging off to the grill.

J fished into his glass for the crushed lime. *Is Mo serious?*

"Hannah … what?" She tugged on J's arm.

"Holly, what are you doing?" cried Lucille, returning with guacamole dip. "Hey, that's not kosher, all his clothes yet!"

"You meshuggeneh!" J laughed and pleaded. He struggled, he really did, but she had the momentum. Plus, she was wiry and determined. The splash reached clear to the barbecue stand. Lucille had two towels ready when he reached the steps.

The temple Friday evening was practically empty. He looked for some candles, an ark, the sefer Torah. The Rabbi was talking to the small assemblage in conversational English. No one in the congregation uttered a word, stepped forward to recite from the Midrash, announce a wedding or death or illness. J twisted the yarmulke in his fingers, scanning the un- covered scalps of twenty-some men. He rolled up the sleeve of his seersucker sport coat, and rubbed his forearm red. He could barely make out the small white scar. Nothing now but a wrinkle. He pinched the skin until it hurt, until he re- membered the outline of blue ink, one of the few memories he could grasp.

He found a preacher that summer. He found a rabbi, tzaddik, pious one, rebbe, teacher, Hasid, maggid all in one, in a Greenwich Village cabaret. Lenny Bruce was on stage, but for J he was an instant pal, this mock rabbi with a Harvard accent: "Children of Is-roy-el ... Where is Is-roy-el? Is yonder Is-roy-el? Out quench yon flaming yahrzeit candle, Is-roy-el!"

J ordered a fresh stein. It was a minyan, here in subterranean Bleecker Street.

"If Moses were to come down, wouldn't he order all the rabbis in their Frank Lloyd Wright shules to sell their tallith for rags and melt down the mezuzahs for bail money for all the Caryl Chessmans who sit in gas chambers or electric chairs ... ?"

J sat there, terrified by the verbal violence, mesmerized by the spiritual theater.

"Now a Jew in the dictionary is one descended from the ancient tribe of Judah ... that's what it says in the dictionary; *but you and I know what a Jew is*—One-Who-Killed-Our-Lord ... Two thousand years of Polack kids whacking the shit out of us coming home from school ... "

J caught the last train to Westchester, but made it back the following night.

" ... Ruby came from Texas, and a Jew in Texas is a tailor. What went on in his mind I'm sure is: If I kill a guy that killed the President the Christians'll go: Whew! Boy, what balls he had. We always thought the Jews were chicken-shit but look at that! ... "

J's spirits soared. Of course this is why Israel is arming itself. Isn't it wonderful? Slaughter the fuckers!

" ... *a Jewish Billy the Kid rode out of the West.* But even the shot was Jewish. The way Ruby held the gun—it was a dopey Jewish way ... "

J slumped in his chair, crest-fallen.

" ... a lot of people say to me, Why did you kill Christ? I dunno ... it was one of those parties, got out of hand, you know ... we killed him because he didn't want to become a doctor, that's why we killed him."

J laughed. He was at a table with strangers, but he

laughed, hard. *Because he didn't want to become a doctor. And with a Jewish mother.* The tears rolled down his hot cheeks. He giggled to himself all the way back on the train, chortling the next day, as well.

"Listen, folks," blurted Seth to the group. They had just assembled for Happy Hour. "Now that I'm twenty one— I'm—changing my name from Ward back to Weicz."

"You're kidding," said Lucille, shuffling over the flag- stones in gold lame slippers, passing a plate of onion dip. "Even I can't spell that one, and you should see some of my sales slips."

"For God's sake," said Mo, re-crossing his legs. "Your great-grandmother picked that when she stepped off the boat. She spotted a Montgomery Ward catalog, pointed to the short word with a 'W,' and shrugged to your great grandpa."

"Listen to the all-rightnik here," warbled Lucille, her mouth full of chip and dip. "Go ahead. Turn your back on your heritage."

"What's so bad about being a Jew?" said Seth hotly.

"Look," said Lucille, waving her arm laden with coral and sterling circle bracelets. "My customers already know I'm Jewish. Why rub it in?"

"Right from the catalog … Ward," said Mo, sliding further down into the canvas captain chair. "American as Grandma Moses."

"What do you think, Jay?" said Seth.

"Well," said J, intoxicated by the continuing family squabbles, all the merriment and silliness and *caring* going on. "What's in a name?"

"Radius. That's a wild one, now that I think of it," said Hannah. "Is it Latin, or Greek?"

"Early Violin Case."

Seth ended the moment of puzzled silence by lunging into the potato chips. "Maybe I'll use both names on the application."

"What application, son?" said Mo.

"To Hebrew University. I've been thinking of post-grad

work before med school."

Lucille wrinkled her forehead, picking up her drink. "Is that the one in Westchester, Seth, or the North Bronx?"

"It's in Jerusalem, Mom. Jay's been telling me a lot about it."

"*The* Jerusalem? Oy gevalt!"

"Now, Lucy," said Mo. "What a great opportunity."

"What? Molotov cocktails, Arabs, sunstroke?"

J laughed and listened to the chatter and wished that summer was the only season.

One afternoon, J decided to read by the pool. The family was gone, the place was serene. He put down his textbook on cell structure and noticed the skin of his arm. It was almost as golden as that iridescent Israeli tan. For just a second he felt alive and determined again, like at the height of his kibbutz weed-pulling career. Can I stick it out, as Mo advised? Become a doctor, be really useful to people? Warmth flooded through him. He peeled off his shirt and picked up his book, but he couldn't read in the glare. *Strip away the sentiments and, no, I don't really miss Franz, our life in a police state. Or Rivka or Shuli or Allon on their deadpan godless work-farm.* Yes, a part of him was a painful void. But he could operate perfectly well despite the cavity. *Who doesn't have a wound? So mine is gaping. So make something of it.* Just look at the joy available in an ordinary Jewish American family! It was blistering overhead. He slipped off his pants and plunged into the pool.

When he surfaced he saw her. Hannah/Holly was smiling, then slowly lifted off her tee-shirt, stepped out of her shorts and panties. She dove to his side and splashed him, dunked him, spun him around. She embraced him from the rear, sliding her lithe body up and down, biting his neck. He laughed softly as their feet barely touched the pool bottom, as her hands stroked his erection. He reached behind and pressed her buttocks closer and closer to him.

"C'mon," she giggled.

She yanked him up the steps, and led him into the tiny tool shed. She arranged herself on the rubbery plastic coils of pool hose, lean legs spread wide, grinning all the while. They wrestled, they licked, they nibbled and laughed. He found himself squeezing her, locking her in an embrace to the point where she uttered a cry. "Easy," she gasped. He entered her and held her with all his might, the two of them motionless as stone. Apparently she understood, and they were still until the flood released itself from his center. Shaking, he did not let her go until they could make proper love, and, even then, until she promised to play her violin. Later, when she got out the instrument for the recital, he agreed, but couldn't remember making the request. He listened and shivered, dozing off on her rumpled bed, amazed the sheets did not itch, his blistered skin did not burn, that his ears were not plugged to muffle the drone of incessant bullets and bombs.

He read alone in his room the following week. He ate and drank and joked with the family. He could not take his eyes off Hannah's trim torso, the way she pulled her silky hair back with the flick of a wrist. Whatever she did would excite him, stir him until it pained in the hollow part of his heart. "C'mon, Jaybird," she'd coo when they were alone, when she wasn't out on dates with her boyfriends, and lead him into the shed, to the bushes, sometimes her bedroom. "It was fun, but let's get up now," she'd say later, always too soon. "Here's my teddy. You can hold him," and she'd tickle his tummy with the fuzzy material. "Jay. I said get up. I'm going out."

I should go back to Germany, J thought, burrowing through his zoology workbook. *To Heidelberg. For that school I was prepared, given full scholarship. I'd fit in, my native tongue, my skills superseding any anti-Semitism* ... With these thoughts he wrestled, even while kibitzing with the Wards. America is so compartmentalized, he was learning ... division of labor has dominated the world, and done great things. But the mind … mine or anyone's … isn't it best *diffused*, letting it stretch *beyond* comprehension? He admired Seth's academic ambition, Holly's too, but … this town, its churches and temples … isn't there a rightful place for *the alleviation of souls?* Home and hearth: he'd done that with Franz, in Munich: the national pastime …

Without telling any of them, J decided to drop out of premed; quit the university in Bronxville altogether. He'd find an apartment in Greenwich Village in the fall. The school scene was just as much of an escape as had been his summer holiday in the air-conditioned suburbs. He had no idea what to do with himself, somewhere in his mid-twenties, but suspected the chances were so much greater of unearthing his mission in the bowels of the city.

The Wards and he were drinking Bloody Mary's one Sunday with onion bialys. It was Hannah's last week home before entering Connecticut College.

"So eat," Lucille was saying to her daughter. "And you're arriving at the freshman dorm with butter cookies, marble cake, and tinned lox."

"Mother, I promise I'll never fast again on Yom Kippur."

Seth burst in the front door with a beautiful blond girl. "Folks, you've got to meet Mitzi!"

"What's the rush?" snapped Hannah.

"Well, we're pretty serious," said Seth beaming.

Lucille, for once, was speechless.

"Would you like a Bloody Mary?" said Mo rising. J figured this was only the tenth girl he knew Seth had laid this summer. She was albino-white compared to the family, her lithe body oscillating like a feather of down.

"Thank you, Mr. Ward. Iced tea would be great, if it isn't too much trouble."

"Of course not, Millie," said Lucille. "Morris, dear, would you please—"

"Mitzi," said Seth. "It stands for Millicent."

"Millicent," repeated Lucille, attempting a smile. "How sweet."

"Millicent Farnsworth," said Mitzi, still undulating, perched on the edge of her chair.

"Mitzi's from Pound Ridge," said Seth.

"Oh. Pound Ridge," said Lucille. "How lovely, there, it must be, this time of year. Leaves starting to turn." She fiddled with the buttons on her floral quilted housecoat, the coils of her springy orange hair.

"Well," said Mitzi, her mouth now extraordinarily wide from relief. "It's so nice to meet you all. At last."

"Yes," said Lucille. Her face dropped. "*At last?* What in holy Gehenna does *that* mean, buster?" barked Lucille to her son.

"Mother!" Hannah erupted, slamming down her drink.

"A shikseh!" Lucille stood, shaking. J rose, trembling himself, and put his arm around her. *Is this a farce? Is this for real? Are they serious?* For J it didn't matter. He held Lucille tight.

"Are you trying to tell me a nice Jewish boy like you, raised in the faith, is turning on his family this way? Are you pregnant with my son's child? Is that what you're trying to say?"

"*Mother!*"

"Lucy, take it easy!"

"Ma, she'll convert. Won't you Mitzi?"

"Oh, yes!" pleaded Mitzi. "I've always had the greatest respect for your people, Mrs. Ward. In my small way, I hope to—"

"How can you get through medical school with a family?" wailed Lucille. "And your kids—half-breeds! Have you thought about *them—my grandchildren?*"

J stood, astonished by Hannah and Mo and Seth. They poured themselves more drinks. Mitzi sat rigid. J was on the verge of tears along with Lucille, who was clutching his forearm, his arm with the little wrinkle in place of the letter, squeezing it for all she was worth. *Yisroel, Yisroel, have you thought about the children, my children ...*

September slipped into October as he somehow postponed his departure, though Seth and Hannah had gone off to school. Mitzi was history; she'd not been pregnant, just in love. The pool had been closed for weeks. Every few days he snuck into the pool tool shed housing the filter, the pump, the vacuum hose and floating easy chair, the site of his summertime flings. The aravah—the willow branches— he found not far away, along a brook through an overly manicured section of Maryville. The etrog was easy, the lulav and hadas—the palm and myrtle branches—less so; these he bought from the local funeral parlor. Maybe Hallmark cards were all that millions of American Jews needed to cel- ebrate the holy days. He was determined otherwise. He said he'd be gone for several days, the fast of Sukkoth was nine to be exact, and he knew they'd never look in here. Finally, the little shed was converted into the sukkav, the hut of the Holy Festival. He locked himself inside. It was quite warm and cozy. The food, of course, was ice cold; he got it from a Jewish deli a few blocks away. Who needs synagogues, he thought. *I'll claim the faith of my forefathers myself,* without the crutch of my fantasy congregation or ersatz family. He arranged the coils of plastic hose as cushions. He shoved the canisters of chlorine and other chemicals into the corners. He lit the candles and began with his Hebrew. *Blessed are You, Lord our God, King of the Universe, who has sanctified us with His Commandments and commanded us to light the festival candle* ... He huddled in the little hut, narrow metal eaves draped with the branches and leaves, plus berries and nuts and other fruits of the season. He intoned the prayers for the tallith, for the sacred symbols, for the bountiful har- vest. Slowly, he was imbued with a sense of unity, of the soil and soul, of the vast distance of time carrying his people for- ward, a simple, ageless, unyielding reliance on their Maker. He lifted the etrog. He chanted. He sang. He blessed and broke and ate the challah. He prayed. He slept. He snuck into the house to relieve himself. He dwelt on the special place of the Jewish people, from one day to the next. Chosen, they were, to endure, to sweat and ache and await the Messiah, to change humanity with the endless call to purification. *Yes, it's possible! I can redeem my people of their sins and conclude their suffering, once and for all.* He had already been granted twenty or so years for the task. He lost feeling in his legs. After three, four, five days, his body weakened, but his mind burned with the mission. *I have to remember my past.* He beat the willow branches on Hoshanah Rabbah, the great deliverance day, the seventh day of Sukkoth, watching the old leaves fall, allowing room for new life to spring forth. He was losing strength. He was losing interest, but he fought. At some point it was Shemini Atzereth, the eighth day of Sukkoth. He vaguely recited the Yizkor, the special prayer for the dearly departed. He strained to feel the agony of his ancestry, cramped in tight quarters. Instead, he became senseless with boredom, with immobility, with longing for relief. He prayed for rain to fall on the dry, sucking desert of Israel, for the fertility of the homeland. If only he could make it to the last and ninth day, Simchath Torah, the rejoicing of renewal, the cycle complete! His head split from the wine, the meager gefilte fish, the stale bread. The sour, burning smell of pool supplies was interfering. He fought off sleep. He mumbled the Kaddish, for over the grave, and slumped against the earthen floor. The thunder rolled, and then the lightning cracked and forced a stab of light upon his swollen lids, prying them open a sliver. The air was thick with a stinging smell. His head was about to explode with the pain. *Please God let me die and try again.* The rain pelted the tin roof with a sing-song yes, yes, yes, yes, yes, his Maker needed him as a celebrant of the faith. And then the sun burst. A new day? The sacred ninth? The blaring light was assaulting his face, his burning eyes …

"Jay! Gottenyu! Oh, dear God," screamed Lucille, wielding a huge flashlight. "It's filled with chlorine gas! What in God's name—get up, you shnook. The cellar's flooded in this downpour. C'mon, we need the pool vacuum cleaner right away to pump the place out. Up, klutz, did you hear me?" She yanked out the hose. "There are fresh blintzes getting mildewed if you don't move this very instant."

Chapter 10

"Frank Mann, Holsum Home." Franz grasped the stout man's hand.

"Of course," said the man in broken English. "Are you here in the Frankfurt office? You sound American, but look German."

They continued pumping arms, the grip becoming more intense. "I'm in Buena Vista, U.S. The headquarters." Franz eyed newly arrived browsers at the display. "I'm product manager for Breath O' Spring."

"What about Plumb Pretty?"

"That's the regular bowl cleaner." Others were now listening as Franz raised his voice. "Breath O' Spring comes in two fla—aromas: lime or lemon. It cleans *and* disinfects." He edged away from the large man, palms pressed together, and began answering questions from the other buyers. A cross-section of an actual, continuously flushing toilet bowl and tank demonstrated how Breath O'Spring's foaming action reached the trickiest lips and recesses. Thousands of business-suited people had milled slowly through the display, most taking a deep whiff from the sample lemon bowl, then the lime.

He listened to himself prattle, first annoyed and then bemused at his lot in life: changing bedpans in the Lebensborn, and now this. And J would reassure him: it's not what you do, but how you do it. Lots of luck believing that in a scene like this.

"They ate it up," said Franz wryly over the phone to his boss in Buena Vista. "Be back next week, Chuck. I'm checking some old—contacts in Munich."

He decided to take a train. He tugged on the cuffs of his shirt to expose the proper half inch beyond his coat sleeves. He glanced out the window at the tidy fields and quaint towns. It's pleasant, and familiar, but no longer home, he thought. The older couple in the seat opposite were planted there, chubby hands folded in their laps, knees slightly apart, rounded ankles tucked into dull shoes. He scanned the impeccably clean cabin, the polished chrome strips of the window. The man and woman gazed steadily at the floor or out the window with vacant expressions. Maybe they were thinking about cream cakes, or what sauce to serve on the Fleischklosschen. *Good for them.* He counted up the sales in his head once more, knowing he'd be greeted in Indiana with a fat raise. Or an office with a window. Big deal. Maybe I should transfer to the Frankfurt office … bi-lingual … large fish in a small pond …

He noticed a uniformed guard at a passing station, his devils temporarily at bay. The guard was ramrod stiff. Franz surmised the guard liked to be ordered about, and to order others. The grating bombast of Nurse Zerbst in the birthing home abruptly smashed Franz's calm. Her constant, shrill hectoring: how he throbbed with stark fear. *Her tongue-lashing like darts hurled from all directions, I outdid her. I seized every task however awesome for a kid and survived.* Sure, it's taken me this long to hold my own with big shots. Most of the time their blather's just to inflate their own wind bags. I should know.

Franz studied his understated cufflinks. He appreciated his hands, the crisp white curves at the ends of his nails. Despite traveling, they were clean. A marvel of design, he thought, of his purchase in Frankfurt at the hotel gift and cutlery shop: a folding nail file and clipper the size of a postage stamp. He glanced at the neat stacks of firewood and hay and bundles of kindling in different sizes, some by every cottage however humble. Such organization, yes, this too was in his blood, but a positive thing. He settled comfortably into the gently rocking rhythm of the coach, closing his eyes. Mocha buttercream: he recaptured the flavor of his second pastry this morning, the "one for the road." He recalled how he and J would surprise each other with treats as boys; how satisfying it had been to put meat on the bones of that poor waif. Franz's anger eventually turned to sadness when J stopped writing, off in his new world, which was good … which was good …

"Greta, you remember Franz?" said Rudi, one of his teenage drinking buddies.

She smiled, holding a sleeping baby.

"What a nice little home," said Franz, gazing at the dowdy stuffed chair, the linoleum floor, the plain laminated table.

"This is Georg," said Rudi of the baby. "Named for Father!" He yanked up his trousers. "And this is Maria." She nodded to the guest.

"Please have a seat," whispered Greta.

They sat down, and Rudi pulled the electric heater closer to the circle. Franz thought of his Evergreen Ridge garden apartment with its central heating, its wall-to-wall carpet and sliding glass doors. He'd normally feel a wave of satisfaction, even superiority, but was inexplicably glum. Greta passed Bismarck herrings stuffed with pickle. Her blond hair was pinned atop her head, but cascades still tumbled onto her forehead and shoulders, encircling her face with a fuzzy, buttery glow. Franz admired the ivory-smooth texture of her skin.

"You've gained a few pounds, eh Franz," said Rudi, serving the beer. "Well, me, I'm a maintenance inspector at the new textile plant. Good job, but I'm sure nothing like your salaries over there." He kept grinning like a tomcat in his hand-knit cardigan. "At least Greta doesn't have to work anymore."

Franz nodded, slipping off his pin-striped suit jacket. Greta was obviously nursing, judging by the size of her bosom. She passed a platter of sliced Weisswurste—veal, his favorite.

"Guten appetit," she said.

"Thank you," Franz answered. "I see you use Kristal Kleer, the soap for your dishes. My company in America makes that."

"Really? How marvelous."

Franz did not impress himself by stating this fact. Being back in Germany only reminded him of his grandiose boyhood dreams. *I'm American, and not even a college grad ...*

"Sometimes I think it would be nice," said Rudi, "to be my own boss—get a little business."

"Rudi," said Greta to her husband. "Kindly get the goose liver. Our guest is very hungry."

"No, please, this is enough," said Franz, startled by this sudden craving for the sausages and flaky crackers he'd not savored for over six years.

"Franz, remember when," said Rudi leaning forward, his elbows on his knees, "we drank dunkels and ate triple portions at the Mathaeser Bierstadt, spending my whole week's wages?"

Franz accepted a re-fill, smiling, and re-crossed his legs to prevent ruining the creases.

"Whatever happened to the tall dark fellow that lived with you, Franz?"

Franz switched to that awful night in the beer hall, J shouting and singing and getting sick on his friends. Was Rudi there? "He went to Israel, when I went to the States."

"Oh, that was best," said Rudi, brushing a bit of wurst from his daughter's mouth.

"Yes. He's—with his people." *I never got to see J soar through university.*

The girl passed the plate of goose paté, but Franz's eyes followed her mother. Greta rose gently from her seat, one arm encircling the peaceful infant. He was transfixed by the milky-rouge hue of the woman's neck. "No thanks," he eventually said to little Maria, who was patiently holding the plate aloft with two hands.

"I delivered a baby, you know," said Franz absently. He was staring hard at the woven placemats, the shiny plates, the polished silver. "Several, in fact."

Franz went to the district he knew so well as a boy. Yes, there were plenty of blonds. Rudi's Greta hadn't even worn lip color. He near melted, just thinking of her hands caressing the baby's tender scalp. American girls talk too much, and too fast. He watched a Fraulein just ahead. She had lovely fair hair and dark-painted nails, an ass like a ripe plum. He caught a glimpse of her blue satin dress.

"Lili," she whispered.

"Let's go, Lili," said Franz.

They were climbing the steps. He felt his hard wallet, so full of cash. Maybe he could have it both ways: live and work for awhile in one of the Holsum Home European sales sectors. No. The action's in Buena Vista. It would be suicide. I have money now. Over six thou a year, not including Christmas bonus and Blue Cross.

He caressed her hair and buttocks. He kissed her energetically. He sank to his knees on the floor, running his hands up and down her shiny stockings. He lifted her dress, and worked his tongue. She loosened his necktie, giggling. "This is going to cost you double, Herr Sex Man," she cooed later. He went on and on, licking her to frenzy, then exhaustion. Craned over her as she sprawled on the bed, he stared down at their torsos as she guided him in once again. He watched their bodies meet, sweating like pistons and valves.

"Higher, Lena."

"Lili."

"Higher, Lili. Oooo. That's it. Like that."

He moved her, manipulated her. He drained, and filled again, finding more energy, more sensation every time. She became a blur, of matted pale hair and raw pink flesh. Their matching blond pubic areas were so locked that he lost track of which belly belonged to whom. He tried again and again, glimpsing his aching elbows, chafed bright red. "I'm almost there!" he pleaded, sobbing, urging her to stay. She slid off the bed.

"How do you like your coffee, Max?"

"What?" he whimpered. Perspiration stung his eyes. He could just about make out her form, fully dressed, arched over his clothes, riffling through his wallet.

Hours passed. It was dark. The screech of brakes, the honking of horns: every outburst was a flare, a bomb, artillery fire at which he flinched. He didn't want to stop. He pulled on himself, even though it was painful. He tried, and tried again, to no avail. It was the middle of the night. He fumbled through his clothes. She had left him a few marks, enough for a cup of coffee, maybe a beer. Everything was closed. He walked back towards his hotel. I shouldn't have used her that way, he fretted. It was wonderful, though. In Buena Vista, he'd be decapitated. It was illegal, even between consenting adults. His stride picked up. I'll go to Las Vegas and find a chorus girl. Who was sick of all that. There were no chorus girls in Buena Vista, just secretaries with circle pins. And the world's largest maker of soap-suds and toilet bowl cleaners. His twinges of pride were always flattened by repeated stabs of regret. At least Indiana was a good place to raise a family. There *must* be girls in America, girls who could fuck and cook great meals and wear sexy underwear and speak a few languages like Jackie Kennedy, and know what to say when Product Account Supervisors came to dinner, even though it was simply a role, for the time being. He took a long hot shower back in his hotel, and then blasted the German germs with Listerine for a stinging sixty seconds. He'd be damned if he'd drive the hundred and fifty miles round trip ever again for the VD clinic in Indianapolis staffed with Sunday school teachers. Blissfully, he wedged between the military-taut, fresh clean sheets.

He had one more day. One more day to retrace the area where they'd hid as kids, where he worked the shadows by night, getting soldiers for the girls. It was a new block of buildings now. Pfeiffer's the Tobacconist was the only place he could recognize. He thought of J and him producing puppet shows and trading cigarettes; his changing bedpans and injecting painkiller; growing the little lettuce and cabbage patch in a cold-frame of broken windows …

All in the past! Forget it. Franz entered the Englischer Garten, following the paths he and J used to race along. He remembered his teenage advertising campaign for blood sausage. Now he was just twenty-five or so, a whole life ahead. How rapidly he had risen as a Munich boy in the ranks of the newspaper and the film company and the fabric factory. It was a bit slower in America because, after all, Holsum Home Products was tops in the world. He passed the pagoda, the Chinese willow-pattern bridge. The garden seemed such a miniature version of the vast forest he roamed as a kid. It was on such a small scale here in Deutschland. *In sprawling America, I have to be patient.* He spotted an empty bench and sat down with his favorite snack, a steaming wiener on a roll heaped with sauerkraut and hot mustard.

His eyes rested on a man and his Doberman in the field opposite. The man was hunched over in his trim topcoat and cap. The glossy black animal, Franz could see, was quivering with restraint, sitting on its haunches, waiting for a signal. The man raised his arm, the dog watching, coiled to spring, furiously licking its snout, shifting its weight from one side to the other. The man lowered his arm slowly to indicate the exercise was postponed. The dog could not contain itself. Nor could Franz, his wiener poised mid-air. What a magnificent display! The man and dog were proceeding once again, with the raised arm signal and the seated, shaking position for the beast. Franz was spellbound, wondering how much longer the dog could withstand it. What pride the man must feel. What time-consuming skill on the part of them both.

Suddenly the dog leaped four feet in the air, sprang round in circles, as his master shouted abuse. The dog cowered on the grass, slinking back into place. Even from this distance, Franz could see the raised eyeballs pleading for mercy. The man kicked the dog first. Then he removed a leather belt, and slapped the animal again and again. Franz put down his snack, clenched his teeth, looking on, aghast. The man arranged himself, adjusted his cap, his coat sleeves. The dog slowly raised itself to the starting position. The man lifted his arm, and repeated the barking of his commands.

Franz looked off in another direction. He could vaguely remember J in a trash heap, the thrill of saving him from starvation. He recalled giving J orders. They both had their jobs. His own was to make most of the decisions. J seemed to enjoy it that way, too. Young mothers with strollers rolled by. He blinked, caught unaware, as if the camera was suddenly pointed at him. I have a mother, of course I did—everyone does—before the Lebensborn. Listlessly, he tossed bits of wurst and bread into the nearby stream. But what was my name before Hartmann? *Perhaps she is alive ...* The ducks appeared from thin air; first one couple, then a flock, strutted up to his feet. It began with an "S," this was as far as he could go. The ducks began honking, and he tore up the rest of his food for them. He clearly pictured this warm, kindly woman reading to him. A tall gallant warrior of a man in a fantastic uniform, rarely around. He had learned, at some point, they were foster-parents. The quacking ducks were becoming more insistent, pecking at his shoes, approaching his hands. He was crouching in fear of that man, praying not to be hit; this, too, he remembered. Yet how much he wanted to please him. The ducks were poking in his pockets, nipping at his wrists. Finally, he flinched with pain.

"J," he blurted at the startled birds, standing up. I wonder if he has a partner now, thought Franz, strolling off. I wonder if he ever finished school ...

Every time Franz took a step inside the barrack-turned-photo gallery, the floor creaked. This upset him. It was plenty bleak enough without straining to re-create the original barren atmosphere. It wasn't officially ready as a memorial, but he knew J had visited here many times when they were kids. Franz was alone except for a single young woman in a raincoat in need of laundering. He wished he had the place to himself to better absorb this, to imagine what it was like for J. He shuddered at the photos of heaps of bones, and the cluster of women in ragged underwear, clutching each other at the edge of an open grave, *to be their own.* He still found it hard to believe that his people were so fiendish.

Franz minded the quiet, as if in a chapel. He felt manipulated, irritated, and then understood: it was normal to feel guilty, so it was said. He glanced at a photograph entitled "Standing Torture," long lines of men standing at attention on the parade grounds. Was J searching for names? That would have been so cruelly in vain. The woman was watching him, but pretending not to. She didn't look Jewish. Her brown hair was plastered to the sides of her head, making her dark eyes radiant and sultry. He stopped at the flogging bench on display. He recalled how J would bait him, make fun of his "anal" housekeeping. Had J been trying to punish me, in his way? There were sunken eye sockets in the next picture. J would often ignore a good meal because he was moody, or tired, or cross with his school work. Then there were those secret Hebrew holy days involving a fast. Franz remembered his own boyish frustration: Why couldn't they just fit in, and behave like normal people? And now, here I am in the U.S., a misfit among a nation of strangers, the country's very reason for being …

Damn it, why had he stopped writing? agonized Franz, as he crunched the gravel underfoot. The empty buildings, the lonely watch-towers, they made him feel all the more deserted. *We shared a life together.* And he ups and takes off to be with "his people." Franz recalled the armed guard he'd glimpsed from the train. He imagined being a guard with a rifle in this particular place. He tried to imagine being patient, not giving in to the torrent of words, not taking aim … You couldn't make up your own rules. You had to support the people in power even if they were full of shit. You tried to *become* a leader yourself. He kicked the gravel, confounded that his country had attempted to stand by its values for the common good. But how did they choose the worst possible man? He picked up a stone and hurled it against one of the endless gray clapboard shacks. "Fuck you, J," he mumbled. "You should forgive me by now."

Franz held his face in his hands. *I'll never be an American. I'm nothing but a witless warrior.* His people, they duped him, told him he was special, saving lives of women and babies, filling hypodermic needles by the light of bombs; told always to remember that his job was to lead. What bunk, the whole world poking fun now, the Jews, at least J, fair enough, with the last laugh. He was startled to feel tears distinct from the rain coursing down.

Franz looked up from the monument of abstract sculpture: broken ribs and undernourished legs, now in solid steel. He caught the feminine curve of a flesh-and-blood leg, the most elegant, graceful leg. He knew she was American, practically flaunting it. Probably not wearing a stitch except a simple raincoat. And she was beautiful! He rubbed his eyes, seeing the little yellow shirt, the pudgy arm waving in salute. No, not now. He stood, and fled. The gravel spit out from under his soaked shoes. The wheels were bearing down on him, huge wheels higher than his head, faster than ever this time. Franz felt his throat closing, gasping for air. He had to reach the next bus back to Munich. The people fled in all directions as the little arm stayed poised mid-air. *Why didn't the boy move? Why didn't he scream? Where was the mother, the father?* It was way too late. He pressed against the concrete wall as the van roared by. And then he ran. He reached the bus stand, out of breath, and checked his watch. Nearly an hour to go. Too exhausted to walk, he collapsed onto the bus stop bench, his head once again in his hands.

His heart stopped. The woman was looking straight at him with a wan smile. She stood very still, her eyes meeting his. And then she moved forward, slowly, to greet him.

Part Two

Jewishness is coziness, not terror.
Let the angels quiver and quake.
They have no option.

— Isaac Bashevis Singer

1965

Chapter 11

*I*t was the middle of the night. Maybe earlier, later, it didn't matter. He was used to being awake. J wondered if his tossing and grumbling would disturb Leonard, his roommate, in the other bed. It was a foul hot summer night. Maybe he should sleep on the living room floor, like when Susan came to be with Leonard. It was stifling. So what if the place filled with soot and fumes from Riverside Drive? J got up and wrestled with the massive, filthy window.

Stale air enveloped him like an unkempt sauna. He slipped back into bed. Leonard was snoring. Once, when neither could sleep, they went to an all-night greasy spoon on Broadway. It was their best talk ever.

He was weary, always a good sign, the harbinger of sleep. And then he closed his eyes.

At first he heard the piano, next, a woman's voice. A muffled aria. No, it was not a recording; it was live. The warbling stopped, started again. At three A.M.? The voice became shriller. Was it across the street, the floor below? He tried with all his might to shove her pitch up a half-note; it was only off by that much. Please, he thought. *Please push higher.* Perhaps he could phone her, politely making the suggestion. He was too tired to move again to the window. Maybe she'd have heat stroke. How on earth could Leonard sleep through this? To think Len used to perform in Village nightclubs, keeping audiences going till dawn, J himself laughing loudest in the front row. Now he was doing daytime TV. The voice faltered, stopped, continued. It would drive him mad. Madder. Their on-going mop-up campaign. What more logical concentration of Jews off West End Avenue in the upper eighties? She was shrieking, like twenty-five fingernails scratching a blackboard. Why hadn't someone called the police? He kept expecting the screech of wheels. They were piping off-key howling into the walls, one target at a time. If they just get me to jump, he thought, they could go on to the next. Leonard, who looked and acted as Jewish as Ryan O'Neal, didn't count. He even ordered sweet and sour pork at the worst Chinese restaurants. She aimed for a high note and missed, again and again. J leaped from the damp sheets. He stood shaking at the window, rapidly scanning the block for lights, for sirens, ladders, police dogs, dozens of hysterical, protesting others. It was totally still, in the dead heat. The aria abruptly ended. Dizzy, he turned on a light and sat down at the kitchen table. He paged through his notebook of hand-written tidbits from recent readings, his ongoing Adult Ed. This will put me to sleep, for sure.

Vatican Council—releases modern Jews from responsibility for "His Passion."

Freudian urge of patricide—Christian "son" remorseful/hateful towards Jewish "father" but basically it satisfies.

Projecting Christian hostility over strict New Testament Epistles & Gospels (Allport).

J fingered the soft, spoiling fruit in the dish, wondering why it wasn't in the fridge.

Hannah Arendt: Theories, theories. They simply hate us.

"You have a rehearsal?" said J the next morning, spreading jam.

Leonard turned the page of the *Times*, intent. "Umm," he answered in the affirmative. J studied the carefully shaped ends of Len's fingernails, the uniform curves, the identical amounts of white edge as Franz would insist upon. He'd never once seen Leonard fuss over such a thing.

"'The Odd Couple' is supposed to be hilarious. Think I'll catch it with Susan," said Leonard. "You wanna get a date and join us?"

"I could try," said J without conviction.

Leonard laughed.

"We have the same Jewish noses," said J. "How come you look like Clark Gable, and I look like I was hit with a baseball bat?"

"Maybe you were."

"Funny."

"God, I can't believe we're sending over more troops." He turned the page.

"Where, Len?"

"Vietnam! Where else?"

"Well. Israel, maybe."

"Jeez you have a one-track mind."

"They're your people, too, Leonard. You just wait."

"Get real, Jay. That war is over."

J picked up a teaspoon and began tapping his thigh. He was sitting there in shorts. He looked at Leonard, his dashing friend in a stylish Madras shirt very open at the neck, pressed chinos, new leather sandals, ready for another day in an air-conditioned studio at Rockefeller Center. Leonard folded the paper and felt his chin for any overlooked stubble, highly unlikely, J thought. "Did you read about Masada, Len?"

"Sounds like a character in Uncle Remus. You reading that to your kids?"

"It's in southern Israel."

"I should have known."

"They're almost finished the excavations. *One thousand* Jews killed themselves on this hilltop rather than be slaughtered by Roman troops. Pretty amazing, huh?"

Leonard let the paper collapse. "I'm sorry about the baseball bat. For all I know, you were beaten to a pulp as a kid."

J, slumping in the chair, two hands resting on the table, finally looked up. The heat was already rising from the frying pan streets, rushing in through the open window. "What did you think about the Eichmann trial a few years ago? Did it mean anything to you … make you sick, or elated?"

"No," he sighed.

J gazed through the window streaked in pewter tones, at the sky, the buildings, the Hudson, three horizontal slabs of haze. "Me neither."

"Looks like you didn't get much sleep." Leonard stood to leave.

"You never heard that lunatic shrieking off-key?"

Leonard composed his face into a rueful smile. "The paper said it's gonna be another scorcher. Stick to the shade, pal." He left.

The inside front cover of the journal was devoted to random dates, two inches per century.

411 BC Egyptian priests bribed Persian governor to destroy Temple near Aswan.

800 CE Toulouse. Slap a Jew at Easter for betraying Jesus. Kill a Jew who wouldn't be baptized, and all sins forgiven.

1012 Expelled from Mainz.

1096 First Crusade. Massacre Christ-killers to cleanse in preparation for Judgment Day.

He closed the window. The noise, the heat, they were already on the assault. He glanced at the sink of breakfast dishes. He walked into the bedroom and looked at his unmade bed. Leonard's was pressed and packaged like one of his shirts from the Chinese laundry. The rows of Leonard's suits and shirts and coats and shoes were arranged, he supposed, by fabric thickness for the seasons, perhaps alphabetically by the labels. It was little to ask that J keep the place straight, other than his closet, for bringing in by far the least amount of cash. The piddling interest from his restitution money that he never touched was plenty enough for him to get by. Assuming Leonard could wrangle free Broadway tickets, assuming J didn't switch from YM-YWHA socials to

Maxwell's Plum. He'd be as much of a hit in the glitter bars as he was with Franz in the Bierhaus Paultz. No way could he drag himself to the library in this heat. He'd keep going with this stack, until the Weimar Republic.

1215 4th Lateran Council. Jews accused of excessive interest rates.

1233 Pope Gregory IX warns Jews getting too prominent as advisors to German princes.

1240 Talmud tried and convicted and burned in public, in Paris, for "Jewish stubbornness."

The sun by mid-day was high enough to remove any hint of color from the haze. J slumped on one elbow, but continued reading and making entries on the inside cover of his notebook.

1235 Simon of Trent. 1st Jew accused of ritual murder.

1290 Expelled from England.

1348 Jews accused of poisoning wells with spiders and lizards causing The Plague.

1394 Expelled from France.

1420 Expelled from Austria.

1424 Expelled from Zurich.

1434 Council of Basel prohibits Jews from university.

1441 Bishop of Valence reminds Jews to wear Jew badge.

1492 Expelled from Spain.

J walked to the local rec hall for boys. Its place in the community was up there with the Temple Issac Mayer and Zabar's Delicatessen. J taught remedial reading and led craft groups. And when there was a large enough audience of tired urchins who couldn't protest, he would read a tale or two of the Baal Shem Tov.

"Alright, Sammy. What's the big deal?"

Sammy crouched in a corner of the damp, subterranean room, its paint and plaster peeling. He clamped his small jaws together, exposing teeth and furiously snorting gushes of liquid back up his nose. He wasn't talking.

"It can't be all that bad."

He was about seven, eight. He was short and homely. He came to the playgroup from a nearby orphanage. J rested his hand on the boy's shoulder. "You want to tell me, or come weave potholders?"

Sammy wiped his tears and suddenly went silent. He sniffed up the last of his running nose. J removed his hand. Sammy lifted his eyes slowly from the floor to meet J's. Neither blinked, neither smiled, neither moved, for the better part of a minute.

J walked back to the low table, a carnival of broken scissors, spilled glue and screaming kids. He demonstrated weaving the squiggly, colorful nylon strips. Just like Franz had taught me, he mused, in some other cellar. Sammy finished three potholders for the Beth Israel Orphanage kitchen staff that afternoon.

"Okay," said J near the end of the session. "Here's a real short one with a long title. 'The Tailor's Work and the Lord's Work.' Any objections so far?" Sammy sat quietly at the edge of the group. And so J read.

"A rabbi ordered a pair of trousers. His tailor promised: 'I shall bring them to you within a week, by next Friday.' The tailor, however, did not keep his promise and brought the trousers three days late. The rabbi tried on the trousers and was well satisfied because they fit him perfectly. He paid the tailor and asked, 'Just explain to me why the Lord only took six days to create the world and to make a pair of trousers you took ten!' The tailor lifted his head and answered seriously, 'My Rabbi. Look at my work. There is not a defect therein! Now look at the world, the work of the Almighty, blessed be He'."

Sammy still didn't smile, but he was clutching those potholders until his knotted little fingers turned white.

As J walked home, he kept seeing Sammy's two large dark eyes, penetrating the dingy shadows of side streets, outshining the hurly-burly of upper Broadway.

"Oh. Leonard. Sorry about the mess. I ran late today."

"No sweat." Leonard continued to bustle with the last of the dishes, went to the window and hoisted the sash.

"I got some watermelon, I did do that," said J.

"I'm not really hungry. Maybe later," said Leonard.

"How about the Thalia. It's air-conditioned."

"I'm just going to crash. I'm really pooped."

They sat, reading, in shorts. J kept glancing up, fighting the lack of recent sleep, waiting for Leonard to mention something about his day, or ask about J's. Give the guy some space! They sat for half an hour, Leonard turning pages of *Time*, J re-reading the same paragraph for the twentieth time. "Ready for some watermelon?"

"Sure."

J cut two big slices and served them on plates.

"Good thinking," said Leonard, spitting out the seeds. "Must have been nice and cool in the Y basement with the kids."

"I didn't notice the heat today." J put down his melon rind, shoring up his resolve. "Leonard. I've been having radical thoughts. I know I've lived in Israel and all that. But I'm afraid I'm becoming a Zionist. Will you still share an apartment with me?"

"Jay." He smirked. "There's more to life than being a Jew."

"I know it's offensive. I'm offensive. They even asked me not to read overtly 'religious' stories, can you believe it, at the Young Men's Hebrew Association? Some parent complained they were too self-effacing and dated. I'm so sick of limp-wristed religion."

Leonard slowly nodded. "Any more watermelon?"

"You know what the Black militants call us? 'Uncle Jakes.' Another submissive minority. I've had it with the Hasidic types, too. Never *blaming* anybody, a bunch of Pollyannas chanting away in blindfolds. I think the only reason to be a Jew is to re-arm Israel. Maybe that could stay alive, a state of siege. Everybody understands that."

"You could start a synagogue at West Point," said Leonard, slurping his fingers.

"Leonard, don't you see?" J perched on the edge of the sofa. "It's slipping away. We were tested, pushed to the extreme to have our spiritual backs broken. God may have proved his point, if no one *responds*."

Leonard let *Time* flop aside.

"We Jews," J continued, "were just the vehicle. Not for hate and evil and ignorance, but utter indifference. See the danger? That it didn't matter a good goddamn. And will happen again and again!"

"Jay, take it easy. You'll be up all night, again."

"I'm going for a walk," said J blankly.

"Stay away from the park, Jay. You know it's late."

J slipped on a tee-shirt and sneakers.

"Have a beer, for God's sake," offered Leonard with a wrinkled brow. "Let me fix you a gin and tonic. You'll pass right out."

"See you later," snapped J, and he left.

He didn't know how late it was. In this heat, people weren't moving around much. Uncollected garbage was fermenting in cans, in tied-up plastic bags composting to the boiling point. He walked west to the park paralleling Riverside Drive. It was mad but it was pulsing with life, and he needed a fix … the water, a breeze, the open sky. He didn't care about the shadows. Those eyes of the child from this afternoon were still emblazoned on every bush, every patch of black in the path. Vast, dark pools, they drew him in. Muggers, knifers, pimps, male and female whores. Beggars, buggers, winos, pee-ers, shitters, fuckers, sleepers, slayers … this park after midnight could compete with the best in all New York. Shapes lurched behind trees. Shadows continuously stabbed the path, a moving branch or a staggering body, it was all the same. The boy's face was all eyes. The mouth, if any, receded, pinched, sucked into the cavity. He leaned on the railing overlooking the putrid water, and locked into position. He couldn't breathe. The air was a paste that pinned him in place, even though there was motion all around. The river raced under him, jerking him slightly to the rhythm of floating mucus, bubbling scum. He tried to picture the hypnotic crack of the train over tracks. His body was stiff, swollen with heat, wedged against the railing and bones and bloated bellies. It was pitch black, airless. No space to even utter a cry. He was absolutely alone, crushed by an inert mass, even though hands—thick, smelly, supposedly loving hands, then as now, were pawing his entire body, his arms, waist, thighs, his neck, his mouth, shoving him over the railing, into the bottomless black. He couldn't scream even if he had the breath. But his eyes were free. They were racing, he was alive. He finally squirmed, and turned enough to see the gigantic dark man with bulging eyes, red and fiery veins instead of white spaces. The coarse sandpaper hands wouldn't let go of his throat. And he could see, in the time it took to blink but lasting forever, the boy and his mother. *I can see her gasping for air herself. And the boy standing without moving, like I am now, as they yank her away, shrieking, kicking, wailing, choking for breath, sobbing a name. I can see hands, vividly, clamped around her throat.* He went totally slack now in the stranglehold, as had she, although that likely pure fabrication, something to fill the void. The ugly eyes suddenly became the boy's this afternoon, silently staring yet demanding him to move, to bite or shove, defy a senseless end.

"Fuck off!" said J, suddenly angry at this interruption in his waking dream. The black man, a drunk, broke his grip at the first resistance, startled, falling over backwards into the gravel, dropping the knife. A knife! J froze. He tasted the rancid air pouring into his lungs. He grabbed the blade and plunged it again and again into the soft gravel, his heart a kettle drum. The man scrambled away. Lurking others approached, then quickly skittered off. Finally, covered in sweat, J flung the battered knife into the river and fled.

He prayed Leonard would be up reading, lights on, the place ablaze. He slipped into the dark apartment, into icy sheets despite the fetid air. He fixed his eyes on the huge, greasy window, until dawn tinted the panes a dusty pink.

He slept late into the morning. Leonard hadn't disturbed him. He delved into his books, the easiest way he knew to forget himself.

1520 Luther calls the Jews "a scourge," "a pestilence," and "a misfortune."

1543 Luther attacks Jews for not converting to his version of Christianity.

1553 Pope condemns Jews as "blasphemous."

1670 Expelled from Vienna; blamed for Empress's miscarriage.

J ran out of space on the inside cover; he scribbled away on an empty page. *Passion Plays: Jewish women accused of washing Christ's wounds with vinegar-soaked rags to induce greater pain. Flagellants of Thuringia, baptism of babies to the point of bleeding. Chiliastic prophets offer hope to miserable, encourage hastening of Apocalypse and Second Coming. Bockelson, leader of Anabaptists, enforced famine: eating hedgehogs, rats, old shoes, whitewash on walls, bodies of the dead. Messianists, Bohemians, Self-Immolators, Beguines, Blood Friends, Adam Cultists, Self-deifiers. Revolutionary of the Upper Rhine—revival of German brotherhood.*

J looked up and out the window, recalled his and Franz's puppet shows, their swearing allegiance forever over their blood-let cocktail … Brothers.

He slumped in his seat. All this fuss over a country no bigger than Connecticut. A lousy one percent of the world's population. For three years with the army in Israel, he mostly put in fence posts and water pipes, no charging through battles like in Tolstoy. The lieutenant was really the mayor of Eilat; the platoon leaders were dentists, eggheads, citrus pickers. Well, he didn't know his mother. He couldn't prove that he was one of them.

He decided the view from his window was a Turner landscape reincarnated. Subtly shifting masses of blur: gray blur, smoky-white blur, a blur of mottled, mildewed yellow. It didn't always have to be Teaneck or whatever, New Jersey. When the sun smeared itself across the upper panes, as now, back-lighting high-rise condos, fork lifts and factory exhaust pipes, why couldn't he squint some and say it was the Canale della Guidecca of Venice, or a sweeping impressionist's view of Marseille at the turn of the century?

Perhaps I'm a gypsy. Maybe it wasn't a "J" for Jud I'd erased from my forearm. Maybe I read it wrong because of the crease and freckle at that exact spot. Maybe it was a "Z" for Zigeuner, gypsy, equally undesirable but more of an admixture—a little Mediterranean, a little Lutheran, a little fallen mountain aristocracy. Despite his nose, his dark hair, he knew he could "pass." And had.

Even if his parents were alive, they'd be silent. For them it was, and would be, unspeakable. They'd have no memory to condemn the wrongs. If memory, no voice. No energy to explain, to understand, to kvetch. It was up to him. He had been there, sort of. What could he say? What had he seen? He had feelings, but who didn't? The buildings, the man-made shapes, now bled into the river. They became one massive, inky black shadow.

No. I must not sink into cynicism. I must believe in Israel, from the bottom of my heart.

J plunged back into his books, sitting upright like a trooper. He was sure a mission would define itself at some point if, as Franz would say, he were disciplined and patient.

"You're getting damn good at chili, Jay," said Leonard.

"It's from the five-minute gourmet cookbook."

"Maybe you can get it down to three, re-heating from night to night."

"Did we have chili last night? Sorry, Len." J could see a remnant of orange make-up on Leonard's neck.

"Listen, ace. I think your work's every bit as important as mine. What were you reading today?"

"The usual. Martin Buber, *TV Guide.*"

"You seem down."

J wondered if Leonard was simply playing another part: strong American savior. He knew it was for real, if only a piece of Leonard's personality. "Why should I bog you down?" J finally said.

"I care about you very much." Leonard flicked his cigarette ash into the tray dead center.

"Thank you, Len. You're a great support. More than I deserve."

"Doesn't seem like anyone can do much for you, this path you're on."

"You eat re-heated chili." J looked directly now at Leonard, who was stabbing out his cigarette and not smiling. "That's the great thing about our friendship. It's just us, sharing this place, no bullshit." He caught Leonard looking up quickly. "Here we are," J continued, "perfectly free to come and go. Yet we've made it—a home."

Their eyes met again and held; this time Leonard's being a deeper, cooler hue of hazel.

Leonard broke the silence. "I've been thinking, Susan and I have been talking about—"

"Len, that's great! You don't have to explain." He lined up the fork and knife parallel on his plate. "When?"

"Jay, I've treasured our companionship. I respect you so much. You're so—serious. You've encouraged me to dig in. No more Drillo commercials, I've made the afternoon drama circuit. It's a solid start."

"Thanks, Leonard. You've opened my eyes to—the lighter side. Remember when I met you at the all-night jam session at the Village Gate, in support of—what? Cuban refugees? I was with Arlene, who introduced you to Susan. I kept yakking, and you all just laughed, you said you were there to listen to the music … "

Still seated at the table, Leonard started stacking the dishes, as if deflecting intimacy.

"And remember when I was so impressed by that play you were in, on radiation," J went on, "and you said it was just a part, that you really didn't … "

Leonard rose and placed the dishes in the sink.

"I'll find another roommate, no sweat," J said. "Not as

pleasant or as well-dressed. Man, that closet is going to be one gaping hole!"

"Speaking of Arlene," Leonard said, "why don't you give her a ring? Sunday Susan and I were planning to—"

"Oh, Arlene's got the hots for what's-his-name."

Leonard picked up his *Variety*. "It was just a suggestion."

For weeks, J went about his business. Leonard hadn't yet moved out, but was rarely around. J was used to being alone. His books kept him company. He had even made two centuries' progress.

1752 Bluttenbach. Identification of white race with Caucasian mountain people: preferred skin shade and oval skull shape. 1764 Jew toll in Frankfurt. 1790 Craniometry: physiological race characteristics; opacity of blacks; unable to blush, morally inferior. 1819 Schlegel: theorist of Indo-Germanic, anti-Old Testament roots. 1800s—Darwin: stratification, classification of types. Pan German League. German Youth Movement. Protocols of the Elders of Zion. Jewish conspiracy blamed for assassination of Czar Alex II. 1890 Fontane: Jews as "irritants." Wilhelm II: Jews as perpetuators of "filthy modern French art." Bochel: "Octopus." Die Juden und das Wirtschatsleben: "Unscrupulous. Rootless." Lagarde: "trichinae, bacilli." Mein Kampf: "spiders."

"Who's in my bed!" cried Leonard, startled, arriving late one night. "What the hell … "

"Shhh," hissed J.

"Who is this? I've paid my share of the rent for another month!"

"Leonard. Would you shut up? You'll wake him." J tugged Leonard into the bathroom, flicked on the light. "Look, Len, he's just a kid from the orphanage. Sammy was having, I don't know, a breakdown or something. I'm letting him sleep here, just for tonight. It's no big deal."

J settled it by giving Leonard his own bed, considered the living room floor, then slipped into the other with the boy.

Thus the love of the Hebrews for their own country was not only patriotism but also piety, and was cherished and nurtured by daily rites until, like their hatred of other nations, it was absolutely perverse. Spinoza. Deuteronomy: the Lord shall return and gather you from among all the peoples among whom God has scattered you ...

J was reading to Sammy and a few others a story from the Baal Shem Tov one day at the youth center. Sammy laughed at the funny names, like the Rabbi of Madzhibozh, which J pronounced with great gusto. Sammy screwed up his face at the end. "How could he do that? The preacher was dead. How could the preacher talk to the other guy, and lead his own funeral march?"

"Well," shrugged J. "Consider it a miracle. Anything can happen in this business."

"I still think it sounds weird."

J smiled. "C'mon. I'll take you out for a pizza. And you're welcome to stay, you know, anytime—"

"We're going to a hockey game tonight."

"That's great." J could feel the myriad of tiny muscles supporting his smile go limp.

The following month, Sammy moved to an inter-faith home for older boys sponsored by Catholic Charities, in Rosedale, Long Island.

J was wandering through the lower Village one morning. He was more or less looking for cut-rate paperbacks. He felt no angst, he kept being amazed. Although numbing, he realized, was in fact how they survived. He preferred living alone. He remembered what a relief it was, finally leaving Franz, no longer having to hoist up his half of the daily bustle and cheer. It was a fantasy, a soul seeking completion outside itself, from a collective, a family, a partner. Even from offspring. He thought of sweet Rivka. Yes, I blew my chance at baby-making. I must be nearly thirty. The people milling about the Village here were zombies, or draft resisters, or sailors on leave, or drifters looking to donate blood. "$5 dollars a pint," said the sign. At first he thought: for givers or receivers? "ID required." At eleven in the morning, men's and women's asses overlapped barstools. The street sweeper bulldozed through, flailing and swirling wet brushes, leaving a cyclone of debris despite the extravaganza of machinery. It was a hopeless task to keep ahead where wrappers—candy, condoms, Rolaids—rained into the gutters like a ticker-tape parade. He shuffled along, free to choose, mature, refreshingly unnoticed. Leonard was probably in some Fifth Avenue salon, his nail polish getting a blow-job. Sammy was playing with kids his own age. He saw the sailor laughing, then the needle. "5 minutes," it said. The five-minute gourmet identification bracelet. He paid ten bucks, and sat on a stool. He rolled up his sleeve when it was his turn.

"Red or blue?"

"It doesn't matter."

"Blue it is."

He waited, to flinch, to scream. He didn't feel a thing.

"J what?" said the man.

"Just J. The letter J. That's all."

"Okay, buddy. It's your ten bucks. Scroll, Gothic, Sans Seraph, Skim-line."

"A simple J is fine."

"Okay, Blue J, you're all set. Fly away, baby. Next."

Chapter 12

Franz strode along his gravel driveway one Saturday morning to collect the mail. The white pebbles had made a smooth and compact lane the year before when he bought them. Solid gravel drive, then solid green and groomed lawn extending towards the house in a graceful sweep. It could rival the color picture on the box of Kentucky Bluegrass seed. Now, the edges were infiltrated by clumps of weed and stubborn dandelion sprigs. He shoved a hand through his hair trimmed to but not extending beyond his collar. He had tried weed killer in the gravel once, but Marcy was fearful Sandy might ingest it. He jogged back to the two-car garage, and grabbed his spring-tooth rake off the wall. He was pleased by hooks over the walls, displaying at a glance the shears, the shovels, the neatly-coiled hose. He trotted back to the unkempt borders. He was eager to deal with this chore and get back to his new workbench and the cabinet doors for the cellar bar complex. That was gonna be a beauty. He could picture Marcy and him entertaining the Trumbulls, the Smithsons, the Strausses, the other fellows of Product Management and their wives, pulling bottles of Michelob and mixers from the built-in refrigerator and cubes from the ice attachment. Railroad ties, he thought. A mostly sunken divider … a lip beyond which gravel couldn't spread, and crabgrass was foiled from sending runners. No way would he put down asphalt. Each house in the sub-division was practically identical. The driveway was only a few dozen yards, but packed white gravel gave it that estate look. And why not a split-rail fence? He squatted up and down the short driveway like a rabbit, measuring the various distances.

The baby drizzled warm milk from her breast. Marcy was amazed how large her breasts had become, how much she enjoyed the continuous wet process of emptying then filling. She loved it with her daughter Sandy, but now she was more relaxed, Andy at eleven months. She nuzzled the hot flesh of his head, his shoulders and pudgy, flailing hands. He was big and strong and blond like his father. So was Sandy at age three, crashing about in her stained turtleneck and falling, baggy bell-bottoms. As Marcy nursed, she thought: What a contrast to her grandparents' home where she was raised starting at age six after her parents died. *Children must be seen and not heard:* the ultimate mantra of those people! And yet, lovingly she pictured her Granddad Herman, hour upon hour in their tidy Jersey suburb, stabbing the sod with his penknife, lifting the tufts of invasive crabgrass and dandelion. How clearly she could visualize it, the roots being perfectly intact. And now Fran out there, a duplicate copy! She changed Andy's warm, gooey diapers, enjoying the aroma, the fluids, the ongoing cycles.

"Foo, foo," said Sandy, biting one of her brother's soiled socks.

"Breakfast ready soon, sweetie." She sprinkled baby powder, watching her own hands, smooth and swift, manipulating the sweet-smelling material around Andy's pink bottom. The soft clean fabric was so much more pleasant to use than Pampers. Besides, she liked the cleaning, the fresh-air clothes pinning, the drying and collecting, then the folding, all out of doors on hazy, late summer afternoons. *Motherhood.* I never would have believed it. Electing abortion to complete my senior year. And settling with just one man? The least likely to succeed. She thought of Paul, the saint, who dropped out of seminary when she got pregnant.

He'd taken up for her Brooklyn Irish Grandpa Tim, with poems and soulful patter. And then Mark, the rabbinical student, had wooed her with new kinds of mysteries from his culture. She always figured she'd get the best of two worlds, like the silly Atlantic City palm reader promised. Two men, but in one: a basically poetic nature in pursuit of the divine while winning bread. She forever dismissed that the palmist also predicted a sudden death … Here and now! She lathered the baby with kisses until he cooed, saliva gushing from his toothless mouth, lubricating his widening smile.

"Me, too," wailed Sandy, stretching her plump arms to her mother's tangled brown hair to be included in the pre-breakfast embrace. Then she wallowed gently over Marcy's thighs, her tummy and breasts, beating on her like an Indian tom-tom.

"Listen, you lazy fools," said Marcy. "I've got to start the sausage frying for your father's breakfast." She strapped Andy in the kitchen door-jamb jumper swing. She swirled hot milk into the children's oatmeal, squeezed fresh oranges for juice, hauled out frozen sausage links for Fran and felt guilty. You'd think I could at least make muffins, a lousy fifteen minutes on the weekend, when there was loads of time.

"Hi, honey. Any interesting mail?" said Marcy, then saw he was empty-handed.

"Oops, I forgot," said Franz, scanning the stovetop, relishing his wife's bobbing tits as she sashayed about.

Marcy unplugged her hand from the potholder mitt and inserted the coffee filter. She poured maple syrup into an earthenware jug and set it on the table. She rolled the browning sausages with the spatula. She grabbed the whisk to beat the French toast batter good and frothy.

Franz paged through the papers as Marcy strapped Andy into his high chair and spoon-fed him oatmeal. She flipped the toast at just the second it turned a golden brown. She felt so much in command, like landing a jet-liner in a thunderstorm, with all these dials and handles and tools at her disposal. "So thoughtful of you, Fran, to build this utensil rack over the range," she said for his benefit, and she meant it.

"What a beautiful platter, Marcy." He began wolfing it down. She joined him at the table with a third his portions, the both of them beaming.

A large plastic sheet was spread under the high chair, well plastered now with gray-brown glop. Franz grimaced as the baby gazed wide-eyed at Franz, a lava-like flow of oatmeal and drool oozing down his chin.

"I can't decide about christening Sandy and Andy," said Marcy, encircling her coffee mug with both hands.

"What's to decide?" asked Franz, pouring syrup. "Why have our kids raised in the bug-a-boo of the Catholic Church? As for the Protestants, it's just not necessary."

"I suppose you're right, sweetie. They can make up their own minds about church as adults." For her, the subject of religion was like her girlhood glass globe that rained snow and then settled. Her latest set of convictions would be stirred by the least challenge and again her mind was a muddle.

The baby hurled a fistful of oatmeal at the floor.

"I'm still frustrated I wasn't at Andy's delivery," said Franz.

"Because they said fathers got in the way?"

"No, about the circumcision," he said.

"That's standard practice now," she said.

"Just seems more of a Jewish ritual."

"Oh. That. We can have him baptized, if you'd feel better. Then you can think of him as a proper Christian." She knew he'd miss her jab; she tried to keep them gentle. "Whatever you'd like is fine with me," said Marcy. She helped Sandy tug a doll arm out of a tangled doll shirt, then paused. "Of course, if we don't expose them to church, how will they have any basis for rejecting it and choosing later on their own? Oh, I don't know."

Franz began on his teeth with a toothpick. Sandy was tugging on his shirt, to no avail. Next, she smacked her brother's scalp. "Hey, Marce, I've an idea for straightening the driveway borders. Railroad ties."

"Fran, you know what happened to your back when you

hauled cement bags."

He patted her ass and strutted outdoors.

Sandy was shredding a woven placemat. Andy was sucking his fist and beating his spoon for more service. The sausages, she thought, mopping up oatmeal. Those greasy little sausages were a flop. *Listen to me.* This is paradise after Brandenburg. So what if he's oblivious half the time. *He's here.* More than my mother could say. And in fairness to Herman and Ethel, her grandparents Burger, Lutherans through and through: they were silent but sincere. Marcy cringed with guilt over the adolescent havoc she had wrought. Her foul Carney Irish temper from the other side! Like the time she smashed Herman and Ethel's TV after they once again averted details of her parents' deaths. She'd forever be compensating for her youth as a brat, repelled by their undemonstrative love. There. One meal done. Two to go.

How could I be so lucky in one lifetime, Franz thought, carefully angling the spade into sod. My wife is gorgeous, smart, orderly, loving with the children. He thought of a use for the sod, to replace the worn section near the back door. Plus, she was supple and eager and energetic in bed. He got aroused, picturing her succulent boobs brushing the curls of his chest hair as his tongue worked its way down. She belted beer from the can; none of that stemmed-glass-gimlet-with-a-twist business. He grunted as he hauled armloads of sod. He had a new wheelbarrow, but wanted the exercise, cooped up in an office all week. He recalled the line-up of pretty blonds he laid as a lad in Germany. They smiled, they complied, but they never seemed to enjoy it. The extra soil … I'll build flower boxes for the garage windows. He relished her fuming Irish temper when she told him off: that, too, caused a swell in the crotch of his coarse Levi jeans.

Sandy was scribbling with crayons on the morning paper and bills. Andy was asleep. Marcy had misgivings about the pacifier. She'd read Dr. Spock backwards and forwards, and still wasn't sure. What if Andy didn't develop enough assertiveness to successfully resolve the Oedipal journey, from break with his father to tough little man? As usual, she was sorting out issues with the laundry. She wasn't doing enough for her family. It was all so pleasant and easy. Something, surely, was wrong. After her month of study in Dublin, just before Munich, she couldn't have conceived of sacrificing art for marriage. What more was embedded in her bones than Grandpa Tim Carney, God bless his soaring wino soul in that piss-soaked cellar in Flatbush? He never married his talent to an energy source, which in turn fueled her all the more, privileged with the Burgers. She recalled working twelve hours a day in the Dublin silversmithing studios. She could trace the designs of the jewelry in the Irish Antiquities Museum over and over in her mind. She had packed them into a good dozen sketchbooks as well. And now instead: cookbooks!

She felt the lovely burning of her nipples against the nursing bra. How long could she protract the best aspect to motherhood without warping his sense of security ... befuddling his libido? She paged through the cookbook that came with her latest kitchen appliance, another present from Fran: a cast-iron meat grinder. "You must have this for leftovers." Tonight's dinner should be special, him wrestling with railroad ties. "Great Sausages from Home-Ground Beef or Pork. Simple as 1-2-3. Polish—Lebanese—Italian—*German* ... " She checked the recipe: spices, seasonings, liquid smoke; she had it all. Fran could watch the kids while she ran out for the casings and meat. There was homemade sauerkraut she had canned with garlic and caraway. Still four dozen or so quarts left in the cellar. Fran said it could pass, but had a few suggestions for when she tried it again. He'll be thrilled ... knockwurst like his foster-mother used to make.

A few hours later, Franz entered the kitchen for a drink of water. He took one look at "this broad who was his wife," making sausage no less, and grabbed her ass. They put the children to bed for a nap in the nursery. Franz ripped off their clothes, and they made furious love on the bathroom floor before they could proceed to their room. Franz was turned on by the tile, the porcelain, the hint of Lysol. Marcy was well acquainted with his pattern of spontaneity. She kept the bathroom floor, in particular, spotlessly clean.

She returned to sausage making. She assembled the equipment; she rinsed and soaked the casing; she finished grinding the meat and fat. It was so simple, and soothing, so wonderfully boring. She especially enjoyed using her hands, her body leading her mind for a change, well, going on three years now. What bliss, after the decade of hammering out differing points of view just for the sake of a good discussion, a passing grade. *Babies*. What could be more basic? Thank God her teenage abortion hadn't ruined her. She'd never experienced this forceful a focus. Marcy could never forget one of the most prized of all German possessions: daVinci's "Madonna and Child" at the Alte Pinakothek. Among the masses of work, this humble virgin was so convincing, so rueful and serene. The flesh tones went from peach to pearly gray, infused with warmth and life and love after this many years. The lips, the earlobes, she could still feel them tremble. They were pulsing with a continuous message of joy at the miracle. Imagine a mother and babe, this everyday event, elevated to such grace! And all this was thanks to Fran. He was a good man, an honest man, an easy man to please. Sexually he had a few hang-ups, but what a distance he'd traveled, from a battered, bombed-out childhood to modern suburban America. What a burden of guilt he had to carry no matter what country or corporation he tried to adopt. Born in the thick of history's most noxious monstrosity. How she admired his silent coping. She cracked the handle with greater effort, force-feeding the grinder with chunks of gristle. He was slaving away for her, for his family, their home, a fresh start. Poor devil. Even with air conditioning, sometimes he worked so hard he couldn't get through the day without a change of shirts. What a relief after the pompous pricks that tried to, and did, get into her pants, during and after college. Of course she'd been in love with their opinions. Liederkrantz! She added it to her shopping list. What a complete use of meat, Marcy thought, gaining speed with the process. Blood and guts, Fran will be so pleased with not a speck of waste. She dug her fingers into the mound from every angle, thoroughly enjoying the herb and garlic distribution process. Maybe I should try sculpture someday? She could see him now out the window, heaving and hauling, open-mouthed, open-shirted. A man needs to use that hard body, she reminded herself, noticing but not bothered by the black and blue she could feel developing on her left buttock. There had been a baby rattle under the bathroom rug. She slipped the tubular sausage funnel onto the end of a roll of casing. She knew "casings" were intestines, but couldn't care less. All part of the natural cycle, in and out and in. Who needed sculpture? Look at my aunt Mary Carol with her brood of five and her brain intact. Marcy had her body to make and nourish life. Her breasts rocked with life-giving fluid. Her belly, her flanks, received her man. She was shaping flesh and bones the whole day long. As Mrs. Frank Mann, she was a conduit for the greatest forces on earth. And for herself? Yoga lessons. Plus Tuesday nights, the anti-baby-seal-slaughter campaign.

God this has been fun, Marcy thought, wiping her hands. Still. How did I wind up with a *German?* When in Munich, she could not deny the vigor and ballsy rush of the place: the belching factories, the children's science museum—girls and boys pushing buttons, yanking levers, speaking sharply to each other to come see *their* discovery. She had entered a mock coal mine operation complete with hydraulic valves, pulleys, carts on steel platforms, a maze of equipment and placards of explanation. The uniformed children swarmed like bees about an angry hive. On another floor was an intricate model of the Krupp forge, which made her think of her Granddad Herman's nail and screw and tool compartments, never a tack out of place. At the time, all this made her itch to sink into real work again, sort of like college, but this time with her hands. Painting, brewing, ventilating, wiring, she had gone to a final floor, to metalworking. There were thousands of hammers, pincers, pliers and tongs. Suddenly, the stamp of heavy commerce was overwhelming. Was there nothing fine or curved or hand-carved as in Dublin? Yet she also appreciated a compelling ferocity about the material—heated, twisted, shaped, painstakingly hammered into a myriad of detail.

She cleaned up the last of the kitchen mess, more or less. It would never be kempt to Fran's standards with two kids this age, although that was just an excuse. Unloading the dishwasher, she was transported again back to Munich, her trip to the potbelly of Bavaria and her conflicting reactions to the homeland of her husband. Nothing had been so flamboyant, so chilling, as Hitler's Camp David, the Eagle's Nest at Berchtesgaden, seen from miles below. It perched on a ridge of the Alps, as close to the gods as it was withdrawn from the people, approachable only by secret tunnels drilled thought rock. For her, there was an appeal, that soaring towards the possible, a great bloated but delicious resolve. She had felt strength of purpose flowing into her from the orderly surroundings, the clear-cut German approach to things. Das Urwuchsige, she'd scribbled in her guidebook. Growth from one's own deep roots. Well, you can't break from your past, she thought, leaning against the sink's edge, but maybe pick out the best parts. *Pray I've got my German for industry but my Irish for soul.*

Franz slammed the sledge hammer to finish a post. His cock and balls were faintly swollen and gloriously tingling. He thought of his homeland and his own two adorable blond creations. It was beyond sick what happened to the Jews, but was it so unnatural to have beautiful, unmarried, otherwise idle German girls, ripe bodies and all, turn out healthy young ones? We're half animal, aren't we, he thought, fiercely gouging the earth with his post-hole digger. He allowed himself such random thoughts because he knew, deep down, they couldn't begin to mollify the barbarity he witnessed. *How can I ever forget Trude dragged and dumped onto the street, eight months pregnant, for cursing Nurse Zerbst?*

He focused again on his work. This is such a wholesome workout, compared to my weights in the basement. And I'm building my "castle." J *did* belong in Israel, damn him, with fighter planes and tractors instead of prayer books and weird foods. Franz stomped the earth around the post to firm it.

He was tickled Marcy was making wurst. He should go in and sniff. Besides, he was aching to squeeze her again, until she laughed and bit his ear, hard, and told him to stop. How he loved to see her face flush red. But usually, she was so easy-going, lolling around with the kids on the floor. He'd step lightly on her fanny with his foot and rotate it until he got the sultry Irish lass hopping mad. Then she'd snap at him, call him a Kraut; swear she'd never flush with Plumb Pretty, until they'd both laugh and tumble into a wrestling match, often their prelude. He fitted the railings into the posts and then pounded them in place with large spikes. He'd seen her through the window with long, whitish tubes, her fingers sliding around on the fat rolls, poking more and more stuffing inside. It looked like she was playing with condoms. At this he'd become inflamed. If the kids weren't around, I should've gone in and taken her from behind at the sink. An erection is to be used, enjoyed; not kept all zippered up. So he was easily triggered and not ashamed. He remembered a Catholic boy at the Lebensborn who peed all over himself because his mother said not to touch it. It was evil. Thank God his foster-mother did right by him. Telling Marcy all the stories in recent years had brought so much detail back to life. They were good people, believing they were doing the right thing. He could even recall a tall man in a uniform. It was a fearsome memory of polished leather and sharp words. Perhaps he was even struck a time or two and in the face. Yes, he was sure that he was. But it filled him with pride even to this day, just the thought of this solid, simple, stern couple taking him on. Hitler was fucked up. Everybody knew that. But they couldn't condemn an entire race, a whole history of hard-working men and women. Now he was doing the same in a young and vital land. Holsum Home had increased their share of market in practically every category of consumer goods since his arrival nine years ago. It was all baloney, but he could share in the satisfaction of a job well done. The sturdy split-rail fence was near to completion.

With Andy behind bars, Sandy jabbering into her toy telephone, Marcy baked apples with raisins and cinnamon in custard sauce, one of Fran's favorites, just in case the wurst didn't work. Took ten minutes. The recipe, actually, was her Grandmother Ethel's. The Brandenburg kitchen was one room there where silence was soothing.

Franz had a long, hot shower. He vowed to get more of this kind of exercise, confronting the mirror. He swore the flab had started to melt with just eight hours of manual labor, although he had a long way to go. Still, he thought, leering at himself: not bad for twenty-nine, more or less. He plotted the next escapade with his wife.

Marcy lit candles, corralled the kids for bed, returned from the cellar with a six-pack of Beck's Imported Dark just as Franz joined her in the dining area for their Saturday night soiree.

The sausage, the whole supper, was a huge success.

"Home sweet home!" Franz smiled and burped.

"Let's leave the dishes," Marcy said with a wink.

They charged from the table to their bed, unfinished beer rocking gently in the ruckus.

Marcy relaxed. She loved it, him lunging away like a greedy little boy. He was reckless, driving deeper, full of brew, no finesse, not tonight. Hell, it didn't matter. No one could abuse her; not this way. She loved the weight of his body, his freshly-soaped muscular torso going all grimy and humid. She loved the smells, his grunts, releasing herself to the wild journey once again. She knew him. He cared. She wouldn't lose him. They meshed, their bodies worked, with no inhibitions. She was building, filling, flushing, draining, building again with pressure to near breaking point, but not quite. It was mad, moronic. She wanted to keep on having babies. He was growing inside her. He was raw. She could shape him, help him, love him, hold him. Her fingernails burrowed into his shoulder blades.

Afterwards, she yanked him down, face to face in the rumpled mess, and covered his forehead with kisses. Her eager beaver, her wayward child; his wounded face, and that just on the surface. Soon he was snoring. Marcy listened to her children breathing through the open door and stared blankly out the blue-black window. She could re-play it word for word ...

"I'm sorry," she had said. "I've interrupted your privacy. But only the two of us here, in this whole place." He seemed shy, despite the icy blue intensity of his eyes.

"I figured you were American," he had said. "The way you shoved your rain-soaked hair, demanding all the explanations of this place, and daring to be on your own."

"And you?" she said. "I can't tell from your accent. American, or German who speaks darn good English?"

"Some of each I guess by now," he said running fingers through his own drenched hair, smiling, but still too shaken to meet her eyes.

"Let me guess. You were born in Germany and now you're living in the States."

"How could you tell?"

"Your Arrow shirt. I can see the label."

He shifted over on the bench. "Sit down, for God's sake. The next bus from Dachau back to the city isn't for nearly an hour." Later, he told her that he figured she was another smart-ass college girl, running around Europe on dividend checks. But she sure as hell wasn't like the secretaries in his office, suggesting miniature golf instead of the drive-in.

She recalled sitting next to this beautiful dazed blond German of her own generation, thinking what an opportunity to share in *his* tangled emotions over this scene. Yet she had wanted to be alone. She was ready to go home after the museums of Ireland and Munich and get to work. Enough of this agonized history.

"You're not Jewish either, are you?" he said.

She shook her head.

"But you lost someone in the war, too?"

Abruptly she looked up.

"I didn't lose my parents," he went on. "I never had any. I was raised in this hospital for pregnant women during the war. I mean, I *worked* there as a boy. My home, my proper home, was in a cellar. The building was bombed, but we found a great basement, right here in Munich."

She stared at him, trying to make room for his reactions to Dachau while hammered by her own. *A prisoner was not excused from work call until his temperature reached one hundred and four ... guards would bend back a fingernail for disobeying. Injection with malaria to study the symptoms ... freezing in vats of ice water to watch the body's reaction ... induced tuberculosis, castration, rates of bleeding from severe wounds ... the potability of sea water.* You, they will point to for generations. The People of the Twentieth Century. *Enough.*

"I lived with my—brother," Fran had continued. "He was a Jew, well, really, an orphan like me." Later he confessed his anger at saying these things to this "nice girl shining like a sexy angel in the rain." He'd wanted to go back to Indiana, to forget the nightmares of Munich. His missing J was punishing enough, let alone this freak show of reminders.

He seemed to be choking over his memories. She had reached out and touched his hand, which was drawn tight into a fist. He didn't flinch; in fact, he grabbed her hand and squeezed it in return. She was shocked—at herself, as well as his response. It seemed the human thing to do, under the circumstances, but still. She hadn't meant it. She wanted to pull it back. She had her own head roiling with doubts and fears about this land, the unsmiling, broad-shouldered matrons who were spitting images of Grandmother Ethel; her "Army hero" father killed in Germany while cavorting on leave, her man-crazed mother dropping dead at the news. "Really?" she said at last. "I'm an orphan, too."

He knew she would come to his room, Fran later laughed, what with her raincoat half-way up her thighs, her skin all silky in the steady drizzle. "I take it you've got some German blood?" he said at the time.

She smiled broadly. "My grandparents would swear in Deutsch through their teeth like they had lockjaw so I wouldn't know they were upset. Now, my Irish ones, they didn't care if half of Flatbush heard them cuss the Virgin Mary—they raised me, too," she said in a rush, as she warmed to his smooth, burning hand, all of this drawing her in, faster, faster, even though she'd been dwelling during this trip on her father, how he, too, lost his life because of all this, but, more to the point, how she had lost him …

"My name is Franz. Or Frank. That's what they call me in Indiana."

"I'm Marcy."

"I *am* German," Franz said. "Up to six years ago, but now I'm as American as Holsum Home Products. You've heard of Plumb Pretty toilet bowl cleaner?"

"My Prussian granddad Herman worked for Otis Vacuum Cleaner. What is it with you people?" she laughed. "Obsessed with filth."

Here you were, Fran said as the tale was often retold. I couldn't believe my luck in that sewer of despair. My chorus girl, Den Mother, wise-cracking woman-of-the-world all in one. I pictured you baking cookies, reading good books, telling happy tales to my children, saying clever things to my bosses, and no-holes-barred in bed!

They had released their lingering handshake as he draped his arm around the bench and lightly grazed her agreeable shoulder.

He was stoically handsome and blond as a god, but clearly a shipwreck of sensitivity underneath. How could she ever admit to him, to herself or anyone after that horrific display, how much the very people who reared her hated Jews? But what was that, next to the contempt people like him had to suffer, typecast as butchers even though he was just a babe during the war?

"Franz," she had whispered, softening further from the heat of his wan, bittersweet smile. "You said your—brother—was a Jewish orphan? How remarkable for you both."

At this his smile turned stale.

Oh but of course, she thought at the time. He must be in mourning. It was she, again, who made a move; she who placed her hand this time on his knee and closed her eyes and tried to forget this awful place, the pale stretched skin encasing memories one could never dismiss, like some malformed fetus in a jar of Formaldehyde, dead but forever intact.

And then we kissed in the rain …

Nowhere near sleep, Marcy approached the end of her yarn in slow motion, as she watched these crazed young strangers run to the nearby woods, the ground, their clothes, and soon their bodies soaking wet. The next bus back to Munich came and left without them.

The autumn leaves turned and fell in Cayahooga County. Andy was launched onto bottles. Sandy had a play group three mornings a week. Marcy seized upon bread-making in the crisp air—Schwarzbrot, Brotchen, Bauernbrot.

"Honey, what are you hammering out there?" said Franz, returning home one afternoon.

"Building a sandbox for Sandy and her playmates." She could tell he was trying to hide his pained look. "No?" she added sheepishly for his benefit.

"It's fine." He paused. "I was planning to use that lumber for window boxes, but I can … "

"Sorry, Fran. Guess I was eager to keep these hands going. I've frozen enough bread for four months."

"And," he loosened his tie, "it'd be best to countersink the heads so the kids don't get cut."

After supper, Franz grabbed a parcel and said: "Marce, could you help me polish this silver?"

"Sure. What's up?"

"A Sho'n Glo in-store display. A silver-plated sugar bowl

offered with a ten-ounce purchase. We're taking some photos tomorrow."

She saw her reflection in the silver. She enjoyed the feel
of the warm glowing metal in her hands. "This one's broken. The handle is coming off." Immediately she started day-
dreaming about the Dublin metalworking studios.

"I've got some solder in my workshop," he said. "I'll fix
it sometime. Marcy, it's okay. I only need to clean the two
bowls. Marcy?" he repeated, as she opened the cellar door.

A week or so later, as Franz was driving to work in his
new Dodge Monaco, he caught himself checking at the
creases of his slacks. On automatic pilot! *As if I still worry
about the small stuff.* As for how the CEO regards me …
Barely thirty. Not bad for managing the world's leading silver
polish. He reviewed the various departments from his years
in the company bowling league: the wimps of Personnel,
the dumbbells of Packaging, the eyeglass brigade of Order
Processing, the eggheads of Market Research, the poets of
Customer Satisfaction, the thugs of Shipping. Well, he finally made it to the top. Senior Product Manager. He could
never go back to Europe. In mass merchandising, it was sec-
ond-rate. Any time he thought of never having enough—the
fist-fighting for a decent meal in the worst of days, people
out to screw even a hungry kid—*it's plenty enough reason to
cast my lot with the red, white, and blue boys.* Ten thou. Five
figures. Maybe there's room for a swimming pool … a small
one, with a redwood deck? They were about to move him up
to Kristol Kleer, with ten times the volume. Marcy would
never have to work. She could read to her heart's content,
become the gourmet cook of her dreams. She was already
the perfect mom, a luscious babe. She could spend half the
day filing her lovely fingernails if she wanted, sitting every
now and then on a charity committee in the living room of
Agnes Leavenworth herself, wife of the company president.
She didn't want anything for herself, so modest and humble.
I'm so in love with her. With Marcy at my side, how could I

not get ahead in this ruthless, money-grubbing, power-mad cockfight? Franz pictured a tall man, an angry, shouting man in uniform. Yes, of course I hated the son of a bitch. And I hated the screaming nurses hurling orders and reprimands. And yet I respected them. They toughened me. They made me withstand it all so I could take responsibility, tons of it and never wilt. So selling soap wasn't highfalutin like being an architect, doctor or professor. He'd like to think he was helping to raise the standards of living in an often slovenly, run-down world. *Nice try, kiddo,* his naysayer heckled him. *So I can't help you're a valid voice in my noggin.* He paused. *Maybe that's what keeps me plugging away!* he concluded with a positive spin. He parked in his designated space, perfectly parallel to the lines.

Marcy could not contain her happiness. The linen closet was stacked with neatly folded diapers and sheets, mattress covers and pillow cases, appropriately labeled shelf by shelf, just as Fran loved it. His boss could walk right in, and she could serve homemade whole-wheat bread on a lint-free Sho'n Glo silver platter, standing on the Nu Blu Lustre kitchen floor. Sandy was flailing torn pages of a Brenda Starr coloring book at Captain Kangaroo. Andy was sound asleep, swollen belly, a smile on his plump, pink face. She understood Fran's addiction, like her Grandmother Ethel's, to cleanliness and order, to open curtains and closed doors. Personally, she didn't care. But it pleased him so much. And this, of course, was a source of pleasure for her. She surveyed the newly vacuumed rooms. She rearranged the display of coffee table periodicals. She wallowed, absolutely, in the independence of having no exams or papers to prepare. Six years out of college, she still could not believe so little, mentally, was demanded of her. She ironed Fran's shirts, twice if she wasn't satisfied. She mended sheets and socks; she scoured pots and baking dishes; she bleached out stubborn stains. Ethel was downright beaming, buried in her mahogany box. Gradually, over the months, with every stroke of furniture polish, she was further seduced by the balm of tidiness, by sheer perfection on this simple scale. The horrors of New York, the ravages of her relationships with Paul and Mark, the derangement of her mother, the repression of her grandparents, the rich ones, the poor ones—all these things fluttered up and away, not quite reaching the shell of her current composure. She was amazed she felt no anger that no one until her aunt Marcy Carol ever told her, during college, the truth about her parents' deaths. What was her father to her, really, but a couple of old photographs? She never blamed the Jews, although their plight dealt his loss, caused his calling up for their defense. She couldn't hang on to the past to paint her self-portrait. So my mother died of a broken heart, well, booze, her Carney birthright, the easiest way out. So my father had been a selfish bastard, like Mary Carol said. And he dumped my mother and me in the madness of war—*that* war no less, for another woman, the beautiful German blond in the snapshot, and their irresistible, fair-haired son. So Fran is my half-brother, let's pretend. So what? Another day, another gourmet meal, organized hours ahead. She, like Fran—although him with good reason, was succumbing to the benign insulation of Indiana, the vast eiderdown patchwork quilt of America swathing her and her loved ones for real, for good. She praised the Lord, although He, too, had assumed a much lesser role in her life. She was doing nothing unholy or shameful. She was living life to its lusty best. She was making up for years of unfilled Christmas stockings, uncelebrated birthdays, Thanksgiving as just another bleak November Thursday: the barren years on her own, after her grandparents Burger and Carney died. She found herself opening the cellar door. Well, this, too, was part of her domain, her daily, mid-day inspection tour, during the baby's nap. It was to be a party room, pine-paneled just like the ads embedded in Fran's brain. She ran her hand over the lovely-grained cabinet work, the little louvered doors and sliding panels of the built-in bar, Fran's masterpiece of carpentry. The refrigerator wasn't yet installed, but she didn't need ice. In Ireland it was always at room temperature. Besides, that would have made it messier to cover up. She opened the door of the main cupboard, choosing a bottle at random. It didn't matter. She replaced them regularly. She selected the tumbler, the same one each day. Seagram's? So be it. She poured and hoisted the amber liquid to the light streaming in through the cellar window, splitting the shadows, and then placed her dry lips on the edge. She tilted it back in one smooth, steady motion. It burned, as usual, but rarely brought tears. All those hours and days of hours when her mind would wander down to the party room; the weeks of days when she could think of nothing else. But no more breast-feeding. She rinsed out the glass, as always, in the laundry sink, and replaced it. She shuffled past Fran's barbells into his workshop of tiny boxes of nails, rows of tools, tools on neat little pegs, everything stacked just so. It was the spitting image of her Granddad Herman's meticulous zoo of caged screws, ever descending smaller jars of hook-eyes, pins, and tacks. A living replica! She couldn't believe it. She thought of his hands, which could be terribly tender. If only she could come. If only she could feel. But for that she would have to have chosen—whom? She kept trying. He held out his heart to her. But if he came any closer, he'd deprive her of all that she did have. She clenched the edge of the workbench, to steady herself. Her vision was still blurred, but she could make out the two pieces, the handle and the bowl. The shiny, mellow glow had a soothing effect. It all fell back into place. She watched her swiftly moving hands, wielding the propane torch, setting the flux, pouring the bowl of pickling solution, arranging the tongs and the vise and the asbestos pad. She stared, amazed, exhilarated, shaking except for those very crucial seconds of soldering the silver, when she was completely overcome with an icy calm.

She worked for several more minutes. She was utterly sober. She held the mended silver bowl in her trembling hands. She raced upstairs and found the one, thoroughly messy drawer she allowed herself, the bottom one in the spare bedroom dresser, crammed with old family treasures, and there, underneath Gramma Gracie's Irish lace and Grandpa Tim's Celtic cross, Granddad Herman's household ledger and Grandmother Ethel's icing spatula, were the idle museum sketchbooks. She fed the children with one hand, paging over and over through the sketchbooks with the other.

He pulled in the driveway early that evening, and like every other occasion since completion of the split-rail fence, Franz was wowed by its stunning impact. Gravel, earth, grass: three contiguous but not overlapping bands. *Man, this is pleasing.* Marcy said a friend labeled guys like me "house-proud." She got that right. His mind ran to possibilities for more projects, getting to the point where they could sell this place and move to a roomier split level in Hemlock Heights. He didn't want to be pushy or appear pretentious to the higher execs in PM. *Just because I'm patient doesn't mean I don't have plans. In fact*, he pondered, *isn't staying the course how the payoff happens?*

"Marcy. Marcy honey, I'm home. Marcy?" He heard a strange hammering in the cellar. He became confused, alarmed.

She emerged from the cellar with filthy hands. "Oh, please don't look, Fran. It's—sort of messy. It's a surprise. Dinner's a little late."

"I'll give you a hand with the lunch dishes."

Marcy began dashing about with pots and pans. "I've got a sitter tonight for the concert."

"Concert?" he asked.

"Beethoven's Ninth. The benefit for the Christian Children's Fund."

"The what?" He tried hard to sound neutral, not annoyed, which he was.

"It's sponsored by Holsum Home."

"Oh."

Later that evening, the chorus assembled after the third movement for the grand finale. In due course, *An die Freude* rang through the rafters of the Buena Vista Bronchos' basketball gym.

Franz fidgeted in his folding chair until the mounting tide of music captured his imagination, until he reconnected with his soaring thoughts of that morning during his ride to work. The violins led the crashing dips and leaps of the most vigorous, most confident rush of music he had ever heard. The huge chorus, too, contributed to the grandeur. Why had he been hesitant to come hear this? The pride and joy of his native Germany, nothing less than Beethoven's Ninth, what he and J had sung as boys in the cellar, here in downtown Buena Vista! Sitting next to his beautiful wife with her pearls and plunging neckline. Him in his black pin-striped suit, no longer a youth but fairly trim. My God, he practically shouted in tune to the rousing melody. I've got the best of all worlds. L.B.J. is right: it *is* a Great Society. Two healthy kids, pushing twelve thou a year. Although a part of his heart ached for J, his whereabouts and well-being, especially compared to his own good fortune, Franz was so happy at this moment he could almost cry.

Marcy sat in stony silence, the tinny hometown orchestra and the shrieking Congregational Church and Y-Fellowship combined choirs filling out the fourth choral movement of Beethoven's Ninth Symphony as convincingly as Fran could sing the lead in *Aida*. Even so, the music seemed pretentious, and cloyingly spiritual. Hosts of archangels assembled like Napoleon's Eighth Army for an assault on Divine Mercy. *Why am I thinking this way?* She loved Beethoven ordinarily. Well, maybe a nice, complicated string quartet She was sitting on a folding chair just outside the boys' locker room in Buena Vista, Indiana. Her thwarted nipples yearned for attention of any sort. The flimflam musicale was crashing helter-skelter to a climax. She was even jealous of that. She sat perfectly still next to her bland, kind, handsome husband. Her orphaned twin. And, in part, her self-absorbed father. She looked down, horrified, at the filth under her fingernails. Pitch, from hot metal. She re-clasped her unsettled hands so they wouldn't show. She pressed shut her eyes as the symphony toyed, retreated, yet hurtled nevertheless to its final bars. She traced the wild calligraphic drawings of Irish antiquities—the stained glass windows, the filigreed silver bowls, the dizzying rush of spiral designs—in her newfound sketchbooks, over and over and over again.

Franz escorted Marcy between rows of folding chairs to meet some of his co-workers. She was such a knock-out tonight, he thought; the dress material stretched ever so subtly over her fantastic breasts, her bangs mostly covering one eye, sexy as Sophia Lauren.

"Great!" said Franz. "Marcy, there's a reception just for PM'ers at Liberty Tavern."

Marcy shoved her lips into a smile.

"Practically on the way home."

An hour later, Marcy held out the plastic cup for a refill. Some dandy in tasseled loafers glared at her. *So where's my dutiful husband?* She went to the bar, tossed one down and got a refill.

"Hi. I'm Jake Trumbull."

"Hi. I'm Marcy Mann." She extended her hand and slipped it into his cool, jelly-fish paw.

"Say, wasn't that a swell symphony?" he asked.

"It sounded like squeaking open a can of tuna."

"I write to the folks in Greenwich," he rattled on, "and tell them all that Buena Vista has to offer, and they can't believe it, you know—"

"Hey, Jake," she crooned in a husky alto. "You ever eaten pussy?"

"Beg pardon?"

"Look at these hands. Filth! Shoved in a hot sink all day. Now why can't you turkeys in that friggin soapsuds factory at least come up with—"

"Jake! Hey there, fella," said Franz. "I see you've met the missus. Jake here is Chairman of the—"

"My husband," slurred Marcy. "He's very good, with *his* hands." She winked at Jake.

Marcy spilled some of her drink onto her dress. Jake Trumbull skittered off, looking like he'd just held a live eel. Franz downed two scotches, on the verge of tears. "Marcy, Marcy, how could you?" he pleaded, got their coats and then tugged her into the parking lot. He kept whimpering like a child. Marcy, wondering why she was in high heels, hobbled across the street to Harry's Quik-Stop Café for a beer. He followed her, and ordered one, too. Franz tried to speak, but his jaw went slack. After another beer, his head crashed onto the table. Marcy got the waitress to help stagger Franz to the car, wedged herself behind the wheel, and drove off. Her head was spinning with the lights and her stream of words that she recognized as anger, pure anger: a roiling river flooding its banks. Next she heard a thud, the faraway thud of metal and smashing glass, and recognized a utility pole. There was a trickle of blood on Franz's face. Freezing air rushed at her through the empty windshield. She sobered instantly. He was passed out but still she spoke, barely audible: "Oh shit, Fran. I didn't mean you, I meant—my father?"

1968

Chapter 13

He awoke to exhilarating violin music. Was it in his head? No, it was real, from another floor. J was suddenly alert, attempting to identify the piece by Bach. Then he relaxed back into the pillow to enjoy it. It was far more entertaining than his dream of bulldozers clearing ruined buildings in Munich over the edge of a bottomless cliff. Had he been sleeping a few minutes, a few hours? Was it morning? He started to roll, to check the clock, but flopped back into place, carried along by the twisting, sliding coils of the strings. He pictured his mother playing the heirloom instrument, his personal myth, but possibly true. Who knew? Her hair fell in such a way, as always, so as to block the rest of her face. Her jaw was set tight, a small mouth poised in concentration, chin tucked into the smooth curves of the beautifully grained wood. Her hands were moving swiftly, the one vigorously dancing over the fingerboard, the other deftly sweeping the bow. They, too, prevented a clear focus on her downcast eyes and brow. He could tell the piece was drawing to a close. He gripped the sheets. Flowers. There was a vase of fresh flowers in the most delicate, smoky hues of blue and rose. Maybe it had been an older sister. Or a grandfather. The music was so vigorous, so intense, it required great stamina just to listen. He was losing it. Maybe the violin belonged to a friend, one of the circle of doctors, musicians, lecturers, poets to which his family was attached, in Vienna, Heidelberg, Berlin. It was over. But he went on, visualizing the lean fingers of craftsmen who built it, the intricate files and saws and fine emery cloths. He pictured the players over the years, a grand, teeming orchestra, hundreds of people with this one, magnificent instrument, each taking their turn. Until him. He continued to clench the blankets and sheets, hoping for an encore. Perhaps they had privilege to be taken so late; stamped in haste. Perhaps his father had been an advisor to an official in the Reich. Perhaps he taught, conducted, composed. From a salon on the Rhine to a West 73rd Street puppet theater for restless kids. Well, it was a way to keep the old YMHA cellar hopping. Not enough to re-paint and re-plaster, but at least parents no longer complained about his "humorless," "arcane," "negative image" storytelling. His latest production was more player piano than first violin: "As the Tablet Turns: The Flip Side of Moses."

Jews are my apron strings. Why can't I let it all go, release myself into whatever shape might emerge? The past was an undersea wreck, but it was home. It housed his soul. The past with all its warts had outgrown pain and could withstand this constant re-cycling, for his living no less. Of course, puppet shows had been Franz's inspiration; brilliant for kids, but now ... He flicked on the light. He looked at the clock. The hour made no sense. His one claim to fame, that he had been partial witness, would never be enough nutrition for another thirty-some years.

He got up and fumbled about the dirty dishes. He found a stale hunk of croissant. He could re-heat it. Instead, he nibbled at the dry flakes. It tasted like Styrofoam, but he wolfed it down. Did I eat dinner? He took out the orange juice which had separated into a thick slurry on the bottom, a watery pale fluid on top. He drank it as it was from the jar. The shiny smudges on the glass resembled the greasy glow of the large window, for years his world view from the westside studio.

A day later, the trousers of the rented tux didn't quite

reach the mirror-finish shoes. J was sure no one would notice with black nylon socks filling the gap. Besides, who would look at him? It was Leonard's night to shine.

"What a fantastic crowd, Jay!" chirped Susan, Leonard's wife, on J's right. "Did you see Sidney Baker over there? *The Times*. Isn't that fabulous?"

J was thinking of Robert Kennedy, Martin Luther King, Abraham Lincoln, shootings in the theater, even on plush seats.

"Listen, Susan. I know it's going to be a smash," said Harry Farb, husband of the famous choreographer, leaning over from J's left. "Cecile hasn't been this excited since 'South Pacific.'"

He was sure the Anti-Defamation League was going to stage a protest during one of his puppet shows. You couldn't please everyone. "Susan," said J. "I'm feeling a little squeamish. I'll take the first half from the back."

"Jay c'mon, I'll hold your hand." Her vivid lipstick glistened like a ruby plum sliced open.

"I'm worried no one's going to laugh at the jokes I wrote for Len."

"At thirty bucks a seat? They'll laugh."

He fingered the *Playbill*, perturbed by a glossy photograph of Ella Fitzgerald in a floor-length mink coat. The show began. He decided to wait for the line on Genghis and Sylvia Kahn bickering over the price of Camels. Thank God it was completely lost in the saxophone intro. "Leonard's so great. Susan, I've got a splitting headache. I'll see you at the party."

The streets seemed to be filled with people pretty much like him, not in any particular rush. He pulled on his raincoat and strolled down into the subway with no destination in mind. With the floppy black trousers and awkward bow tie, he decided he must look like one of those tired trombone players on his way home to the Bronx from the first shift at Radio City. You see them all the time in the subway, wellworn overcoats or ski parkas over faded tuxedo uniforms and a five o'clock shadow. He joined the platform crowd, swaying ever so slightly to the rhythm of the distant rumbling sounds. He didn't look at the signs, just at the sea of serene faces—black, white, brown. Maybe he looked like a waiter at Mama Leone's. Didn't they have to dress like penguins at those places for the folks from Davenport? People stirred somewhat as ears caught the beat of the train's approach. For some reason, he was standing on the edge, studying the grime, the tracks, the trash. People were set into motion now; there was a purpose, to be aligned near a door. Papers were folded, watches checked. The train was definitely to arrive on his side of the platform. One of the lines was electric, wasn't it? If you just stepped on it, you'd be home free? Or would it take the train? Make a tuxedo sandwich, messy but quick. He saw the light around the bend. There was general bustle now, the chance for people to spit and cough, clear their throats, notice kids, reprimand whatever they were doing wrong. Always, always doing something you weren't supposed to, like life with Franz. *Franz, Franz, Franz.* Why bother? He balanced over the edge, the soles of his feet acting as fulcrums. The blaring light was now dead ahead down the tracks. What was so funny about making people laugh? He felt himself losing balance. It was just a little dance. He was kicking up his heels with the noisy throng of black teens, cheery, adorable really, flashing teeth and shouting shits and fucks, playfully punching and shoving. The train was screaming along, practically up to his feet, a few yards away. The mob pressed close and he pitched forward, yes in fact he was falling, feet still glued to the platform. Just like they said it would happen, in slow motion. Someone grabbed his coat from behind. He fell against cold metal as people let themselves be sucked inside. He returned to the street, and somehow wound up walking to his westside apartment. He dropped into a deep sleep for several hours, until the phone rang in the early dawn and Susan, near choking in hysterical sobs, read him the rave reviews.

A group of eager types took charge of the puppet shows. He simply wrote an occasional play from his treasury of German and Hebrew folklore. With time to kill, he found himself holed up in his apartment, sleeping by day, emerging by night to read. He wasn't straining, as before, with his latest set of books; he was merely drawing it to a close. He started in, week after week of transcripts, word for word. Testimonies at the trials. Kicking pregnant women in the stomach, defecating in slow, hot streams during forced marches. Could he bring himself to see, touch, smell—a physical wound rather than a fragment of his imagination?

He waded for the first time into the mind of the demented one, word for word.

... one of the most patent principles of nature's rule: the inner segregation of the species of all living beings on this earth ... Any crossing of two beings not at exactly the same level produces a medium between the level of the two parents.

Here was the very blueprint, years before the fact.

The Aryan is not greatest in his mental qualities, as such

He smiled and thought of Franz with affection.

... but in the extent of his willingness to put all his abilities in the service of the community ... Our own German language possesses a word which magnificently designates this: Pflichterfullung—fulfillment of duty; ... not to be self-sufficient, but to serve the community.

J's own family at least had each other. No internecine, mental battles, no three-decade hunt for explanation. A bloody madman, pure and simple. There was "no meaning." It happened. A crumb of bread became a crumb of bread, capable of sustaining life for another paltry hour. Period. So what were the five thousand pages of Babylonian Talmud all about? J thought, brightening. The Nazis for a few decades are one thing. Isn't some religion defined and empowered for centuries primarily by glaringly similar persecutions another?

In hardly any people in the world is the instinct of self-preservation more developed more strongly than in the so-called 'chosen'. Of this, the mere fact of this race may be con-

sidered the best proof. Where is the people which in the last two thousand years had been exposed to so slight changes of inner disposition, character, etc., as the Jewish people?

He began seeing the maniac's point. He flipped his Bible to the famous lines in Deuteronomy, the fifth book of Moses. *For thou art an holy people unto the Lord thy God, and the Lord hath chosen thee to be a peculiar people …* He returned to *Mein Kampf, My Struggle: … never in possession of a culture of his own … the Jew is led by nothing but the naked egoism of the individual … For what sham culture the Jew today possesses is the property of other people, and for the most part it is ruined in his hands.*

He thought of his popular puppet show, kids and parents laughing. He began twitching, reading the manuscript of just one man, this verdict written only forty years ago and executed to the letter. Was it far off from expressing the sentiments, in truth, of multitudes?

To what an extent the Jew takes over foreign culture … can be seen from the fact that he is mostly found in the art which seems to require least original invention, the art of acting.

J looked up and out his vacant, dim window. He thought of Leonard and of his own penchant for wisecracks.

… he is not the creative genius, but a superficial imitator.

So he was burying his family and lying to rest his past. But Hitler was right: no one survives without support. He was sure Franz was busy building his network. Tribes, families, it was all based on simple, settled collectives with a stake in the soil. So the Germans managed the soil business with a little too much enthusiasm. But why on earth had he, like a few millennia of his forebears, managed to go to the other extreme? Base their community by-laws on airs of moral superiority, inviting not only antagonism but massacre, and then, for those who were still standing, celebrating its working for another generation of cats and dogs?

Here the Jewish press most lovingly helps him along by raising such a roar of hosannas about even the most mediocre bungler, just so long as he is a Jew, that the rest of the world actually ends up by thinking that they have an artist before them, while in truth it is only a pitiful comedian.

He looked at his clock. It read three A.M. He put on a coat and tie, for what reason he had no idea. He left the apartment building, finding the rush of cold air a welcomed relief. It was perfectly calm except for the odd taxi or lurking shadow. Central Park was only a few blocks away.

Three A.M. His timing was perfect. It made Riverside Park look like a Kindergarten. I can devise my own Inferno, here and now, thought J. I'm dressed like a gentleman, tie and coat, there'll be no question. I can come out alive or not. It's that simple. But if I do, I will survive. I'm a man without a past. I'm a man with nothing but the past. After this stroll, this sojourn into hell on earth, the next best thing I'll ever find in this century to qualify as such, I could create the dawn. He stepped faster. I can make friends. I could be a lover, a father, a funnyman, a rabbi. *I can get beyond myself.*

He entered the park. It looked so innocent. Not a soul in sight. Oh, please let me live and have another chance! He wanted, more than anything, to run back to Rivka and Lucille, to Leonard's stupid show business friends. To Franz! He was assaulted by shadows and lumpy figures, but he would not turn around. There was still time. *No.* He walked further yet slower into the silvery moonscape of pulsing shadows and menacing trees. He had to serve as target. He had to approach that cluster of boys. He could see the flash of knives, like the Riverside Park knife at his neck. He had to flaunt himself, play the victim with downcast eyes, just asking, just aching for it. His heart was hammering in his throat, behind his ears. *I haven't felt so murderously alive in all my life!* They turned and sneered at him. They shoved him away, flashing needles, armbands, money. He walked on, through bushes carpeted with condoms and cigarette butts and broken glass. He knelt down and availed himself, as chopping block, urinal, pin cushion. He took out his wallet, trembling at every rustle of the leaves, and threw his bills around. "Here!" he warbled in a quaking voice, fumbling with his money. "Here," he tried again. A drunkard staggered by. "Here!" cried J, racing up to him with a ten dollar bill. The drunkard trundled on. And so did J, realizing he hadn't allowed enough of a chance to look like a victim, nervous and shaking. He walked faster, as if he were in a hurry to reach the other side of the park and had something to lose. He was being followed by two men. There was no way he could run. Is it a dream? Am I actually beginning my death? Hallucinating? Have I been stabbed, already, by a needle, yet another needle from my still-born past? They were gaining on him. And suddenly, for the first time, he was stark, cold afraid. He fought off the urge to flee. No, he had to withstand it; I have to be reduced; it's now or never. She had flowers! There were fresh flowers in a vase by the violin! No, this I must forget! A desperate twist of my imagination, evanescent as the corona of the moon. He began to shiver violently. And slowly, as the men closed in by a matter of yards, he felt himself submitting, relinquishing his life, his name, his craving for Franz and family, for normalcy, for a wife and a child and a country of his own. In just a fraction of a moment, as the men stepped within his shadow, his body went totally limp. Hot urine trickled down his leg, stinging his flesh. He went numb with terror one second, and released even that as they grabbed his shoulders. He could only feel his body turn to rubber as his bowels emptied themselves as well. There wasn't a scuffle. He lay in a heap at the side of the path, unharmed, untouched, as the men strode on, drunk, jeering. Moments passed. He picked himself up and shuffled on, pants covered with excrement, shirt coated with sweat and filth. He was exhausted yet wild with thoughts. I'm a charlatan, a flop. I'm trying to erase myself, defile myself, yet here I stand, stinking of piss, plastered with shit, strong as an ox. Suicide was not the answer. That was too easy. *I am not walking out of this park with my old self intact. God damn it to hell and back.* He darted in and around the clusters of shrubs. Men fucking girls. Women sucking boys. Staged homosexual assaults; performers in leather, in chains; masters with slaves queuing up to be fist-fucked, in broad moonlight, the more on-lookers the better. Maniacs. But such innocent puppets, pathetic freaks. He approached the shadowy building, a public latrine. There was just enough light inside from a single bare bulb to see the row of red-eyed wizards, glaring anxiously at the new arrival, penises gleaming and greased with spit. He stumbled into the section of proper toilets, dazed, nauseous, determined. More men, giving, receiving, grunting in groups of two, three, four. Older, fatter men, masturbating on the sidelines, drooling and slurring encouragement. Action, too, in the stalls behind closed doors. He didn't have a dime. He went to the last booth, the only one without a coin device, for the common trash. He entered, inhaling the stench of urine and semen and sputum which soaked the floor. He bolted the door and vomited into the bowl which hadn't been flushed, couldn't be flushed. He heaved, again and again, now on his knees, delirious, knowing full well what he had to do. He put his hands on the edges of the bowl. It was in his power; it was now or never. He had exploded his insides. He had nothing left but blind rage and disgust and humiliation and fear, and those, too, had to go. He lowered his head. He licked the seat. The books, the money, the languages, the travel, the tender care and protection from Franz, from Rivka, from Lucille and Leonard, they were obliterated in one foul moment. For good. He lifted the seat and licked there, too. He was shaking again. He was retching, again and again. He was hot with sweat and caked with filth. He was finished. He lowered the seat. He pulled himself up by the empty toilet paper rack and sat down. He managed to yank off his wretched pants, as rank as the toilet bowl. He had to get them washed in the basin. Otherwise he could not proceed. Perhaps then he could swallow the scum. A hand rushed under the door and grabbed his pants. "Hey!" J bleated, and swallowed. He opened the door. The youth, laughing, dashed around the corner and outside. J stood, convulsing, as the men began to back away from him. He tied his shirt around his waist, apron-style. His undershirt was saturated with debris. He staggered outdoors in uneven steps.

It was dawn. He re-traced his path through the park. He felt nothing. Not even the stares on the streets, already bustling at this ungodly hour. He could sense the fever throbbing, at a level of concern that was very far removed. His tongue, his throat, his eyes were aflame. Now, he couldn't swallow. His vision became blurred, but not so much that he couldn't recognize his street, his building, the button to push in his elevator. He found some money and tugged on jeans, a jacket. That was all he could manage, as the aches and throbs along his entire alimentary canal began to intensify. He scrambled down the steps. He was in too much of a rush to wait for the elevator. He huddled, shivering and squatting, in the recessed entry to a Broadway Woolworth's until it opened three hours later. He wanted to get the crayons first. A jumbo box of Crayola crayons. It was simpler than paints, the varieties of which he couldn't really comprehend. Also, a large pad of paper. The flowers were the easiest. Discarded snapdragons. He had been clutching them all this time, drinking in their fuzzy, warm tendrils, their twisting, graceful curves, their showy splashes of pink, mauve, and the most delicate hazy blue, the high blue of a summer sky without clouds. He got the materials assembled on his kitchen table. He placed the battered, lovely flowers in the orange juice jar with extra water. And without bathing himself, oblivious to his own putrid stink and furious fever, he broke open the seal of that box of crayons. His hands shook wildly now, but still he could approximate the shades, the pearly blues and soft roses, the rounded and fluted edges of the bulbous flowers. Make-believe dragons in a small child's tale. The evil part was only to exaggerate, to make a point. Bell-shaped, they sang, and he sang, in the dim light of his greasy, stained window overlooking Riverside Drive. He actually hummed, his fiery mouth and throat without a speck of fluid. His fingers clenched the crayons, usually breaking them in his fierce grip. He drew the stems, the riot of broken leaves; he scribbled the hollow shapes of the tubular vegetation, the proud spikes of glossy bloom, tossed as garbage but still bursting with color. He craned over one page of the sketchbook after another, sometimes flailing away designs with reckless abandon and, at others, tightening up like a seamstress executing the finest of needlework. They were lips! They were mouths, they weren't bells. They were kissing, their lovely curls spilling from smooth oval faces, one above another, from the largest and most fully developed to the ever-smaller and daintier buds on top. Who were the sufferers, after all? The victims who wouldn't complain, or the torturers whose hearts pumped bile instead of blood? The viceroys of death, of degradation, if only they were here, to see, to touch, to guzzle in the fragrance. It was so simple! There was no reason to be afraid. It was written in the flowers, from sprouting birth to rotting flesh in a single stem. There was no reason to deny the process for a lifetime: to slaughter in order to forestall one's own demise. They could see it all in a single day, an unfurling flower. The tears came as he grabbed the Cerulean blue, a fresh one from the box he'd overlooked.

1969

Chapter 14

Franz propped himself up with pillows and shifted his ass. He wished the swollen hemorrhoids would burst and be done with it. The unmown lawn, the inbox at work, were also driving him nuts.

"Sorry you're missing bowling tonight," said Marcy as she headed downstairs with his empty oatmeal bowl.

Franz grimaced at Marcy's having to wait on him, she already overloaded with the kids, itching to be back at her cellar workbench. Guilt compounded his throbbing anus as would a black eye in public be worse than the pain.

"Daddy, why aren't you raking the lawn?" said Sandy crashing in, hiding her brother's toy under her shirt. Andy bolted in as well, screaming, pounding his four-year-old fists at her.

Marcy followed saying "I'll corral them in the kitchen," and scooted them downstairs.

Franz acknowledged his stomach pressed tight against and drooped over the elastic of his pajama bottoms. *I'm becoming like too much soft ice cream packed into a cone.* His exercise routine, sporadic at best, was indefinitely on hold. He clamped shut his eyes.

Saturated with misery, room for no more, he dozed off, soon entwined in a tangle of limbs, humid and smooth. Once again, they were his and Gretchen's under her covers, her sliding his young hands and forearms over her center, her silk nightgown rolled up to her neck. So delicious, so spine-tingling it was; plus, the fleeting release of his aches, fear, exhaustion. This he strained to savor as she continued to caress him, but every time the image shifted into her bloody cunt, her carcass inhumanly sprawled across his linen closest floor, the skin of her legs and neck gone ice-white and lifeless as he jiggled her for response, before he managed to haul her off. Then he was mired in the worst of it: Gretchen begging for mercy as the boy—*was it really me?*—stood gaping at the officer's ugly buttocks slamming between her still-pink thighs.

The kids were fighting peacefully in front of the TV. Marcy retrieved their plates of mostly fingered food. She stood at the sink and watched the trees out the window ripple like the surface of a broad lake. Pleasant, yet somehow unsettling. She nibbled the children's food. So I'm a careless mother, an unsympathetic wife, she reflected. Well, I didn't have a role model. The kids were now yelling. She was spellbound by the rustling leaves and couldn't move. His boyhood in busted sewers, she thought, while I'm making out in rumpus rooms. And at least I was weaned by a flesh-and-blood mother. She started in on Andy's goppy orange spaghetti. Funny how she could picture her mother more clearly with the passing years … Annie being a little each of her high-strung father Tim, her all-heart mother Grace. She'd been a scrambler, fleeing her "Shanty Irish" Brooklyn for the WASP suburbs. Marcy could distinctly remember hearing tales and songs on her mother's lap, before the lap of her Grandpa Tim. Annie was there for six years, before and during the war, making us a home albeit in the Burgers' spare room. I can't fault her for dying of a broken heart. I can be angry for her wasting tears on my bastard of a father. I used to hate her, in fact: her insecurity, recklessness, immaturity, inability to hold her liquor, cavorting after hours with the town rejects, choking to death on a lousy crust of bread learning of her husband's deceit, *leaving me …* Marcy gouged out pink peppermint ice cream for the kids and served them, finishing what was left in the carton back in the kitchen and then, without thinking, poured herself a beer. She choked on the first swig. *It takes him immobile upstairs, like daytime at work, for me to be myself?* She dumped the beer down the drain.

Franz, restless in bed, was leafing through magazines, peppered in the back as usual with small ads for rupture relief and denture paste and sex technique. At least the products he oversaw at Holsum Home were of worldwide consequence. Maybe it was good to have this break, this perspective on his talents and managerial skills. He saw, like a neutral observer, his capacity to seamlessly fold others into the decision-making process, leading them through a funnel, saving his own conclusion as the agreed-upon outcome. *Thirteen-and-a-half thou and just thirty-three.*

The next day Franz wasn't well enough to take the kids to Sunday school, a time Marcy reserved for her jewelry making. So he read them fairy tales. The dainty rings and necklaces of small silver loops, he thought, were so pretty. He wished Marcy would wear them once in a while. He wasn't so crazy about the way she could look these days, coming up from the cellar.

Marcy craned over Fran's former workbench, covered with her metalworking apparatus. Their new house in Hemlock Heights had a full basement, so she had plenty of room. She warmed the thin-gauged sterling wire in her hands, feeling the metal soften slightly, responding already to her emerging design. Her first things had been way too complicated, or eager: literal copies from the chaos of swirls and interlacing patterns in her Irish sketchbooks.

"—there's a horrible witch sitting in the house who scratched my face with her long claws ... and by the door stands a man with a knife who stabbed me in the leg; and in the yard there lies a black monster who beat me with a wooden club ... "

Sandy and Andy huddled closer to their father's feet.

Marcy was gripping the stylus, carefully scratching the

smooth and hard charcoal block, her stylized falcon and claw in relief. She worked quickly in the small circle, concentrating her energy, aware, vaguely, of the time bomb upstairs.

"—the daughter was taken into the forest where she was torn to pieces by wild beasts, but the witch was cast into the fire and miserably burnt."

"Oooo," Sandy and Andy crooned in unison.

She fired the torch and melted the end of the silver chunk over the recessed charcoal. The metal grew dark and then blushed purple and finally glowed a rich, luminous crimson before dripping. She strained to maintain the wafer-thin flow; the thickness of a dime was all she needed. The metal was oozing from her fingers, from her very being. She was as taut and calculated as the eye of the noble bird she etched, about to pounce. Her mind, as always, was flying around the Antiquities Museum.

Franz made carrot sticks for the kids, obsessing about his overgrown shrubs in need of pruning, while Marcy carried on in the cellar.

Back in his office on Monday, Franz slumped at his desk. He checked his calendar, near-empty of appointments. He gazed at the frames featuring Marcy and their kids, dolled up in some photographer's studio, all fake smiles and stiff backs. Idly he fished for his wallet to check his cash: did he have the usual three twenties, for just-in-case, tucked into the hidden flap? Yes, they were there, along with the gleam of worn brass, his half of the violin case clasp sewn in ages ago. Was this why he could never bring himself to buy a new wallet? He supposed, rubbing his finger over the smooth, ancient metal, he needed to be forever reminded of his dustbin beginnings and how far he had come. Would that be so for J, too … with all his smarts that he, Franz, had stoked along with the fires to keep them warm and alive in that city of ruins …

He thought of J reading books, learning new languages, telling them stories of Parsifal that slid them cold but content into sleep. He, Franz, made tickets for their puppet shows, counted and hoarded the cash. Still fingering the metal, with its tiny tabs worn to nubs, Franz wondered for the first time in all these years: did J keep his matching piece with the small recesses? Surely not. *You sentimental jerk!* he snapped at himself, slapped the wallet closed, and lurched back to work.

Franz announced that he was going to attack his on-again, off-again Royal Canadian Air Force regimen. This prompted Marcy to try once more with the Yoga Journey to Inner Peace. She set aside an hour for asanas, the posture routine. Perhaps with Sandy in school and Andy at play group, she could find the discipline and strength to pull it off.

She reviewed her old yoga manual, horrified with every page to realize how she was squandering her life-force; how compromised had become her Alternate Nostril Breathing Awareness. She had to shift from her ordinary self, thinking of what to serve for supper, and concentrate. She rehearsed by picturing her Granddad Herman on his little lawn stool, searching for crabgrass, hour on end. There was no reason to be afraid of losing touch with reality. She had everything to gain by becoming partners with the Collective Unconscious. People ridiculed the Flower Children because they were threatened, terrified by the utter simplicity of it all: giving up, letting go.

She placed her instruction book in a music stand with clothes pins. She stood calmly in loose clothing, the window open for fresh air, and began the complete breath standing routine. She stood straight, with head and shoulders slumped, exhaling deeply. She raised her arms and came up on her toes. She thought of reaching to the top kitchen shelf where she had hidden the Swiss milk chocolate fudge from herself. She inhaled instead of exhaling, stiffening instead of relaxing. She lowered herself to the floor for the cobra position, settling on her belly, forehead on the floor, her arms at her side. Slowly, she raised her head and back without the support of her arms and hands, looking to the ceiling, straining, feeling herself dissolve as it said in the text, feeling the pain in her back leap from pulsed throbs to continuous screams, as she groped also to blend night and day, beginning and ending, to weave herself into the Universal Tapestry. She farted and flopped to the floor.

Franz declared war on fat. He'd never get his next promotion looking like an amateur tuba player from the lower Rhine. He chose that quiet stretch when Marcy was reading to the kids to slip into his "body shop." Repeating, grinding, pumping unmercifully: there's no short-cut to getting hard. Her voice from the family room was so calming, just when he was trying to be fierce.

"Seeing a white shape in the garden in the half-light, Nasrudin asked his wife to hand him his bow and arrows. He hit the object, went out to see what it was, and came back almost in a state of collapse. 'That was a narrow shave. Just think. If I had been in that shirt of mine hanging there to dry, I would have been killed. It was shot through the heart.'"

"Isn't he silly!" squealed Sandy. Andy was asleep.

"Yes," said Marcy, frowning, studying the back cover blurb to the strange book of tales. Something about the Sufis, she read, confused, pestered and intrigued.

Franz heaved and grunted freely one Saturday doing push-ups between two folding chairs. His hands were placed on the chair seats, and his feet were on an ottoman so that he was forced to lower and raise himself through a much-extended push-up than ordinarily. *Eleven, twelve.* He thought his teeth might break, so locked they were. Truman Coates, Holsum Home CEO, must be all of seventy, yet looks as lean and hard and hungry as a young stud half that age. *Sixteen, seventeen.* Damn Marcy for making that mocha torte. *Twenty-three, twenty-four.* I'll show those candy-assed college boys. I have the ideas, the stamina, the brawn and good looks. *Thirty-one, thirty-two.* He pressed his weighty arms, sweating heavily. *Thirty-six, thirty-seven.* It was his own blasted body; he would *command* it. Enough of Elliott Limp-wrist mealy-mouthing another order over the phone.

Forty—ten to go. Nostrils ablaze, gasping for breath, he made to it only to forty-four.

Marcy propped the little book of Middle Eastern folktales upright on the kitchen counter. *Nasrudin was throwing handfuls of crumbs around his house. "What are you doing?" someone asked him. "Keeping the tigers away." "But there are no tigers in these parts." "That's right," said Nasrudin, and he added: "Effective, isn't it?"* She licked the bowl of icing, and read on.

"Honey, I think we should talk about the children, and school, and their manners," said Franz, believing he needed to offer Marcy more support on the home front. It irked him that, in telling the tale of some lady friend, Marcy cited the wife's thinking of herself as raising three kids, not two, to include her husband.

"Fran, I agree Sandy and Andy need more structure. Cheryl and I have been thinking of starting a nursery school for kids Andy's age. I met Cheryl at the Crafts Center."

"What's that?" Seated, Franz corrected the fold of the cloth napkin.

"You know, on Buena Boulevard. Where people display, sell—"

"For money?"

"Of course."

"Like a jewelry shop?"

"Yes, they'd—display my pieces. Listen, Fran," she said, side-stepping this threat to his ego. "The snacks these women make—carob cola, soy fudge. He's better off at a good nursery school than here eating Spaghetti-O's."

She left the sink and sat at his side. "Wouldn't it be great, Fran, to pack up, for just a week, and leave the kids," she said in a breath, fingering Grandpa Tim's Celtic cross on its chain which she'd been wearing non-stop. "How I'd love to show you Ireland, the museums."

Franz smiled wanly. "That'd be great," he said, and thought: deadlines, deals, could I ever drop them, *for her?*

He couldn't get to sleep that night. Over and over, the grin of the driver, the blank efficient stare, the steady course of the olive-green Army truck. The earth even at this point trembled from the hurtling tonnage. The moss clinging to the damp brick wall chilled him as he huddled against it, pressing his body in a tight embrace. The air tasted of ashes. The roar of the great machine, a whole convoy on four wheels, became deafening. The pudgy flailing arm, it was waving to *him*. The little yellow shirt was flopping to the rhythm of hard rubber crunching over gravel or street debris. He pulled away from his shelter. Yes, he tried to release the grip of the moss and vines plastering his white uniform to the wall. He strained in the direction of the child, still waving to him. Franz struggled to move, but his feet were glued in place. No, the child couldn't see the truck. It was towering too high overhead and bearing down too fast. Yes, he was positive he ripped himself from the wall and shouted at the tops of his lungs; and he rushed into the street a second too late, nearly getting crushed himself, as the spit of dirt and gravel stung his legs and arms, him wailing and shrieking for the truck to stop. It was over. *I barely escaped myself.* The yellow shirt kept flapping like a toy flag in the dust as he reached for Marcy, unsuccessfully.

The next morning she said she'd slipped into the guest room bed because he'd been kicking and flailing so in his sleep.

"That's weird," he said, staring over her shoulder. "I had this horrible dream about J. I always thought I had saved him, but now I'm not so sure."

A few weeks later, Marcy's nightstand was piled high with things on Eastern religion, a few from the local library, but mostly from new friends in the crafts' collective. One morning, the children in school, a day that was scheduled neither for her yoga workshop nor the crafts center, Marcy decided to vacuum while contemplating the Universal Mind. Thomas Moore counseled that any activity, however humble, could be infused with *soul*. And her Zen manual instructed her to "cultivate emptiness." This seemed the perfect opportunity. She was filling the vacuum with cookie crumbs, cat hair, and silly extraneous particles of thought: the constant flow of trivia that contort, cloud, clutter the Buddha's Truth. When you vacuum, vacuum, she thought. Don't digress. Don't scout for little piles of mangled Oreos, flagellating yourself for being a lousy mother, serving machine-made, gut-rotting crap instead of wholesome homemade. Just hold the hissing tube and evaporate, personally, into nothingness. Be in the world, not of it. Enlightenment was available not just to the Bhagavan, but to housewives, houseflies. To paw the shag rug, to discover stray staples which could puncture children's tender feet or a husband's calisthenic bottom and do nothing more than acknowledge the litter and allow it to be sucked was to sit zazen, to go with the flow. They hadn't swallowed those open safety pins or bits of apple covered with ants and mold, so why get in a flap? It was an overdue housecleaning of her mind. She observed without emotion the cavalcade of rusted hairpins, raisins, quarters, filthy children's socks sleeping quietly under the sofa cushions. She was building, with Oriental grace, the lovely attitude of *nyu nan shin*, the "soft and flexible mind." She noticed the gray-blues of Fran's shirt collars not so much as neglect on her part, but rather a natural stage in the harmony of cycles. She touched the cracked earth of houseplants which had shriveled into brown twigs, smiling as she wiped the table around them, wonderful, loving reminders of her progress in detaching, in allowing her Mind Weeds, as the Zen Master called them, to flourish along with the wilting flowers and fruit, the whole of them eventually returning, as with all things, to fertilize the soul. She flipped the Dylan record, and finished her transcendental dusting.

"Fran!" Marcy exclaimed one night, side by side with her husband in bed as she paged through one of her metalworking magazines. She was riveted by a very familiar object.

"Here's a photo of that fantastic steel sculpture at Dachau. You remember," she went on, captivated by the article. "The one right there, where we met!"

Franz grunted, but didn't raise his eyes from his folio of market research.

"It says the piece was commissioned by a man who sold an heirloom violin, an authentic Stradivarius, that actually survived the death camps. Incredible."

"A violin?" He looked up.

"What an amazing sculpture—twisted steel. Makes my silver things look spineless."

"Whose violin?" Franz said as if his pulse was on hold.

"Jay something. Here, you read it."

"J something?" he managed and reached, trembling, for the magazine. "Radius," he said, sounding relieved but also crushed. "No, no it's someone else."

Chapter 15

There were masses of cut flowers around the room in various states of decay. The mums and marigolds, more or less intact, could pass for dried flower arrangements, but the tender, totally withered lilac and daylilies bore no resemblance to their original shapes and hues. The clear glass containers displayed water that was slime green from the gradual decomposition of stems. The dirty plaster walls were teeming with life. J had thumb-tacked his crayon and pastel chalk sketches over all available space. The colors alone created a bouquet of jungle-fresh brightness. There were hot peppery pinks of dahlias, or zinnias perhaps. There were delicate puffs of carmine, lavender, and pale blue on coiling long stems. These last represented, most likely, bunches of sweet pea or cosmos or larkspur. They looked like variously nodding, papery bells, or those gay ropes on pleasure ships, fluttering with bright pastel flags.

J was not keeping an exact count of the days to which he had confined himself to his apartment. A month was the specification in the Shulkhan Arukh for mourning, that portion of the Halakhah attributed to Rabbi Karo of Safed in the sixteenth century. He also learned that a funeral procession must make way for a bridal procession; that when a funeral and a circumcision affect the same people, the circumcision takes precedence. He learned the corpse was to be accorded great respect, however, even that of a supposed suicide, unless he or she was witnessed in the act. If one could pull it off in secret, one might catch God off guard?

He gazed continuously at the tubs of rotting plant material and then at his frenzied, soft splashes of color on paper above them on the walls. The colors were pulsing. He could just about, although not quite, pique his nostrils with their vapory perfume. He could shut his eyes and trace in his mind the meandering veins of the petals at their peak. So which was the more real: the putrefying flesh in full dimension, or the mental snapshot at full bloom?

It was odd he didn't itch. Thirty days without a bath. Thirty days without rejoicing or greeting others. Thirty days without washing his clothes, in this case, his white tunic, his kittel, symbolic of freedom as well as of the final days. Thirty days abstaining from intercourse, work, the cutting of one's hair. These last three did not represent a break with his routine. It was the last mitzvah—thirty days without the "vanity" of leather shoes—which posed the greatest problem. Because whether he sat and stared out his great, filthy stretch of window overlooking the Hudson barefoot or in cloth sandals, he could not escape obsessing over the trainloads of children's shoes. Trainloads, mountains, truckloads. *They saved the little children's shoes.*

No matter which interpretation of the Halakhah, a line is drawn positively at one year. No more mourning. The departed soul, if it is ever going to, has long since joined forces with the divine.

He read and re-read from the only portions of the Torah that were permitted during this period: Job, The Lamentations, the sad parts of Jeremiah.

He nibbled some food. It was not permitted that he cook for himself. His freezer was jammed with Chinese take-out. His phone unlisted, it was wonderfully peaceful. He glanced at his unopened mail. Just more requests for more puppet plays to trivialize their heritage. He was amazed they kept repeating his old ones.

Was his only option being a Jew? How could he fight the weight of all these years? His family, or whoever, were denied individual deaths. Collectively, namelessly, they died, and so must they be honored. He was sitting shivah going on thirty years. He wanted to praise them, love them, part from them, and recite the Kaddish for the final time.

Jewish community, Jewish continuity! You come, you go. Never mind you leave no son, no namesake. You're still theirs. You've had them, for your past. You haven't technically felt an orphan. And they're right there, as you sign off. At least they have you for their future, which in turn will be as backward-looking as was yours. The whole system infused the soul, a single sponge at the bottom of the sea. Hell of a way to run a religion.

... remembering mine affliction and my misery ... wherefore doth a living man complain, a man for the punishment of his sins ...

He was hiding, but he was not contemplative. Nor was he grieving the fate of true victims. Yes, he was being blasphemous to the faith with his mock-rituals, but only in so far as he'd been reaching for a substitute family, a father on earth. He knew all along that the Lamentations were shaping him: *We are orphans and fatherless, our mothers are as widows.* But Jeremiah said *The punishment of thine iniquity is accomplished.* Maybe they were finished with their handiwork, have I ever thought of that? He yanked himself up from his sagging chair for the copy of Baal tales on his bed. There was one line in particular—yes, here: *As the gentiles say: "A demon has his teeth in me."* For Jews, the absence of a deliverer; for Christians, the presence of a devil: it was all the same. The demon perpetuating faith was identified as being without instead of within. Suffering was meant to be borne, not to destroy, he reasoned. So there *was* another option, if he could bear it. Of course he had a family. Who else had served so long and hard as his mother? And this parent—he was alive!

It had been months since she'd made any jewelry. Her cellar bench was now a parade ground for works-in-process: goblets, graceful sinewy sculptures of leprechauns and friendly lizards. Her arsenal of equipment had multiplied during her first full year. She had installed a second and larger anvil, and covered a nice old tree stump in soft leather for planishing and also as a pleasant arrangement to sit and pound on her work. Marcy ran her finger over the smooth expanse of her new silver box—the sides and the dragon's feet as dainty pedestals. It could serve as a keepsake for a deck of cards. The hinged serpent-head lid opened and closed with bank-vault precision. This pleased her, the sharp, cold cut of metal, one layer carefully pressing another. What an Irish fetish, she thought, feeling the reptile's fangs, St. Patrick having shooed every last one of them back to the sea. For its christening, she lifted the chain over her head. Both it and the little Celtic cross collapsed perfectly into the recess, the delicious, polished, hushed secret hiding place.

The doorbell rang. Fran was in New York on a business trip. The kids were at Barb's for the afternoon. The bell buzzed again. She was in no rush. Upstairs was another world.

She could see the Girl Scout uniforms through the curtains. "Come on in, kids," said Marcy. "So it's cookie time again?" The girls smiled and assembled their materials on the kitchen table, although it was piled with unfolded laundry and dirty dishes. One was decidedly older, probably thirteen or fourteen. They were so sweet, so dedicated, carefully printing on the order form. Marcy made her selections.

"Did you say mint cremes or mocha cremes?"

"Oh why not both?" Marcy answered wondering what she had been doing at that age. Baiting her Grandmother Ethel … masturbating … dissecting frogs …

"One or two boxes of vanilla wafers?"

"Two, what the heck. Fran'll always eat them."

"Thank you," said the younger. She couldn't have been a year older than Sandy. Marcy beamed, handing her the check, fretting over her maternal failure, Sandy being the only Brownie drop-out on the block.

The older one addressed Marcy making direct eye contact. "Are you a Christian, Mrs. Mann?"

Marcy batted her eyelashes and smiled. How touching. "Yes. I am."

The older girl twisted a pamphlet from her stack and thrust it forward. "If that's so, do you realize you're a tool of Satan? You're praying to a fake Christ, Mrs. Mann. The world as we know it is coming to an end!" Her fierce little eyes centered themselves in their sockets, not budging.

"Oh, I agree, girls. The assassination of our leaders, the lip-service to racial understanding. I really, truly, am heartsick."

"Mrs. Mann, that's wonderful. Have you already sworn yourself to the New Society? Are you already a witness for Jehovah, the one true God?"

Marcy flinched. "Well, I'm not really affiliated with a church at the moment. I don't necessarily think there has to be a connection." The switch from cookies was too abrupt. She functioned more slowly now, more thoroughly, like soaking the casserole dish baked with crud for a day or two—whatever it took. What was the point of struggling with the dishes? Silverwork, yes, but not baked beans.

"Are you a mother?"

Marcy nodded.

"Then you especially should be warned. Jesus is man-made, and corrupt like us. To celebrate Christmas is a sin, part of the hoax of the Devil to undo us! Did you fill your children's stockings with candy?"

"Why, yes."

"And cookies?"

"Of course!"

"What about *love*, Mrs. Mann. Did you include that in your heathen holiday?"

Marcy was flushed with resentment, also wonder.

The younger girl withdrew a copy of *Watchtower*. "Will you help us? Could we have just ten cents … "

Marcy reached for her purse.

The older one continued. "Of course, you know Jehovah's Witnesses were persecuted and murdered, too, in the Nazi concentration camps, Mrs. Mann."

Marcy fumbled again for her checkbook.

"In Micah 4 it's recorded that there will be no more national boundaries—"

Marcy had written a ten on her check and changed it to twenty.

"—no political divisions—"

"No political divisions," Marcy mumbled, handing the girls the money.

"—and no war."

"Yes. No war. That would be wonderful."

"Thank you, Mrs. Mann. We'll expect you tomorrow night at seven at our Local Kingdom Hall. Bring your whole family. They, too, have to be saved!"

Marcy tried to calm herself when they left. She recited the sutra, but it required a clear head. She descended to her cellar laundry room, her zendo, and breathed deeply. She needed her mental workshop, the entire basement, to organize the frayed bits of her life. She lacked conviction, commitment. She always expected everything to come to a crashing halt. The girls' point about the end of the world, for her, was perfectly valid. She was too agitated even to twist some silver wire in calligraphic Sanskrit, two of her currently favorite media. She had smoked her last joint the evening before, after Sandy refused to say her prayers while her father was out of town. She thought of rummaging through Fran's biodegradable refuse heap where she hid the roaches in a plastic baggie with the coffee grounds. She flipped through the pages of her book of Sufi tales, but found herself thinking of her husband. Fran, this Siegfried among Germans, for all his superficial discomfort with Jews, had saved the life of one. Jewishness, otherness, had shaped him, her too in anti-Semitic New World Brandenburg. Well, she shrugged, returning to her workbench: all stripes and colors, certainly

Jehovah's Witnesses, have their place in the patchwork quilt.

Franz poked idly about the vast floor of the New York Coliseum presently housing the National Premiums Buyers' Show. In the corridors of Holsum Home, his head was filled with deadlines and the grating voice of Elliott Reed. Here, gorgeous models or unemployed chorus girls paraded around in tight miniskirts, demonstrating gadgets like push-button lemon squeezers and disposable auto ashtrays, embellishments for box-top offers and glossy magazine ads. It was a kaleidoscope of color, twirling batons, flashing panty-hose, overweight execs like him. For the moment, his nay-saying demon on hold, Franz was enjoying it all to the hilt.

He was representing Holsum Home, one of the giants of industry. The premiums, the trite gimmicks that really push product, he had brain-stormed an entire history of them, from Styrofoam toilet bowl cleaner display bins to miniature videotape, in-store commercials of their five-minute, self-polishing car wax. He came to a stop, his gaze at the circus of bright lights gone blurry.

A statuesque blond tapped him on the shoulder holding a tray of little wieners in puff pastry. "Holsum Home?" she read his tag, smiling. "I bet you got a pretty big account wrapped up there, mister." She winked.

Franz felt a tingle in his groin. He laughed, then wolfed down the hors d'oeuvres, raising his eyebrows coquettishly at the sultry dish.

He went for a walk outdoors, overheated with lust ogling those broads for six hours. He headed south from Columbus Circle along Seventh Avenue, the neighborhood getting seedier with every block. It was like parts of Munich when he was a kid but too young to take advantage. Whores, orgasm gadgets, sexy magazines—he browsed through the porn shops getting hard, holding his briefcase strategically. Suckable falsies, "staying creams," flimsy outfits for your sweetheart. He chose some lacy things in more of a lingerie shop, and shoved them into his briefcase. He figured Marcy was ready for a naughty nightie after all these years. The plastic mannequins with angry painted eyebrows and nipples arching through tight, shiny fabrics actually looked more convincing than the poor painted ladies at the Coliseum. He was now rock-hard.

He paused in front of a bulletin board on a grubby wall. It was plastered with calling cards, three-by-five cards, slips of paper with phone numbers and sex routine shorthand. "WHPS, CHNS, BLK LTHR BTS. Will kick, claw, bite on command." "Suck Semi-Congealed Jell-O From My Pussy. Cherry, Grape, Lemon-Lime. You Choose." His eyes raced on, his blood thumping. This anonymous demi-world of fantasy sin where one could be swallowed, for a few minutes, by the swamp of total pleasure. Toss away one's company name tag. *How have I come so far from these sensations I felt all the time as a kid?* "Ida the Master. You the Slave." In short, nervous strokes, he copied down the number.

He bought a bottle of Listerine on the way, stashing it in his briefcase.

She had a wig on, so he knew it wasn't for real; he could let himself be afraid as part of the act. She was taller, more attractive than he'd expected, still like a lady wrestler with large, strong, exciting hands, but no match for his strength if he let it go too far. The windows had fake bars, like a make-believe dungeon. His heart was fluttering in overdrive. She was the perfect degree of smart-ass. He started to slip off his tie and coat.

"Uh-uh, pretty boy," she said, adjusting her black leather wrist bands. "That's for Ida to do. *If* Ida wants. *When* Ida wants." She shoved him onto the padded floor and straddled his face. "Now shut up," she added, undoing her belt. He couldn't help fixating on her false eyelashes, the left one in particular sagging at an odd angle: pathetic, really, as himself.

"Sorry, Ida," he said, leaping to his feet and thrusting her a twenty. "I got all the fantasy, love and big tits a goon like me could ever want, right back home in Indiana."

Striding again on the streets, he knew he'd tell Marcy

of this zaniness. If anything, that woman has a sense of humor, when she isn't buried with a blowtorch. Finished with this thought, gloom followed by shame seeped into the void. *Marcy, my beloved, my life-mate.* He would never, ever, think of squandering himself so stupidly again. He was nearing Times Square, that infamous oasis of porn. Imagine if every city in America had a hell-hole like this ... society would crumple at the drop of a dime in one of these peep-show machines. Imagine the men, buyers and sellers, who make this *a way of life?* You have to hand it to New Yorkers, likely Jews, he mused: whatever it takes to make a buck.

Franz. You are *a Jew.* J shaped me as much as I shaped him. He felt slightly better for the slur, like an Italian referring to himself or another Italian as a wop without offense.

He passed a faded poster for a girlie show, he assumed. He didn't know why it caught his attention, amid the life-sized nude cut outs and teaser crotch shots. "SIEGFRIED FOLLIES" was the banner, plus a picture of some sad-sack with dark eyes. He sighed, walking off. Something about a puppet show. *Siegfried.*

He froze on the sidewalk, people pushing past in both directions. His hand gripping the briefcase started sliding from sweat. He raced back and stared at the rest of the words. "Puppet Theater for Children of All Ages by Jay Radius. A Playground of German and Hebrew Folk Heroes." *Radius. The name connected with the Dachau sculpture, the ancient violin.*

He tried to copy down the address, but his hand was too unsteady. He ripped the poster off the wall and shoved it into his briefcase.

Franz held his briefcase on his lap on the plane to Indianapolis that evening. He was relieved he'd decided to keep the sexy underwear in there, too. If his luggage ever got lost and was opened for inspection, with his company name and address—he shuddered and gripped his prized possessions. He had a burning sensation in his gut. He slipped out the poster. Of course it couldn't be *him*. He stared at the beady-eyed bloke. He pitied the face, staring out so blank like he'd just encountered the Devil himself. Droopy eyes as if he'd been kicked in the shins but would never complain. It reminded him of J when they were kids, J silent, brooding, always triggering Franz to think he himself had been brainless about something or other. He re-read the poster, remembering the excitement of show-time with their puppet theater, the thrill of collecting the money, the heavy breathing of people packed into the place. He recalled the great dragon-slaying heroes from the stories they read and made up into puppets. He could almost pull on the curtains and feel the gadgetry he'd devised for sound effects while his hands were busy otherwise. He could just about touch the fantastic fabrics they cut up from the treasures of old opera house costumes stored in their cellar, the layers of velvet and silk they slept in that were crawling with lice but so nice and smooth and warm. He remembered that sullen expression on his partner, how it never budged but how it lit up just before curtain-time when Rudi rattled the kettle drum and both of them had their hands full of puppets and their mouths bursting with memorized lines. He remembered J's face—

Jay Radius ... *German* ... and *Hebrew* ... *Puppet* Theater ... Folk *Heroes* ... YMHA *Basement* ...

No, he thought. Impossible. He shoved the poster into his briefcase, angry and upset with himself.

He didn't wait to claim his suitcase. He went right to a phone. He used his company credit card, and placed seven calls before reaching the 73rd Street YMHA. "I'm sorry," whined a woman. "Mr. Radius has had his phone number unlisted. We only contact him by mail ourselves. We'd be happy to forward your inquiry."

"It's important, damn it," Franz shouted. "I—I'm his brother."

"I'm sorry. He left instructions not to—"

Franz slammed down the receiver. He was shaking. He was overcome with fear he didn't understand, and with

disgust at his loss of composure. Paying the parking atten-
dant, the little brass clasp sown into his billfold which he
rarely noticed shone as if on fire.

J took down the flower sketches. He laid the stack carefully in an old suitcase he'd found rejected at the trash bins.
They were already smudged, his papers. They would fade in
time. The only things that could be pictured were the magic
and the energy, and these he carried in his head. He looked
around. What else was there to pack? The last of Leonard's
hand-me-down sport coats? He would wear the clothes on
his back. He closed the window, that view of the indefati-
gable and colorless Hudson, the hazy impenetrable mass of
Jersey shoreline, those gently shifting, sluggish scenes that
had offered him so much comfort and companionship over
the years.

In his pocket was a bank check from closing out his
Certificates of Deposit. It was well into six figures. He'd had
no idea. He couldn't fathom how this had happened to him.
This hoard, too, like the violin money, he would surely give
away when he was in his right mind. For now, it took every
ounce of will to hold himself upright, to grip the handle of
the suitcase even though it was feather-light, to twist open
the door, to enter the hall, and push the elevator knob. The
rest, he knew, would be all downhill.

He also knew he would never return to New York. After
Indiana, who knew? It didn't really matter *where* you lived.
He clutched Franz's telegram and letters in his pocket. Franz's
invitation, his appeal. Franz was waiting for a reply. J knew
how impatient Franz was. It seemed so much simpler just to
show up.

Marcy had developed an aversion to the doorbell. She had
even hallucinated about lecherous, hunched gremlins stepping out from behind their masks, revealing Girl Scouts.

"Yes," she said curtly, not as a question but a barrier. The
peddler simply stood there. She waited for him to withdraw

one of his salvation booklets. Not Fructarians like the other day, condemning her for cutting living, breathing blades of grass. Not Hari Krishna, she thought, with that much hair.

"Is Franz here?" he finally said. He was still dizzy from the assault of fresh air, the glare of uninterrupted blue sky. The long taxi ride from the Buena Vista airport had swept him farther and farther into woods, higher into green hills, but mostly into a tomb-like silence after the city. J was totally disoriented but elated, too.

"Fran? Frank? One moment, please," said Marcy, skirting away from the foul-smelling stranger, assuming he was a day-laborer Fran had hired to fix the lawnmower. She hoped he was paying him a decent wage.

Franz stared at the hippie with greasy long black hair, his forehead carved with frown lines making him look so much older than he himself. He was repulsed then infuriated thinking this creep could get away asking for hand-outs in the Heights.

"Franz?" J said staring in turn, as motionless as his old friend. "Is that really you?" J could only connect with the eyes, those amazing steel blue eyes, frosted even further by expanses of puffy skin and pale hair. His hair was so thin on top ... the side-burns shaggy and matching his paunch.

"J? *Mein Gott im Himmel.*" Franz's mind exploded into a self-inflicted shotgun blast of disgust ... shame ... sheer thrill. He recovered enough to utter, "You're so rundown." He twisted his torso, extending an arm towards the interior. But motionless, their eyes held for seconds that stretched into an endless, shapeless gridlock from which Franz knew they'd never escape. "Komm herein." Franz sucked in his gut, standing tall, finally beaming. "Marcy? Marcy! J is here! My old—the playwright." At this, he cringed from his own cowardice. "It's J-a-y now, isn't it?"

J took a half-step forward as Marcy smiled shyly and extended her hand. Her lips parted, but no words emerged. She was seized by his eyes: devastated, cavernous, wise. Her mind couldn't engage the whole. It was too much, these two men. How could it be? This wild stranger, this enormous but faraway piece of Fran's past. They walked into the living room to sit down but still stood, so many more hurdles until approaching any semblance of ordinariness. How could she conceivably feel drawn to him, as if she knew him better than her husband of eight years? "Let me get coffee," said Marcy, weak on her feet. She took her time, but could still overhear them. *It's reading his eyes, above all, I have to avoid.*

"Well," blustered Franz. "You got my telegram." He tried again. "Enough of manual labor in Israel, you're back to the books."

"No, I loved working outdoors," J said. "It's a very beautiful home, Franz. And you have a beautiful wife. Thanks for getting in touch and inviting me." Guilt, so long under glass as a relic, was insisting upon being held and inspected from all angles. *J, the deserter ...*

"The guest room's waiting," said Franz unsteadily. *He looks as much the battered oaf as ever. Good God, I want to cradle him, stink and all.*

"A guest room would be nice," J said, wringing hands.

Each observed their facial muscles, unable to sustain smiles, going slack. Instead of words, to continue a discourse, they lazily nodded their heads like wobbling toy tops at the end of their spin, as if still appraising each other in wonderment; in truth, being speechless.

Why have I come here? J thought, panicking. *Interrupting his family, their warm, sensible, uneventful life.* How he wished he'd made a nest with a loving wife long ago.

Finally, they sat. Franz squirmed in his seat, feeling his hemorrhoids react, his skin rash flare on his shoulders and neck. *Where the hell is Marcy?* "Well. You've come pretty far in the world, J, for an incurable egghead. A poster in the middle of Manhattan!" He hated sounding patently false, floundering.

"There were only a few hundred printed."

"Nonsense. We get what we work for. I'm sure you struggled to write and rewrite and dedicate yourself all these years."

"I've been pretty much a drifter."

"Never found the right little Jewish princess?"

"Guess not," J said, incredulous this man still held out a hand of friendship under the mock-gruff talk.

Marcy returned with mugs. "This is unbelievable!" she exclaimed. "First, that we read about you in the magazine. And then, you two cross paths in New York … Fran the businessman and you, Jay, the artist." She adjusted her newly completed silver pendant so that it rested more squarely between her breasts.

"Oh J here is a businessman, Marcy. When I started to make dough back home, he always had shrewd advice."

"I remember standing on line making deposits for you."

"I hope you'll feel welcome here, Jay, for a good long visit," blurted Marcy without forethought. "It must be a very hectic life for you, for anyone in New York. I can't even guess how it's changed since I lived with—lived there." Mentally she started cataloging Middle Eastern recipes: olives, lemons, white fish and oil.

"Thank you," J said, in awe of her radiance. "That's very kind."

"Well," Franz said, sizing him up, a tad more at ease. "You never were a natty dresser."

"Fran," scolded Marcy softly. *He needs to put Jay down to puff himself up, Fran's self esteem clearly the lesser of the two.* But this she gleaned the instant she laid eyes on Jay.

"That's alright, Marcy," J said. "He always harps on me for stuff like that. He knows I'm not much interested in clothes."

Marcy smiled weakly, excluded, her own tie to Fran so fragile at times. *Whatever did they share in common?*

J felt slightly ill from the coffee, so rich with sugar and heavy cream. It was delicious but way too much, like the over-stuffed chair into which he was sinking and the bright-patterned wallpaper that was practically screaming in neon colors, after the grungy walls and windows of New York.

"Marcy, the kids. For God's sake, get the kids. Wait'll

you meet them. You don't know what you're missing." Franz
was oddly relieved that J was still a misfit. *Shame on you,* he
reacted.

"I've spent a lot of time working with children, Franz.
With orphans, in fact." He couldn't believe he found the energy for a retort.

Marcy left to fetch Sandy and Andy. Franz leaned closer
to J, who was insulating himself increasingly with the cushions. She returned with her fidgety, protesting kids whom
she had yanked away from "The Avengers" on the color console. *The Christian Science Monitor,* she opined, called it a
"festival of sadomasochism," averaging a violent incident every three and three-quarter minutes.

"Mommy, we're missing the rescue!" cried Sandy.

Franz did the introductions. "Now listen, Sandy and
Andy. I want you to pay attention to J while he's here. Maybe
some of his smarts will rub off." He beamed at Marcy, who
looked tense. "Your mom's razor-sharp, of course. But old
J—he had the brains in the ... "

The children scrambled off.

J looked steadily into Franz's eyes. In place of the dare-
devil boy was the petty official. Marcy stopped breathing,
leveled by the intensity, the despair, while excited, too, by
the unknown, the perhaps yet-to-be. Franz felt hot flashes
around his asshole, his war zone. He was thoroughly confused, as if he was not reuniting with his brother but—the
birth father he'd never known.

J fumbled with his top shirt button. He pulled a cord
and revealed the small, tarnished bit of metal, the matching
clasp of brass.

Franz was thunderstruck. "In my wallet ... " He was fal-
tering. "Hey, listen," he chortled. "We've had the tea party.
Now some beer and pretzels, for old time's sake."

Marcy arose, the words of the silly palmist in Atlantic
City during college suddenly ringing in her ears. *Two men,
all very loving, the three of you, oh my dear—a sudden death
... Hush! I'm such a slut for anything ethereal. "Or maybe

Jay would like," she offered, "something stronger?"

"How many years," said Franz as if they hadn't heard her. "Sixteen, seventeen, half our lives?"

"I wouldn't know," J replied. "I never celebrated a birth-day."

Franz's smile faded. "Me neither."

1970

Chapter 16

He'd been there half a year. Their lives went on. He hadn't especially interfered. He did most of the shopping, with his own funds. He took his turn to cook. He read stories to the children, chauffeured them to lessons, school, movies and friends so Marcy could get in an extra hour or two in her garage studio or finish her tearoom meditation. He raked leaves for Franz's compost heap. He weeded, watered, trimmed and swept without being asked so Franz could relax and enjoy his day at the golf course. Once, when Franz complained, jokingly, about being underpaid compared to those who struck it rich as war orphans, J bought him the two thousand dollar riding lawn mower he'd mentioned so often. When Franz remarked on another occasion about his tight-fisted employers, he presented Franz and Marcy with air tickets and paid expenses for a weekend in Las Vegas plus petty cash for the slot machines, with his minding the house and the children. Quite recently, even joshing about the "showiness" of some people with their money, instead of just shrugging, as usual, J thought of mixing gasoline in Franz's mouthwash. Of course, he knew these quips were from Franz's surface, the toxic flak they'd both grown up with. Plus, with Franz's attempt at humor, it only underscored how deeply he cared for J that he was comfortable making light of him.

Franz and he had reminisced a bit. But J seemed to have severed his past. Not that he could see tomorrow. His mind had gone blank. The Manns and he had never discussed a departure date, or J's ultimate plans. His room was full of books. Franz's family didn't disturb him. They thought he read all day and night, that he was writing. He was actually suspended in a beatific stupor, by piano lessons, kitty litter, yoga partners, bleeding hemorrhoids. In a way, it was all vaguely familiar, Franz doing battle on the streets, he himself tending the hearth.

The Manns were compulsively engaged. The children at nine and six had separate sets of friends. Just in the space of his visit, Marcy's metalwork had outgrown her basement headquarters, which was now devoted to her ceremonial tea service. She had installed large platforms and benches in the garage. She kept her own car in the other half, accumulating grime, but Franz was quite happy to park his BMW 2002tii in the double driveway. In the metalworking portion of the garage stood a four-foot tall cylinder of acetylene fuel and an octopus of rubber tubes and torch nozzles. J watched her frequently. Their protective masks reminded him of city street crews, blasting and jack-hammering away with their shrieking utensils. It made it more like home, here in the halcyon hills of central Indiana.

One evening after dinner Franz and J were quietly relaxing in the den. Marcy had retired to the basement. J had finished reading from a book of Gaelic fairy tales to Sandy and Andy, who continued to study the marvelous illustrations with him and gambol on the thick pile, wall-to-wall carpeting with the puppy Bruno. Franz was leafing, reluctantly, through the latest market research.

J observed his friend's ever-thinning crown of baby-soft blond hair, and his ever darker, longer sideburns now well below his ears and cut at a widening angle across his cheeks like meat cleavers. His robust moustache, however, was remarkably light. It was more like the mop of hair that used to flutter as he did the thirty-yard dash between approaching soldiers, trading shoe-shines for cigarettes.

Franz looked up and beamed at J and himself dressed in identical golf shirts with the snappy alligator emblem, J's red, his own yellow and a full two sizes larger and still stretched, dammit, in a seated position like this, over tell-tale rolls around his waist.

J could see himself reflected in the black-paned window glass of mid-evening, his hair now just shoulder length, with fashionable bangs and covering his prominent ears. He shampooed daily at Franz's insistence with an acid-balanced, protein-enriched brand, three times as expensive as Holsum Home's product, but scientifically engineered in the youth-and-body-conscious laboratories of coastal California.

Franz noticed J's bicep stretching the golf shirt's cinched armband. He'd outlined an exercise program for him, but still: why wasn't J getting fat on the frozen pizzas and Boston cream pies? "You think we're better off with a variable annuity at six and three quarters, J, or staying more liquid in CD's at five and a half?"

"Let me think about it."

"Uncle Jay!" wailed Andy. "I want another story."

"To bed with you, buster," said his father.

"I want Mommy," whimpered Andy.

"She's meditating, you brat," hissed Sandy, keeping all the cards to herself.

"I want Uncle Jay to put me to bed."

"Quiet! Both of you," Franz said, putting down his sheaf of statistics. "It's my turn," and he scooped them up, one under each arm. The puppy began biting, fiercely, J's white athletic sock while the kids squawked. "Alright, alright. He'll listen to you say your prayers. D'ya mind, J?"

Later Franz presented two frothy steins of beer. "Marcy works herself into a fever out there, skipping meals. Can't even count on her to split a beer any mere." He crashed into the soft leather armchair, creating a great, farting whoosh.

"She's really driven."

"Like how we were in the war days, J. Go, go, go."

"That's how you were, Franz. I sat there stirring the soup."

Franz shook his head, grinning. "We really came out on top, didn't we? Just a couple of scrawny kids. And look at these two at that age. Not a care in the world. Thank God for them, for all of us, it's this way now." He took a long gulp of beer.

J listened, slightly smiling.

"What a clever devil you were," said Franz, glancing off, "even back then. Reading all that stuff we found. Devising those puppet shows … "

"You read too, Franz. And helped write the lines. And you built the stage and fixed up the seats and the lighting. And made the posters and sold the tickets and organized half the street kids to help without paying them more than a few cigarette butts. It was another of your fantastic schemes. I was just the helper."

"Helper? You ran the whole show! I busted ass, hopping all around fetching you stuff to cook with, getting you the medical supplies you needed and the money you said it would take to send you to school when they reopened, a proper one for the brighter boys."

"Franz, my friend. *You're* forgetting. I was the orphan. You had been living in a nice, clean hospital for women and children."

"I lived in filth! In bloody rags and vomit basins and carcasses of bloated bodies."

"You had to pick lice from my scalp every night, I remember that. I was too weak to reciprocate. You put knives to the pus in the wounds on my arms and legs, and pressed clean cloth with stinging fluids to the sores until I couldn't find the strength to continue screaming, I'll always remember that. And you healed me."

Franz re-crossed his legs. His ass was on fire. He shoved the small of his back into cushions to ease the pain. "You act like I was doing you all these favors—"

"You were."

"—so you can play the victim, on and on, and make me feel sorry for you, and for what happened to—your people."

"You *should* feel sorry. What's the matter with that?"

"It's crazy to go on thinking this way after twenty-five years," Franz moaned. "No excuse for the horror, but the Jews as a sliver of the population were taking over the newspapers, the theaters, the banks and import businesses."

"What of it?" J waited to have his head smashed open or be flooded with guilt.

"Wasn't that out of kilter?"

"If Jewish prominence was out-of-kilter," said J, baffled by uttering these things he'd wanted to say all his life, "what do you call what the Germans, not just the dictator, ended up doing to the Jews?"

"I am suggesting," stammered Franz, "how understandable it was, the compliance of ordinary … I mean, look how upset you have made me here and now. I think we had better get another beer. J, you know I hate to argue."

"Yes," J said, aware of irritation in place of his usual sympathy or indifference.

Franz scooted into the kitchen, flushed. *It's true,* he thought. *My career is all about* not *arguing, but accommodating all points of view. But with J?*

"It seems you were always on the right side, the winner's, in a way," he said, again facing J. "You *have* led the world, in thoughts, opinions. They editorialize your peoples' ideas in publications while I pay them to run my detergent ads."

"No one said your work is unimportant, Franz. Cleanliness is next to Godliness."

"I should wrap a golf club around that skinny neck!" he said, half meaning it. He chugged his beer. And, for the first time in all these months, it dawned on Franz that J was seething underneath, as always. *Can I be patient, like when we were kids?*

J wished for his poisonous peroration he'd at least suffer remorse. As was getting to be his habit, he felt nothing. He focused on the curves of pasty white flesh on Franz's face, the tides of breath of the sleeping puppy, a German shepherd he finally realized.

A few days later, J was sitting on the hood of Marcy's beat-up Mercury station wagon. She was directing the cutting torch along a chalk line she had drawn on the rusted sheet metal. Sprays of sparks jetted out from the tip of the torch. The sparks cascaded onto the concrete floor in a continuous stream and bounced off again with equal velocity before extinguishing themselves. They danced over a propane tank and Marcy as well. She seemed unconcerned in her heavy jeans and work-boots and soiled lumberjack shirt.

Marcy guided the flame with her right hand. With her left she pressed a lever releasing a flow of oxygen from a second standing tank, to intensify the heat and speed of melting. Given the spark guard she wore over her face, with its slanted slots for the eyes, she figured she must look to him like an overgrown armadillo, up on its haunches, flailing thick, canvas-covered paws. She bent big hooks once they glowed malleable orange, doubled over now in surgical concentration. She had switched from silver to steel.

He was paging casually through one of her sketchpads. There were soft-leaded pencil lines swooping in large, bold waves across the space. They were clean lines, gracefully curving, a foundation of strength for the flutter of nervous zigzags which crossed their path. He didn't see the relationship between the sketches and the more violent welding, the sharp-edged, rather unfriendly forms emerging from the cutting, burning torch.

Marcy thought of Jay's flower sketches, which she loved. She wondered why, since arriving, he hadn't felt fueled to move a muscle in that direction. For her, an active pair of hands was a short-cut to peace of mind. When things got wobbly, she had her other workshop, her tea leaves and her new ceremonial hut she'd been assembling in the cellar. Amazing how many demands you could handle by recharging the batteries in a sanctuary all your own. The torch slipped, but she caught it. *Concentrate.*

She was a strange woman, straining awfully hard, he

thought, to remove herself as she ricocheted from one playground to another. She was also strikingly beautiful with high, prominent cheeks and strands of soft brown hair falling gently over her shoulders that weren't quite included under the strap of her spark guard mask. The baggy outfit could not quite conceal her curves; in fact it accentuated them by their sudden revelation as she swiveled and arched. Once again, J thrust himself back into the clutches of sweet Rivka, acrobatic Hannah after that.

"I wish I'd studied more languages like you, Jay," said Marcy at supper. "It's amazing—your reading to the kids in dialect."

"Uncle Jay, I need to practice my piano lesson again, don't you think?" said Sandy. "First though, we'd better do my math."

"A pro we have here," beamed Franz. "Listen, buddy. How's the checking account? Marcy bounce two or twelve this month?"

They were alone one evening in the den, Franz and J. It had become a routine, Marcy often being out with colleagues in her metal craft or Japanese tea ritual. Franz had had a bit too much beer. His head swayed like a bowling pin deciding whether or not it had been struck. J remembered how he worshipped this man, his "Jewish Mother," his savior in truth. Franz still takes such interest in my hair, teeth, my health and food. It was very satisfying to J. But it isn't the same, he reflected. I'm no longer so helpless? There's nothing to be protected from, nothing else to lose?

Franz was momentarily at peace. He liked the way the armchair and ottoman were angled so that they formed with the sofa and his own leather Eames chair a nice little group. J looked rested and several pounds heavier than at his arrival, which pleased Franz enormously. "So, how's the new play coming?"

J stared back without expression. "I don't even have an idea for another play."

Franz nodded in response while absorbing this blow. It

fractured his calm like so many ear-splitting sirens of the past. Putting all his brainpower into minding the store? *This will never contain him.* This was a gut-level threat that Franz hated to admit.

"Remember when you had that bit part in the Hollywood movie, in Munich?" said J. "I thought you were destined to become a leading man." He, too, was feeling the beer.

"Don't remind me. And you, the scholar, wind up with your picture on Broadway!" Franz laughed but gripped his beer with both hands. "I was too good-looking, you always said, to be believable. And you, the runt with that kisser like a discarded fig, in print on a poster. You snuck back to fight the war with words. Because you never could raise your voice, you twerp. Oh I can guess what those kids' shows are about. The Jews come out smelling like a rose. Where were your people *then* when they should have been resisting?"

"You and *your* people should have been resisting." J was exhilarated. *How can I be this callous? We both need a lifetime to heal.*

Franz seized the armrests of his leather chair. "I had my hands full, a million kids to watch, only a year or two younger. I was just a boy, for God's sake."

"You let one of them get killed, I always remember. You used to shout about it in your sleep." He continued, despite Franz's twisted, scarlet face. "You always used to feel guilty about letting it happen."

Franz watched his own hands twitching. "You see what I mean? I set up our home and when things fall apart, I take the blame. I was running ragged. I was a nursemaid to practically half the ward. The boy ran into the road. I yelled for him, but he didn't listen."

"Why didn't you run after him? You were older, larger, faster."

"I did!" Franz yelled, his neck veins popping. "They were making me do two errands at once—delivering another package to the head nurse's house, and smuggling this kid someplace."

"Where?"

"I can't remember."

"Sure you can."

"I can't remember. To his real mother, maybe. To his home. I'd done it before, for other women."

"The address was in your pocket. You used to holler about that, too, Franz."

"No. I never said that." His eyes were stinging.

"You wanted to go home."

"He ran away! He thought it was a game."

"You were jealous of him. You wanted to run away, too."

"No! He disobeyed my order. He wouldn't turn around."

"He was only four years old. You were in charge."

"No. Mein Gott."

"You thought he was weak, and inferior, for wanting his mother."

"Nein … "

"You thought he was weak for not having to stay in the Lebensborn and work hard like you."

"Nein, nein."

"You always used to brag about your foster-mother, how devoted she was. And your foster-father, some Army hero. In fact you hated them for abandoning you. Then you went and did the same to a helpless child. Because, admit it," J was spitting the words, "somebody ditched you even before your foster-parents, even if it was just a birth mother in that home. The little arm waving goodbye in the road, Franz. That was you at the very same age!"

Franz was shaking his head.

J saw Franz making fists. He didn't care; they were both drunk. "You punished him, your helpless mirror image."

"I swear I tried to save him."

"You stayed by a wall, I remember you always repeating."

"I almost got run over myself!"

"You let him get killed."

"No! *Please.*"

"And the step-father, Franz. He hit you. He hit you again

and again because you *disobeyed.*" J was grinding together his teeth.

"J, my God, stop!" Franz lowered his face into his bands, sobbing.

J watched the shoulders heave. The sleeping dog awoke with a snarl. J was jolted into sobriety. "Franz, I … "

Franz heaved himself up, staggered to the stairs.

"Franz … "

Franz held up a hand, climbing one step at a time. "Shhh, we'll wake the kids." And then he stopped. He was gripping the banister like a vise. He turned and rushed at J, suddenly aflame with strength. One fist seized J's shirt, the other aiming for the head but pummeling a shoulder.

J tripped Franz, who crumpled onto the shag carpet. "I wouldn't, Franz. I excelled at Israeli martial arts. A side to me you've never seen." He extended a hand and yanked Franz to his feet.

"Fuck you," mumbled Franz, and he lurched towards the stairs.

For days, J prosecuted himself as the evil Hagen betraying his partner Siegfried, piercing the hero's back as he lay down his sword to drink from the stream … another fable from their self-invented past. Even the child getting killed had a dozen versions in the black matter of Franz's nightmares. What relevance for them now? Why not concoct and follow a brand new myth from scratch?

Marcy had taken the kids and their friends to a matinee one Saturday several weeks later. It was early summer, and very hot. J was helping Franz plant evergreens, the thick hedge screen Franz had always wanted from one brassy neighbor in particular.

J inhaled the aroma of warm, sweet earth. He hadn't remembered such fragrance since his sketching fresh flowers in New York, all that now a vague memory of ache and unendurable loneliness. He tried to recall the kibbutz garden, but that too had shrunk to a fleeting impression. They grunted in unison as they shoveled. This was altogether new: doing the same thing at the same time with another soul. What about their teamwork in the Munich puppet theater? With each shovelful of soil, J felt he was helping to repay Franz for his savage outburst that awful evening, his merciless stabbing into Franz's private parts. The worst of it was, he realized later, that he'd been unleashing this torrent at his own desertion, however justified in that hysteria. Franz was the first and only person to have shared his tragedy. And here, hoping to move beyond, he had picked at the scab like some vicious bird gone berserk.

"Let's call it quits," said Franz, rubbing his soft gut and straining for breath.

J wanted to keep on digging and sweating.

"Race you upstairs!" said Franz, once inside, leaping ahead and remembering how he used to outrun J every time in the Englischer Garten.

J climbed the stairs in a measured pace, enjoying the salty taste of his skin with every lick of his lips.

After each had showered, Franz strutted into J's room, toweling himself and beaming broadly, the house momentarily turned into a locker room. "Boy, a cold beer's gonna taste great."

It was odd to see Franz's body after all these years. The voice and motions, as always, were so boyishly eager, slapping the towel across his back, assaulting his skin. He still looked like a bleached koala bear, only ten times as big.

J feigned a smile, quickly wrapping the towel about himself. They hadn't been naked together since they were boys, experimenting with sex.

"See you downstairs," said Franz plodding off.

That was weird, thought J dressing: sudden intimacy. *Is it only Franz compelled to revive our bond? I must forever remember the acid stains on Franz's frontal lobes, and mine, too.* And then followed a flood of memories: of breathing each other's breath, of pressing together for warmth. Suddenly J's nostrils were infused with the moldy, burnt rubber smells of the cellar and Franz's flanks, both briny and sweet. He tried to visualize the sturdy body of the boy, now this battered ox of a man, going through the motions of a human being but at least partially brain-dead. *It's time to move on, and leave well enough alone. Who knows what treason this tongue of mine is capable of,* he thought, *ironically liberated by Franz?*

Franz was folding laundry when Marcy sidled by in a new silk kimono. She'd lost so much weight that he couldn't see her lovely ass. But the dress fit nice and snug over the boobs, still in A-1 shape in that department. If only she knew how sexy she looked, thought Franz. How slithery and feminine, after running around in sooty overalls and greasy work-shirts. He got aroused and plotted their next scenario in the sack, ambling out to the lawnmower. Plus, he realized: *she's wearing* silk *to titillate me, God love her.*

J stuck to his room and books. Most of his family time was spent helping Andy with reading and math, Sandy with her piano and poems. He slid further into this exotic, unfamiliar tranquility without questioning it. Even Marcy, increasingly concerned about his solitude, did not rile him. Her quickened step and weight loss, the bravura of her latest work, *her blinding purpose in life,* this distanced him all the more from the fracas. Interestingly, his dream life was frightful, often suicidal but in a celebratory way, and so very vivid, as if his subconscious was doing overtime to balance his quotidian lull.

Circling the lawn on his riding mower, Franz fumed about being so unsettled at work, waiting for his next promotion. He felt downright nauseous at the thought of *Elliott Reed* becoming his boss. He glanced at his BMW, coated with tree sap and insects, parked in the driveway since she'd taken over the garage. But Marcy was looking spectacular. He didn't mind her getting occasionally dolled up was likely compensation for spending every waking minute in the garage. Just anticipating her jumping in bed these days was enough to make his dick stiff.

J was cogent enough to see he was obliterating his past, so encrusted with doom. Franz's own slice of their history was apparently insulated by the sweet here-and-now, deflecting J's periodic attempts to expose the scar tissue. Both Franz and Marcy acknowledged his blood relation to Franz, and had opened their hearts to him, despite his inability to reciprocate Franz's bovine warmth. The dog and J had not made friends. Luckily Sandy did the lion's share of tending. J fixed himself iced tea, skirting Bruno, and retreated to his room. The dog, he considered: like his master, bulky and smooth on the surface, but basically unstable at the core.

Elliott Reed popped his head into Franz's office. Franz pictured a harmless grass snake poking its slithering snout from a rock wall, all flipping tongue. Franz had a proper office now, but with a window and carpeting and philodendron plant. "Say Franko," he said, clicking teeth. "Ya got a sec? In my office."

This is it. Sixteen and a half thou. Thirty-four years old, as best J and he could figure.

"Have a seat, fella. That was a swell idea—that fake diamond ring deal."

"Thanks, Elliott."

"Ted and I have been thinking. You've been with Holsum how many years?"

"Twelve. Going on lucky thirteen."

Elliott chortled, ever the chameleon. "How about a new assignment?"

"Great!"

"Director of Premiums. For the *whole* company, worldwide."

A lump formed in the back of his throat and wedged there.

"It's the culmination of so many years of hard work and bright ideas."

"It's the world of trinkets and cheap tricks."

"Yeah but it pushes product. Frankie, you're our man!"

At the supper table, Marcy quipped: "Sweetie, it's just as

well. You forever in Product Management with that ballet class of Ivy League pansies?"

They all burst out laughing, prompting Bruno into a vicious growl, bearing teeth and seizing J's leg, J wincing in pain.

No, Marcy, *not forever*, Franz beamed to himself. My next move will floor you both.

1971

Chapter 17

The following year, Franz was well installed as Director of the Merchandising, Special Sales Support, and Collateral Material Department at Holsum Home Products. He appreciated his spacious, two-windowed corner office with its commanding view of the Cayahooga River valley industries. Even though he and his new colleagues were situated a floor below the company's highest echelon of executives, Product Management, the complex itself towered over the region's string of manufacturing plants, warehouses, and railroad beds. He enjoyed the company of his secretary, Christine, a new administrative assistant, Pearl, and a few other amply-chested staff members. Otherwise, he was miserable, blaming no one but himself. To keep the business trotting along, it took a handful of brainstorms. These came to him, appropriately enough, in a flash. *Superficial is simple*: one of his agonizing aphorisms. Thus he spent most days plotting his escape. His boldest ideas—becoming mayor of Buena Vista (given his skill at corporate team-playing), running a fitness center (acknowledging his soaring cholesterol), or, better, a nightclub with showgirls and poker on the side—were fun but untenable; the soundest—self-employed at his trade—somewhat dull, but doable.

Marcy progressed with her steelworking. The two-car garage had a new concrete floor for improved fire protection from the steady flow of sparks. The pieces of scrap metal and odd bits of steel she labored over were larger and bulkier; the varieties of acetylene torch nozzles more complex. She assured Franz she knew what she was doing, given his growing concern. All three cars were now parked outdoors, much to the dismay of neighbors, one of whom complained to the Hemlock Heights Town Council of the Mann's unsightly driveway. Well, she had a message for all passersby on the bumper sticker of her new but very used Ford pick-up that at first resembled an enlarged Master-Charge card, with its overlapping orange and yellow circles: "Give CHRIST CHARGE of your life." Her spirituality had shifted from The Way of Tea to a simplified, re-invigorated Christianity.

She was outgrowing the garage. Marcy welded a twelve-foot gantry from which to suspend, by chain, various works-in-process. The contraption resembled a swing-set for Goliath, and straddled Franz's former rose bed between the house and the garage. Whenever it rained, the various tubes and chains dripped a steady flow of rust into pools at each of the six gantry feet. The former area of grass and now patch of bare earth was stained rich sienna. Franz had offered to paint the fixture, but Marcy insisted the corroded effect was more in the spirit of raw metal.

J had bought Marcy the pick-up truck to facilitate the hauling of factory-seconds of two-inch steel pipe and other bargains around town. He kept the station wagon for his own use, which primarily involved the transporting of Sandy and Andy, ten and seven, to their various activities. He now did all the shopping, laundry, cooking, and cleaning. He paid the bills, managed the family finances; arranged dental appointments and cash allowances for the two adults and two children. Sandy won an interscholastic piano competition under his tutelage. There was a handwritten note on Andy's first grade report card saying he was the most cooperative boy in the class. J, himself, neither wrote nor drew nor read anything very demanding. He and Franz would watch "The Mary Tyler Moore Show," drink some beer, but not have much to say. He would sit on a bench in the garage, watching Marcy at work for hours. It was there, in the blackened garage interior, between his short bursts of household activity, where he felt most at home.

She was working on an enormous abstract sculpture, a configuration of interlocking cubes and flat discs, a sort of cell division with signals crossed. Presently, she was cutting the two-foot square panels of steel with their jagged edges, six for welding into one of the three-dimensional cubes.

J sat idly in the corner, in awe of her determination. He adjusted his goggles and aspirator. He felt so secure and anonymous. He could not connect to the dozen or more years of his life in New York. He could vaguely sense how far he had withdrawn from the promise he'd made to his nameless forefathers. The more self-absorbed Franz and Marcy became, the easier it was for him to recede. The fumes became a dense gray fog that was suddenly rent by a violent spray of florescent sparks. They would change color, depending on the angle and speed of the torch, from a fiery orange to a sinister hot white. He thought of industrial ovens and blast furnaces. He was suddenly transported to his homeland, the Ruhr Valley steel works spitting sparks and belching smoke. It was that kind of power; she had that kind of fury.

Marcy relaxed her grip on the torch. It was almost as if the deadly tongue of flame could follow the line of its own accord; she was just the intermediary, the design consultant. Her concentration and musculature were riveted by the reddening, swelling parts of steel. Still, a fraction of her was aware of him, feeding her his intensity, elevating her thoughts as had Grandpa Tim, the besotted Irish would-be bard. Yes, she could feel herself the outsider, the newcomer to her husband's original partnership. The square she completed crashed to the floor as she gently guided the torch in a graceful, sweeping curve to the next cut-out, some of the cob-web filigree connecting the massive cubes and discs. She became a conduit for a force that included every iota of her stamina, her guts, her dreams; perhaps her observer's, as well.

Later, she took a break. His hair and nails were starting to go, she noticed. He seemed perfectly sane, even loquacious, especially in her workshop. She joined him on the bench, yanking the goggles back over her head.

"Something about you, Jay, confounds me, even frightens me a bit." She couldn't look him in the eye, but felt the better for saying it. "Maybe it's your Jewishness."

He watched her tug off the coarse gloves. "How do you mean?" he said.

"You're so excruciatingly private."

"Doesn't that also apply to you?" said J. "Isn't that how we've come to share a home?"

"I almost feel vulgar with you, Jay. Take Christianity— so public, unsophisticated. Many Christians hold hands, shout creeds."

As usual, he was shocked but beguiled by her bluntness. "Have you ever been to a synagogue, Marcy? We mumble, not in unison but individually." She was now facing him eye to eye. "We're born this way. We don't need to take a vow."

"To me that's a loss. I like that Christians take their pick. But once I accepted Christ, from whatever voting booth, I acknowledged the Other, the Higher in a true community of believers."

"How nice for you."

"Don't be such a defeatist."

"Are you trying to convert me?"

"Convert you? I was just suggesting you accept the core of your own faith."

"And if I do," sighed J, "that will help you justify yours?"

Marcy felt her Irish rising. "Just think, Jay. If your Messiah actually showed up, you'd have to pack up your groaning boards."

"You just feel guilty because of all that compared-to-Christ crap in your head. So you're taking pot-shots at the patriarch here. You forget I'm the founder of monotheism! Show some respect."

Marcy smiled. "Let's have a cup of tea," she said, slipping

off the bench. "You know how I love to talk shop." They re-settled at the kitchen table.

Her lips had always enchanted him, ripe with a readiness to shift moods in a second. Her face, though, was becoming more complicated, with long, straight furrows in her forehead indicating stress, and shorter, squiggly lines between her eyebrows which could go either way: a smile or a frown.

Marcy stared over her steaming cup at his piercing dark eyes. She was getting him engaged. There was a vacillating soul in there quite desperate to reclaim itself. "Jay, I agree. As you say, how could the Messiah have come and gone when we're still such a mess. The Christian act of faith is just a quick fix."

"But why must that come after life instead of during it?" J said. "You people, to earn what you call salvation, have gloried in the wildest, goriest trail of blood ever spewed upon the face of the earth!"

Color was rising to his pale cheeks—*yes*.

"Jews are just as bad," he continued, "if you go back enough. The same prohibition against intercourse with, contamination by, the other. The same tug of war instead of devotion. It's all so hopeless."

"How so?"

"Both Christian and Jew, we're each mired in guilt, corruption, the breaking of covenants."

Her eyes widened. She rested her teacup. "No, my friend," she said. "Not your people, in this lifetime, this generation. I can claim to be a moral failure, but not you."

She had that look in her eyes. "You Christians are so hooked on hero worship," said J.

"You have suffered like Him!" she lashed back. "Don't desecrate the martyrdom of your people by denying it."

"What claptrap, Marcy, like your pictures of Jesus with a Breck shampoo. A celebration of death, a denial of life."

The blood was banging her temples. "I've been so angry at your passivity, yet so inspired by your silent struggle to resolve it all."

"You see," he cried, his cheeks ignited. "This crazy 'chosen' mystique Christians have blown so out of proportion."

"It's true!"

"To confirm your own lust for inferiority!"

She nodded, rapidly.

"Marcy, I'm sorry. I didn't mean to attack you."

"You're right, you're right. How could a physical man be a go-between for me and my Maker? It's a cop-out." She shoved back loose strands.

Why am I accosting someone so impassioned? J railed at himself. It's the failure of *my* faith to give people hope. "Look at all the Christian after-life holds for humanity at its most wretched, much of the world still living like mud-worms. Christianity's been a noble framework for the preservation of souls."

"No. The *Jewish* tradition works in the here and now, living life to its fullest, swallowing the bitter with the sweet." She peered into his eyes. "You're an amazing man. You must tell me about your people, cross-pollinating yourselves in every culture on earth, propagating non-violence; the highest standards of artistic and scholastic achievement, a defense of a just God beyond all human reason." She grabbed his hand across the kitchen table. "Jay, I need your help. You know I'm still searching. Maybe I should become a Jew!"

The door burst open, Franz crashing in with Sandy and Andy. "Would you two grown-ups stop arguing. Holy-moly, I could hear the racket outside."

"We weren't arguing, Fran," said Marcy, her head spinning like a gyroscope. "We were discussing. A few ideas."

"J, what's for dinner? I'm starved. Christine sent out to that new deli, and you needed a magnifying glass to find the Swiss cheese."

J glanced at the broad, blond man, struggling out of his suit-coat, revealing the tremendous beer barrel of a gut where once resided the hard, slim torso. He tried, in that instant, to recall the dashing young entrepreneur, but lost that image as rapidly as he did the evaporating content of his roiling conversation with Marcy. He rose from the table and started to heat pots of water for the various blocks and bags of frozen food.

Marcy listened to her children prattle without taking her eyes off Jay at the stove. He was more than a saint for his lack of fanfare, the privacy and dedication of his inner quest. She watched thickening plumes of steam coil up from pots and pans. He was in danger of destroying himself. She was all Jay had as an understanding friend, Fran so mired in the muck of his work, at times so depressed. She gave in to the tugs and followed her children to the family room so she could praise their latest projects.

After supper, Franz tossed his feet onto the ottoman, unfolding his briefcase as Bruno nuzzled a wet snout onto his master's lap, pleading for a feel after a day of inattention. Franz tried to address a drain opener report. He watched J twist and contort his eyebrows at the kids, reading a story and making them shriek with laughter. Franz was almost jealous of how wonderful J was with the children.

"Uncle Jay," insisted Sandy, elbowing her brother away. "You have to help me with my six-times table."

Her eyes were flashing and eager, like her mother's. Her fingers were pinching the corner of a page into a neat, nervous triangle. This reminded him of her other parent.

"Six times seven," he said.

"Forty-two."

"Six times eleven."

"Sixty-six," she snapped, her smile breaking into a beam.

"Six times, ah, zero."

"Zero!"

"I thought you said you needed practice?"

The child's eyes widened. Her hands were resting now on the arm of his chair. "You knew my father when he was my age," she said.

J nodded.

"He didn't have a mom and dad like me, did he?"

J placed one of Sandy's hands between the both of his, pressing gently, making one of their famous hand sandwiches.

"Or an uncle, even?"

J smiled, looked up quickly, and shot out: "Six times six!"

"Ah—ah—I can't remember," said Sandy giggling, collapsing onto J's lap.

Franz felt his smile waver between happiness and hurt.

Marcy dwelt for days upon the neglect of her family, not the least of whom included Jay. She had taken advantage of his willingness to run the household. Surely by now he was near the boiling point of resentment. She knew very well he wasn't writing up there. Or drawing or reading. He was brooding upon his fate: his irrevocable, damnable, heart-wrenching ties to his past. Most likely unaware of his own bizarre influence, he had fueled her zest for metalwork and spiritual practice, while she ignored nurturing what was now their chief source. Usually, she dashed off to her sculpture. This particular morning she lingered in the kitchen with J at the sink. His limp dark hair needed cleaning; his expression, as usual, was sullen.

"Jay. Enough. I'm cleaning that skillet."

He wouldn't release it.

"Give it to me, Jay! You go and … "

"What are you talking about?" he laughed.

She pushed hair behind her ears. Her soft brown eyes widened, now glinting amber. "You were in a camp, weren't you?"

"Oh brother," he said.

"Tell me the truth. They were all gassed except you."

He averted her eyes.

"C'mon, now, damn it. Answer me."

"I don't know. Marcy, there's no point."

She shoved him into a kitchen chair but she stood. "Why didn't you tell me you were a real Jew, not just Jewish?"

"What on earth … "

"I mean, here you've been living with us, eating eggs and bacon, pork sausage, shellfish. I thought you were mostly a German gypsy, perhaps part Jew. Two vagabond war orphans. Jay, you've been hiding this rich heritage from us."

He looked at her impassively. He thought of all his Jewish communities, one as in-turned and atrophied as the next.

She put on a kettle of water. "For twenty years I've ignored my share of responsibility for the Holocaust."

"Oh, Christ."

"My grandparents Burger even swore in German! The first synagogue in Brandenburg had its windows smashed. This is *my* story, Jay. *Dr. Konvitz has the only swimming pool in Brandenburg, of course,* a topic in my home as common as the weather. *Always the best grades, the flashiest cars, imagine fur coats at Easter-time. Straightening noses, changing names. What do you expect it to cost from a Jewboy if you don't Jew him down yourself.*"

"You're on an ego trip."

"We're taking our tea into the cellar. I'll light some candles in the old tearoom."

"At nine in the morning?"

"We have to get away from this clutter, the dishes and crud, the telephone, this stage set you've constructed for yourself with my tacit approval. Jay, I'm sick to death of seeing you stir pots and pans. How about my mind for a change?"

Her beauty was now raging through every pore, the curves of her chest and the flash of her eyes, so infused with *her* choice of armor, her list of projects to fill the void, as he had had his. "Oh Marcy, I'd so much rather see you pour this energy into your blowtorch."

They talked the whole day. And the next, and the next, in the cellar sanctuary, face to face in the lotus position. The more indifferently he discussed religious formats, the more compelled she was by his wealth of knowledge. She agreed with so much of what he said, in terms of how irrelevant it all was; and yet she could see the possibility of reaching him, softening him, helping him ease the pain.

"So Judaism," J was saying, "is rooted in the Greek culture, as a national concept. And Christianity is rooted in the Roman Empire, on a universal scale. One intensely inturned, chauvinistic, narcissistic. The other outbound, bullying; aggrandizing from day one. The whole system stinks."

Marcy locked her eyebrows in concentration, practically a postgraduate course in her laundry room.

"A Jew must accept the physical revelation of God to Moses on Sinai," he went on. "A Christian must accept Jesus. They're both nursery rhymes."

She was consumed by his face, carved dramatically into midnight blue shadows by the low candle flame. "Neither may be very good," she said, "but one is clearly worse. Jay, do you realize not until this very moment has Dachau held meaning for me? I'm still craving to connect with … " She paused.

"Shame?" he suggested.

"Shame? Well, yes."

"At Dachau," J said, "you met somebody to help shoulder the German burden. The outer layer, the manifestation of your guilt—"

"I truly love Fran, a basically good man."

"—who lets you feel not nearly so prejudiced, so you can live with yourself as well as avoid real intimacy, just like you've described your girlhood home. You had to seal yourself off to survive."

"What the hell are you saying?"

"That your shame is a fake."

"Jay! God Almighty, I am trying."

"Yes. Again. As an ordinary person, just living and being here, I'm not good enough." He tried to stop his stabbing tongue. He thought his bile was spilled, that he had dealt with his past for a third of a century. Meanwhile, he heard these words: "Now, you want to climb aboard my twisted Jewish train wreck. You can claim more credit for your tolerance … your zeal to save lives. You can assuage and even deaden your perfectly justifiable overload of guilt."

"You ungrateful bastard," she moaned, forehead flopped into hands.

"You had nothing to do with the Jews, Marcy." He froze, but the sounds had already left his lips. "You just murdered your mother."

Marcy could not raise her arms to wipe the downpour from her eyes. She felt a scream forming deep in her guts. The power of steel and fire was solidifying her entire body. She felt capable of killing him in a flash. He was full of poison. "You're a masochist. You're warping truth to perpetuate your own pain. You love drawing out the pain in others, to join you. No!"

She sprung forward and throttled his neck. She knocked over the candle. He grabbed her arm and pushed her backwards. She bit his shoulder. He pounced on her, grinning. The words were such a waste of time. But, oh, he felt so miserable for hurting her. He lost his strength.

She tossed J on his side and pinned him on the soft bamboo floor. "You think I'm just trying to heal myself. That you and Fran don't mean a shit, you fucker." She gritted her teeth.

Her wild eyes, her dangling hair, excited him. They clubbed each other's arms, shoulders, legs. It was the first time, ever, that an adult woman seized his entire body. She slapped his neck. He winced with pain but started laughing.

"You think it's a joke, do you Jay?" She flopped onto him fully. "What's this?" She maneuvered her hand. "Oh, my! So there's life in there, o pious one! Who's calling who a fraud?"

"Marcy," J gasped.

She pressed his neck back with one forearm and unbuttoned his fly with her free hand.

J was starting to cry but she didn't notice. He was protesting, kicking, calling her name. She was fumbling, swiftly, and soon fondling. Her center was a swamp. He was swelling, aching, pressing her warm lips and tongue to his. They tore at each other, gripped each other like magnet to metal then rolled from one side of the tattered tearoom to the other. She disrobed him in a frenzy and covered his chest and belly with kisses. He partially slid down her jeans and panties, mostly managed with her shirt but not her shoes and socks as they crashed to their knees. He stilled her great rolling breasts in his shaking hands attempting to caress her nipples but biting them into stiffening, magenta knobs. Her milky skin was sweet as spring grass. His skin, to her, was shiny and tough and tart as lemon rind. They locked eyes. They sank back to the bamboo pads.

He drank her in. Never had he been so aroused. *What's happening?* Some splinter, some irritant aching to be dislodged which he could not see or touch was being yanked by an incredible force.

She was lost. She had left herself. Her body had become too saturated and could absorb no more. And so it encircled him, entered him, though he was slamming into her. His mind, his heart, his cock, his past, whatever else he was willing or able to share, were hers.

"Marcy," he whimpered.

"Jay … it's not too late."

They pinched and cried. They shuddered into each other's ears. And then, for many moments, they lay still.

I'm happy, was his first thought; and he could almost taste the honey on the raised Hebrew letters, learning the alphabet as a little boy.

I've conceived a child, was her first thought, if she believed in God and the purpose of orgasm. He was denying life and creating life. That was his contradiction. And his reason for being, keeping whole each component.

They clung to each other, licking, whispering, sighing, dozing, and then started again.

"Shouldn't we do something about the kitty litter?" Franz said at supper.

"Yuk. After we eat," said Sandy, pinching her nose.

"That's my point," said Franz, his frown carved in grays against the sunless skin.

Marcy poured rich brown gravy over her second helping of mashed potatoes.

J excused himself to dash to the Seven-Eleven. He'd let them run completely out of ice cream and Oreos. He was sunk into a state so foreign that it did not encompass guilt, Franz, broader implications, the usual machinations of his mind.

There were plenty of opportunities. Marcy's metalworking deadlines were strictly of her own manufacture. And she bought a new diaphragm. Always capable of obsession—hell it was her life force—Jay, for now, obliterated all else.

"I thought intercourse was forbidden between Christians and Jews," said J unbuttoning her blouse. "Each was afraid of conversion by the other."

"Shall we begin," said Marcy unzipping his fly, nibbling his neck, "with the *missionary* position?"

Marcy got J to join her for flower sketching in a nearby field. It was pulsing with so much *color* compared to the grimy garage: pink mallow and black-eyed Susans, proud, heady spikes of purple loosestrife. They shared a bottle of wine and a fresh box of Winsor-Newton pastels. He tried, but couldn't capture it. He much preferred to watch her, the strong arm shooting over the paper in jet-stream arcs, followed by her silky hair flopping over her shoulder as she mussed up portions with smudged fingertips, those essential, counter-pointed dollops of confusion and angularity.

She missed her period. For this she was prepared, along with her doctor's confirmation. She made her decision, but kept it to herself.

Marcy started gaining weight. She relieved J some in the kitchen, making fondues, sauerbraten, mocha tortes. She returned to her steelwork with a new enthusiasm. She completed her Cell Division I and began another, this time a vast assemblage of metal sticks and skulls, sharp points as well as carefree curves, one connecting to another in hallucinogenic fashion if the eye stayed glued to the circuitry.

J watched the steel concoction grow from scratch. He saw the limbs of the woman swell with a new and awesome vitality. Franz was losing hair and becoming stouter week by week. He received a considerable salary advance for a successful, international kids' soap-carving contest. As for J, he was not convinced it was he she was after as opposed to another stepping stone in her path to enlightenment. They'd each lost their mothers, brutally, face to face. From this both their journeys began. She was wonderful, stimulating, loving and kind. *How can I ever return it, the way I'm wired?* He remembered sipping from the gushing fountain at Ein Gedi once on patrol. Jehovah Himself knew it was a mistake. He was not meant to be a soldier. Nor a German scholar nor red-blooded American social worker nor Carmelite monk reincarnated. Least of all: head of the family of Mann. He didn't mind, really. In fact, it was interesting to have watched the sequence of possibilities, the inevitable, painless, dissolution of self.

She was gaining strength. She was gaining steam in her collection of offspring. Flesh and metal, they were much the same: recipients of her outpourings of love and creativity. She was shaping with her hands and with her thoughts, giving life. She was even animating sheets of eleven-gauge steel. If she could do that, she could make it work for Jay. For this she could take no credit. It was simply a power, God-given and available. It was too easy to whine and vegetate; too easy to read and think and never touch, like the barren years of university before Paul and Mark. It was even easier to blame, especially Mother and Ethel, which had summarized most of her past. I've crudely latched on to labels—Catholic/WASP, Celtic/ Kraut, wife, whatever—to make the going smoother, when *I'm no bloody different from any other ladle out of the melting pot.* Yes I'm good with my hands. Very good at making this pizza dough, for instance—a bratwurst and olive pizza; that says it all. She wasn't brave, though. She did have to steady her nerves. She knelt down and opened the cabinet door with her flour-smeared hands. She uncapped the nearest bottle and took the merest sip; her fetus! With her becalmed hands, her renewed sense of purpose, she sliced the

wurst into paper-thin, gourmet slivers. The Irish were persecuted, too; the Jews didn't have a corner on it. It's possible
to plod on, or gallop. Jay has no excuse. She reached down,
for a slug this time.

Franz and Marcy competed for the final crusts of pizza,
nibbled and rejected by the children. The Chianti bottle was
completely drained. The children raced off to the television
with the dog. The three adults sat there, waiting as always
for a review of the day's marketing circus at Holsum Home.

"I'm pregnant!" erupted Marcy, near choking on a piece of
crust. She should have opened another bottle. Wine must be
fine for Mediterranean women. She beamed at both her men.

J's heart stood still. He was prepared for the void beyond
Indiana. But it was so wrong betraying his best and only
friend. How cowardly and selfish! His earlobes were ablaze.

"Marcy!" cried Franz, slapping the table. "That's wonderful. Our family continues to grow. And at twenty-two
thou we can easily afford it." It was so long since he'd been
jubilant, he forgot such an emotion existed.

"Jay, my sweet. Why so glum?" Marcy sang, gripping the seat
of her chair, gushing with excitement. "It's your child, too!"

No, J's mind raced, *she can't do this to me, especially to him.*

"Yes, J," added Franz. "You've been like a mother to
Andy and Sandy. Thank God you are here to help us manage
so beautifully."

"No, darling," said Marcy in a rush. "He should also be
the father. Of this one. Along with you, of course." She was
ecstatic.

"But he's still the uncle, even though he's be here from
the start this time."

"Labels, whatever, we're all in this together," laughed
Marcy.

"I think," began J. "I think it's probably time for me to
leave." Franz's and Marcy's mouths went agape. "We should
all think about it, at least."

"What you should think about," pronounced Franz,
"is getting your ass in gear, and focusing on yourself for a

change. With all your brains."

"Yes," cried Marcy. "You're so wonderful with kids. They're forever needing substitutes at the school. I'll introduce you to Deborah from my old crafts group. She teaches second grade. Jay, please, let's talk about it." She glared at him.

And so they did, the following day, over tea, in the kitchen this time.

J sat motionless. He had called a halt to their lovemaking weeks before, but never suspected *this*. "It's totally my fault. I've been an intrusion from the start."

"Don't be ridiculous. This is your home, too."

"I'm not fit to be a father. I should have a wife."

"Then get one! But is that any reason to not accept me, us, your child, as family?"

J looked off, to avoid her laser-like, olive brown eyes. "You can't have us both," he said, "like a pair of faucets, him for body, me for soul."

"That is so bloody stupid. Life is complicated. Look. Franz has probably fooled around with his secretary. So what? I care for him deeply; we have a past, the kids. You! Fran needs you, as his brother. And I … " Her eyes now were swimming, about to overflow.

He took her hands, kissed them tenderly. "You make it seem so easy, Marcy. It's just not right, for you as well as for me. It's sounding so much like the mess you came from, your mother carrying on with another man."

"*You*—another man?"

Again he avoided her now red and pleading eyes. "What if Franz, too, has been unfaithful? Face it: it's like your father! Children should have a solid foundation."

"You're being so cruel. And cowardly. This is biologically, emotionally yours!" she wailed, clutching her belly.

"You're making a new union, a new offspring, just like your father did, that's as doomed to failure, or at least as compromised, as your first."

"Jay, no!" She was terrified as never before in her thirty-four years. "*I love you.*"

"There was a time," he said vacantly as if he hadn't heard her, "when I would have given anything to feel your throbbing crashing veins as mine. Oh Marcy, you're so full of life. You're all the life I have. I'm so withered, and weary."

"Jay, you have given *me* a new life, and not just this," she said cradling the curve of her front.

"You're crazy!" he shouted, and then mumbled, spent. "It's just plain wrong. It won't work. I have to go, far away, and start on my own. Teaching, yes, you're right about that. I am good with kids—who don't talk back." He attempted a sour smile.

"Life is complicated," she said, "or should be."

He hung his head, the hair a mass of dark tumbleweed.

Suddenly she rose, grabbed the teapot, and hurled it to the floor, bursting it like a hand-grenade. "No, damn it, I will not let you leave! You left him once, and now us? *Never!*"

"I don't know if I'll leave. But I should. And definitely I must tell Franz, and face the consequences."

"My God. *Please.* I love him as my husband. He's had so much more pain than I. It's the only wish I'll ever have: to share my baby with the two men who make sense of my life. Finally, we have a *real* family, fuck what others say."

She was on her knees, frantically picking up shards of sharp ceramic, cutting herself clumsily.

"Marcy, this is *my* life. You already have one. *Franz is my brother.* I made my decision to tell him even before you just confirmed it."

J stood in the plate-glass-windowed hall, a colorless blank space devoid of personality, matching his own state. Waiting for the receptionist to buzz Franz, he stared moronically at the framed, five by six foot color photograpghs of Kristal Kleer, Sho n' Glo, et cetera, like long-dead movie stars lined up in the lobby to glorify a cheap suburban cinema.

"J, what's happened?" uttered Franz as he raced into the room, his forehead tightly crenulated with his usual worry lines.

"I have something to tell you, Franz. My wagon's parked outside. Come, please. No one is hurt," he added in a momentary flash of his right mind.

They settled in the car, Franz behind the wheel as if this was clearly his turf, while J slipped into the passenger seat.

J clasped Franz's sweaty hand. "I had to tell you face to face. I … "

"J, it's okay. I realize you want a life, a family of your own." He half-smiled. "Please just promise you will stay in Buena Vista. Or in shooting distance."

J released Franz's clammy grip. Now numb, he stared point-blank through the windshield. "You know how you joked I was overdue to make some woman happy like you've always done, but you did strike a vein of truth."

"Yes?" He punched J's shoulder. "So you and Marcy's friend—"

"No, Franz. I—I've spent so much time with Marcy, you know, talking to her for hours on end, in her studio, the kitchen, all day long sometimes. She's gotten under my skin, she's so intense, she's aroused all these feelings I've never had before, never thought I could have … " he rambled on.

"J, that's good."

"No, it's not, Franz. We've done more; we've hugged and kissed, and she's, we've gone wild, she's stirred me. *It's so wrong.* I never meant … "

Franz sat up straight now behind the wheel, glancing ahead himself. "Yes. Well, she's the most loving, feeling, female of women. It is only natural, yes, that she would, you would respond … "

"I've never made love before, never felt that way; so totally lost myself with a partner. Forgive me, Franz. *You must.*"

"So," he caught his breath. "You made love. I have shared my wife with you. You are being honest. You are my brother. You are my family."

"Franz, you've had sex all our lives. I never could, that way. I've been so fucked up. I could never feel anything, enjoy sex like it's normal to. You urged me to do it, forever.

And now, here, I've gone and done this to *your wife*. To you! You shouldn't forgive me! This is unthinkable. Please just let me apologize and don't you say a thing. To me, to Marcy. I will just go. And we will all heal. Please, Franz." Again J touched Franz's hand.

It was vibrating spastically on the steering wheel. Suddenly Franz withdrew it and turned the ignition key.

"No, Franz. Good God. What are you doing?"

Franz stabbed the shaft into drive, pressed the accelerator, swung the car into a mindless circle, to the left, then to the right. He clutched the wheel with one hand, ran the free one through his messed-up hair, over his face, rubbing his eyes, barely missing one parked car and then three in a row.

"Franz! You'll kill us both!"

Franz steered the vehicle sensibly, gasping for breath, nodding to J, and drove slowly to the edge of the lot, the fence, the steel posts, the barricade before the long steep ditch into the river bed below. J slumped back in his seat but jerked forward like a puppet as Franz floored the accelerator, and, as quickly, one foot from the fence, slammed on the brake. He dropped his head on the wheel, slobbering with tears.

"Forgive me," he whispered, turning off the ignition. "I'm furious at myself, not you. Who on this earth better deserves a piece of ass?"

"What? You're nuts. Got nothing to do with it."

"I've abandoned Marcy, years ago. Our sex is always about me."

J reached over and slid out the key. "Let's go home, Franz. You can call in sick. There's more to discuss, but later. Now please, let me drive."

"No, no. I'll be alright. I'll follow you."

"But promise me, as your brother," said J, "for just a few days, *please* don't say anything to Marcy. We all need to calm down." He wrapped his arm around Franz's big, soft shoulders. "Give me your word?"

Barely glancing up, Franz nodded.

Marcy was in the garage and had not seen the two men return. Franz called in sick, mumbled to Marcy about a hemorrhoid attack, said he'd skip dinner, and retired to their room. Instead of facing Marcy over a meal, J told her he had finally called Deborah, her ceramicist friend from the crafts collective, for a movie date. In fact, he drove alone to the Cinema Six, picked a dark room at random, closing his eyes for three hours then driving to the cremee stand and back without ordering.

She waited until the kids were sound asleep, well after ten, locked their bedroom door, and slid into bed beside Franz. Gently, she stroked his forehead without fear of waking him; she knew, even in the pitch dark, that his eyes were wide open.

"I know you know," she sputtered, reaching for his hands which were folded tightly over his chest, and extracted one to clamp in hers. "Oh God, why couldn't it have been me to tell you. *It was not his fault.* Fran, I'm wretched. I know he told you, damn it, he's incapable of guile, of deceit like me. I've never let anyone into some place in my heart that I've never found. You are my rock, our breadwinner, my partner, my pal. The father of our children! I love you for everything you've always been. You screw up and you change and you learn. I'm hollow at the core, and keep all this shit hurling around me; totally selfish! I hate myself for causing you pain; Jay, he's dealt with it all his life. I should kill myself." She was crying now, on his stiff, folded hands. "At least I will kill this baby."

He grabbed her. "No," he said hoarsely. "I've seen enough cruelty. I cannot be greedy. What person, what man especially, should own another? Own a woman? What is a husband, a wife? You know we both think that's a crock. It's love, Marcy. It's commitment. We said till death do us part, and I know, you know, we both mean it. And besides: how much can one partner offer another? I love you as best I can but we both know there are ways we are worlds apart. I've been so grateful J has constantly supported you with your artwork. Is that any excuse for my lack of involvement? No, but your sculptures have made me happy for you. Marcy. Marcy?"

She was still weeping, stuffing her hair, his pillow, into her mouth to muffle the groans. *The children.*

"I meant it, too, with J," he continued. "And I know you understand that. We're family. He needs you now, more than ever. You've given him a gift that I never could, and I don't mean just your fabulous body. That's the least of it."

They tried to laugh. He could, sort of. She gagged in her attempt to speak.

"Oh Fran, I've cheated on you. You know I can't help but look at it that way, too—my goddamn religions. I almost wish you screwed your secretaries silly. You know it wouldn't faze me."

"I know, angel." He chuckled. "But the truth is, I never did cheat on you after we were married. No cigar, but close a few times. Didn't need to. So why the big deal about this once, this one time you were carried away? You're a passionate woman! And with love-starved J, no less. Hell we do it three times a week. Plus, you put up with all my fantasy silk stuff. We've all got to let it wash over the dam. Okay? Honey, okay?"

She was wailing again, this time into her own pillow, her body arched against his, curling farther and deeper into her middle, cramped tight as a fist.

When J crept up the stairs and into the hall, the lights were out, but he could hear them attempting to muffle their sounds.

Franz went to work the following morning, the kids went to school, Marcy went into her garage-studio, and J called Deborah Abramson for real, arranging a lunch date at the Buena Vista coffee shop to talk about substituting at Sandy and Andy's grammar school at which she taught. Afterwards, he visited Deborah's ceramics studio, returning home too late for dinner, and with a replacement teapot.

1972

Chapter 18

No one was home. The old station wagon stood empty and waiting like a hearse. J watched himself approach the parked vehicle slowly, wondering if they had something to serve Sandy and Andy for supper. His fingers poised on the door handle. He looked at the house and then at the evergreens serving at Franz's tightly pruned foundation shrubs. They were lined up, precision trimmed, like upside-down ice cream cones. The garage area, too, was fairly well ordered. She was doing figures now, graceful shapes. And she had a huge chunk of green Connemara marble he'd seen her eyeing.

He drove off. It was a stretch of unexpectedly bitter weather for early March. The opaque egg-white sky gave no indication of breaking up into brightness. If anything it felt like snow. He was sweating and gripping the wheel.

He'd left nothing in the way of a note. He'd bought the children boxes of candy. And he did the breakfast dishes. And cleaned the kitty litter. He turned on the windshield wiper, finally noticing the splashes of wet snow. He headed north instead of south, on the outskirts of Buena Vista. Drier, thicker snow seemed appealing.

He started humming the Kol Nidre in time to the windshield wipers. It was a low dirge, a plaintive tune which was fixed in his mind more as Beethoven's Quartet in C sharp minor than as chords of a kantor. What had he wanted from Franz other than to push it back to point zero? Franz would be relieved. Upset for awhile. An office, a routine, a family, a sales quota: these things had a way, he gathered, to work quite nicely for some. The havoc wrought by their three-some had been ameliorated by the sheer forward march of Franz's steamroller, Marcy's infatuation with metal, the children with distractions of their own.

Behold, said David to his son. *I am now about to go in the way of all the earth.* The road was dusted with a thin, powdery glaze. He pushed the pedal down farther. There were crossroads passing overhead, supported by massive concrete slabs. Stationary. Indestructible. He pressed the accelerator to the floor. He kept waiting to hear Franz's voice, yelling for him to stop. *Hear O Israel, The Lord Our God, The Lord is One!* There was no traffic, he was free, it was clear; he kept aiming, aiming at the massive wall ... *Hear O Israel ...*

He swerved back into the lane and raced on.

They fail, again and again, to stamp us out. But how do we find the conviction to stay malcontent, a one-man diaspora, to listen and to learn from the Maggid? How odd of God to choose the Jews. The road was getting slick. He hammered on the brake. The car fish-tailed over two lanes including the shoulder but kept on course. The snow was coming down much heavier up here in north country.

He began singing the Passover campfire round from the kibbutz Ben-Yaakov, the dizzying version of "Uncle Moses Had a Farm" or "A Partridge in a Prune Tree." Soon he was on the last verse. "Ten laws in God's command, nine months before a birth, eight days before a b'rith, seven days to make a week, six books explained our laws, five books contain our laws, four mothers in Israel, three father patriarchs, two tablets of the law, One God, of heaven and earth ... " He spotted a bridge. He veered off the highway, onto a lesser road, and gunned with all possible speed square into the railings. *Hear O ...* The wooden posts were buoyant. The car bounced back like a rubber ball and thundered down the road, spraying the ever-thicker snow like sea foam to the sides.

He shut off the wipers, to let the pounding snow accumulate to the point of blinding him. He felt the thrill of steering absently, waiting for the thud, the long-belated crunch. Why of course! You had to repeat the path of your father before you could let it go and carry on. He twisted the wipers on again just as the sound of tires indicated he was careening off the road.

He recalled that Israel was sending her athletes to the summer Olympics, to his hometown of Munich no less. Was it possible the globe could come together in the former nest of fascism? He thought of the thousand at Masada refusing to be Roman chattel and falling, at the last moment, onto their own swords. He thought about Abraham binding his boy and lifting high his blade as an act of God. He tried to think hard about what he was doing. *It's time, above all, for Franz and me, Marcy too, to go our separate ways.*

The tires were losing their traction but the sheer weight of the big car propelled it farther and deeper into the nameless hills. He was totally lost. The sky, the road, it was all a heavy, dull, bird-dung gray. A soft eiderdown was descending and smothering everything in sight. There were pale blue forms as accents to shapes, but these, too, were fast disappearing.

Though I walk through the valley of the shadow

He saw his foot shove down the accelerator. Despite the fishtailing rear-end, the car picked up tremendous speed. He was apparently going downhill and around curves. Finally, he let go of the wheel. The car crashed softly down a steep bank, through evergreen branches that slapped the windshield like the view of giant brushes of an automated carwash. It traveled quite a distance off the road into the snowy woods, snapping birch trees in half and shoving off from larger trunks with a chorus of thuds. It came to rest, tilted at a forty-five degree angle, with him sprawled comfortably over the front seat, wedged up against the down-hill door. He stared out the smashed windows which allowed icy air to flow in and reach his nostrils with a spicy, woodsy perfume.

He followed the course of every enormous snowflake that was accumulating on his face and folded forearms.

He chose not to move. Something had happened to his neck. All was silent. The snow was being poured forth, thick and furious, from some galactic vat of the stuff with an endless supply. It was very satisfying. He was insulated like the pine needle mulch of the forest. His chest and lap and legs were already covered with the lacy crystals. *I will fear no evil.* He suddenly understood the boxcars and why they had not burst open at the seams with outrage and useless emotions. He saw survival as vanity. The snowflakes covered the hood of the car, the dashboard. On his lap alone it was now a good inch thick. He could not feel his feet. What use was there for them now? His soul was right here making friends with every flake of snow.

He drifted off.

Slowly, he lifted his eyelids, glued with frost. He could vaguely see the rounded, chalky white outlines. He was in an igloo. It was colorless. But as he waited, the variations of hue, from ivory to eggshell, from pearly gray to milky vanilla, began to announce themselves. The Eskimos, of course, have a thousand words for snow. Like the Arabs, for camels; the righteous, for holy.

He started singing his favorite Village cabaret tune. "Sons of the thief, sons of the saint. Who is the child with no complaint? Sons of the great, sons unknown, all were children, like your own … " It was a song-poem, from Jacques Brel. *"But sons of tycoons, or sons of the farms. All of the children ran from your arms. Through fields of gold, through fields of ruin. All of the children vanished too soon."* It was Elly Stone, warbling the Kaddish to him in his snow cradle, the closest thing on earth to his mother's voice. *"Sons of the sons, and sons passing by. Children we lost in lullabies. Sons of true love, and sons of regret. All of the sons you cannot forget … "*

I'm a son! I'm a father! I'm to be a son again!

Jan Hartmann, Yod Hertzl, Yankele, Jay Radius, all that we have done is for your forgiveness. He lay perfectly still during the ceremony of the pines as they shoveled heap upon heap of pelting snow over his stiff frame. He was being laid to rest in the traditional white garment, just as specified in the Halakhah!

Yitgadal veyitkadash shmeh rabba, he heard the wind whistle the Aramaic phrases through the branches. He found the words of Shema Yisrael upon his lips, breaking apart the mounds of snow, the words for the final prayer. He listened to the simple, vacant words, the mouthings of a mechanism, a gentle echo of Zion, nevertheless, calling its sons and daughters to the Herodian wall for a final view. *Hear O Israel!* They persisted. *Hear, hear.*

Gradually, seemingly for hours, he wiggled like an earthworm, maybe just a few feet. His mouth was full of rotting pine bark. It was totally black now, but his eyes were wide open, wiped by eyelids and washed with tears. *I will give them an everlasting name,* said Isaiah. *Nie wieder,* never again, say the children. His head kept rattling with a lifetime of words. *Lebensraum,* said the Germans. Living space! *Nisht fargesen!* said the Jews. "Father!" he cried, his lips smeared with pine gum. "I forgive you." He could still make a fist. Enough of waiting for the Messiah like a robot with a canker sore. Who is the child with no complaint?

He could feel his toes.

So there is evil. So there is shadow. Ignite it! Faith is there, as nutrition not painkiller. So take it! he accosted himself, in Marcy's voice.

His lips started to move in time to a tune. "Come dance the Ho-ra! Light the Meno-rah! Now's the time for joy-a!"

He could move his neck, and he yanked the brass pendant off in a grand flourish, tossing and letting it vanish forever in the mountains of fluff. *I'm free.* The snow, forgetting individual specimens, was blindingly white in the dawn as he struggled out of the woods.

"Jay! What's the matter?" said the woman in the dead of the night. She reached for his shoulder.

He stared wild-eyed into an indigo blur. "Good God,"

he said breathless, collapsing back into Deborah's arms.

"You're shaking."

"I'm fine." He buried his face in her neck.

"Good," she murmured and squeezed him tighter, soon nodding off.

He lay there for hours, eyes strained open, preferring the soft umber shadows to sleep.

Marcy was five months pregnant. Her focus was her children now that J spent several nights a week at Deborah's. Her hands, however, were still active with her sketchpads and charcoal drawings, shapes of steel gestating along with her next child. She hadn't touched a drop of alcohol for all these months, oddly content, coming to terms with a looming, inexplicable uncertainty over her and her family's future. *I have to let Jay go in order to keep him.*

Franz, thinking of himself these days as a carnival barker in a three-piece suit, was optimistic enough to see this as the last straw before his leap. His ongoing funk was relieved by tidying up the yard now that Marcy was on hold with large sculpting materials. Marcy's and J's fling: history. *She's having my baby.* Her health and happiness were all that mattered to him, bottom line.

J had been urged by his colleagues at the grammar school to get the necessary credits for certification to teach full-time, not just substitute, at which he'd been highly popular. In addition to the regular curriculum, he'd introduced an expanded story hour and puppet-making during art period. He was happy, as far as he could know, since he had never dwelt in that layer of the atmosphere. And kind, intelligent, steadfast Deborah: she was like a candle in a silent cloister, quietly burning with resolve to love him.

Marcy, Franz, and J found themselves amid the clutter of dishes seated at the dining table one night, after Deborah left for a meeting and the children were arguing agreeably in the family room. Franz, thought J, seemed especially fidgety and excited.

"I couldn't wait to tell you," said Marcy in a rush. "I got a call today from the head of the town library. They've chosen my sculpture for the lawn, at the new entrance! Cell Division I."

"Fantastic!" cried J.

"The big one out back? Hallelujah," gasped Franz, "that's a quarter of our backyard."

"And they're paying me—three thousand dollars."

"Hey Marce," said Franz standing to grip her shoulders and kiss her. "How wonderful."

J was swooning over this sweet news as the three of them babbled on.

Franz cleared his throat. "I have an announcement, too," which totally silenced his partners. They waited. "I've given notice at Holsum Home. I know I should have discussed it with each of you, but—I wanted it to be a surprise." He placed his large fleshy hands smack on the table. "I'm starting my own business. Mann Marketing. I've been talking to Mac Sorrens, the ad manager of the paper, for months. *He* convinced *me* to start an agency to help his hundreds of piddling accounts. Their coupons, offers, premiums. Special sales stunts, the whole bit. It'll pump heaps more profit into the paper. All these ideas I have the company pisses and farts on, meeting upon meeting, day after day. No more."

Marcy now rose to embrace him, from the rear. J wore a giddy smile.

"Four thou *a month.* They're guaranteeing me a minimum fee, plus mark-up on all the collateral crap. And I can do extra projects for dozens of outfits in Buena Vista, hell, in all of Indiana. What's to stop me?"

J was still beaming, shaking his head. "It was just a matter of time."

"Listen, J, I'm gonna need lots of help on the financial side. We're talking big bucks."

"You can hire people, honey," said Marcy, smooching her husband's ever-thinning pate, the blond of baby down. "Jay has his hands full. Deborah. School. Here," she added plaintively, a hand resting on her thickening waist, her eyes searching for J's. But J had cleared the table, scraping dishes, focused on the sink. Marcy winced from a stab of panic.

1973

Chapter 19

Franz studiously sharpened the knife. He wanted to make a clean cut so as to lose as little fluid as possible. Anything more blunt than razor-sharp would crush the carrots and cause them to bleed before he could pop the fresh wedges into his new Gush-n-Health Juicerator.

Marcy nudged her nipple gently into place. The baby's wide eyes were glued to her own. She lifted her swollen breast, beginning to dribble now, even closer to his open, gaping little mouth. The eye correspondence, at this moment for the baby, was more pressing than the liquid lunch.

"We should never peel carrots, Marcy," said Franz, scrubbing fresh ones in the sink under a vigorous jet of cold water. "Most of the vitamins are in the outer layer."

"Uh-huh." The baby was licking the dribble and just beginning to show signs of an appetite. She was aching, pleasantly.

His machine whirred quietly, its blades spinning at such a rapid rate that the juice was separated from fiber and pulp in seconds after each insertion. He could feel his stamina building every day. He tilted his head back slowly to let the trickle of earthy, unadulterated orange slurry impart the maximum flavor to his taste buds. He could visualize the maze of minute root hairs of each carrot piercing his earthworm-infused, humus-filled topsoil. He could picture the roots seeking out a cornucopia of trace minerals and essential nutrients and sucking them up through capillary action into the fat golden tube for storage in cellulose. Wasn't the common carrot a clever vessel! He was drinking from the earth. He was growing celery. Not the pallid limp whitish stuff you get in stores, but the bittersweet, bright green stalks that absorb sunshine and manufacture vitamins. The fabulous outer stalks, usually stripped away by some poor wetback in California because they'd wilt in transit, were even better than the castor oil he used to swallow as a boy. These homegrown beauties, too, he would shove into his Gush-n-Health along with his blood-red, vine-ripened tomatoes, bell peppers, his emerald parsley, his beets and the cabbage left over from canning sauerkraut. "Marcy," he erupted, almost amputating his pinky. "I'm gonna make our own V-8!"

The baby spit out Marcy's nipple and duplicated his mother's startled expression. "That's wonderful, sweetie. Would you mind reaching in the fridge for an ale?"

"Sure. But sometime I can make you a Brewer's yeast banana shake in the blender. I bet it'd be super for nursing mothers."

Marcy lowered her eyelids. She hadn't touched a drop in nearly a year. Now, at least, the occasional beer was recommended. She rocked the child and partially covered her breasts with a clean, sweet smelling diaper which she'd been using as a bib. The baby's eyes continued to wander, bright and involved. He was questioning from the first moment she laid eyes on him. The eyes weren't as dark as his but every bit as penetrating. He never cried nor fussed as had Andy, nonstop. He was simply too busy. She pushed the hair from her face with the back of the hand holding the bottle of ale. She set her bare feet a little wider apart for easier rocking. She wore long skirts everywhere now, even in summer. She loved the way they kept her spreading body to herself. She was still eating for two, she would chuckle, helping herself to cold chicken or salami or paté whenever she pleased. She was tall, so she wasn't really fat. She rather liked the way she looked at thirty-six. She knew this was her last bid for immortality, in terms of flesh. There was always her metal. She actually missed being pregnant, after six months. She cuddled the hot wet little creature and wrinkled her eyebrows in a dizzying series as he followed her every move. But this phase was still intense and almost as good. She did mourn some every day, as his fingernails and hair follicles sprouted forth, as his pinching grip became more insistent, as he continued to sculpt his own universe.

Franz poked his huge index finger into the baby's clenched fist. "Oh he's got his mama's quick smile but he's got his daddy's tough forearm, doesn't he? And his chin!" Franz thrust forth his own in an exaggerated silhouette.

Marcy looked aside.

"Such dark hair," Franz said.

"It's the Black Irish genes," she replied.

"I remember so many babies in the Lebensborn," reflected Franz. "Their mothers were so upset, but it's just the first growth. He could be blond, too."

Marcy opened and then closed her mouth, weary of debating whether or not to regurgitate the circumstances of her conception if not the bald truth. But what was that? How could she, any of them, know for certain? Hadn't she clouded, no, besmirched, three lives enough with her heedlessness? Enough wounds for a lifetime. Of course hers couldn't measure up to Fran's and Jay's, but if she prodded things further and skewered herself, wouldn't that just be a feeble attempt to inflate her own grief, to more equate it with theirs?

Franz, meanwhile, was wiping the counters spotless. He began preparing the beef for the rouladen, trimming fat and slicing wafer-thin pieces. Marcy was careless about her body and exercise yet seemed so at ease. *Not fair, me forever waging war with my own.* To shape it, to keep it stiff when he wanted or to slow it down and relax. A little gristle wouldn't hurt. Maybe he could remember the exact proportion of spices Frau Mueller had taught him when he learned to cook in Munich, when J was in school and he was keeping house. He pounded the raw slices on the butcher-block with gusto. *Yes, at home is where I'm truly happy. Always been the case.*

Marcy was humming softly to the baby as she settled into her other rocker, cradled the little boy and stared intently out the small nursery window on the second floor. She was glad Fran agreed with her to call their son Timothy after her beloved Grandpa Tim. Timothy J, without a period; just J, for that special person, too. TJ, could be his nickname. Timothy J Mann he was, someday claiming each of his important parts, she could hope. She was calmed by the drone of the lawnmower in a far section of the yard, and, after that trailed off, the steady whine of the locusts doing their mating rituals in the linden trees. She could smell the fresh-cut grass wafting in through the screen. It all became the familiar, diaphanous, yellow-green haze of high summer, the safety of hedges; the continuity of a smoothly clipped, spongy cool carpet upon which one raced about barefoot. She could hear her grandparents Burger talking softly, exchanging ideas for staking the dahlias, listing fresh vegetable possibilities for the evening's meal, discussing whether or not to hang the laundry since it looked like rain. She watched Granddad Herman, stooped over his pen knife, removing clumps of dandelion with surgical skill, stacking them in little piles for later collection for his compost heap. She traced Grandmother Ethel's elegant hands as she iced the wobbly angel food cake with that lovely worn and flexible spatula that never once ripped the fluted edges. She stared in amazement as Ethel deftly slipped it out the Bundt pan that had molded it in the first place, steaming and fragile yet holding its shape. She placed the dreaming child in its crib and returned to the rocker. She folded her hands in the mountain range of ridges formed by the yards of printed India cotton of her floor-length skirt. She strained to recreate Jay's eyes, to match them with the child's. He still kept his room here, but was mostly at Deborah's. And Deborah and he were planning to rent a place together in a matter of weeks. Again this evening, it would be just she and Fran.

Once Jay had said she set herself up for loss, leaving so many relationships in her past, as had he. Well, she savored the people or tried to, while they were in her midst. The metal works had a sort of permanence, but that was not the same. She could see Fran in the yard now with Andy, Fran's left arm akimbo, pointing with the other to the next assignment for his son. Andy trotted off, not before Fran tapped him on the behind. He too was the father of this child, every bit as much as Jay. *I have to not only think this but believe this to the marrow of my bones.* She could do that; she was determined. She had to juggle it all, and represent whom she suspected would become the missing parent to the baby. So, by one person was how she was raised, in her earliest years. One parent was a hundred percent more than either of these men had had. Except for each other. Her husband was kneeling now, with Bruno, sharply waving his forearm and barking louder than the dog. The German shepherd sat quivering on his haunches as Fran rose and slowly backed up, the two of them in a fierce ballet of restraint. It was Herman, and his hound Heinz, in another backyard. The orchestra of insects reached a feverish pitch.

She went downstairs and got another beer, the baby fast asleep. The blender, as usual, contained the remains of a wheat-germ eggnog. She curled up in the living room. She looked at her hands. They were knobby and gashed from her years of metalwork. He'd be teething soon and crawling off. Would she return to the garage? It was hard for her to remember the regularity of it all: the nine to four-thirty routine she'd followed for years, enforced by some wondrous embedded wiring, salmon spawning upstream. The beer was warm and fuzzy and spread throughout her bulky frame. She inhaled deeply, the new-mown smells still lingering. It was her big chance to take a nap. She tried to close her eyes. As always, he sat there, silently brooding, fueling her and haunting her. Why hadn't the creative juices seeped into his fingers as well as hers? She glanced up at the framed pastel.

She was staring into the cylinder of a daffodil, her favorite of all he had given her. The corrugated edges varied from fiery yellow to a soft moist buttery hue. The pistols were aiming straight out, like vipers' tongues of thalo green: on the alert but recessed enough in their chambers to do no harm. The six-pointed petals were another yellow altogether, a pastel lemon with ridges of smoky gray. And then the onionskin encasing the frail flower's shaft. It thrilled her, so life-like it was. She could almost smell the damp spring soil. Not that the rendering was very precise; on the contrary; it must have been executed in a rush, full of smears and dashed strokes and vapory washes. It was the flavor of transience that made his flowers, like him, so alive. "Damn you," she muttered, lowering her watery lids.

Franz could feel the strong sun burning the top of his balding head. But it was tempting to complete all the weeding at once. The straight rows looked so nice with nothing but mellow brown, loosely crumbled earth right up to the plant stalks. Just like the beautifully manicured borders of the Englischer Garten—the inspiration J said he carried to his work on the kibbutz. The idea of ragged unruly weeds grabbing more than their fair share of fertilizer and sunshine repelled him. He liked the thinning of the feathery "fingerling" carrots, the tender green beans that actually snapped they were so fresh and succulent. He loved filling the root cellar, formerly Marcy's spiritual teahouse, with acorn squash and braids of Ebeneezer onions that could make it till spring. It gave him a good feeling like when he was a boy squirreling away surplus in Munich. He remembered doing more than the other kids in the home, earning the privilege of sleeping alone on clean sheets in the linen closet while all the rest were spreading infectious disease on piss-soaked mattresses. He liked his boy Andy now earning pocket money in the neighborhood, tending yards. He squatted among the tomatoes, sweating and pinching off the tricky suckers. He could almost taste the ice-cold brew he'd get as his reward. He thought of Marcy acting so contrite about J, for months on end. She could love to suffer, take on the plight of the world; argue herself bananas from one vantage point and then the other. Everything turned out beautifully: Timothy, J and Deborah, Franz's new job on his own. His heart near burst with joy just thinking about that sweet woman and with all she'd put up with over his years of pussy-footing at Holsum Home, his edicts about raising the kids, his compulsions about their yard, their kitchen, their bed. Did she ever complain? She'd had it just as tough as him as a kid, in her way. She, too, believed in Selbstaendig: self-reliance. He dug his toes and knees and elbows deeper into the soft loam, examining cabbage leaves for worms and squishing them on the woody stems. She and he had made a team of two outsiders. He thought of all the poor bastards stuck with lily-assed wives who would bust a gut if they so much as pinched a secretary on her backside. He swore he was going to use something stronger than wood ash for these slugs. No wonder he'd made it, at long last, his very own business, ten employees, full-time, three freelancers on call, option to buy his building within view of his alma mater, Holsum Home, about which he had no regrets. Sheer bloody perseverance. Eighteen years at the factory, starting at age seventeen in the mailroom, with English classes every night. He never once stopped believing that he at least should aim for the top. Not that he could take sole credit for it. But let's face it, he thought, leaking a little wind as he stooped low to yank up an especially ornery clump of witch-grass. I finally showed those Ivied prisses with their endless Choate schoolboy chatter what it was all about. *Moving product off the shelf.* It's not talent, it's not how well you can slice a backhand at the Hemlock Heights Racquet Club. It's pure piss and vinegar that pays off in this world. What that skinny shit of a sidekick of mine is finally learning. J was even earning extra cash outside of his school now with his theater for kids in an abandoned gas station ... although he claimed it was strictly non-profit. And at last, *getting laid,* understanding what these arms and legs and things are all about. He pinched two centipedes copulating on his Bibb head lettuce. Franz started composing the salad in his mind, the fantastic choice of crispy, crunchy greens, the tangy Bermuda onion slices and the garlic croutons he'd whip up, just as soon as he rolled the rouladen and minced the potatoes for the Kartoffelklosse.

"Fran," said Marcy after supper as they sipped their freshly-brewed Irish coffees, her long glossy brown hair pulled back and secured at the nape of her neck with one of Sandy's broken barrettes. The older kids were playing ping-pong in the reclaimed cellar rumpus room. The baby was asleep. "That was a wonderful dinner. Thank you."

"Helluva pepper sauce, huh? More whipped cream? Schlagsahne mit dem whiskey?"

"Sure. Listen. I've been thinking—"

"Oh no!"

"—since I have to get up so much during the night, and you're complaining about getting a sound sleep, that I'll go into the guest bedroom with the baby when Jay moves out."

Franz put his mug into the saucer with a clatter.

"It'd be nice, too," she went on. "My own john for all my junk."

The beautiful dinner, the day of great gardening, shrunk to oblivion.

"We can still fool around," she added.

He was at a loss for words, until these emerged: "What'll the kids think? They'll tell their friends. Their friends' parents talk ... "

She looked at him through sleepy eyes. "I hate to upset you, honey. But I need my rest these days. We can still snuggle. Sometimes shoot for the stars."

Hot fear seized his neck, his veins there whip-lashed. *It isn't what anybody in the neighborhood would say. It's losing her ... her warmth and belly and legs next to mine ...*

She suddenly sobered. She realized what she'd just said: practically evicting him. She resisted the temptation to speak, reached for her mug but saw it was empty. She gripped the handle, nevertheless.

"Sure," he finally said, trying to conceal the wound. "You always hit me over the head with these ideas. But they make sense. I mean, it'll almost be a relief not to feel we should make love all the time. We can be tender, when we really mean it." He managed a smile. "I'll never understand how that head of your spins around, but I know I love you. And I always will." The beer, the sweat, the rouladen sauce and Rhinewein and Irish coffee were working upwards, to his heads and face and eyes, making them glaze, then toppling over the rims.

She relaxed her hold on the mug, awash in guilt but also pleased. And then she softened. "Just for the time being."

"I know we're not the same," he said, "and never will be. And good for us for that. But damn it, Marce, I'm still crazy about you. Just promise me one thing. Please don't bolt your bedroom door."

She had been there twice before: once with Jay to humor her and once on her own. The men nodded, whether to acknowledge her or to continue chanting, she had no idea. The bet hamidrash, the small chapel, was used for early Thursday morning minyan. There was no way she could downplay her presence. And this time, clutching the child, she might be taking too much license with the laws. The place was dark and gloomy. She fixed her gaze on the elaborate silver menorah, the multi-branched candelabrum, as a glowing sign of life. Beginning to tremble, she glanced down. His eyes were more alive and eager than ever. And still, he didn't utter a sound. She slipped into the caucus room, the cluster of widowers or otherwise bereaved and generally older males squinting at her. She hoped they'd stay distracted, pronouncing Hebrew, consoling their individual pains while keeping up the chorus. The baby began to whimper, or croak, or sing, she couldn't tell. The hell with it, she thought. So he doesn't have a Jewish mother, the definition according to The Book. So we've reversed things, in this case. I'll teach him the Kaddish to say after one of his fathers. I don't want to buck tradition. Just the opposite! Some were staring at her. Fran probably didn't even realize there was a synagogue in Buena Vista. He would die. "Yitgadal veyitkadash shmeh rabba," she recited, loud enough to be heard. Baby Tim started hiccupping, or protesting. She tightened the fringed tallith she'd picked up at the entrance and draped it around his wriggling shoulders. A few of the men stopped chanting, glaring at her flagrantly violating the scheme of thousands of years, intruding her needs, and his, into the community of true mourners. "Yitgadal veyitkadash," she muttered even louder. The baby started bawling. She didn't mean to be defiant. But, Jesus Christ, it was his birthright! Her knees wobbled. She acknowledged the nausea. "Shmeh rabba." Rubbish. She was trying to dignify her shallow incentive with their horrendous ache. They themselves couldn't do it justice. How in the name of God could she ever find a ve- hicle? She was trying to do it on her own but she needed help. She could still press her face against the windowpane and hear her mother cackling, crashing in at midnight. She could still press her ear against the door and hear grand- mother Ethel bemoan her insolence. The baby's face shone vermilion, wet with tears. The men continued chanting and slowly shuffled to encircle her, the icy white stony faces of Jewish elders tediously working jaws without skipping a beat. The sterile hospital circumcision wasn't satisfactory? A symbolic one is in order? She caught the flash of a sil- ver blade, like Abraham's over Isaac, and other sacramental instruments poised on the ark. She tried to chant louder, to drown out her squawking child, to shatter the terrify- ing porcelain faces and ink-black airless room. Finally, the most white-haired of the group rested a brittle hand on her shoulder, and directed her to a folding chair at the edge of the droning circle. She looked down, to relieve the pressure, and saw the baby's fist clamped like a terrier's onto Grandpa Tim's Celtic cross and chain around her neck. The eyes were Jay's; the grip was Fran's.

It was a typical Sunday afternoon, Franz ensconced in his study on work due the next day, both kids off to help J at his children's theater. Sandy sold the tickets and counted the cash; Andy served as usher. J was scheduled to collect his things from the house the coming week, the week Marcy and the baby would take up his room. Franz felt his naysayer's ice-pick jab his innards. He had to see the positive side to this, for all of them. *My life, if anything, at least at first, was open to wild change and adventure. I mustn't lose hold of that.* Maybe someday I *will* start a saloon here in the Bible Belt.

The baby was so easy, her third; she found the free minutes stretching idly and pleasurably into hours with her old sketchbooks, eyeing her garage. The energy was never extinguished, just lurking patiently under wraps.

Marcy was seized with a thought. She put down her beer; she'd already had one. She asked Franz to keep an ear on the nursery and then changed into her old jeans, a struggle but she made it. She backed the vehicles out onto the driveway, shut the doors and began, lovingly, to touch the sheets of metal, her tools, the myriad nozzles and propane tanks. The crude edges of one especially mottled piece she wanted to tame; not compromise it completely, not mask the material's black earthen essence, but to ask its permission to collaborate. The goggles were cross-hatched with scratches; she'd have to get clear new ones, but these would do. She burped and wiped off her head gear, tripped over a steel rod that had rolled out of place. Her hands and wrists were thicker; the gloves barely fit. She may be rusty, but so was the metal! Her forward momentum, like Fran's, yes, that was still hot as hell.

Franz cracked open the door of his home office, really the far third of their living room which rarely saw much action any more. All was silent upstairs in the baby's room. He smiled at his desk, plastered with works-in-process. My very own clients, my sole responsibility, honest folks paying me a lot and respecting me for what I'm worth …

The boom shattered every window in the living room. Franz gaped in horror as the glass crumpled and drifted like dust from the frames to the floor.

"*Marcy!*" he screamed, first bounding up the stairs to seize the baby, still sleeping, then crashing down the stairs and racing to the garage. He stopped short in the kitchen, thick with eerie orange smoke. "Dear God," he cried rushing back to the living room, thrust the baby onto the sofa and bolted outside to the garage.

It was no longer there. A few flickering flames were licking their way in a futile attempt to penetrate clouds of black fog. He dashed back for the baby, handed him to a neighbor, one of a dozen now encircling him on the lawn, as he sank, sobbing, to his knees.

They set up home, temporarily, in a rented house farther out from the city, Franz, the children, and J. J postponed his marriage to Deborah. They did it all without saying very much, as Franz proceeded to have the remains of the house in Hemlock Heights razed, landscaped, and put on the market. He had found the Celtic cross in the ashes. He gave it to his daughter, who wore it from that day forward. J was saving his own chain with its brass clasp for the baby someday. He took charge of the children, the paperwork, and even Franz's business. His kids' theater, of course, was put on hold. He adored Deborah, but saw her much less, at least for these anguished weeks, punctuated only by Franz, the kids, and himself taking one step at a time: it was all they could do. Once the property was sold, the men, without much planning, purchased a huge wreck of a place, fifteen rooms begging for renovation, out in the country but still close enough for them all to commute. It had acres of yard, forgotten orchard, garden, even a small barn, which J eyed as a puppet playhouse while Sandy negotiated for a horse. She also demanded, sounding more all the time like her mother, that the men finally celebrate a birthday, together, the first of July, mid-point of the year.

Franz closed his office in the city, and said he'd set up shop at home; for now, there was no rush returning to work.

All he wanted was to be with his family—Sandy, Andy, the baby, and J. "I'm taking over," he told J, referring to the kids. "You're hauling your ass out of here, J, before the end of the year, and taking that sweet woman as your bride."

"You won't have time to cut the lawn," J said.

"Let it turn into a jungle," Franz replied.

Going through all these motions, they were leaden with grief, which surprisingly was lightened the afternoon the flatbed truck arrived and its crew unloaded and installed, out back by the old orchard, the rangy, graceful labyrinth of steel, Marcy's Cell Division II. The new household cranked ahead with Franz and J as equal partners, but Franz commandeered the making of TJ's formula, it coming right back to him after a million years.

Breinigsville, PA USA
06 October 2010
246840BV00001B/2/P